ARCHANGELS / BOOK 2

HEART AND SOUL

Jan Dunlap

FaithHappenings Publishers

FaithHappenings Publishers
7061 S. University Blvd., Suite 307
Centennial, CO 80122

Cover Design ©2016 FaithHappenings Publishers
Book Layout ©2013 BookDesignTemplates.com

Heart and Soul / Jan Dunlap. -- 1st ed.
ISBN (Softcover) 978-1-941555-30-9
This book was printed in the United States of America.

To order additional copies of this book, contact:
info@faithhappenings.com

FaithHappenings Publishers,
a division of FaithHappenings.com

For all who know that prayer heals, and for those who have yet to

believe

"What am I to do? I will pray with my spirit, but I will pray with my mind also."

1 Corinthians 14:15

PROLOGUE

R aphael Greene had seen much worse. During his last tour of duty in Iraq, he'd often made the helicopter flight from the bloody scene of a roadside mortar attack back to the forward operating base desperately holding pressure on the mangled parts of a soldier's almost-severed limb. Compared to that, the old man on the stretcher here in the back of the Dane County ambulance had it easy. Thanks to the quick thinking of his friends and a makeshift tourniquet fashioned from a leather belt, his sliced femoral artery wasn't going to bleed him out. Rafe figured that the man's chances were more than good he'd keep the leg, along with his life, which was pretty near miraculous considering he'd been at ground zero of a tornado touchdown in rural Wisconsin.

The ambulance caught the edge of a pothole in the road, rattling the racks of supplies that were mounted on the inside surfaces of the emergency vehicle. With one large hand, Rafe grabbed at the man's backboard to balance himself, while his other hand steadied the bag of IV saline swinging near the unconscious man's head.

"Heart rate's dropping! He's going into cardiac arrest!"

Rafe's eyes flew across the patient's body to his fellow paramedic. Jimmy Blue was a kid, hardly out of training, and Rafe wasn't convinced that the guy was really cut out for ambulance work. In the past two weeks of their shared shift, Blue had lost his lunch at accident scenes more times than Rafe could count. Even now, the patient's pale, clammy face wasn't enough to warrant the unprofessional panic in Blue's voice. Deftly opening the IV line to pour more fluids into the patient's vein, Rafe checked the old man's breathing and told Blue to get another bag of saline.

"He lost a lot of blood, man," he reminded the kid. "Keep it coming."

He swapped the empty IV bag for a fresh one just as the ambulance abruptly swayed around a corner. An alarm screamed in the cramped cabin of the vehicle.

"No pulse!" Blue yelled.

Rafe didn't think twice. He grabbed the old man's hand and squeezed tightly while his partner leaned forward to begin CPR in what Rafe knew would be a useless attempt to keep the dying man alive.

But Blue was too late.

Instead of the steady screaming sound of the monitor alarm, a sudden silence filled the cabin.

Silence, except for the soft, reassuring beep of a normal heart rhythm back on the monitor.

The old man's heart had restarted itself.

Stunned, the young paramedic took a second, and third, look at the readouts on the ambulance monitors.

"He should have died," he whispered. "The bleeding, the shock, his age—his heart couldn't have bounced back like that, unassisted."

His wide hazel eyes slowly locked onto Rafe's calm brown ones. "That makes it twice in one week, buddy. People just don't die around you, do they?"

Rafe smiled half-heartedly.

Not if I can help it, he thought, his eyes filling with a distant pain. He pushed the awful memory away and looked at the old man on the stretcher, Blue's comment echoing in his head.

"His heart didn't stop," he told his partner. "It was just a glitch in the equipment when we took that last corner. That crazy man Hansen behind the wheel up there thinks that driving an ambulance is a time trial for the Indy 500."

Rafe turned up the wattage on his smile. "I guess that makes us the pit crew, huh?"

Suspicion continued to cloud Blue's face. Inwardly, Rafe sighed.

It was time to start looking for another job.

Again.

CHAPTER ONE

I think you might need a larger size."

Rafe lowered the tiny shirt he'd been holding up for examination in the hotel gift shop to find a petite woman in a well-tailored business suit smiling at him from the other side of the display table. Beyond her, bright sunlight filtered into the lavish, palm-lined lobby of the Orlando Suites Conference Center, where a crowd of people were busily checking out and loading bags onto luggage trolleys. Rafe's own small duffle bag sat at his feet, already tagged for his departure.

"I'm sorry, I couldn't resist," she said, her dark eyes twinkling at him from beneath a long fringe of jet-black bangs. "You looked so serious studying that little tee-shirt, as if you were trying to figure out a way to make it fit you."

"It's for one of my nieces. She's crazy about princesses," Rafe told the woman, pointing to the silk-screened tiara on the front of the shirt. He held the child-sized shirt up against his own extra-wide chest. "So you don't think I could borrow it from her?"

The woman laughed. "Not unless you're planning to use it for a handkerchief."

Rafe looked down in mock alarm at the glitter-dusted image on the shirt. "Heaven forbid I would even consider wiping my nose on a tiara. I'd lose my favorite-uncle status in a heartbeat."

He glanced back at the woman, who was still smiling. Really nice smile, Rafe thought. Pretty, too. Short. Then again, compared to his own six-foot-three-inch frame, most everyone was shorter than he was anyway. Nothing new there—he'd gotten used to being the big black guy his sophomore year in high school when he'd shot up four inches and put on twenty pounds of hard muscle. His football coach had been thrilled and moved him from defensive tackle to offensive back.

"Just mow 'em down," his coach had told him. "You get that ball and don't stop for anything."

His mama, on the other hand, spent the next two years lecturing him about the moral responsibilities that came with his size.

"Don't you ever take advantage of others because you're big and strong," she'd reminded him daily. "God gives us our gifts in this holy web of life for good reasons, even if we don't know what those reasons are. No matter what, He works through your heart and your hands, and you got to respect that, baby boy. You hear me?"

Oh, he'd heard her all right, and he made sure he respected his gift: he had let God work through his hands—and his extremely quick feet—every time he hit the football field. In fact, he'd respected it all the way to a full-ride football scholarship at LSU. After that, he'd done a stint with the United States Marine Corps as a medic for eight years, seeing more action than he ever wanted to in combat zones in the Middle East and Afghanistan. And it was during those years that he had discovered he had another gift from the good Lord.

He hadn't told his mama about that one yet, though. Truth be told, he was still trying to figure out for himself if it was really a gift after all.

Miraculous healing was a heavy load to bear, especially when guilt hitched a ride on it. One day, he hoped, he'd find the right place to set it all down, but so far, he just kept moving on.

"Heaven forbid," the dark-eyed woman in front of him agreed.

Rafe returned her smile and placed the shirt next to the register on the gift shop counter along with a twenty-dollar bill and then turned back to the woman. He nodded at the dark blue computer travel bag hanging from her shoulder. "Just arriving, or on your way out?"

"Leaving," she said. "I'm waiting for the shuttle to the airport."

"Me, too," he replied.

"Here you go, sir," the store cashier said, handing him his change.

"Thanks." He took his bagged purchase and stuffed it into the top of his duffle, zipped it shut, and looped the strap over his shoulder. "The name's Rafe," he said, extending his hand to the woman, "Rafe Greene."

She smiled that pretty smile again and shook his hand. "I'm Ami Kim."

Her small hand was delicate, but her grip firm and sure. Rafe liked that. Too often, people's handshakes with him were tentative and fleeting, as if they were frightened by his size and couldn't wait to end the contact. This woman, however, didn't seem in the least bit intimidated—in fact, she held on to Rafe's hand just a split second longer than he was accustomed to.

He liked that, too.

He watched her as she bent slightly to her right side and grasped the handle of the wheeled suitcase next to her feet. As she straightened back up, it tipped onto its wheels, just in time for Rafe to see a small red dot traveling up the side of the case to land on Ami's hand.

Rafe reacted instantly. He grabbed Ami around the waist, spun her off her feet, and dove with her behind the display table piled high with Disney princess t-shirts.

A mere breath behind him, a bullet plowed into the stacks of clothing, leaving a small wisp of smoke to trace its passing. Out in the lobby, hotel guests were shouting and screaming, though Rafe didn't hear any gunfire. He looked down at Ami, who was lying sprawled on her side in the shelter of Rafe's big body, her almond-shaped eyes incredibly wide and her face a white mask of shock.

"So," Rafe said, "you come to Orlando often?"

He watched her blink several times while she took ragged breaths.

"That's good," he encouraged her. "Breathing is good. Wakes up all those cells in your body. Most of the time, people don't know how to breathe properly."

"Funny you should say that," Ami said, her voice strained and low. "I tell my patients that all the time, but there's generally not someone shooting at them when I'm saying it." She stared at him. "How can you be so calm? We're hiding behind a table, and there's someone shooting a gun in the hotel!"

"Actually, I don't think anyone's shooting anymore. Aside from the one bullet that hit the table, I haven't heard any other gunshots."

"And that's supposed to make me feel better?"

Rafe nodded. "Yes. That and the fact that no one's going to get to you without having to get through me first. And as for anyone who wants to try that, well, I hope they've got lots of medical coverage, because they're going to need it. I'm a fair-sized guy, in case you hadn't noticed."

He saw that a little color had returned to her face, and the pupils in her eyes weren't quite as dilated as they'd been a minute before. "You said 'my patients,'" he recalled. "Are you a doctor?"

From beyond the gift shop came the voices of the hotel's security team members reassuring guests that the gunman was gone, that the area was safe. When Ami began to sit up, though, Rafe laid his hand on her arm and firmly held her down.

"Give it a minute," he told her. "Let security thoroughly sweep the area before you make yourself a target again. There's no reason to rush here."

Ami blew out a breath that ruffled her long bangs. "I'm not a target. Why would you say that? That's crazy."

"Is it?" he asked. His brown eyes pinned hers. "Someone had a laser scope on your hand. That doesn't seem like a random thing, if you ask me."

For a split second, Rafe saw a flash of fear in Ami's eyes.

"My hand?"

"Yes, your hand," Rafe repeated, then rose to one knee and offered his own hand to help Ami lift herself up from the carpeted floor. As soon as she took it, though, he winced as her slight weight pulled against an old football injury.

"Oh, I'm so sorry!" she immediately apologized. "It's your MCL, isn't it? Hitting the floor like that—that couldn't have helped."

Rafe stood up, too, and brushed some carpet lint off his jeans. He studied the woman's attractive face, wondering how she knew about the damaged ligament on the inside of his left knee. Sure, he'd seen plenty of ace medical practitioners in his years as a paramedic, but he'd never seen anyone diagnose a specific knee problem without at least touching the joint in question.

"How did you know about my knee?" he asked her. "Are you an orthopedist?"

"No," she said. "I'm a cardiologist—a heart doctor."

Her eyes slid away from his for a moment, then returned.

"I just guessed that a 'fair-sized guy' like you probably played sports at some point—maybe in high school—and I also know that knee injuries often come back to haunt you later."

Rafe studied her again. She was right, knee injuries were par for the course for men who played sports. But the most common knee injury for old football players was a tear in the ACL, not the MCL. Unless she'd practiced orthopedic medicine before she went into cardiology, what were the odds that a heart doctor would guess the less common ligament injury?

For that matter, what were the odds that a cardiologist would have a laser gun sight locked onto her hand in a hotel gift shop in Orlando?

"Excuse me, ma'am. Sir?"

Rafe turned to find two uniformed police officers standing on the other side of the damaged display table.

"I'm Sgt. Hernandez and this is Lt. Loch. We need to take your statements about what just happened here," the older policeman said. The younger officer flipped over a fresh page in his small notebook.

"I really don't know," Ami promptly volunteered. "I was just chatting with this man here in the gift shop, and then I was on the floor. And then people were screaming. I'm a doctor," she added. "Was anyone hurt?"

Loch shook his head. "No, ma'am. It appears to be a random act of violence. We think the shot came in through the open doors there."

He pointed across the bright lobby to the hotel's main entrance.

"You can see it's a straight line from here. We've had some trouble lately with gangs trying to move into this area, so my guess is that we're going to find out that's what this is connected to."

"Pretty high-tech gangs," Rafe said. "The shooter had a sniper rifle with a laser scope."

Almost in perfect unison, the two officers took a step closer to Rafe. He could see the sudden wariness in their eyes.

"I'm a former marine," he explained. "Medical corps. I saw the red tracer move across the lady's suitcase just before I moved her into cover."

Hernandez turned back to the diminutive doctor. "Who did you say you were?"

"Dr. Ami Kim," she told him. "I'm a cardiologist at the University of Minnesota Medical Center. I was here for the medical convention that ended last night. I was just waiting for the airport shuttle when the shooting started."

"Sorry to have your visit end on this note," Loch told her. "Gang violence isn't exactly the kind of publicity we want in Orlando. Could you walk me through what you do recall? You first, Doctor."

Rafe watched Ami's face as she spoke with the two men, answering their questions as they scribbled notes for their report. Now that she wasn't flat on the floor behind the display table, Ami Kim was the consummate professional. Cool and collected. Rafe had to admit to himself that she impressed him with her quick recovery from the surreal shooting; caught in a violent situation, she'd only given in to a few moments of panic after he'd knocked her out of the gunman's sights. Most people would be experiencing some adrenaline letdown just about now, fighting off the shakes, but Rafe didn't see a single tremor shake her composure while Ami talked with the policemen. Despite the close encounter with a bullet that had just missed her, the doctor apparently had nerves of steel.

In fact, looking at Ami now, if Rafe hadn't seen the red dot on her hand himself, he wouldn't have believed that she'd been in the sights of a rifle just minutes ago.

But she had.

And then there was another thing Rafe wouldn't have believed: a gang member not only had a laser-scope sniper rifle, but he had the skill to use it proficiently enough to accurately target the small hand of a woman when a lobby half-full of people stood between them.

If he were completely honest with himself, Rafe still didn't believe it, which could only mean that no matter what Ami thought, it had been no fluke of fate that a single bullet had been fired through the Orlando Suites front entrance to bury itself in a bed of cotton t-shirts just inches from the pretty doctor's hand. The truth was that if it hadn't been for Rafe's lightning response, Ami's hand would be bleeding right now all over the gift shop carpet, and he'd be applying a pressure bandage until the ambulance arrived. Best case, she might have sustained only a little nerve damage; worst case, she could have lost the use of her hand.

For a physician who had spent years in training to perform intricate, complex procedures inside the heart, an injury like that would be devastating both professionally and personally. Rafe had spent enough years around emergency room doctors to know at least that much, and Ami's momentary reaction had clearly confirmed that assumption. A cardiologist who couldn't treat hearts was a lost soul.

Like a healer who had failed to heal . . .

For what seemed like the millionth time, Rafe pushed the memory away. He knew it would come back later, just as it always did, but right now, he needed to keep his attention on something he didn't know, which was why someone wanted to put a bullet into this particular physician's hand. Because, whether she wanted to believe it or not, Ami Kim had definitely been the sniper's target.

That little red dot he'd seen knew exactly where it was going.

"The laser locked on her right hand," he told Hernandez.

Loch looked from Rafe to Ami, then back to Rafe again. "That would be a real problem for a doctor, wouldn't it?"

He swung his attention back to Ami. "Maybe this wasn't such a random shooting after all. You sure there's nobody holding a serious grudge against you, Doc? Maybe a malpractice suit pending? Some grieving relatives of a patient you lost?"

"I've never lost a patient," Ami said.

Rafe was certain he hadn't heard her correctly.

"You've never lost a patient?" he asked, disbelief clear in his voice.

Ami turned to look at Rafe.

"No, I've never lost a patient," she repeated, slowly this time, so he couldn't possibly mistake her words.

"That's . . ." he started to say "impossible," but caught himself. After all, "impossible" was what he did on a regular basis.

"Phenomenal," he amended, his eyes pinning hers.

"Yes," she agreed, returning his gaze with an equal intensity. "That's exactly what it is."

Rafe felt a frisson of awareness travel down his spine.

There was something very special about Dr. Ami Kim.

"Let me get this straight," Hernandez interrupted. "You cure all your patients?"

Ami briefly shook her head. "I didn't say I cure them all," she tried to explain. "Curing and healing are not the same thing. There are nuances in those terms, and it gets rather complicated and involved, Sergeant, and I don't know that you really want to get into that right now. Suffice it to say, that no, I don't have any litigation pending against me, nor is there anyone I know of who would want to hurt me. Besides which, I was here for a conference—I don't even know anyone in Orlando."

The policeman exchanged a glance with his partner, who nodded towards Rafe. "Anything to add to the doctor's comments?" he asked him.

Rafe shook his head. "She covered it all."

Hernandez looked over at his partner's notes and sighed. "Then let's just get your contact information, and we'll let you two folks get on with your day," he said. "I imagine, at this point, you're more than ready to head home."

Ami pulled a business card from her computer case and handed it to the lieutenant, while Rafe verified his name and address for Hernandez. Beyond them in the lobby, hotel security people milled around, apparently waiting for further instructions from the investigating policemen.

"I hope you catch the shooter," Ami told the two men. "Gang violence is the last thing you want around here."

"You can say that again, Dr. Kim," Loch assured her.

He offered his hand to her and then to Rafe.

"Thanks for the cooperation, folks. I'm sorry your trip had to end on such a bad note."

He gave Rafe a little salute with his fingers. "Thanks for the sharp eye and the save, Mr. Greene. If it hadn't been for you, we'd be looking at a lot messier crime scene. We'll be in touch."

"Yes, thank you for the save," Ami said as the police officers walked away. "I don't think I've said that yet. You're obviously a good man to have around, Rafe Greene." She brushed a few bangs from her eyes and smiled at him. "But I really do have a plane to catch."

"So do I," he reminded her, lifting his duffle back onto his shoulder. He reached for her suitcase handle, but she was quicker.

"I've got it." She pointed to the people still filling the lobby. "You lead the way for us out to the shuttle. I think people will get out of your path faster than they will mine, and since I now have almost an hour less to make my plane, speed is of the essence."

"We're out of here," Rafe replied, striding out across the reception area. Behind him, he could hear the wheels rolling on Ami's suitcase as she hustled to keep close on his heels.

"Don't worry, we'll make your flight," he told her over his shoulder, stealing another glance at the woman trailing him.

No doubt about it, Ami Kim was someone his mother would call "a person of interest." His mother's criteria—friendly, polite, and unmarried, judging from Ami's bare ring finger—was not, however, necessarily shared by Rafe. Unlike his mother, the eternally optimistic matchmaker, Rafe found Ami interesting because of what he didn't know about her. He felt an echo of the shiver he'd experienced when she'd insisted she had never lost a patient.

Never?

How was that possible, especially for a cardiologist who worked with a wide range of patients in a large medical center? Statistics alone dictated that some of those patients wouldn't survive. Even claiming an eighty percent recovery rate would be utterly astonishing when it came to patients with heart disease. Ami Kim would have to be more than an extraordinary physician to post a success rate of one hundred percent.

She would also have to be more than a cardiologist if she could instantly recognize that Rafe had a bad MCL. Nobody could diagnose that condition without first doing some kind of physical exam, yet the good doctor had correctly and instantly identified it without Rafe even mentioning his knee pain.

And last but not least, why did someone want to put a bullet in the pretty doctor's obviously very talented—and valuable— hand?

Yes, Dr. Ami Kim was, by far, the most interesting woman that Rafe had encountered in a long while.

Interesting was good.

In fact, it was so good that Rafe decided to change his current flight destination from Milwaukee to Minneapolis. He had some time on his hands since he was between jobs again, and a little visit to the Twin Cities might be just what the doctor ordered in this case.

Or, rather, what the paramedic self-prescribed, because Rafe was getting that gut feeling that there was a lot more to Ami Kim than a successful heart doctor who had come to an Orlando medical convention and unexpectedly got caught in the middle of a gang turf battle.

Besides, Rafe really did like her smile.

CHAPTER TWO

.

Tapping impatiently on the padded steering wheel of his new BMW, Niles Villome waited for yet another red stoplight to turn green on Lake Street. He hated driving in this part of Minneapolis; no matter what time of day, the traffic slowed to a crawl through dying neighborhoods of barren yards and the occasional boarded-up building. How some urban developer had managed to entice any store owners, let alone so many upscale restaurants, to open shops in the area he was heading for, he'd never been able to figure out. If Niles had had his choice, the entire neighborhood would have been leveled and rebuilt from the ground up to get rid of all the transients and relocated refugees that populated the district. Unfortunately, though, taking Lake was the quickest route from his office near the University Medical Center to the Black Forest Inn, and he was already running behind schedule for this mid-afternoon meeting.

Niles hated being late.

When a pedestrian started to step into the crosswalk just as the light turned green, Niles pounded on his car horn, sending the elderly man reeling back onto the sidewalk.

"Drunk," he muttered, spinning his wheel hard to make a sharp right-hand turn onto a small side street. "Or blind. Either way, stay off the streets."

He barreled north a few blocks and took a left turn onto one-way Twenty-Sixth Street. Barely a minute later, he slipped the BMW into a parking space on Second Avenue, or "Eat Street," as the optimistic city planners had dubbed the restaurant-filled row. Grabbing his briefcase, Niles shot out of his car and headed for the German restaurant. As he pulled the heavy door open, he glanced at his watch to check the time.

He was four minutes late.

Which would never have happened if Pieter Hallenstroem had agreed to meet Niles in his Minneapolis office.

But as Niles had learned in the past six months, the last thing Hallenstroem did was consider anyone else's schedule. As the founder and CEO of the infant Calyx Pharmaceuticals, Inc., the Belgian boy-wizard expected everyone to accommodate him.

Niles stepped across the tiny entrance lobby of the restaurant to check with the hostess at the reception stand. Paneled in dark wood and adorned with the impressive heads of full-grown bucks and bighorn sheep, the Black Forest Inn could have been plucked right out of a Bavarian village—not only could Niles smell the red cabbage simmering, but the aroma of the restaurant's signature fresh-baked *brotchen* reminded him he'd skipped lunch a few hours ago. He waited for his eyes to adjust to the Inn's dimly lit interior while the hostess checked her table chart for where she had stashed Hallenstroem.

"This way, please," the young woman said, leading Niles into a side room of seating. She ushered him to a table near the back wall, where another deer head hung mounted, its glassy eyes forever focused on nothing. Below the hunting trophy, two men in expensive suits were drinking mugs of dark beer and quietly perusing the menus.

"Pieter." Niles reached out to shake Hallenstroem's hand. "I'm sorry I'm late. I caught all the stoplights, I'm afraid."

The younger of the two men clasped Niles's hand in a sure grip.

"Not a problem, Doctor. It's good to see you again, Niles."

He inclined his head toward his table companion.

"Have you ever met Diedrich Mahler? He's just come on board at Calyx as my executive vice president of new product development. I stole him away from one of my competitors because he is a genius at new drug introductions. Diedrich, this is Dr. Niles Villome. He is going to make us all rich."

Pieter laughed.

"I mean, richer."

The older man rose slightly out of his chair and extended his own slim hand to Niles.

"It's a pleasure, Doctor. I'm looking forward to our collaboration. Please, join us."

Niles shook the offered hand and took the third chair at the table, setting his briefcase near his feet and trying to mask his sudden annoyance.

He'd only expected Pieter at this meeting.

In the eleven months since he had first approached the Calyx CEO with his proposal for the new drug, Niles had become accustomed to reporting directly to Pieter; the news that a third person had been added to their intimate party for two was upsetting, if not insulting. Noting the men's comfortable camaraderie at the table, Niles also couldn't shake the feeling that he'd just been relegated to odd man out, when he'd been anticipating being the sole recipient of Pieter's undivided attention.

Niles didn't like agenda changes, especially when he wasn't the one making them.

A black-clad waitress with a stud above her lip appeared at his side and asked him what he'd like from the bar. Not caring for the Inn's heavy German beers, he opted for white wine and ordered a glass of Piesporter Michelsburg.

As she hurried back across the empty room, Hallenstroem leaned his elbows on the table and fixed his sharp gaze on Niles.

"So, where do we stand with the trials? The last time we met, I was less than pleased with your team's progress. But if I am remembering correctly, you promised me some substantial data today that would assure me that my money was being well spent." He threw a glance at Mahler, then turned his attention back to Niles.

"I've decided I want CardiaZone on the market within the year."

Niles tensed and bit his tongue to keep himself from blurting out a protest at the short deadline—a deadline that was considerably sooner than the two years they had originally agreed upon. True, the drug already had the FDA's stamp of approval for its original application, but even Phase IV testing for alternative usages took time and patience. Patience that Pieter Hallenstroem apparently lacked. Not for the first time since he had sealed the deal with Calyx, Niles wondered if he was really going to be able to pull the whole thing off.

"CardiaZone?" he repeated.

Pieter smiled indulgently. "Our marketing agency came up with it. They have the whole introductory campaign already mapped out. I can't tell you how eager they are about getting started. Perhaps as eager as me."

Niles felt his stomach seize and a wave of panic rise in his chest. His eyes jumped from Pieter to Mahler, and he realized that the new Calyx vice president was watching his reaction closely.

"Not to worry, Dr. Villome," Mahler assured him. "Everyone at the ad agency has signed a confidentiality agreement, so no word about your research has leaked out."

Niles swallowed with difficulty and quickly looked around the room for any prying eyes or listening ears, but the room was empty save for the three men at the table.

"There's no way you can guarantee that," he choked out. "There are industrial spies everywhere, and the pharmaceutical development business has got to be one of the most lucrative places to ferret out secrets."

He could feel both his temper and his blood pressure rising. How could Pieter have made such a stupid move as to bring in more people at this point in the process, potentially jeopardizing everything he had invested in Niles's project? All it would take was one loose-lipped copywriter talking about his day over a happy hour drink at the local bar to tip off the bloodhounds from other big pharma companies. Pieter's million dollars of funding and Niles's months of research would run right down the drain if competitors caught a whiff of what the two men were developing. The pharmaceutical industry thrived on the game of one-upmanship, and Niles was furious that the boy-wizard had put Niles's work—and his ultimate big payday—at risk by jumping the marketing gun.

"I can't believe this," Niles continued, his voice pitched low, his anger barely contained. "We've got the biggest pharmaceutical coup of the decade—the century—under wraps in my lab, and you paraded it in front of a bunch of publicity people? People whose jobs require them to talk about their clients' products? I'm amazed my cell phone isn't already ringing with calls from your competitors, Pieter." He closed his eyes and massaged his temples. "We haven't even finished the third set of trials yet."

"I own the marketing agency, Niles." The Belgian grinned at the doctor. "If there's even the smallest leak about CardiaZone, they all lose their jobs. It's as simple as that. So you see, I'm not worried at all."

Niles let out a ragged breath. He still wasn't convinced there would be no security breaches. More than that, however, he was inwardly shaken by Pieter's rush to release a drug that he was still in the midst of testing for efficacy.

Or rather, that his research team was testing for efficacy. So far, the drug was exceeding expectations, but until the final trial was completed, Niles refused to guarantee its unqualified success. The history of pharmaceuticals was littered with great prospects gone terribly wrong, thanks to premature enthusiasm and inadequate long-term studies, not to mention pure bad luck. Niles could name two such nightmare scenarios without even thinking about it: TGN1412, the so-called "Elephant Man" drug trial in England that was supposed to yield a new drug for leukemia treatment but instead led to organ failure in its first human clinical trials; and the Phase III trials of a touted lung-cancer drug that were suspended after the patients in treatment were dying at a faster rate than those not in the trials.

Not only did such failures result in patient deaths, but they also irrevocably decimated doctors' careers and drove drug companies into the financial sinkhole of massive insurance settlements. Maybe Calyx could survive that kind of catastrophe, but Niles certainly wouldn't.

Niles didn't have the money to cover that kind of a mistake.

Especially since he'd already been taking some liberties with Pieter's funding.

As the director of his clinic, Niles had naturally assumed all the administrative duties for the project, leaving his research team leader free to immerse herself in the actual research protocol. Likewise, he'd very willingly grabbed the financial reins that Pieter had generously provided him—along with a lion's share of the funding to which he felt entitled for his bringing the drug to Calyx's attention. Busy CEO that he was, Pieter had never questioned the fiscal reports Niles had submitted for review, nor had he indicated he wanted to push for a release of the drug earlier than the two years they had negotiated in their initial agreement.

Now Niles wondered why Pieter was bent on speeding up the work, and, at the same time, taking a step back to hand the project to Mahler.

Almost as if the man had read his thoughts, the new vice president took control of the conversation.

"So tell us how CardiaZone is coming along," Mahler suggested, leaning back in his chair and focusing his dark eyes on the doctor. "I'm assuming you have some things to show us in your briefcase."

He nodded towards the valise that Niles had set on the floor. "I'd very much like to see this miracle drug that Pieter is so excited about. He says it will change the face of medicine, Dr. Villome."

Niles quickly studied the man who was so obviously trying to put him at ease, which only made Niles more suspicious of him. Weathered and lined, Mahler's face looked much more like the face of an outdoorsman than a corporate executive. His prominent cheekbones cast shadows over his jaw in the subdued lighting of the Inn, and his cropped silver hair reminded Niles of the retired military men he often treated in his cardiology practice. Like those men, Mahler held himself straight and tall, even while leaning back in an old wooden chair at a make-believe Bavarian restaurant. Unlike those aging patients, however, the Calyx vice president projected an unmistakable sense of power and authority that had Niles suddenly deciding that it would be in his best interests to stay on the man's good side.

Which meant he'd better take another look at those financial reports when he got back to the office after this late afternoon meeting. A few adjustments might be necessary.

Niles leaned over and pulled out a sheaf of papers from his case.

"I only have the one set of the data with me, so you'll have to share, I'm afraid."

He spread three pages on the table between Pieter and Mahler and pointed to the bottom lines on each sheet.

"These are the results from the first two trials. They document the percentages of arterial blockage improvement after three months of using the new drug—CardiaZone."

He watched the men's faces for their reactions to the numbers. As they eagerly scanned the numbers and remained silent, Niles shoved another set of three pages in front of them.

"And here's the data on blood pressure and lipid panels for those two trials. By my estimation, we should have the third trial completed in another month, and it will document the patients' results six months out after beginning use of CardiaZone. But you can see on this sheet," Niles paused to hand them yet another piece of paper covered with bar charts and percentages, "where the trial subjects are sitting as of today."

The waitress finally returned with a glass of wine for Niles and set it on the small area of the table not covered with pages of paper.

"Are you ready to order?" she asked the men, all of whom were intently reading the columns of numbers.

"Give us a few more minutes," Niles brusquely told her.

She raised her eyebrows at his sharp tone, then nodded silently and left the room.

Pieter looked up to shoot his boyish grin at Niles.

"This is exactly what I wanted to see, Niles. This is my billion dollar baby, right here. I just may have to increase that little bonus I promised you."

Actually, Niles was already counting on it. Pieter's obvious pleasure with the reports finally relaxed the knot that had formed in the doctor's stomach. A moment later, Mahler raised his eyes from the data, too.

"This is unbelievable. You are seeing total reversal of heart disease, using a drug that has already been approved to treat—of all things—personality disorders. You're right, Pieter, we should be marketing CardiaZone within the year." Mahler whistled softly between his teeth. "Gentlemen, we are not only going to become unimaginably wealthy from this, but we are going to change the world with this drug."

"I'll drink to that," Pieter said and hoisted his beer stein. Niles and Mahler clinked their own glasses to Pieter's, and the three men all took a long drink.

"Now, where is that charming waitress so I can order my Wiener schnitzel?" the boy-wizard asked. "I'm going to go find her. You two talk some more. Get acquainted."

And with that, Pieter rose and left the room.

"He is very relieved," Mahler told Niles as soon as Pieter was out of earshot. "You may not be aware of this, but he is staking Calyx's future on your CardiaZone. The sooner we release the drug, the easier he will breathe."

Niles swirled the remaining white wine in his glass and considered what Mahler had just told him.

"I was under the impression that money was no object to Pieter Hallenstroem."

Mahler's dark eyes narrowed.

"Money is always an object to someone like Pieter, Niles. Just because he tosses it about with much more abandon than perhaps you or I might, it doesn't mean he doesn't want it to return to him with a sizable increase. The success of Cardia-Zone will do three things for Pieter."

Niles watched as Mahler laid his right fist on the pile of paper beside his beer mug and extended his right index finger.

"One: it will position Calyx as an industry leader in the treatment of heart disease, which will ensure that future innovators of drug therapies will come to the company for exclusive development contracts."

Mahler's middle finger joined its neighbor on the table.

"Two: the success of CardiaZone will render the whole range of heart-treatment drugs of other pharmaceutical companies obsolete, wreaking havoc with those companies' bottom lines and probably putting some of them out of business, clearing the field for Calyx's domination of the worldwide pharma market.

"And three," he said, his ring finger sliding into place on the papers, "Pieter will have his place in history as the man who introduced the world to a cure for heart disease. Any one of those things would ensure Pieter's place in entrepreneurial history, but all three? The man will be a legend for all time."

Mahler lifted his mug and drained the beer, keeping his eyes locked on Niles. "Wouldn't you be anxious if you were in his shoes, Dr. Villome?"

Niles nodded, almost mesmerized by the intensity of the man's dark stare. The full weight of what his research project could do, and what Pieter Hallenstroem expected it to do, came crashing down on his shoulders. Despite the light taste of the wine that lingered on his lips, his tongue felt thick and his mouth dry. Niles suddenly realized that personally appropriating a disproportionate percentage of Calyx's funding was probably the least of his worries. If the final results of his Phase IV drug trials came up short, the Belgian boy-wizard would probably come looking for someone to blame for the collapse of his glorious house of pharmaceutical cards, and it didn't take a brain surgeon to figure out that Niles would be on the short list of candidates.

"What do you suggest I do, Diedrich?"

Mahler finally broke eye contact with Niles and casually pulled the menu out from under the papers that Niles had laid on the table. He took a quick glance at the laminated sheet and passed it to Niles.

"I think you should authorize overtime for your researchers and ask them to expedite the trials. In fact, I'd like to return with you to your office and speak with them myself. Offer them encouragement and, perhaps, incentive."

Niles dropped his eyes to the menu, but registered nothing, except a deep sense of foreboding that Mahler wasn't going to like what he was about to say.

"They're not in the lab or offices today," he told his new boss. "My lead researcher is attending a conference out of the state, so everyone is taking a few days off."

Mahler tipped his head a fraction of an inch in silent response.

"I see. I assume your people all have signed non-disclosure agreements as well. As you so vehemently pointed out to Pieter earlier, there are industrial spies everywhere."

Niles nervously swallowed the last of his wine. "Of course they have."

"Good," Mahler approved. "But I think we would all sleep better at night from this point on if you kept your research team close to home and focused on the prize here. Don't you agree? After all, travel poses certain risks beyond delayed departures and mechanical difficulties. I'm sure you've seen it as well as I, how the close confines of traveling can make casual companions out of total strangers."

His eyes locked again on Niles.

"Or even friends of those who might otherwise be our enemies."

Niles felt himself bristling at the implied suggestion that any of his team might be leaking word of their research, deliberately or otherwise.

"My people are completely trustworthy," he assured Mahler tightly.

"I'm glad to hear it," the vice president replied. "Especially since we are so close to the finish line."

His eyes lifted briefly beyond Niles's shoulder.

"I see Pieter has our waitress in tow." He lowered his voice to a whisper. "I want us to cross that finish line sooner rather than later, Doctor. Make it happen."

An hour later, Niles slid into his BMW and turned on the ignition. Somehow, he'd have to convince the team to accelerate the drug trials. He checked his side mirrors and pulled into the lane of traffic. His team leader wouldn't like it; knowing her obsession with perfectionism, Niles could only imagine the fight that lay ahead of him when he told her to push up the schedule of her research. The woman was brilliant, no doubt about it, but in this case, her perfectionism might just cost him not only a very big bonus from Calyx, but his whole medical career. After spending part of an afternoon with Diedrich Mahler, Niles was sure that if he failed to deliver the drug that Pieter Hallenstroem wanted, the Calyx vice president would make him miserable—and probably unemployable—for the rest of his life.

Since Niles had no desire to give up either his prestigious university teaching position or his lucrative medical practice, however, he found himself rehearsing arguments to throw at his business partner as soon as she stepped into the office tomorrow morning. With any luck, Dr. Ami Kim would, for once in her life, see the wisdom in his reasoning, give him what he wanted, and speed up the research. True, Ami had never been one for life in the fast lane, but then again, neither had Niles.

Or at least, he hadn't been until he'd realized that a young, hungry pharmaceutical CEO would virtually write him a blank check to test a drug to reverse heart disease—a drug that had already passed FDA approval for human use. The fact that the trials Ami had designed were simple and almost cost-free was icing on the profit cake, and certainly no reason to inform Pieter that his funding was almost unnecessary. Niles had quickly learned that big pharmaceutical companies expected to dole out millions for drug development, and rather than dispel that assumption and thereby earn the ire of his medical colleagues, he'd kept his mouth closed and quietly shunted the money into his own pockets. Since then, he'd been discovering a growing taste for life in the fast lane.

With a quick look at the merging traffic on his left, Niles roared up the ramp to I-35 and headed back towards the medical center. He had a four o'clock appointment with a patient and he hated being late.

Perhaps he needed to remind Ami of that, too, especially since his deadline with Calyx had just been moved up.

A deadline he absolutely could not afford to miss.

CHAPTER THREE

There was something decidedly different about Rafe Greene, but Ami had yet to put her finger on it.

She took a quick look at the man belted into the seat next to her in the first-class cabin of the Boeing 727 as the jet lifted from the runway in Orlando and pointed its nose towards Minnesota. Part of it, she knew, was the way he carried himself. For such a big man, he was surprisingly graceful and light on his feet, and though they'd been maneuvering through tight crowds in the airport, she hadn't seen him bump into a single person.

She, on the other hand, had taken plenty of knocks from harried and hurried travelers as they'd sideswiped her with too-large carry-ons or cut in front of her to dash down a concourse. Finally, she'd fallen into step just behind Rafe and let him clear a path for her in the terminal. When he realized that she'd shifted behind him, he laughed and told her that she was the daintiest back he'd ever blocked for.

"Not that I mind," he'd been quick to add, his eyes sharp with wit and intellect. "And forgive me for being sexist here, but I'd much rather have a beautiful woman watching my tail than any of the bruisers I used to play with."

"Because a woman is smarter and makes better decisions?"

Rafe laughed.

"Yes, ma'am. That too. You can call the plays on my team any day."

That was another thing about Rafe that impressed Ami: not only did the man have a sense of humor, but he was the calmest, most relaxed traveler she'd ever seen. As far as she could tell, the former marine didn't give traveling a second thought. When the hotel shuttle dropped them off at the main terminal, they had checked the departures listing only to find that Rafe's flight to Milwaukee was canceled, and Ami's plane was already boarding. Without missing a beat, Rafe told Ami he'd catch her plane to Minneapolis with her and worry about a connection later.

"There's no way you'll get a seat," she'd warned him as she'd trotted along in Rafe's wake to her gate. She knew that if she'd had a last-minute ticketing change, she would have already been frantically laying out alternate flight possibilities in her head.

"These flights are always overbooked," she'd told him. "Besides which, they're already making the last call for boarding. That means they'll have already given away any seats they did have available to people who were waiting for them. You're going to have to find another flight."

"Oh ye of little faith," Rafe had replied to her over his shoulder. "I'll get a seat. Just watch."

"There is no way that is going to happen," she'd insisted again as Rafe dumped his duffel in front of the gate's ticket counter and aimed a broad smile at the chestnut-haired Latina airline agent behind it.

Two minutes later, a freshly printed boarding pass in his hand, Rafe followed Ami down the jetway.

"I can't believe it," Ami said. "Not only is there one seat left, but it's the one next to mine."

"I'm not stalking you, in case you're wondering," Rafe laughed. "I'm just lucky when it comes to traveling. Always have been."

Now Ami had to wonder if Rafe's traveling luck was rubbing off on her. She couldn't remember the last time she'd made a flight with only moments to spare, let alone actually taken off on time. And as for her seating arrangements, she could probably count on one hand the times she'd flown with an attractive, interesting man seated beside her.

Not to mention the fact that the man in the seat beside her had knocked her hand out of a sniper's gunsight and probably saved her professional career.

Or maybe her life.

For the first time since Rafe had tackled her in the gift shop, Ami let herself consider what might have happened if she hadn't been flirting with the big man looking at princess shirts. Would the sniper have adjusted his aim to somewhere other than her hand? Or was her hand never his target at all, and Rafe had said that only to minimize a worse scenario?

Had someone tried to kill her at the Orlando Suites?

"Are you all right?"

Ami realized she was staring into Rafe's brown eyes, her jaw clenched and her knuckles white on the armrest between them. Her teeth were chattering uncontrollably.

Rafe laid a big hand over her smaller one, and immediately, Ami felt some of the terror slip away.

"It's the adrenaline letdown," he explained, his voice just above a whisper. "It usually hits just about the same time that your brain finally begins to process the trauma. You're doing the 'what ifs?' aren't you?"

She nodded, her eyes still locked on his.

"Don't," he breathed. "Either the adrenaline will kick back in or you'll fall apart." He gently squeezed her hand beneath his. "But either way, I'm right here, Ami. Like I told you in the shuttle, I've got years of paramedic experience behind me, so no matter which way you swing right now, I'm going to help you through it. Okay? Do you trust me?"

Ami hesitated.

Trust him?

She didn't know Rafe Greene at all. Aside from the trite, polite, conversational exchange they'd had on the way to the airport in the hotel transport, the only thing she knew for sure about him was that he had extremely quick reflexes and maintained a remarkable cool under pressure. Both were traits she admired in any situation, and if she had to find herself in the midst of a crisis—exactly as she had in the Orlando Suites' gift shop—they were exactly the traits she'd most want to see in a paramedic attending her.

But did she trust the man?

She could almost hear the bitter laughter echoing in her head, but then another sound overlaid it—the nearly silent whoosh of a bullet speeding past her shoulder.

Rafe had pulled her back from harm's way.

Ami nodded.

"Good. Breathe. Breathe with me," Rafe instructed her. "In through your nose. Out through your mouth. Again. In. Out."

Ami synchronized her breaths with his. After a few more inhalations, she began to smile. Her teeth stopped their chattering and the tightness in her lungs eased. In its place, she felt warmth creeping back inside her veins. She'd been on the verge of shock, she realized shakily, but Rafe had pulled her out of the danger zone.

Again.

"Okay, that's the second breathing lesson you've given me today," she said, her voice betraying only a little shakiness. "The first one was behind a table in the gift shop while someone was spraying bullets around the hotel lobby. Are you, by any chance, a yoga instructor, as well as a paramedic?"

Ami watched the tiny lines of tension that had creased the outer corners of his eyes start to smooth away as his full lips lifted into a smile.

"Now there's an idea," he said. "Maybe I should forget working as a paramedic and just hang out my shingle: Breathing Lessons with Rafe Greene. Do you think I could make a living at it?"

For a second, her gaze held by his, Ami had no doubt that this very appealing man could make a living at whatever he chose to do—and if her own sudden physical response to him was any indication, Rafe Greene would have women lining up to learn to breathe with him. Feeling a hot flush blooming on her cheeks, Ami dropped her eyes to his hand where it still lay, covering hers. She didn't want to acknowledge how comforting it felt, so she tried to make light of the chemical attraction she felt growing inside herself.

"Tell me," she said after a moment, "do you pick up a lot of women this way? Rescuing damsels in gun sights and telling them to breathe?"

Rafe's smile grew broader.

"I don't know yet. This is my first try. Is it working?"

Ami glanced up at him through her long bangs, just as the plane's captain announced that passengers were free to get up and move about the cabin. She could feel more warmth spreading through her chest.

"I'll let you know when we get to Minneapolis."

He squeezed her hand one more time before releasing it to wave at the flight attendant approaching their seats. "Can I buy you a bottle of water?" he asked Ami. "Talking patients down from shock makes me thirsty."

"I'd love one," Ami answered, relieved at his change of subject. "I think avoiding shock does the same thing to me. Not that I want to repeat the experience in order to verify that hypothesis."

Rafe asked the flight attendant for water bottles and turned back to Ami.

"As a matter of fact, I really am looking for employment at the moment. That's why I was in Orlando—I had a job interview. What do you think my chances are of finding a paramedic position in Minneapolis?"

"Dr. Kim?"

An elderly man stood in the aisle, his left hand grasping the seat back in front of Rafe.

"Excuse me," he apologized to Rafe as he leaned in to offer his right hand to Ami. "I'm Dr. Uttam. I heard you speak at the conference last night, and I was very impressed with your work. I'm on staff at the Mayo Clinic in Rochester, and I'd very much like to have you see the exploratory research we're doing there. I think you will find that it closely mirrors what you are doing, but with leukemia patients rather than heart patients."

Ami shook the doctor's hand and smiled.

"Thank you for the invitation, Dr. Uttam. I've heard a little about your work, and I'd love the opportunity to visit sometime. I agree—I think we could definitely find some common ground."

The doctor slipped his hand inside his suit jacket and withdrew a business card to pass along to Ami. "I'll look forward to hearing from you."

He again glanced at Rafe as he moved back into the aisle. "I'm sorry to intrude."

"Not a problem," Rafe replied.

The elderly doctor turned away and took a seat two rows ahead in the front of the first-class cabin.

Ami tucked Dr. Uttam's card into her own jacket pocket and looked back at Rafe to find a puzzled expression on his face.

"What?"

"What was an oncologist doing at a cardiology conference? I'm assuming Dr. Uttam is a cancer doc, since he mentioned working with leukemia patients."

"Your water bottles," the attendant said, interrupting Rafe.

Rafe thanked the younger man, took the two short bottles, and gave one to Ami. He picked up the conversation where it had left off. "It seems a little out of his area of specialty, don't you think?"

"Not at all," Ami answered. "You assume wrongly. Dr. Uttam is a neurologist, a neurophysiologist actually, not an oncologist. His area of expertise focuses on how the brain can rewire itself. He's a pioneer in TMS."

"What's TMS?"

"Transcranial magnetic stimulators."

She took a sip of her water and threw him a quick smile. "Do you want the short version or the full lecture?"

"Be gentle with me," Rafe told her. "Layman's terms, please."

Ami laughed.

"Okay," she agreed. "Here's the introductory lecture. Basically, the human brain is electrical. It has thirty billion neurons, and when these neurons communicate with each other, they form synapses—sort of like electrical bridges that carry information from one neuron to another. That's how the brain processes data."

Rafe nodded. "That's why cochlear implants work at helping the deaf to hear. A microelectrode is inserted into the patient's auditory nerve and the implant converts sound into electrical impulses that are carried to the brain."

"That's right," she said. "And then the brain learns to interpret this impulse as a sound with meaning to it. It's similar to learning a new language, in a way. The bottom line is that the brain responds to electrical stimulation. TMS is a type of electrical stimulation. It's magnetic, and it has the ability to affect the behavior of neurons in some surprising ways."

"Such as?"

Ami took another drink from her water bottle and then set it on her knee. When she looked back at Rafe, her eyes were filled with excitement.

"The brain is plastic, Rafe. It can be molded, or remolded. Given the right kind of stimulation, the human brain can re-wire its synapses, reshape itself to adapt to change. It's the rea-son that people who have had strokes can regain the use of their paralyzed limbs even though a part of their brains have been damaged. The neurons can grow new connections to heal the body."

Ami searched her seatmate's face to see if he understood the implications of what she was telling him.

With a deep sigh, he leaned back in his seat and tipped his head to stare at the smooth white ceiling over the cabin. Rafe pursed his lips and frowned. "So you're saying that the human brain can heal the body."

"With the right kind of stimulation, yes," Ami agreed.

Rafe rubbed his chin with his left hand and continued to in-spect the ceiling. "And this connects to your cardiology confer-ence in what way?"

For a moment or two, Ami was silent. "I never said what conference I was attending," she corrected him. "You assumed it was a cardiology conference because I told you I was a cardi-ologist. I was attending a neurology conference. I presented a paper on the neurophysiological indications of cardiac recov-ery."

She could almost see the wheels spinning in Rafe's head as he remained silent.

He took a few long sips from his water bottle, then turned his whole body in his seat to face her.

"This paper you presented—it has to do with the fact that you've never lost a patient, doesn't it? What have you done, Dr. Ami Kim? Discovered a drug therapy that empowers the brain to heal heart disease? Or is it the cure for cancer?"

Rafe's sheer size suddenly seemed to fill Ami's vision. Yet she didn't feel intimidated by the big man, or by his questions. All she felt was the complete confidence in her research that had fueled her work for the last two years. Confronted by this man she hardly knew, but to whom she felt inexplicably drawn and somehow connected to, Ami realized she didn't want to say goodbye to Rafe in the Minneapolis airport.

"It might be both," she whispered.

CHAPTER FOUR

Speechless, Rafe stared at Ami. "You're kidding me, right?" Ami shook her head.

Rafe collapsed back into his seat and locked his elbows on either side of his head. Inside his mind, a thousand thoughts spun and reconfigured themselves as he tried to make sense of everything that had happened since meeting Ami Kim in the hotel's gift shop. Knowing now why she had been in Orlando, and what she had been doing there, he began to see the shooting in the hotel in a different light, and he was convinced that his initial impression—that she had been the actual target—was dead-on. He inwardly winced at the unintentional pun. The fact was that someone wanted very badly to put a stop to Ami Kim's incredible research.

But if that were the case, why was the laser's sight on her hand, and not her head?

Rafe had met enough sharpshooters during his service in the Marines to know that snipers didn't make mistakes when they aimed, nor did they merely wing a target when they wanted him dead. Which could only mean that Ami's shooter wasn't looking for a kill, but instead was delivering a message.

What that message was, Rafe couldn't begin to figure out, but he was certain it had to do with her work.

For her own safely, he wanted to grill her with questions the police had never thought to ask. Who knew about her research? Who was funding her? Were there competing research projects?

He could barely stop himself from laughing out loud as he realized the sheer idiocy of his inquiries.

Who knew about her research?

Well, duh—everyone who attended the neurology conference along with everyone who worked with her in her lab in Minneapolis, not to mention probably a whole legion of patients and family members who had participated in her studies.

Who was funding her?

If Rafe had to guess, if there were any kind of drug involved, it would probably be some pharmaceutical giant salivating over a huge profit in future sales of her discovery. If it didn't involve drugs, then there might be some health foundations or medical think tanks or even some government agencies backing her. Any way he sliced it, there had to be plenty of people who not only knew about Ami's research, but had a serious stake in it, too. And in the competitive world of medical care, that probably meant there were also people who, for their own reasons, were hoping she failed with her project rather than succeeded.

Were there competing research projects?

This one didn't make Rafe want to laugh. The idea that someone might want Amy to fail was bad enough, but in a worst case scenario, it had the potential to get very personal. If someone was vying with Ami for funding, that researcher might have real motivation to put some obstacles in Ami's path. Short of killing her, what would stop the research? Perhaps ending her medical career, which, Rafe guessed, would be almost as fatal to Ami as any bullet to her heart. And based on the near-miss this morning in the hotel gift shop, Rafe couldn't deny that a worst-case scenario was a distinct possibility.

The woman needed protection, but Rafe was pretty sure Ami didn't know it. Nor did he think this was the moment to apprise her of the extent of the danger she might be in. He'd already talked her down from the verge of shock once on the plane; he didn't think he wanted to go a second round in the same spot. Maybe, instead, he could talk her into a late dinner when they landed, and then he could lay out his suspicions over salad and steak.

"Rafe?"

He dropped his elbows to the armrests and looked at Ami's solemn face, her eyes narrowed with suspicion.

"You think I'm crazy, don't you?" she asked him. "That I've blown my research completely out of proportion. How unbelievable—a neurological cure for cancer and heart disease. You save my hand, possibly my life, and I thank you with letting you know you've got a lunatic sitting in the seat beside you."

Rafe shook his head, thinking that if Ami wanted "unbelievable," he could show her a thing or two.

Unfortunately.

But this wasn't about his situation, he reminded himself. This was about a brilliant woman who had found a key to unlock the deadly grip of two of the world's worst diseases. For all he knew, that key might eventually lead to a revolution in health care that would improve the lives of millions of people. If that happened, Ami's work would change entire industries and involve mind-boggling amounts of money poured into international markets.

It would, in effect, change the world.

In more ways than one, Rafe realized, Ami Kim was walking on the edge, and making herself dangerously vulnerable while she was at it. With that kind of money at stake, she might as well paint a red target on her back.

What the good doctor really needed, he decided, was a guardian angel.

Rafe smiled.

Lucky for her, he was available.

"Then we can be lunatics together," he told her. "Because I believe you, Ami."

She tilted her head to the side to consider him, and Rafe could tell she was wavering between a smile of relief and a nagging doubt.

"And why is that?" she prodded him. "You don't know me nearly well enough to make that kind of a judgment. You heard one doctor compliment me, and that's all. You have no idea what kind of work I do—whether I'm sloppy, prone to self-aggrandizement, overly critical. For all you know, maybe I've falsified my research in hopes I can land some plum clinic job somewhere, or become a media medical darling and make a million dollars for guest appearances on television talk shows."

"Why do you want to argue with me?"

"What?"

"I asked why you wanted to argue with me. All I said was that I believe you, and you start giving me reasons not to do that. If I thought you were any of those things you suggested, I wouldn't be sitting here, talking with you. Although I really don't have a problem with someone who's sloppy," he added, his lips twitching into a smile. "I grew up in a house with five sisters and two brothers, none of whom ever learned how to hang a coat on a hanger so it wouldn't fall off. You open the back hall closet door and you'd be buried under coats."

He took an appreciative look at Ami's tailored suit.

"I'm betting you know how to hang up your coat, Ami. And I'm willing to bet your research is as well put-together as you are. And," he continued, lifting his hand to stop her from commenting on his compliment, "on the off-chance that you do become a media darling, I'd be happy to be your chauffeur and share in some of your millions. I am looking for a job, you know, and I do have experience driving an ambulance. You should see me take dirt roads at over eighty—you'll think you're floating on air."

Ami laughed. "Five sisters and two brothers? No wonder you became a paramedic. Lots of broken arms and skinned knees to tend to?"

"More like broken hearts and bruised egos, really. Everybody survived, though. And now they're all producing babies. Last count, I had seventeen nieces and nephews."

"And you only bought one princess t-shirt?"

Rafe covered his heart with his hand. "Okay, I confess. I play favorites. It's for my youngest niece, Tasha. Her dad—my brother—he didn't . . ."

Rafe cleared his throat and turned his head briefly away before looking back again at Ami. "He didn't make it back from Iraq."

"I'm so sorry," she breathed.

"Yeah, me too," he said.

Sorrier than anyone could imagine, he wanted to tell her.

Samuel should have made it back, but he didn't.

Because of me.

"Have dinner with me when we get to Minneapolis."

Ami's invitation stopped Rafe's slide into guilt.

"I mean, if you have time before you catch your connection to Milwaukee," she amended. "There are a few good restaurants in the terminal. We could get something there."

Rafe liked the kindness and earnest appeal he saw in her dark eyes, and he knew that if he hadn't already decided on an unscheduled layover in Minneapolis, he'd be scrambling right now to come up with a good reason for one. Not only was Ami Kim intelligent and intriguing, but she was also kind and sensitive. True, she did seem to enjoy arguing, but Rafe wasn't afraid of locking horns with her. He had, after all, grown up with five sisters.

And then, of course, there was the little matter of her claim to have found the cure for both cancer and heart disease, which was utterly mind-blowing. Or rather—according to Ami—neurological.

Not to mention the mystery of who had tried to shoot her in Orlando.

Yes, without a doubt, Ami Kim was a woman of interest.

"Actually," he told her, "I was serious when I asked you about medic jobs in Minneapolis. I'm going to hold on to my ticket back to Milwaukee and take a few days to check out the Twin Cities. Would that be a problem for you?"

Ami smiled. "Not at all. I've got a car at the airport. We can have dinner, and I'll drop you at a hotel. Will that work?"

"Absolutely," he assured her.

Rafe pulled the glossy airline magazine from the seat pocket in front of him.

"Guess I'll check the hotel listings," he said, returning her smile. "Hopefully, getting a room shouldn't be too tough in Minneapolis in February, right? A little too cold for a vacation destination, I'd say."

"You'd be surprised," Ami told him. "There's always something going on in the Twin Cities, even in winter. St. Paul had the Winter Carnival two weeks ago, and there's always at least one home show or medical convention somewhere in town. Really, all sorts of people show up in Minneapolis."

She stopped talking and looked at him, her lips quirked into a crooked smile. "I'm arguing, aren't I?"

Rafe shrugged his wide shoulders. "I didn't want to point it out, but yes, you're heading in that direction."

Ami smiled again. "Let me try this one more time. Yes, Rafe, I'm sure you can get a hotel room in Minneapolis. You should have no trouble at all."

Rafe laughed with her. The petite doctor was a fast learner, too. And she had that quick wit that had opened their first conversation together. All in all, watching over her for a while wasn't going to be a hardship at all, he decided. In fact, as long as no more snipers took a shot at her, this was going to be one of his better ideas. He flipped to the back section of the magazine and started reading ads for hotels.

"What do you think of the downtown Hilton?"

"It's comfortable," she told him. "It's a short ride from there to the medical center, which is also where my office is located."

Rafe smiled. "Works for me. The Hilton it is, then."

Ami gave him a questioning look. "And you're so sure they'll have a room available for you?"

"I got this seat, didn't I?" he replied.

"Yes, you did," she conceded. "Against all odds, too, I might add."

"So maybe I'm just a very lucky guy," he said, still smiling.

Ami's eyes locked onto his. "I suppose that's possible, but something tells me you've got a lot more going for you than just dumb luck."

"Who says it's dumb?"

Ami laughed and pulled her own magazine from the pocket in front of her.

Yes, Rafe told himself, this was definitely one of his better ideas.

CHAPTER FIVE

Diedrich Mahler stepped out of the black stretch limousine and walked into the ticketing level of the Minneapolis-St. Paul main terminal. His boss, Pieter Hallenstroem, was already airborne on his company jet in route to a big charity bash in San Francisco, while Diedrich had opted for a commercial flight back to Calyx headquarters in Belgium. With another two hours to wait until his flight departure, Diedrich made a beeline for the exclusive Gold Elite Travelers' Lounge located halfway down the A concourse of the airport. Once inside the thick, sound-dampening doors of the lounge, he found the room empty of passengers and took a seat on a creamy leather sofa near the big windows that overlooked the busy runways. A moment later, the lounge hostess stopped by his spot and offered him a cup of coffee, which he asked her to place on the end table beside him.

"Sugar or cream?"

The attractive redhead laid out a napkin on the polished wood of the table and set a cobalt-blue mug on it. Steam rose from the brew, wafting a rich coffee aroma into the recirculated air of the lounge. If he closed his eyes, Diedrich could almost imagine he was back home in Brussels, savoring the first cup of coffee of the day.

Instead, he was sitting in one more airport executive lounge, waiting for one more plane to take him on a sleepless flight back to Europe.

"Neither," he told the waiting woman. He was just getting old, he reminded himself. Only a few years ago, he'd been doing twice the traveling he did now, and he had loved every minute of it. The jets, the limos, the food, the women, the coveted invitations to exclusive parties—he had embraced it all for almost forty years. So why was he tiring of it now, when it was everything he had ever wanted?

He absently rubbed his chest before a prickly sensation reminded him of the shaved spots on his skin where the doctors in the emergency room had attached the sensors to monitor his heart. Was it just last week? Diedrich had been in the middle of touring the production facility of one of Calyx's chemical suppliers outside Frankfurt in Germany when he'd experienced sharp shooting pains in his upper abdomen. His host had insisted on calling an ambulance, and within an hour, Diedrich had found himself admitted to the local emergency room, having his heart rate monitored and needles poking his arms for blood samples. He'd ended up spending the night in the hospital for observation, and while the doctors found no evidence of a heart attack, they'd recommended he get a complete heart examination, including a stress test, once he returned home.

Which he had yet to do.

And while he was quite certain his heart was healthy, and that the pains had probably had more to do with heartburn than heart disease, he couldn't entirely shake the sudden and awful fear that had assailed him in the emergency room.

He didn't want to die.

Coming on the heels of that realization was a restless feeling that although he had achieved all the success he had ever imagined, it had never been enough. He was missing something, but he didn't know what it was.

Against his will, his thoughts relentlessly turned to the news that had shaken the world a few months back. An American physicist had announced that he had located the eleventh dimension predicted by string theory, and that in the process, he had uncovered positive proof of the existence of Heaven. Naturally, his discovery had been hotly contested and debated in every media arena on the face of the planet, but so far, no one had been able to debunk the man's work, or at least, that was the latest word on the affair. And while Diedrich remained convinced it was all a publicity stunt aimed at generating revenue for spurious research, he had to admit that in the darkest hours of the night he had spent in the hospital, he had briefly considered the possibility of Heaven and an afterlife.

And been even more terrified.

On the other—saner—hand, his health scare had given him new insight into the potential of the CardiaZone project. If he did have heart disease, no price would be too high to pay for a cure. Who wouldn't want to buy his way out of death? With a drug like that to market, a pharmaceutical company could set its own price and profits would rip right through the roof. The cost of medical insurance plans would probably skyrocket, too, but that wasn't Diedrich's concern. Who cared if CardiaZone was only available to wealthy patients? If you want to play, you have to pay. He'd seen that line on a computer gaming site somewhere and thought it aptly summed up so much of what he'd seen over the years in his career as a corporate executive. Success never came cheap.

No wonder Pieter had been so distraught before their meeting with Niles. The Calyx CEO had begun to fear that the doctor had grossly overestimated the efficacy of the drug in order to keep the money pouring into his clinic's coffers. At their last meeting, in fact, Pieter had warned Niles that his patience was wearing thin, and that he'd better have some excellent results to share with him the next time they spoke, or he would be forced to take drastic measures. It was, Pieter had confided to Diedrich, the reason he'd hired him to act as the executive vice president of new product development—he wanted a second opinion on the wisdom of continuing to fund Niles's project, and someone else to ride herd on the doctor while he was otherwise engaged in running the corporation.

Even a boy-wizard needed some help sometime.

By the time Diedrich had put him on his corporate jet, though, Pieter had all but forgotten his concerns with Niles's management of the CardiaZone trials. He and Diedrich had finished their late lunch by picking through the data that Niles had supplied, searching for errors or inconsistencies. The data was clean, impeccably documented, indisputably demonstrating that a drug that had previously only been used to treat certain personality disorders caused reversal of organ damage in heart disease patients.

The drug was a phenomenal success, and Diedrich held its future in his hands.

"You're looking pleased, my friend. I take it the meeting went well?"

Diedrich turned away from the big windows to watch his other employer cross the room towards him.

Tall and athletically built, the man was dressed in an expensively-tailored suit, a heavy wool overcoat draped over his left arm. His streaked blonde hair and silver eyes caught the attention of the redheaded hostess, who rushed over to offer to hang up his coat and bring him some coffee. He handed her the coat and refused the drink, softening his rejection of her eager attention with a warm smile and a quick wink.

The man was incorrigible, Diedrich thought. He also looked much too young for his age; when they had begun working together all those years ago, Diedrich had assumed they were both in their twenties. These days, though, Philip Arden could pass for an elegant forty-something, while Diedrich looked every inch his sixty-plus years.

"Very well," he replied to the striking man. "It would appear that CardiaZone is the miracle drug we've been waiting for."

"And Dr. Villome's results will satisfy the FDA for Phase IV testing?"

"I believe so. I've gone through every line of the drug trial report and everything seems to be in place."

Arden took a seat on the matching leather sofa opposite Diedrich. "What do you think we should do?"

"What are the options?" Diedrich asked.

"Oh, the usual, I would guess. Create mayhem and chaos. We could sell the formulation of the drug to one of Hallenstroem's competitors and ruin Calyx. Pieter would probably kill himself over it. Or we could make some fine adjustments in Calyx's manufacture of the drug so that instead of curing heart disease, it would kill several thousands of patients before anyone could do anything about it."

Arden lifted his left wrist to check the time on his Rolex watch.

"Of course, that would also ruin Calyx and kill Pieter," he added, almost as an afterthought. "Either way, I'd get my revenge for his refusal two years ago to come into my corporate fold."

He glanced out the big windows at the runways, then turned back to Diedrich.

"Or we could simply let Calyx supply the world with the drug and very discretely reap a generous portion of the rich financial rewards it will yield. By the time Pieter knows he's leaking income, he won't have any choice but to turn to me for help."

A slow smile crossed Arden's handsome face.

"Now, that would be sweet. I like it. And at the same time, we can shore up the old 'Better living through chemistry' campaign. I've always loved that concept. It's so seductive . . . deceiving."

He lowered the pitch of his voice.

"Diabolical, wouldn't you say?"

As he had for forty years, Diedrich waited to feel the telltale hint of danger his body always registered in Arden's presence. Sometimes, it was the fine hairs rising on the nape of his neck. Other times, he felt a sudden chill in his bones. Exactly why he felt it, he didn't know, but he had, over the years, become as addicted to the sensation as any junkie who needed a fix. As long as he could count on the thrill, he did whatever his employer asked of him, be it industrial espionage, the purchase of politicians, the orchestration of terrorist funding, or the devastating destruction of personal reputations.

Diedrich did it all.

And so he waited for it.

And waited.

But it didn't happen.

"Diedrich?" Arden lifted his right hand in a small wave. "Are you all right?"

It didn't happen.

Stunned and shaken, Diedrich rubbed his temples with his fingertips to cover his distress.

"Yes, I'm fine," he lied, shutting his eyes for a moment. "I think jet lag is catching up with me."

He heard his employer stand up from the couch and walk over to stand beside him.

"Perhaps you're working too hard." He laid a hand on Diedrich's shoulder. "I hate to tell you, but you're no longer the young man you once were. And I know what a toll our business can take on a body."

Diedrich doubted that, given Arden's unfailing vitality and trim physique. He looked into the man's silvery eyes. "You mean on a soul, don't you?"

Arden quickly scanned the lounge for the hostess. Apparently satisfied that the redhead wasn't within earshot, he took a step back from Diedrich.

"Don't tell me you're getting cold feet after all this time. We've waited years for someone to develop a heart remedy, just so we could step in and control it. People all over the world will put their—pardon my pun—'heartfelt' faith in a drug that offers them a cure for their cardiac disease. And if I'm the one controlling that drug, then their faith is in me, isn't it?"

He leaned towards Diedrich and whispered, "I own them."

Diedrich shook his head and sighed. "I should have guessed. This isn't about the money, is it? It probably never was, just like it never seems to be with you. You're probably the richest man in the world thanks to all your companies and 'activities,' but I swear you could care less. You just want to be in control. Of everything. You have a God-complex, Philip. Do you know that?"

Arden threw his head back and laughed. "A complex? I don't think so, Diedrich. I'd say it's more of a 'wish,' or maybe 'plan.' No matter what you call it, though, the end result is the same: I want everyone to put their trust in me. And if I can give them the drug to heal their broken hearts," he winked again at the lounge hostess who was walking towards them with a pot of fresh coffee, "then they will, Diedrich. They will absolutely trust me."

Thirty minutes later, Diedrich left the lounge to check in at his departure gate. He hadn't expected to see Arden at the airport, but it wasn't a complete surprise, either. His employer had the uncanny knack of showing up in unexpected places at exactly the right time. Diedrich supposed it was just one more of the other man's traits that made him such a master at his trade of empire-building: the ability to see opportunities where others saw nothing. Philip Arden had enterprises all over the world, many of which he controlled through holding companies, while others—the less reputable ones—were hidden behind layers of subterfuge in dark corners all over the world. It was one of his more legitimate enterprises that had brought him to Minneapolis on short notice, though, Arden had told Diedrich as he finally accepted a cup of coffee from the insistent hostess in the lounge. He was in town just for the evening, and the limo picking him up was delayed, so he'd thought he'd spend his wait in the comfort of the lounge. He'd never imagined he'd find Diedrich there at the same time.

Diedrich knew his employer better than that. Arden was many things, but spontaneous was not one of them. The man was a meticulous and obsessive planner. For this job alone, he'd had Diedrich digging for months into Pieter Hallenstroem's business ventures before he wrangled the position at Calyx, and it was because of that effort that Diedrich knew just how little Villome was involved in the actual drug trials and how much depended on his Korean clinic partner, Dr. Ami Kim. Rather than expose the self-important doctor to Pieter, though, Arden had instructed Diedrich to play the game out and see if a cardiac wonder drug would result from Kim's research. When he'd asked Villome earlier for a tour of his clinic, in fact, Diedrich had been well aware that Niles's lead researcher was in Florida, but he hadn't been able to resist the temptation to put the overbearing doctor on the spot and watch him squirm. As Diedrich had learned long ago from his own employer, it never hurt to remind your subordinate who was boss.

Which was why the recently hired Calyx executive vice president of new product development knew there was no way on earth that his own employer just happened to walk into that Gold Elite lounge as he was contemplating the possible ramifications of the success of the CardiaZone project.

Philip Arden was spying on him.

For a split second, Diedrich wondered if Arden knew about his hospitalization in Germany. He knew from their long association that his employer detested any sign of weakness on the part of his employees, claiming that it showed a lack of the personal toughness that he required of everyone in his corporate empire. As a result, Diedrich had never missed an annual physical or failed to follow a healthy regimen, which had made his heart scare even more disturbing. The idea that despite all his discipline and efforts to ensure his physical health, he might be betrayed by his own body, went beyond unsettling to life-shaking.

Like Arden, Diedrich needed to be in control.

He was so lost in his train of thought that he almost didn't see the woman in time to avoid walking right into her. Catching himself at the last moment, he sidestepped around the small brunette and headed for his departure gate.

Arden's showing up at the airport was not a good thing, Diedrich was certain. But until he knew the reason for it, he would exercise even more caution than usual as he wrapped up this Calyx project. Diedrich really didn't know what Philip Arden would do if one of his grand schemes fell apart, but there was one thing he did know: he didn't ever want to find out.

CHAPTER SIX

Violet Winters turned to glance briefly at the silver-haired man who had almost knocked her over without even so much as an "Excuse me."

Not that she was surprised, since she was used to other travelers practically mowing her down in airports. At barely five feet tall, she seemed almost invisible to many people. Her shoulder-length brown hair was typically pulled back in a short ponytail, and the only makeup she wore was mascara on her eyelashes and pale gloss on her lips. Her twenty-nine-year-old face was unremarkable, and the faded denim jeans and jacket she habitually wore left her indistinguishable from the thousands of other passengers who passed through every airport in America. In fact, Vi was very happy with her innocuousness, since it played a crucial role in her success in her chosen career field.

After all, no one should be able to recall what an assassin looked like.

She pushed through the door into the Gold Elite Lounge and instantly spotted the tall, strikingly handsome man sitting on the sofa by the windows. Making her way across the room, she returned the man's inviting smile with one of her own. He stood as she neared him and extended his hand in welcome.

Vi took his hand in her own steady grip and reached up on the tips of her sneakers' toes to plant a quick kiss on his right cheek.

"How was your trip?" she asked.

"Uneventful," Arden told her. "I got on the plane, the pilot flew, I ate a few peanuts, and here I am. I trust your trip was more exciting."

Vi frowned. "Not quite as exciting as I had planned, actually."

She threw a look in the direction of the hostess, who was busy refilling the coffee pot at the service bar. "Do you mind if we sit?"

"Not at all," Arden replied. He motioned for Vi to take a seat on the leather couch, then sat down close beside her, their thighs lightly touching. "Tell me," he said, his voice warm with invitation.

Vi looked into his silvery eyes and smiled. "It's good to see you, but I'm afraid you won't be happy with me."

"Nonsense. I'm always happy with you."

Vi chuckled lightly. "Right. Apparently you've already forgotten that little fiasco in New Hampshire last month when I put a bullet into the president's double on the ski slope."

"Not your fault," Arden assured her. "We didn't know it was a double until he was dead. My sources obviously slipped up on that one."

"So I'm forgiven?"

Arden lifted her hand from where it lay in her lap and pressed her fingers to his lips.

"Of course."

"I missed her hand," Vi said. "I had my sights on it, and this man—incredibly—pushed her out of the way."

Arden said nothing for a beat or two.

"She wasn't hurt at all?'

Vi shook her head. "Not that I could see. In the confusion, I was able to stick around and check it out. There weren't any injuries, other than a few hotel guests getting banged up when they hit the floor after I fired."

In her mind's eye, she could still see the chaos in the Orlando lobby. She'd only taken the one shot, and though no one else had been in any danger from her bullet, every person in the hotel reception area had dropped to the ground when they'd heard her sniper rifle's report. It had been a simple thing to dump the gun in the thick bushes near her position, then run into the panicked crowd in the hotel lobby to see for herself what damage she'd done.

When she'd seen her target rise from the floor, unharmed, she'd been furious. Coupled with the recent failure of her New Hampshire job, Vi's missed shot had almost tempted her to go back outside and try to line up another shot just to redeem herself, but her professional instincts forbade it. Frustrated, she had hung around the edge of the milling guests until the police had arrived to investigate, hoping that she might learn something useful about the mystery man who had ruined her shot.

He had, after all, interfered with her work. For that, she owed him, and sometime, somehow, she was going to pay him back.

"Dr. Kim and the man with her answered questions from the police after they arrived, but no one needed an ambulance," Vi told Arden. "The man who saved Dr. Kim was just another guest at the hotel. It was a total coincidence that he was in the right place at the right time, and, on top of that, had the reflexes to help her out."

Vi looked repentantly into her employer's face.

"I'm sorry, Philip. It should have been a slam dunk."

Arden was quiet, lightly running his thumb over the back of Vi's hand.

"Only a fluke, then. It happens, I suppose." His gaze caught Vi's. "Do you think you shook her up, at least? Frightened her?"

"I don't know how she couldn't be frightened," she replied. "The woman's a physician, and physicians prize their hands."

Arden nodded in agreement. "Then I'm sure you scared her. Now that I think about it, and given the news that Diedrich had for me, it's better that you didn't make the shot as planned, Vi. It turns out that Dr. Kim is ultimately going to be more useful to me by finishing her research than by failing to complete it. I need Dr. Kim to be at the top of her game right now, and fear—thanks to you—should fuel her drive to succeed quite nicely."

"But I'm not sure she'll take the shot personally, Philip. The police were insistent that it was gang-related." Vi frowned. "If she doesn't know she was targeted because of her research, how does that help us pressure her?"

He sat in silence for another moment. Vi watched his thumb trace a line over her knuckles.

"She'd be a fool not to consider that she was a target," he finally said. "A laser sight lands on her hand in a crowded hotel lobby? What are the chances? Dr. Kim is a very bright woman, and while she may have accepted the police report at the time, I guarantee you that she will be replaying the scene in her head all through the night. It's human nature, Vi. The more she tries to process the experience and make sense of it, the less sense it will make, and the more she'll wonder. And fear."

He patted her hand. "Yes, this is definitely a good thing, Vi. It allows for new options."

"Such as?"

Arden's eyes narrowed and his voice sank lower. "Distrust. Suspicion. Our dear Dr. Kim will convince herself that the shot was not random after all, and then she'll begin to wonder who would want to hurt her. When her partner Dr. Villome hears about it, he'll do more than wonder—maybe he'll think a competitor has gotten wind of the project and wants to sabotage it. Or maybe, even better, he'll suspect Pieter or Diedrich of trying to pressure him to accelerate the drug trials by threatening Dr. Kim."

He smiled slowly.

"Either way, to cover his own back, Villome might have to finally break down and tell his partner that he's been appropriating her research for his own and has already sold it to Calyx. I can't imagine that will make Dr. Kim very happy, let alone bolster her trust in him."

"She doesn't know?"

Arden's smile broadened. "No, she doesn't. Diedrich thought it odd that Pieter hadn't met Niles' lead researcher yet, so he did some investigating into their clinic—Heart something or other. According to Diedrich's information, courtesy of the office night janitor, Dr. Kim has been working alone on a study of 'personal interest.' Apparently, she's befriended the janitor, who often finds her working late in her office, and they chat. She told him that to keep her partner happy, she works on her project mostly after office hours, when she won't be interrupted by patients. She's hoping that sometime soon Dr. Villome will recognize the value of what she's working on, but at this point, her partner is only interested in practicing medicine and the income it produces."

"I'd say there's something else he's interested in," Vi observed. "Stealing research."

"So it would seem," Arden agreed. "It appears that Dr. Villome is a true opportunist—a man after my own heart, I must say."

He kissed Vi's fingers one more time and returned them to her lap.

"Perhaps I should pay Dr. Kim a visit myself and see if she'd like to leave all this treachery behind and come work for me, instead," he mused. "It would certainly cut out a few needless middlemen."

Out of the corner of her eye, Vi could see the lounge hostess casting curious looks towards their hushed conversation. She gave Arden another light kiss on his cool cheek.

"But it wouldn't be as much fun, would it, Philip?"

Arden's teeth flashed white in his grin.

"No, it wouldn't."

CHAPTER SEVEN

Hot air blasted out of the heater at the front of the Eco-noPark shuttle van as it ferried Ami and Rafe to the remote parking lot where she had left her car before flying out to Orlando for the conference. With only her wool suit jacket to keep her warm, Ami rubbed her hands together and looked out at the dark and frosty landscape. Beside her on the shuttle's bench seat, Rafe pulled over his shaved head a knit cap he'd taken from his duffle before he'd stowed it on the luggage rack.

"You're prepared," she said, eyeing his cap. "I've lived in Minnesota for almost half of my life, and I still can't believe how frigid it gets in February. My fingers and toes are already feeling frozen, and I'm not even out of the shuttle yet."

Rafe produced some gloves from his hip pocket and offered them to Ami, but she refused them.

"Suit yourself," he replied, tugging them on. "I'm a delicate southern flower, you know, and these northern climes are hard on my fragile nature."

Ami scoffed. "Southern, maybe. Fragile? Somehow, I doubt that."

Rafe looked offended. "You don't know me very well, Doctor. I cry at the movies and adopt stray dogs."

"And tackle unsuspecting women in hotel gift shops."

"I had a good reason," he reminded her, then changed the subject. "So where were you the other half?"

"Excuse me?"

"The other half," he repeated. "Of your life. You said you've been in Minnesota for half your life."

"Oh," Ami said, rewinding her attention back to her earlier remark. That should have been an easy thing to do, but she was having trouble focusing on anything at the moment besides Rafe's warm brown eyes that were fixed on her own. Did he have a clue how mesmerizing that look of his was? She swore she could swim in those eyes.

"Ah, let's see," she said, closing her eyes briefly to get a grip on her distracted thoughts. She heaved a small sigh and looked at him again.

"I grew up in Busan, on the southern coast of Korea. When I was sixteen, my parents sent me to California as a high school exchange student, and by the time I was eighteen, I was enrolled pre-med at the University of Michigan. I did my residency here in town, and I haven't left."

"Any family?"

"Still in Busan. My father's a retired pharmacist and my mother gardens."

The van slowed down and turned into a filled parking lot.

"Here we are," Ami announced. "My car's in the third row."

The shuttle lumbered to a stop in the middle of the lane between two rows of parked cars. Ami hoisted her laptop bag onto her shoulder and made a grab for her rolling suitcase, but Rafe was quicker and pulled it into the aisle at the same time he swung his duffle onto his back.

"I've got it," he told her. "You open your car's trunk when we get off, and I'll toss our bags in. Less time for my tender skin to be exposed to the elements that way."

Ami followed the man who had shared the shuttle ride with them off the van and hit the trunk button on her remote key. A cascade of snow slid back onto her Camry's rear window as the trunk lid rose, and Rafe lifted their luggage into the baggage compartment. More than six inches of heavy white flakes covered the car.

"You get it started and I'll start swiping off some of the snow," Rafe offered, taking her laptop case from her and laying it beside the other bags. He grabbed the snowbrush Ami kept in the trunk and started sweeping big swaths of the packed snow off the car and onto the pavement.

Ami headed for the driver's side of her car, noting that their fellow van rider was likewise trying to clear the snow from the roof of his vehicle parked next to Ami's. "Are you always this—" She stopped her comment to Rafe in mid-sentence as the man suddenly dropped from sight.

"Sir?" she called over the roof of the car.

No answer.

Ami spun on her heel and lurched around the back end of the man's car, throwing her hand out to catch her balance on the car's back bumper.

He was lying crumpled in the snow.

Ami fell to her knees beside him and quickly checked for a pulse in his neck.

"Has he got one?"

Rafe was crouched beside her, already dialing 911.

"Yes, but it's too fast."

She picked up the man's right hand and held it between her own two. The stranger's eyelids fluttered, and he looked up at Ami vacantly.

"Sir?" She tried to make eye contact with the man, but he seemed confused and disoriented.

His eyelids shut again. Despite the frigid temperature, Ami could see beads of sweat forming along the man's hairline. She closed her own eyes and blocked out the sensation of the icy cold on her knees.

Almost as if from a distance, she could hear Rafe giving information to the emergency dispatcher. "Older man. Maybe a heart attack."

"Not a heart attack," Ami interrupted him.

Rafe paused.

"He's hypoglycemic. Diabetic. We need some glucose right now."

Rafe dropped the phone in the snow and bolted back to Ami's car trunk. A moment later he was beside her again, shaking a small blue can in his hand.

"Pineapple juice."

He popped it open and handed it to Ami, then lifted the stranger up to a sitting position so Ami could put the can to the man's lips.

"You need to drink," she urged the fallen man.

She pressed the can against his mouth and cautiously tipped a few drops of the yellow liquid in. A dribble of juice ran down his chin. Groggy and shaking, he drank.

When the can was empty, Rafe leaned the man against the side of the car. The sound of an approaching siren cut through the night.

"We've got an ambulance coming," he told him. "You're going to be okay. Lucky for you, I always carry a supply of sugar with me."

The man nodded weakly.

Ami rocked back on her heels and looked at Rafe.

"You're diabetic," she guessed.

"Guilty as charged," he responded easily. "It runs in the family, so it wasn't a total surprise when my glucose levels came in high at an annual physical. Of course, that made it my last annual physical in the service. The Marine Corps showed me the door when I was diagnosed; you can't be active duty and diabetic."

He hoped that Ami couldn't hear the twinge of disappointment and anger that always seemed to creep into his voice when he talked about his discharge from the Corps. Being a medic had been a perfect fit for him and his unconventional gift; amidst the chaos of war, nobody had the time or interest for keeping track of his miraculous record for healing. Busy with the demands of a battlefield, Rafe had simply done his job—no soul-searching required, which suited him just fine.

Civilian life, though, had been another story, a story that was leaving him with too much time for regrets and questions he couldn't answer, not to mention the unwanted notice of colleagues. He mentally slammed the lid on the Pandora's box that haunted him, and changed the subject.

"How did you know that was the problem and not his heart?" Rafe asked, glancing at the man whose eyes had drifted shut again. "Any paramedic, including me, would have bet on a heart attack."

Ami reached over and gently slid up the man's left jacket cuff to reveal the silver bracelet around his wrist that she had glimpsed when Rafe pulled the man up against the car. She turned the tag on it for Rafe to see its metallic glint in the streetlight.

"Medical identification tag," she said.

Rafe nodded. He wore a similar tag on the silver chain around his own neck.

And then all of a sudden, they were surrounded by flashing lights and emergency personnel cramming into the tight space between the cars. Ami detailed what had happened, and then she and Rafe retreated to wait inside her car while the paramedics tended to their patient. She turned the key in the ignition to warm up the engine so she could start the heater and rubbed her cold hands over her icy knees. Beside her in the passenger seat, Rafe peeled off his gloves and offered them to her.

"Just lay them across your knees," he told her. "On you, they're almost a lap robe."

Ami did as he suggested and almost immediately could feel some warmth seeping into her chilled skin. The leather gloves were enormous and seemed to have retained a remarkable amount of Rafe's body heat.

"Thanks," she said. "Nice gloves. I never would have guessed that they doubled as space heaters."

Rafe laughed in the darkness of the car, and the sound warmed Ami even more than the gloves on her lap. She smiled at him, quietly regarding the big ex-marine who twice today had been in exactly the right place just when he was most needed.

"That man owes his life to the fact that you were here, and that you happen to share his disease," she observed. "If you hadn't had that can of juice, I don't know if he would have been able to avoid a seizure, or worse, before the ambulance got here. He was in pretty bad shape."

"It's what I do," Rafe quietly said. "I'm just a big, black Florence Nightingale. Without the skirt," he solemnly added. "Or the goofy headcovering thing."

Ami laughed.

"And how about you, Ami?" Rafe's voice remained soft in the car. "What do you do? I mean, besides being a cardiologist and researcher who's found a neurological cure for cancer and heart disease?"

Ami's pulse raced at the tone of Rafe's question.

"What do you mean?"

Rafe shifted in the car seat so he was facing Ami directly.

"You knew that man was diabetic before you saw his ID tag. His left hand—the one with the bracelet –was underneath him in the snow when you told me he was hypoglycemic. Just like you knew about my MCL. You weren't just guessing, were you, Ami?"

She didn't respond.

"You're a medical intuitive," he said. "You can sense disease."

CHAPTER EIGHT

For a split second, Rafe thought Ami was going to argue with him, but then he watched as her facial features visibly relaxed and her shoulders lightly dropped their tension. She drew a hand through her long black bangs and let out a little sigh.

"Yes, I am. But I don't let it interfere with my work," she quickly insisted. "And I certainly don't broadcast it."

"I would think it would make your work easier," Rafe pointed out. "If you can intuit—know—what's hurting people, just by touching them—that's how you do it, isn't it?—that's got to make diagnosing problems a snap. No tests, no waiting for results, no false positives. Why not use it?"

A loud rapping noise on Ami's car window prevented her from making a reply.

She rolled the window down, and the face of one of the policemen who had answered the 911 call at the EconoPark appeared.

"You folks can leave if you want," the officer told them. "And thanks for being good Samaritans. But I've got to say, that fellow is one lucky guy to have parked his car next to a doctor and a paramedic who just happened to be getting in their car at the same time he was."

He touched the brim of his hat with two fingers in a small salute. "Have a good night, folks."

Ami thanked the officer and hit the "up" button on her automatic window. She put the car into reverse and waited for the last emergency vehicle to leave, finally clearing the lane behind her. Just before she backed out of her slot, she took Rafe's gloves from her lap and handed them back to him.

"So where do you want me to drop you off?" she asked. "Still planning on the Hilton downtown?"

Rafe shook his head. "This conversation is not only not over, but it's barely begun," he told her. "Besides which, you asked me to dinner, and I accepted. So let's go eat."

He pulled on his gloves, enjoying the welcoming warmth they had absorbed while laying on Ami's legs.

"You don't want me to go hypoglycemic next, do you? That little snack on the plane was hours ago. I need carbohydrates."

"What? Don't you have another can in your duffle bag?"

Ami shot him a look that he thought was equal parts sarcasm, frustration, and amusement. He'd briefly wondered if his comment about resuming their conversation might have pushed Ami too hard, but the lady was obviously standing her ground.

Rafe added another trait to the growing list of what he liked about Ami.

"No, Dr. Kim, I don't," he said, shaking his head in mock despair. "I am totally dependent on your mercy. My life is in your hands. Please save me by finding an excellent establishment of fine dining that will quickly bring me a platterful of carbohydrate-rich appetizers."

He thought he heard a stifled chuckle from Ami's side of the car, but decided not to remark on it. Instead, he buckled his seat belt and kept his mouth shut while Ami paid her parking bill and zipped up the entrance ramp to I-494, the beltway around the Twin Cities. As he watched the traffic flow around them, he pieced together what he had learned about the woman beside him and began to realize he could probably answer the question himself that he had put to her about her intuitive gift.

Why not use it?

Rafe, of all people, knew why not.

Fear.

Ignorance.

Distrust.

Disbelief.

He'd seen all of those reactions himself whenever a coworker began to suspect what Rafe was really doing when he laid his hands on critically ill or injured patients in the back of an ambulance. As long as he'd been in the Marines, it hadn't been an issue; surrounded by enemy fire, no one had time or opportunity to look too closely at why a wounded man lived, instead of died, on the way back to the base.

But emergency medicine in the civilian world was different, Rafe had discovered. There weren't crowds of casualties to distract his shift partners every time an ambulance was summoned, and all the high-tech monitoring equipment they had on board precluded any anonymity he might have had when it came to miraculously saving a life. And when he did save a life, he could expect his partner to take note and become increasingly uneasy around him, just as Jimmy Blue had during Rafe's final month at his last job. In the weeks since then, Rafe had found himself, more than once, weighing whether he should even use his healing gift at all.

And then he'd hear his mama's voice, telling him that God works through the hearts and hands of His people, and he had to respect that.

He had respected it. He'd used his gift and healed.

Except for that one time.

Rafe winced.

Imagine what it's like for Ami, he reminded himself. *You can have a pity party for yourself later.*

Shoving aside his own problems, he thought about Ami's situation. In a university's medical center, she wouldn't have the anonymity and the relative freedom, either, that he'd experienced in the Corps. Regardless of what he thought—of what he knew—to be true about the role of spirit in healing, Rafe was sure that Ami's medical career would be jeopardized, if not destroyed, by an open acknowledgment of her gift. Some people would say her intuitive skill was a bluff based in wishful thinking, while others would label her a fraud and clamor for her medical license to be revoked. Still others would just call her "crazy" and avoid her like the plague. Despite the tremendous service she could render as an intuitive diagnostician, the world of medicine would chew her up and spit her out. As long as she admitted to anything as unscientific as medical intuition, all of her work would be suspect, including the cure she claimed to have found for cancer and heart disease.

Who was he kidding? A cure like that would be suspect most of all, if not rejected outright.

The truth was that unless a treatment or procedure was scientifically validated, borne out by repeated research and detailed documentation, most modern medical practitioners didn't want anything to do with it, or whoever might be proposing it.

Actually, Rafe reflected, if it wasn't good science, it didn't even exist, according to the vast majority of the medical establishment. True, there were plenty of "alternative" medical traditions with which people could experiment, but when it came down to "real" medicine, that territory belonged to the world of objective and measurable science.

And that was the heart of the health puzzle, Rafe knew. Too many people had put their trust in technology alone, and forgotten the power of God. Even after that physicist, Dr. Carilion, proved the existence of Heaven with his string theory research, people still didn't conceive of themselves as partly spiritual beings, or understand their own connection to God. Instead of seeing the whole picture of existence, most people focused on just one piece of it: the physical piece.

Which, to Rafe's mind, was both sad and crazy. Why settle for just a piece of life, when you could have so much more?

Without a doubt, technology of all kinds—medical, geological, biological, social—had much to offer the whole world. It just didn't offer everything. Only God could do that, whether it was done with the assistance of technology or without it altogether.

"A penny for your thoughts," Ami said, breaking the long silence.

"A penny?" Rafe scoffed. "My thoughts are worth a whole lot more than a penny. Especially in this economy. My thoughts are worth at least a quarter."

"Italian okay for dinner?"

Rafe noticed that Ami was no longer driving on the interstate, but had turned off into a suburban neighborhood filled with old homes constructed of brick and boasting wide front porches. It looked a lot like the neighborhood in Milwaukee where he'd been living the past year.

"Sounds great."

Ami drove another two blocks and parked on the street in front of a little family-owned pizzeria. Before she could get out of the car, Rafe laid his hand on her right arm.

"I understand why you don't let people know you're a medical intuitive, Ami."

Bathed in the red light from the pizzeria's neon sign, Ami's face was a study in stillness.

"It would kill your career. You'd never practice medicine again."

"That's right. So don't mention it to anyone, okay?" She shook her head and her voice was barely a whisper. "I don't even know why I told you. If you didn't think I was crazy before, you certainly do by now."

"You didn't tell me," Rafe reminded her. "I guessed. And I don't think you're crazy, either."

"And why is that?"

He could almost feel the bleakness emanating from her. He fixed his eyes on her pale face and said, "There's something you should know about me, Ami."

He paused and licked his lips while he considered how to tell her.

"I can heal . . . with just my hands."

CHAPTER NINE

C hinh Nguyen padded down the silent building corridor to the heavy paneled door that marked the entrance to the Minneapolis Heart Partners Clinic. Using his master key, he unlocked the door and pushed his cleaning cart into the empty lobby, flipping on the overhead lights as he passed by the switches on the wall. He made a quick circuit of the seating area, dumping the contents of the four small trash cans tucked between the chairs into the larger can mounted on his cart, then unhooked the vacuum to begin his sweep of the lobby's burgundy carpet. Chinh was halfway down the short hallway that led to the examining rooms when he noticed that one of the doors at the end of the hallway was slightly ajar.

Frowning, he went to check. The door belonged to Dr. Kim's office, and she had told him last week that she would be traveling to a conference in Florida for a few days. He liked the young Korean doctor and frequently told her that she worked too hard when he found her in the office late at night, her reading glasses perched on her nose as she peered at rows of numbers on her computer screen. Dr. Kim was always kind to him, inquiring about his numerous grandchildren and offering him the appropriate respect for his age and best wishes for his continued good health. He hoped that her trip had gone well and not been cut short by an emergency with one of her patients, but who else might be in her office at this hour? He turned off the vacuum.

"Hello!" he called, watching the doorway to see who might emerge. "Dr. Kim?"

A slim, brown-haired man stepped into the hallway, and Chinh immediately recognized Dr. Kim's partner, Dr. Niles Villome, from the framed portrait of the man that hung out in the lobby by the receptionist's desk.

"I'm Dr. Villome," he said. "Can I help you?"

"No, no," Chinh responded, shaking his head quickly. "I just wonder who is in Dr. Kim's office. I clean it."

"I can see that you do," the doctor assured him, nodding pointedly at the vacuum. "She's been out of town, though, so her office doesn't need cleaning tonight."

Chinh stood in the hallway, unsure what to do. He didn't think it was right for anyone to be in Dr. Kim's office while she was away, but he certainly couldn't say that to the man who co-owned the clinic that employed him. In the fifteen years he'd been in America, he'd often been confused by what was considered correct or polite in the unfamiliar culture, and he'd given up long ago trying to figure it out. For all he knew, perhaps Dr. Kim's partner regularly used her office.

After hours.

In her absence.

While his own office was right across the hall, empty.

Chinh's eyes narrowed.

"I just check trash can," he said, taking a step towards the open doorway.

The doctor moved with him, effectively blocking Chinh's path.

"I said it's not necessary."

Chinh met the younger man's glare for only a moment before he lowered his gaze to the floor.

"I clean the examination rooms now," he said, turning his vacuum and himself around to face the opposite direction. But just before he flipped the appliance's power switch back on, he heard Dr. Kim's office door closing behind him and then the faint click of the inside lock.

And even though who used Dr. Kim's office was none of his business, Chinh Nguyen felt a distinct sense of unease creep into his bones.

He did not trust this Dr. Villome.

Niles sat back down at Ami's computer and resumed reading her notes, combing through them for anything he could use to pad the expense report summaries he'd already given Pieter Hallenstroem. Since it was public knowledge that the drug Ami was testing was already commercially available for treating personality disorders, he couldn't write in extra costs for private lab fees to manufacture experimental dosages or new pharmaceutical concoctions. Nor had Ami offered any of the patients in the trials travel or time costs to defray expenses for their participation; from what he could determine from her records, she'd had more than ample volunteers who required no monetary incentive to try out a cure for heart disease. And while Niles had, at one point, briefly considered adding in fake costs for patient reimbursement, he had also decided it was just too risky a move. All it would take would be one happy patient giving an interview to a reporter about the chance to get a free heart cure, and Niles would be busted by the Calyx accountants.

Or more likely, now, by Diedrich Mahler, Calyx's very own new vice president of new product development.

Niles had gotten the distinct impression over their late afternoon rendezvous that the tough-looking, silver-haired man was already suspicious of Niles's management of the project. Had Pieter found something questionable in the earlier expense reports that Niles had filed with him? Or was Mahler's intensity his own brand of management style? Either way, Niles was sure he didn't want Mahler hanging over his shoulder, and to guarantee that, the doctor was convinced he'd better slip in a few more big ticket-items to the expense reports to justify the financing he'd demanded from Hallenstroem.

Despite the soundproofing of the offices, Niles could still hear the high-pitched whine of the cleaning man's vacuum. He wasn't concerned that the man had found him in Ami's office. After all, Niles was a partner here. He had every right to be in his colleague's office doing paperwork. He wasn't about to worry what a low-paid Vietnamese immigrant thought about his work habits.

Ami, on the other hand, worried endlessly about what other people thought of her work. More than once he had argued with her about her obsessive concern with the opinions of others, and each time, the argument had ended with her vehement insistence that she was, unconditionally, responsible for not only her own reputation, but also the reputation of her family, her workplace, and even her native countrymen and women.

"You need to ship your antiquated ideals back to Korea," he'd told her after one particularly loud argument. "America is the home of the individual, Ami, not the group hug."

Ami's altruistic streak had been the primary reason he'd taken full control of their practice's finances when they'd set up the clinic after completing their medical residencies. If he'd left it up to her to manage their money, they'd be working out of a bare-bones office in some gang-ridden sector of the city, barely earning enough to pay the rent and themselves a minimal salary.

Thankfully, though, Ami had desperately wanted to do research as well as practice medicine, so it had been an easy sell for him to talk her into affiliating their office with the university's medical clinic. As a result, their practice had exploded in the last few years, and the fees had come pouring in. Even when Ami occasionally "forgot" to bill her overtime or extra patient expenses.

Which might just be his salvation, he suddenly realized.

He scrolled through more of Ami's records, looking for overtime hours that she may have neglected to tally and report to him for the drug trials. Finding none, he jotted a note to himself and stuck it in his pocket. On second thought, he pulled it back out and hastily added a few more words.

"That should do it," he told the computer screen as he closed Ami's files and brought up the late newscast to check the weather. "Both Dr. Kim and I have put a lot of overtime into these trials, and time is definitely money when it comes to the free market economy of medical research. And that's something not even Mr. Mahler will find fault with, I'm sure."

He waited for the podcast to get to the weather, but was suddenly glued to his seat when he saw a teaser for the next news segment.

On the computer screen, a camera panned across a hotel lobby that was filled with people and police officers. Standing in front of a gift shop was Ami.

"No serious injuries have been reported from this gang-related shooting at a posh Orlando conference center earlier today," the smooth voice of an invisible journalist informed him. "And while we've heard rumors of a young woman doctor being targeted in the attack, we don't have any confirmation of that so far."

Niles blinked at the screen.

He was sure it had been Ami in front of that gift shop. She was supposed to be arriving tonight from the conference in Orlando—the conference he hadn't wanted her to attend in the first place. Why in the world did she want to go to a neurology conference anyway? And why now, of all times? He'd argued that she needed to be focused on her research and she could pursue other interests later, after the drug trials were completed. She'd retorted that she needed to get away and clear her head, or she wouldn't be able to finish the trials at all. As usual, she'd done exactly what she wanted to do, despite his objections, and flown to Florida.

He slumped back in the desk chair as a terrible thought occurred to him.

What if she had been hurt?

What if she had been killed?

Niles fought to drag air into his lungs. Without Ami, his project with Calyx was dead in the water.

Or rather, he, Niles Villome, would be dead in the water. He needed his partner to finish the third trial to get the drug approved and his final payments from Calyx.

Especially since he'd already spent the money.

Mahler had been right to tell him to keep his research team close to home until they finished the project. Life could be full of unwelcome surprises . . . like drive-by shootings and financial disaster.

Then an even more frightening possibility popped into his head. The newscaster said there was a rumor that a woman doctor had been targeted.

Targeted.

Niles jerked upright in the chair. His comment to Mahler came back to haunt him.

'There are industrial spies everywhere."

That meant that the danger of industrial—in this case, pharmaceutical—sabotage was very real. And what quicker way could there be for a rival drug company to stop the development of a new, miraculous, money-rich product than to kill the lead researcher?

Niles felt his stomach lurch. When he'd signed on with Pieter Hallenstroem, it never occurred to him that he could be putting Ami in any kind of danger. He'd never considered himself naïve, but this was a wrinkle in his plan that he would never have imagined either.

And then he had an even more frightening thought.

What if he was now a target, too?

He was, after all, the man in charge of the project. If a competitor had come after Ami, what would stop that person from coming after him?

Niles needed Ami to finish the trials and get the drug into the hands of Calyx, for both of their sakes.

No wonder Mahler had voiced a concern for urgency; as an experienced pharmaceutical developer, he must have known that the closer a project came to completion, the more likely it was to be compromised. Viewed in that light, the executive's reservations about Ami traveling were more valid than Niles had realized.

And then another wave of nausea hit.

He glanced at the computer screen, but the news report was over. A weatherman waved his hands tracing a winter storm's approach.

How coincidental could it be that the very day Mahler warned Niles about Ami's traveling, she was involved in a shooting?

Niles felt a cold sweat break out on his brow.

Maybe it wasn't a warning, and maybe the shooting wasn't random, either.

Mahler's last words came roaring back at Niles.

'I want us to cross that finish line sooner rather than later, Doctor. Make it happen."

Niles bent over in the chair and took deep breaths until his head stopped spinning. He stared at the gray carpet beneath Ami's desk. The truth was that no matter who was behind those shots in Orlando, the stakes in the pharmaceutical poker game he was playing had just gone sky-high. He was going to have to do something about it, for both Ami's and his own protection, but at the moment, he was uncertain what that might be. One thing he did know was that he couldn't turn to the police for protection because then he'd have to admit he'd sold Ami's work without her permission. How many years in jail would that little admission cost him?

He rubbed his hand over the headache that had begun to throb in his temples.

Niles needed to fix this, and he could think of only one way to do it. As soon as he saw Ami in the clinic in the morning, he was going to demand that she give him something she'd been stubbornly withholding for the last ten months. Something he not only wanted, but now felt he desperately needed for his own insurance to finish out his winning hand with Calyx.

He was going to get the name of the drug Ami was testing.

CHAPTER TEN

Vi swallowed another mouthful of warm coffee from the large paper cup in her hand and gazed out her windshield at the entrance to Dr. Ami Kim's condominium building. Though she hated doing any kind of surveillance, she knew it was always crucial to her successful completion of a contract, and few things mattered to Vi Winters more than her success ratio. She also knew that her gut instincts were rarely wrong, and though Arden had told her he had a better use for Dr. Kim, her gut instinct was telling her that at some point, her employer was going to ask her to get rid of the doctor.

That was why, after delivering Arden to his dinner appointment with another one of his various business associates, she'd taken a room at a hotel near the airport and looked up Dr. Kim's address. Sitting near a frozen lake not far from the bright lights of the Minneapolis skyline, the building had been easy to find and even easier to watch with its glass-fronted lobby. It wouldn't take much to pick out a target, Vi noted, especially since the building's elevators were plainly visible there in the open lobby.

Privacy was obviously not one of the architect's priorities.

As she watched several groups of people entering and exiting the building, Vi decided that security wasn't one of the residents' priorities, either.

More often than not, people leaving the building held the outer door open for those coming in, making it unnecessary for the new arrivals to produce a key to access the lobby. Deciding to test it for herself, Vi turned off her rental car's engine and left the vehicle, quickly walking to the designated crosswalk

77

that led to the condo building's entrance. Since no one was using the lobby, she kept on walking, sticking her cold hands deeper into her jacket pockets and trying to breathe in as little of the frigid night air as possible. When she'd reached the next block's corner, she reversed directions and made another pass towards the building.

This time she was in luck. An elderly couple was just entering the glass-walled lobby ahead of her, so she sped up her pace to close the distance between them, catching the handle of the door as it started to swing shut.

"It's a cold one!" she told the old man as he turned to see why the door had not closed behind him. She made an elaborate production of stamping her shoes on the lobby's rubber mats to shake off the slush and snow she'd picked up on her short walk.

The elevator's doors opened and the couple stepped inside. The woman leaned slightly out of the doorway and looked questioningly at Vi.

"Oh, don't hold it for me," she told the old woman, waving her away. "I'll catch the next one after I get more of this snow off. I hate tracking it in upstairs."

The woman nodded knowingly and the elevator doors closed, leaving Vi alone in the lobby.

As she continued to brush at her clothes and stamp her feet, Vi surreptitiously studied her surroundings. Bare of any furniture, the lobby consisted of a blue-veined marble floor and two brightly lit crystal chandeliers hanging from the ten-foot ceiling. To the left of the three elevators, a bank of numbered brass mailboxes filled the wall space; to the right, a stained-glass door marked "Office" sat next to a solid door that had a handle but no lock. It was probably a stairwell, Vi reasoned, making a mental note to check it out before she left the building. If she wasn't mistaken, residents probably had secured underground parking beneath the lobby, and the stairs would lead down to that garage as well as up to the floors of condos. Since only one emergency exit wouldn't satisfy fire codes, however, another flight of stairs was most likely to be located at the opposite end of the building, and that door was most assuredly only opened from inside. Vi reminded herself to check that out, too, since an emergency exit that let out behind the building would be her exit of choice if she had to make a kill in the condo.

The elevator door quietly chimed, and a man with a small dog wrapped in a tiny sweater walked out into the lobby. Vi turned away and headed towards the wall of mailboxes, where she bent slightly at the waist, pretending to peer into a box window in one of the lower rows, looking to see if she had mail. As soon as the man and his dog went out into the cold, Vi made a beeline for the unmarked door, overly aware of how loudly her sneakers squeaked on the marble floor. Once she was through the door, however, her shoes no longer made any noise. Here the floor was poured concrete that led immediately to a flight of stairs that both ascended and descended. Just as she had expected, a sign on the wall marked "Parking" pointed downward, while the upward-pointing arrow was labeled "Condos."

Vi ran down the stairs to the garage and emerged into a well-lit parking bay that was filled with expensive cars and SUVs. She counted twenty slots in each of the four rows and noted that the red Emergency Exit sign at the far end of the garage was missing lights in two of its letters. It still told her what she needed to know, though. There was definitely a back door out of the building.

As she turned to go back up the stairs, the large garage door in the middle of one long wall began to clank and move upward. A second later, a sleek sedan passed by Vi on its way to a numbered slot. Without thinking, Vi took a quick look at the driver's face as she went by.

Dr. Ami Kim had made it home from Orlando.

CHAPTER ELEVEN

It was almost midnight by the time Ami let herself into her condo and dropped both her laptop bag and carry-on in the front hall. She was exhausted.

No, she was shell-shocked.

No, that wasn't quite right either.

Ecstatic?

Whatever she was feeling, she would have to sort it out in the morning because she felt like her brain was on overload and ready to short-circuit.

Rafe Greene was gifted with healing touch.

Though his descriptions of his ability had far outstripped anything she'd ever heard, Ami was actually very familiar with the concept. When she'd been in medical school, there'd been an uproar about the introduction of "therapeutic touch" courses into the curriculum of several regional nursing programs. Detractors and skeptics denounced it as outright fraud or well-meaning psychological manipulation, but the fact remained that therapeutic touch produced positive results for patients, alleviating pain and restoring health.

What intrigued Ami the most was the history of therapeutic touch. Not only had drawings depicting the practice been found on ancient cave walls around the world, but accounts of healing touch appeared in the Bible as well, under the guise of "laying on of hands." The concept was simple: a skilled healer simply placed his hands on a sick person and passed along his own energy into the body of the patient.

It was an act of sharing, an act of love.

In the nursing courses she'd heard about, the practitioners never actually touched the patients, though. Instead, they learned to sense the movement of energy in the patient's energy field by moving their hands over the body, and smoothing out any imbalances with gentling gestures. Whether or not a nurse ever sent her own energy into the patient was a hypothetical point, although Ami had heard nurses comment that they themselves felt physically depleted after a therapeutic touch session.

In contrast, Rafe had told her that he physically laid his hands on people when he attempted to heal. His results were more spectacular, too, if she believed even half of the incidents he'd recounted during dinner. In his eight years with the Marines, he figured he'd probably saved at least one hundred men from dying on the battlefield or en route to a camp hospital. Since he'd left the Corps to work as a civilian, he'd added another twenty to his list of miraculous healings.

Of course, she hadn't seen him in action with his gift, but after spending almost the whole day with the man, she had no reason to doubt his sincerity. When he'd told her about it before they went into the restaurant, he'd seemed as hesitant and reluctant to talk about it as she had felt about admitting to her own ability of medical intuition. People didn't make that kind of stuff up, she reminded herself. Or if they did, they either didn't tell anyone about it, or they did the opposite: talked about it at any and every opportunity in order to get the attention they craved, which was why they made it up in the first place. But Rafe clearly wasn't looking for attention. If anything, Ami would guess that the opposite was true: Rafe wanted to avoid the spotlight. She'd been in his company nonstop for ten hours before he brought it up, and even then, it had obviously been very difficult for him to speak about it.

He said he'd never spoken about it before, in fact.

So why did he tell her, a virtual stranger, something he'd never entrusted to anyone else?

"Because you know what it's like," Rafe had explained over lasagna in a quiet corner booth. "To have a gift that you know you have to use, but that you also know is going to complicate your life if anyone else knows about it."

That was exactly how she felt about her medical intuition.

No one understood it, so people typically ascribed all kinds of ignorant and inaccurate suppositions to the skill. The most harmless conjecture was that it was simply wishful thinking; the scariest was that it was the work of the Devil. In her experience, however, most people just dumped the idea of medical intuition in the category of "delusional," if they thought about it at all.

In that regard, she and Rafe had the same problem: as far as the general population believed, their gifts were non-existent. And on the very rare occasions that those gifts were made indisputably visible, the witnesses still couldn't believe what they were seeing.

Rafe had told Ami about the times that he'd been forced to leave a job because of the growing discomfort he felt from his co-workers when his healing abilities became evident—they weren't sure if he was evil incarnate or just plain crazy, but he could feel their mistrust of him increasing, and that compromised how well he could work with others in an emergency situation. For Ami's part, she'd never demonstrated what she could do—she'd always gone the route of providing patients with conventional diagnostic tools, even when she could have saved everyone a lot of time and money by simply holding their hands and focusing on their bodies.

Her mounting frustration in hiding her skill was the goad that had driven her into research, seeking ways to explain what she could do in terms people could accept. When Dr. Michael Carilion shook the world with his proof of the eleventh dimension, she knew she had found the key to that explanation. The eleventh dimension was pure energy, the same energy that she "read" in other people's bodies. For some unknown reason, she—Ami Kim—knew the language of that energy.

And Rafe Greene was able to manipulate that energy physically. The presence of the eleventh dimension was the reason that Rafe could heal with his hands.

"So you're saying these gifts of ours have scientific explanations?" Rafe had asked her over their tiramisu dessert, after she had outlined her understanding of her medical intuition.

"Yes, absolutely," she'd said. "They're a form of energy medicine. The same energy medicine that the Chinese have been practicing for five thousand years, and quite possibly the same type of healing that Jesus and his disciples utilized. Think about it. When people don't have the understanding or the language to explain something that's happened, they call it miraculous—unbelievable and filled with a mystery they can't penetrate. But now, with Carilion's discovery, we can start to unravel what has been, up until now, a mystery. We can begin to explain it in acceptable scientific terms and integrate it into conventional western medicine."

"The life energy of chi meets the American Medical Association?" Rafe winced. "I don't know, Ami. Scientific prejudices die hard. So do medical ones. It's been forty years since the World Health Organization endorsed the use of acupuncture, and there are new studies coming out every day about its effectiveness, yet most people still reject it as legitimate treatment."

She knew Rafe was right.

Never mind that acupuncture was routinely and effectively used in many parts of the world to treat asthma, anxiety problems, gastrointestinal and neurological disorders—in the United States, most people preferred to rely on complex medical, usually invasive, typically expensive, protocols than to even consider ancient cures shrouded in an alternative system of healing the body with natural energies. Even studies that speculated that acupuncture worked by manipulating the body's release of its own natural painkiller endorphins—hormones that promote healing—had been largely ignored by the medical establishment. Though, to be completely fair, there were a few trail-blazing hospitals across the country that had recently begun to offer acupuncture as an alternative to anesthesia in their surgery suites.

Like Rafe said, medical prejudices die hard.

Even in the face of evidence.

But the study that had captured Ami's attention and ignited her current path of research was the one that grounded itself in the body's natural electromagnetic fields. In that report, the researchers suggested that the points of acupuncture utilized by Chinese medicine were charged with the body's own natural electricity. After being stimulated with needles, that same human electricity altered chemical neurotransmitters which, in turn, caused the body to heal itself. Infrared images taken by the researchers clearly displayed the change in the body's electrical field, convincing Ami that the true vehicle of healing was the movement of energy throughout the body.

"Which is exactly what traditional Chinese medicine has always claimed," she'd pointed out to Rafe. "It's like the story of aspirin. For a long time, no one really knew why it worked, but it did. The effect was there, but we couldn't explain it. Science had to catch up."

She'd leaned forward over the table, her excitement pushing aside the travel fatigue she'd begun to feel when they'd landed in Minneapolis.

"And that's the same thing that's happening here, Rafe. Science is catching up to acupuncture. We're getting closer to explaining it in scientific terms, in the words of chemistry and biology and physics. We're using the language of cells, which is ultimately where change occurs in the human body. And the language of cells is energy."

Rafe's eyes had bored into Ami's with understanding.

"And you and I—we have a gift for reading and using that language. Is that what you think, Ami?"

It was definitely what Ami thought.

"And at some point in time, we'll be able to explain how our gifts work, scientifically," he'd concluded. "Like with the aspirin. Science will catch up to us."

She had nodded in agreement.

"Now, see, I've got a simpler explanation," Rafe had quietly insisted. "No physiological neurotransmitters, no electromagnetic fields. I think I can heal and you can intuit because God is working through us."

For only a fraction of a moment, Ami had let herself gaze deeply into the dark wells of Rafe's eyes.

Yes, she'd wanted to say. With all her soul, it was what she ultimately believed to be true—that God was the energy that worked through her.

But her years of professional training wouldn't let her say the word.

Suddenly terrified at how easily Rafe had slipped under her disciplined defenses when it came to her medical intuition, Ami had ruthlessly stamped down her admission of faith.

Right, she'd reprimanded herself. *The day I go down that road is the day I kiss my medical career goodbye. And disgrace my family. Again.*

She'd dropped her eyes to her empty plate.

"Speaking of working, are you going to start looking for a new job tomorrow?" she'd asked.

And with that, Ami had deftly steered the conversation back into safer waters.

Shortly afterwards, they paid their bill, and Ami dropped Rafe off at the downtown Hilton in Minneapolis. He'd wanted to see her to her condominium's front door, saying he was concerned for her safety, but she'd assured him there were no gang members trying to stake out territory in her upscale neighborhood. He'd laughed and asked if he could meet her for lunch the next day.

She'd told him yes.

"Do you not have enough complications in your life as it is?" she scolded her reflection in her front hallway's full-length mirror. "Not only did you admit that you are a medical intuitive to an almost complete stranger, but now he's coming back tomorrow for Round Two."

Ami studied the tired face that looked back at her. At the outer corners of her eyes, the finest lines were beginning to appear, lines she'd earned through long years of building her medical reputation—a reputation she'd been apparently willing to jeopardize after spending only a few hours in the company of a certain paramedic.

What had she been thinking?

Focus on her work was what she needed right now, not an irrational attraction to a man she barely knew. Besides, she'd been promising Niles for the last month that she'd get the research proposal finalized, and she well knew that the last thing he'd appreciate now was for her to delay it any longer.

She scrubbed her hands over her face and looked again at her reflection.

"Okay," she granted her mirror image, "that was at least one smart thing you've done: collected all the data to support the proposal, rather than going to Niles with nothing already in hand. He's always saying you need to put in more work upfront to validate unique research. Wait till he gets a look at this data. He's going to go crazy."

Ami shook her head.

"Yes, I am really tired when I start talking to myself. Go to bed, Ami."

She reached for her carry-on to walk back to her bedroom and froze.

There was a scraping sound coming from her front door lock.

She watched in silence as the doorknob twisted the tiniest fraction of an inch, then stopped.

More scraping.

Ami slid her hand into her laptop bag and pulled out her cell phone. She stepped close to the door and slowly leaned in to look through the peephole.

Fury spun through her.

CHAPTER TWELVE

Rafe stood at the big windows of his seventh-floor hotel room and looked out at the bright lights of downtown Minneapolis. Somewhere out there, Ami was—hopefully— already home.

When she'd left him at the Hilton's curb just a short while ago, it had taken every bit of restraint that Rafe could muster not to hop in the nearest cab and follow her to her condo just to be sure she was safe. Only by reminding himself over and over that the odds were unbelievably slim that someone would launch a second attack in one day on the lovely doctor could he take the key card from the hotel's desk clerk and go up to his room for the night. He also reassured himself that Orlando was states away from Minneapolis, and while another gunman could show up in the Twin Cities to hurt Ami, Rafe just couldn't believe that whoever was behind the shooting could make alternate arrangements that fast.

Although, if Rafe's stint in the Marines had taught him nothing else, he had learned that assuming anything was the fastest way to failure. In boot camp, assumptions got you twenty more pushups when you thought nobody noticed you'd slowed down on the last one.

On the battlefield, assumptions could kill you.

Nevertheless, he'd finally pushed his fears for Ami's safety temporarily aside and locked his own door. For at least this one night, he was going to trust that her regular guardian angel was awake and on duty. After all, when he'd gotten up this morning in Orlando, he'd had no idea he was going to find himself signing on for a mission by noon.

A dark-eyed mission by the name of Dr. Ami Kim.

At least now he could see a reason behind the irresistible compulsion he'd had to take that job interview in Orlando, despite his ambivalence about returning to the southeastern part of the country. Rafe couldn't help himself from laughing out loud.

When it came to matchmaking, no one, not even his own mama, could compete with the Big Guy.

Rafe sat on the edge of the queen-sized bed in the pastel-shaded hotel room and dropped his head into his big hands. He'd never dared to imagine how good it would feel to finally tell someone about his healing gift, but when he'd told Ami, he felt like a mountain of weight had slid off his shoulders. She didn't think he was a freak or crazed, because she was hiding a similar gift, though she insisted it was scientifically grounded, rather than a spiritual talent. He would have to work on her about that, he knew. From his own experience, he'd found that the gift only grew in proportion to the faith he brought to it.

And Rafe had always brought a lot of faith to his healing.

From the first time he'd laid hands on a dying soldier and felt the rush of power roar through his body, he'd known it was a gift from God, just like his physical strength and size. Stunned at his ability and the soldier's miraculous recovery, Rafe had spent hours on his knees, praying that the Lord would continue to use him as a healer.

And He had. No one ever died in an ambulance when Rafe was riding along. After a while, his fellow marines started calling him "St. Rafe" when one of his buddies explained that St. Raphael was the patron saint of travelers, as well as being known for healing. At the time, they'd all joked about it, but Rafe wondered if there weren't more to his gifts than he had realized. He still hadn't found a big neon sign from God telling him he was, in fact, a twenty-first-century archangel, but some things, Rafe knew, were better left unsaid.

And then, in one awful moment, his healing power had failed him.

'Hang on! For God's sake, hang on!"

Blood was everywhere. The ambulance bounced over the edges of the holes blasted into the dirt road, but Rafe wasn't yelling at his brother to get a grip on the sides of the vehicle.

He was yelling at him to keep living.

'Don't you die on me, Sammy! You hear me? Don't you die!"

The blood was gushing through the wads of bandage as fast as Rafe applied them to his brother's belly. Samuel had been riding in the first truck in the convoy when the rocket-propelled grenades started slamming into the column of Marine vehicles on the way to Baghdad. Rafe had thrown himself out of the ambulance and dodged his way past two Humvees and enemy fire to locate his brother.

What he'd found brought him to his knees in the sand beside Samuel.

His brother's body was almost torn in half.

Rafe lifted him in his arms and ran back to the ambulance, where he'd laid him on the stretcher and tried to staunch the hemorrhaging.

'Hang on, Sammy!"

Rafe closed his eyes, laid his hands on his brother's body and prayed like he'd never prayed before.

No power roared in his bones, and Rafe howled in despair.

His brother was dead.

In his pants pocket, Rafe's cell phone sang out the tune to "She's a Brick House." He took a moment to let the awful memory slide away, then flipped the phone open.

"Hey, Mama," he said. "You've got perfect timing, you know that? I was just thinking I could use some of that big love of yours."

The familiar warmth of his mother's voice reached out to him across the miles.

"Poor baby. What's going on? Didn't that hospital down in Orlando want you? You want me to call them up and give them a piece of my mind?"

Rafe smiled. That was his mama, all right. Not only did she have perfect timing with her phone.calls, but she always knew exactly what to say to make him feel better. "I love you, Mama."

"And I love you, too, Rafe, honey," she responded. "As a matter of fact, I've been thinking about that, a lot, and how much I wish you'd find a job back here at home. Your nieces would love to have their favorite uncle right here in town, and then I wouldn't have to worry so much about you being alone, either. There's this little house, cute as a button, just two blocks over, that's for sale."

Rafe rolled his eyes, knowing what was coming: the "time to settle down and raise a family" pitch. He had to give his mother credit for pure determination because CeCe Greene never gave up. She'd been on his case about getting married for at least ten years now. Let the woman into boot camp for six weeks, and she'd be the toughest Marine in the Corps, Rafe was sure.

"It's just the right size for a young family," she continued. "Lorraine Taylor's grandniece is moving back here next month, too. You remember Lorraine's grandniece? She got a job at that new trauma center that just went up. Lots of good jobs, I hear. Pretty girl, too. Single."

Rafe stifled a yawn and not-so-subtly changed the subject. "Hey, Mama, guess where I am tonight."

"You back in Milwaukee?"

"No, ma'am. I'm in Minneapolis."

"Minneapolis? What're you doing in Minneapolis? It's just as cold as Milwaukee. Colder, even."

Rafe looked out the big windows at the frozen city. "It sure is," he agreed, "but I hear it's got a couple good things going for it."

"Such as?"

"They've got a winter festival with ice sculptures and a treasure hunt. Lots of home shows and medical conventions."

"I see," she replied, sounding thoughtful. "Home shows, huh? Lord knows, you like those kinds of things," she laughed. "Okay, baby boy, who is she?"

"What do you mean?" Rafe pretended innocence.

"This is your mama talking, son. I can tell when there's a woman in the mix. I don't think you even know what a home show is."

In his mind's eye, Rafe could still see Ami's lovely smile. "Anybody ever tell you that you are one suspicious woman?" he asked his mother.

"Just you," she said. "I believe it was the morning after you came home smelling like a skunk, and I asked you if you knew anything about that senior class prank that got pulled on the high school principal."

Rafe coughed to cover his laugh. The man's office had stunk up the entire school for the last two days of classes. No, three days. Because of the prank he and his buddies had played, the whole graduating class got to spend an additional day in their classrooms.

Breathing in skunk stench.

"All right, Mama," he relented. "I did meet a woman in Orlando, and she told me that Minneapolis has all kinds of medical jobs. So here I am."

"And where is she?"

Rafe laughed out loud. "At home, in her condo."

"She like home shows?"

Rafe laughed again. "I don't really know. But I think I'd like to find out. We have . . . some other things in common."

And for the first time in my life, I could tell someone what it's like to have healing power at my fingertips, and she understood how amazing, and how frustrating, it can be to do something no one else can.

He couldn't tell his mama that part, though. That would require him to tell her about his gift—the gift that should have saved his brother, but didn't. Two years later, the grief he still saw in her eyes whenever he dropped in for a visit broke his heart all over again. It was the reason he kept the visits short, and why he'd been unable to shake the shadow of doubt that had crept into his faith in his gift even while he'd continued to heal others.

Why me, Lord?

"I might look for a job here, see if anything develops," he finished, trying to lighten his thoughts and the conversation. "You know me, Mama, I'm just a rolling stone."

"This girl know you're interested in her?"

"Yes, ma'am," he replied, "and we've got a lunch date tomorrow."

"That fast, huh? She must really be something."

"She is."

"Well, I guess I could come up there in the spring to visit you. Get away from this humidity for a while. That might be real nice. What's this girl's name?"

"Ami. Ami Kim. And I don't know that I'll be living here, Mama. Like I said, I just want to see what develops."

"It's high time you develop getting married. Minneapolis, huh? God does work in mysterious ways, I'll give Him that. Love you, baby boy."

"I love you, too, Mama."

"Sleep like an angel," she said.

"I always do," he replied, wishing it were true.

Rafe closed the phone and lay back on the king-sized bed. His mama had been tucking him into bed with that line ever since he could remember. A pillar of faith, she'd endured the tragic deaths of her husband and her son, and never once had she faulted the Lord. With her whole heart, CeCe Greene believed that everything turned to good in God's hands.

Gazing blankly at his hotel room ceiling, Rafe wondered what she'd say about Ami Kim's adamant insistence that energy, not God, was what made everything right in the world.

Recalling Ami's obvious reluctance—no, avoidance—of talking about a spiritual source of her medical intuition had made Rafe a little uncomfortable at first. Whether he understood exactly how he could heal or not, he'd never considered that it was anything other than God's own power working through him. After hearing her explanation about pure energy sources, though, he'd been tempted to try them on for himself.

What if his ability to heal was some kind of electromagnetic activity that he unconsciously directed? Wouldn't that explain why he'd been unable to help Samuel?

Maybe there'd been a solar flare or a flux in the earth's energy fields at the particular moment that his brother was blown apart, and so Rafe's ability failed to function. Maybe God didn't have anything to do with Rafe's healing gift at all, and Rafe just happened to be exceptionally adept at managing physical fields of electrical energy, just like Ami insisted.

Tempting, yes.

But also an easy way out of responsibility, and if CeCe Greene hadn't drummed anything else into his adolescent head, it was that he had an awesome responsibility to respect the gifts of God.

Responsibility was a heavy load, especially when it involved saving lives.

It was even heavier when lives were lost.

Then the responsibility became a curse and not the blessing it had seemed to be.

And Rafe knew what that felt like.

It felt like being completely, irrevocably abandoned, because why would God give you a gift that failed?

Ami felt the burden of responsibility, too, though it came in a different guise.

As she'd pointed out, and he'd agreed, she had the responsibility to her patients and colleagues to produce research that was recognized as scientifically credible. That was why she omitted any mention of her diagnostic intuition to others—she had no way to objectively verify its existence. As a licensed physician and serious researcher, reputation and integrity were critical responsibilities to Ami, and when Rafe pressed her about it, she'd sighed deeply at the dinner table.

"Do you remember the cloning scandal in the early years of this century?" she'd asked him. "A South Korean doctor claimed to have produced the world's first cloned human embryos. It was a monumental breakthrough which suddenly promised to make miracle cures possible through therapeutic cloning."

She'd dragged her fork around on her empty plate.

"It brought hope, Rafe, to millions of people with debilitating diseases that human cloning could be the answer to regenerative medicine."

Rafe knew what she was talking about. He recalled the shock waves of excitement that shook the military field hospitals following the announcement of the research findings. Some doctors speculated that cures might be found for paralyzed patients. Battlefield wounds might not be irreversible. Perhaps the lame could walk again, and the blind see.

"It was like a new age in medicine was just about to break open," he said.

Ami agreed.

"But then when the doctor admitted he had faked the data, he was disgraced," she reminded him. "He was fired from his post at the university, and his research license was revoked. Koreans everywhere had hailed him as a national hero, a medical genius. Now we were humiliated as a people that we had been taken in by a fraud. I may be an American citizen," she added, "but I am also a South Korean, and I share my country's shame."

She laid her fork down beside her plate. "I refuse to risk bringing more embarrassment to the Korean people."

"That's quite a load of responsibility," Rafe noted. "Although I can't help but wonder what kind of place this world could be if more people thought like that—that they're responsible for people they don't even know, that their actions don't happen in a vacuum. Sort of like those rings that spread out from a pebble dropped in a pool."

He took his napkin from his lap and tossed it on his own empty plate.

"Maybe the human race would be in a better place today if we all took a page from your book, Ami. Claiming responsibility for our culture doesn't seem too popular these days."

He took a sip from his water glass, eyeing her over its rim.

"And so, to avoid embarrassment, you cover up your intuition with science."

Rafe made it a statement, not a question.

"But what about this miracle cure you've found for heart disease and cancer? If you have proof, Ami, you must be planning to make it public."

He hesitated, trying in vain to read Ami's mind.

Now that would have been a helpful gift, he silently mused. *Sure would save a lot of time in conversations.*

"Is that what you presented at the neurophysiology conference?" he finally asked. "Your proof of a cure?"

She shook her head. "No. I'm still completing my studies for that. I simply presented my findings on the correlations between cardiac improvement and neurophysiologic change."

"Meaning?"

"Meaning that I have evidence that with the right stimulation, certain features of an individual's neurophysiology that affect heart function can be altered."

"The brain heals the body."

Ami smiled. "Yes, Rafe, the brain can heal the body."

But someone didn't want that happening, if Rafe was seeing the morning's attack on Ami clearly.

Yet she insisted that she hadn't announced her stunning conclusion at the conference—she'd only presented a piece of her research, the piece that said the physical organ of the heart was connected to the head when it came to healing. That alone, though, must have been enough to convince others at the conference, Dr. Uttam in particular, that her work had important implications for other mind/body medical issues. Uttam's patients had leukemia, which led Rafe to conclude that Ami thought her work could be extended into cancer therapy.

He suddenly realized what he was missing in understanding Ami's theory.

She'd claimed that the brain could heal the body with the right stimulation, but she'd never revealed what that "right stimulation" was. Did that have something to do with the shooting this morning? Did Ami know something so important that someone had hired a sniper to . . . do what?

Rafe knew that if a sniper wanted her dead so she wouldn't divulge some big secret, then Ami's hand would not have been in the laser sight—the back of her chest or her head would have been the target, and he would never have seen that red dot in time.

But that wasn't what had happened. Her hand was in the crosshairs, so the sniper didn't aim to kill.

A warning, maybe, to back off from her research?

If that were the case, then a hand wound might make sense.

But why would someone try to stop a medical breakthrough?

The only reason that Rafe could imagine would be that a breakthrough might make someone else's medical procedure obsolete. He'd been around the medical block long enough to know the kinds of money that health care involved, and that the advent of a superior treatment usually meant big financial gains for its developer at the expense of the previous provider.

Was Ami unknowingly wading into someone else's profit pool? Someone who was greedy enough to shoot trespassers?

Rafe rubbed his hands over his eyes and then headed into the bathroom for a shower before bed.

"What have you not yet told me, Ami?" he queried, catching sight of his tired face in the mirror over the sink. "What's really going on with your research? Then again, I guess I haven't exactly told you all my secrets either, have I? Dr. Kim, meet St. Raphael. I'm a good traveler, a great healer, I love puppies, and I'm a twenty-first-century archangel. Are you free for dinner tomorrow night?"

CHAPTER THIRTEEN

W hat do you think you're doing?"
Ami practically spit out her words as she jerked the door open and the man outside in the corridor nearly fell into her front hallway.

Dr. Niles Villome caught his balance and pulled himself shakily up to his full height.

"We have to talk," he announced.

Ami could hardly breathe for the fumes of alcohol that poured off her partner.

"You're drunk, Niles. Go home, sleep it off." A moment of real terror gripped her. "You didn't drive over here, did you?"

He shook his head in a wide arc. "No. Got a taxi from Paddy's. He wouldn't let me drive. Took my keys."

"Thank you, God," Ami said, rolling her eyes to the condo's ceiling.

Paddy's had long been a favorite bar of doctors who worked at the University Medical Center, for two reasons: the Irishman who owned the pub carried the tastiest microbrews in the Twin Cities, and he never let an inebriated patron leave his establishment with car keys in hand. Ami made a mental note to give Paddy a call tomorrow and thank him for minding Niles. Even when he was stone-cold sober, Niles was a terrible driver; Ami cringed to imagine the havoc he would have caused behind the wheel while intoxicated.

"We need to talk, Ami," Niles repeated, weaving slightly. "I'm worried about you."

"You better sit down," she told him sternly, "before you fall down, because I'm not going to pick you up if you do."

"You are so mean to me," he complained.

He gave her a drunken scowl and then headed into her living room, where he dropped into the nearest couch.

Ami sighed. She wished she hadn't opened her door but had left him out in the hallway. The problem with that solution was that the next morning would be even harder to face than it already was. The last thing she needed was for her neighbors to find Niles on her doorstep, passed out and stinking of stale beer.

Though all she wanted right now was a dark bedroom and a soft bed, she figured she had to at least get Niles loaded into another taxi and sent on his way home.

She punched in the number for the city service and ordered a cab.

"You coming in here or not?" Niles called from the living room.

Ami closed her phone and walked over to a chair positioned a good six feet away from Niles. She had twenty minutes before the cab showed up at the curb downstairs. On the one hand, it might take her that long to move Niles into the condo lobby, but on the other hand, she couldn't bear the thought of waiting with him as he slurred his words, all the while enduring the curious and reproving glances of anyone passing by the big windows of the entrance.

"I was afraid you were dead."

Ami threw him a hard glance. She wasn't sure she'd heard him correctly.

"I mean, I knew you weren't dead," Niles tried to explain, waving his hands in the air, "because you were on the news. But I was afraid someone was trying to kill you. And that maybe they're going to try to kill me, too."

Ami shook her head. "I've seen you drunk more times than I care to remember, Niles, but this is ridiculous. No one is trying to—"

She abruptly stopped what she was going to say because Rafe's words suddenly rang in her head.

'Someone had a laser scope on your hand. That doesn't seem like a random thing, if you ask me."

A tremor shot through Ami's spine as she remembered the surreal feeling she'd had on the airplane when the adrenaline from the shooting wore off. She'd actually considered the possibility that she had been deliberately tagged by a gunman's laser rifle sight.

She looked sharply at Niles.

"Just for the fun of it, let's say someone was shooting at me in Orlando," she said, her voice tight with a growing anger she didn't understand. "Why in the world would that suggest to you that someone might want to kill you?"

Niles blanched.

"Niles?" Ami demanded through gritted teeth, her suspicion mounting from a vague bad feeling to something more frightening. "What are you not telling me?"

"I did it for both of us! For the clinic!" he defended himself.

An icy-cold finger trailed the tremor's path down Ami's backbone. Her voice was almost as frigid.

"Did what, Niles?"

"I sold your research. We're going to be richer than sin," he drunkenly proclaimed.

Ami's knees buckled beneath her and she fell heavily into the chair. She could feel her teeth snap together when she hit the seat cushion, sending a jarring stab of pain through her head. She stared at Niles through a haze of fury and disbelief.

"I already bought a new car," Niles said. "BMW. I always wanted one."

Ami blinked and shook her head, trying to get her mouth to produce a word, any word, but she couldn't seem to engage her brain in the action.

"It was going to be a surprise," Niles slurred.

Ami started laughing. She laid her head on the padded back of the chair and laughed until she was out of breath, because if she didn't, she would probably lunge across the room and choke the life out of her partner.

"What's so funny?" he asked when she finally stopped.

Ami wiped tears from the corners of her dark eyes and looked again at the man sitting on her couch.

Niles Villome looked like the affluent young doctor he was, his expensive wool overcoat fashionably unbuttoned over his tailored navy suit. Even his tie was still neatly knotted at his throat and his thick rusty hair carefully groomed. In fact, if he didn't reek of liquor and just kept his mouth shut, no one would guess that the handsome doctor was an unrepentant alcoholic.

But disguising and justifying his addiction had been an art with Niles from the first days Ami had known him in medical school, and despite her own pleadings with him to get help, he'd never abandoned his illusion of being in control of his habit. Even now, when he had gone behind her back and shared her hard work—no, stolen it—she was still torn between the urge to dropkick him out of her life once and for all and her desire to rehabilitate him. It was a part of her very nature that she'd never been able to shake.

No matter how hopeless the case, Ami just couldn't accept that she was helpless to make a difference.

Niles wasn't the only one with control issues, she reminded herself.

"The fact that I could possibly be surprised at any asinine, self-centered thing you might do," she finally answered him.

"Not selfish," he indignantly, drunkenly, protested. "The money's for both of us. You can get a car, too, if you want."

"I don't want a car!" Ami shouted at him, her nerves nearing the breaking point. "I want you out, Niles. I'm going to get you down to the lobby where your taxi should be waiting and send you home. We'll talk about this in the morning. In the office."

Niles leaned forward on the couch and lowered his voice.

"I could stay here, Ami. For old times' sake."

"No, you can't." She stood up, her face gone to stone. "We're going downstairs. Now."

When he didn't move, she lowered her voice, too.

"Don't make me call the police, Niles. You know I'll do it."

To her relief, he didn't challenge her on it. Instead, he lifted himself carefully from the couch and walked unsteadily to her front door.

"I can see myself out," he told her. "And I'm glad you're all right."

He patted the pockets of his overcoat as if he were trying to find something.

Ami sighed. "You don't have your car keys, Niles. Paddy has them. You got a taxi over here."

Niles didn't respond. He just kept patting his coat.

"Niles. You need to leave now."

He opened his coat and fished in a deep inside pocket. "Here it is," he said and pulled his hand out.

In it was a gun.

I'm going to die, Ami thought. *There's a drunk in my condo and he's pointing a gun at me.*

The morning's events rushed back at her. A bullet had barely missed her in Florida.

Now here, in her own home, Niles was pointing a gun at her.

Rafe was right. Someone did want her dead.

She just never would have guessed that it was Niles.

"It's 'kay," Niles slurred, holding the gun out to her, a foolish smile on his face. "It's for you, Ami. Protection. I told you I was worried about you."

He took a step toward her, weaving on his feet.

Before she could think twice about it, Ami snatched the gun from Niles's fingers. It felt cold and heavy in her small hand and her stomach roiled at the thought of it going off. She didn't know anything about firearms, and she wasn't sure if Niles did, either. All she could think to do was to put it somewhere out of reach as quickly as possible. She steeled herself to carry it into her kitchen, where she carefully laid it in the cupboard underneath the sink. When she returned to the living room, Niles was leaning against the wall beside the door, rubbing the shadow of stubble that had risen on his chin and cheeks.

"I'm worried about you," he repeated, his eyelids drooping. "I want you to be safe."

Too tired and emotionally drained to argue with him—even if she had wanted to, which she didn't—Ami took his hand and gently pulled him toward her front door.

"Go home, Niles. I'm sure your taxi is downstairs waiting for you. We'll talk tomorrow."

"Promise?"

She nodded wearily.

Ami opened the door and Niles went out into the hallway, where he headed crookedly for the elevator. She watched until the elevator's doors closed on him and the chime signaled that it was on its way down before retreating into her condo and locking the door. As she threw the deadbolt, she noted the time on the thermostat that hung beside the doorframe.

It was already tomorrow.

CHAPTER FOURTEEN

"Everyone loves Dr. Kim," the round-faced woman behind the desk told Rafe. "What a coincidence that you would meet her on your flight here."

Rafe gave her a dazzling smile in reply while he continued to fill out the application form for employment.

According to her nametag, Ethel Anderson was the Human Resources assistant manager for the University Medical Center, but Rafe already had another name for her: the Ethel Express. About ten minutes ago, he'd walked into the office and inquired about job openings, saying that Ami had referred him, and that had been the one and only time he'd managed to get in a few words. The woman had immediately begun a non-stop narrative that related her own interactions with Ami, her satisfaction with working at UMC, her concerns about the rising costs of health care, her grandson's bout of strep throat, and her daughter-in-law's refusal to find a new daycare provider even though her grandson had already had strep twice in the last two months.

When he realized that Ethel had stopped talking and was apparently waiting for a response from him, he looked up from the form with a blank look. "I'm sorry, I didn't quite catch that."

Ethel leaned her heavy bosom over her desk and spoke a little more slowly than she had during her monologue.

"I said everyone loves Dr. Kim, and what a coincidence that you met her on the plane here."

"Yes," he agreed. "Quite a coincidence."

Although he couldn't agree with her other comment. There was definitely someone in Orlando yesterday who didn't love Dr. Kim.

And even though he'd pushed his fears for Ami aside last night, he knew he was going to feel a whole lot better this morning once he saw for himself that she had weathered the night safely.

"You know, you are the tallest EMT I have ever seen," Ethel commented. "How in the world do you fit into the back of an ambulance? I'd think you'd be much happier working in an emergency room where you could have a little more space to maneuver. We have a whole new emergency department, did Dr. Kim tell you that? It's state of the art. A really gorgeous facility. She's down there pretty often, you know, consulting with our emergency docs about cardiac patients. She's got to be one of the best physicians around, if you ask me. I swear she worked a miracle with my brother-in-law last year. We thought sure he was going to have to have at least one heart stent put in, but she put him on this new therapy she's testing, and he's made a full recovery. You know, I'm sure you'd really like working in the emergency department."

She paused for a breath.

"I love ambulance work," Rafe said, jumping on the break in the torrent of words. "That's the only position I'm interested in, Ms. Anderson."

"Oh, well, that's fine. As a matter of fact, I think we just got a new opening last week."

She rolled her chair sideways to the big corkboard that covered a section of her office wall and removed a tack from the top of a sheet of yellow paper.

"Here," she said, handing Rafe the sheet when she rolled back behind her desk. "This is the job posting. I'll send your application right down there, and my guess is that you'll get a call sometime today."

She craned her neck towards the application Rafe had placed on the front edge of her desk. "It looks like you have plenty of experience there."

"Yes, ma'am, I do," Rafe assured her. Then, in an effort to avoid the inevitable question of why he kept changing jobs, he added, "I'm looking forward to getting settled somewhere, and Minneapolis has a lot to recommend it."

"If you like winter sports and lakes, it certainly does," Ethel said. "Me, I'm not so crazy about the cold, you know. But it's a pretty city, and we don't have too much crime. The schools are good. There are parks all over the place. Do you want me to walk you down to the emergency department?"

"Oh, no," he insisted and shot to his feet. "I've already taken up way too much of your valuable time."

He stuck his hand out to shake Ethel's.

"Thanks, Ms. Anderson. You've been a great help."

And before she could say another word, Rafe was out the door of Human Resources and into the building's wide corridor, congratulating himself on a smooth escape.

"A tour with the Express," he muttered. "No thanks."

He checked his watch. Another forty minutes and he'd meet Ami in her clinic office to go to lunch. He pulled a map of the medical complex out of his leather jacket's inside pocket and located the building that housed the Minneapolis Heart Partners Clinic. With over fifteen buildings in the complex and at least that many skyways weaving between them, getting from one office to another promised to be an adventure in itself.

"Good thing I like to walk," Rafe said under his breath as he started the hike to the far side of the complex.

The brown-haired woman with the ponytail watched him disappear around the corner of the long hallway before she pulled open the door to the Human Resources office.

Vi was certain he was the same man who had shoved Dr. Kim out of her crosshairs yesterday at the Orlando Suites, and the same man who had sat next to the doctor in first class on the airplane. Seated across the aisle and only four rows behind them in coach class, Vi had noted the constant conversation the two had engaged in during the flight. At one point, she'd even gone up to the lavatory between the two sections of the plane, hoping she might catch a few words of their exchange. She hadn't, but she also hadn't missed the way they had exited the plane together and walked companionably down to the pick-up lanes for the remote lot shuttle vans, where they climbed aboard the same shuttle.

Seeing the big black man here on the medical campus where Dr. Kim worked, however, disturbed Vi deeply.

Yesterday, she'd been sure that the man's role as a spoiler was just an unexpected, albeit disastrous, variable that had skewed her carefully laid plans. Then, when they'd traveled together, Vi had wondered if, perhaps, the "chance encounter" was actually not a chance at all, and was, in fact, a contrived meeting between the two. Hadn't Philip himself floated the idea to her in their conversation that a competing corporation might try to approach Dr. Kim about her research? Maybe the big man was doing exactly that, working for another pharmaceutical company and worming his way into the doctor's confidence. From what Vi had seen on the plane, the man wasn't even going to have to work very hard to win that trust, thanks to her own botched shooting that had placed Dr. Kim squarely in the man's debt.

Regardless of the man's intentions, though, it was clear to Vi that she now had another player in this game to manage. Granted, she already had her own grudge to settle against the man, but when she was on assignment for Philip, she made it an unbreakable rule that his needs came first, and hers, second. That meant she would keep her professional focus on the petite doctor just as her employer had commanded.

But her personal radar was going to stay locked on the man from Orlando. Vi wasn't fooling herself about the man's abilities, either. He was obviously former military. Throw a bunch of men in a room, and Vi could pick out the soldiers in half a second by the way they carried themselves and interacted with others. If she had to guess, Vi would also say that Dr. Kim's new companion was a combat veteran, judging from the lightning-fast reflexes he'd demonstrated in knocking her down in the hotel gift shop, not to mention his apparent recognition of the red laser sight that had galvanized him into protecting her unsuspecting target.

All of which meant that Vi had a lot more surveillance to do, because Vi Winters was nothing if not thorough when it came to doing her job.

If Dr. Kim had suddenly acquired a new companion, Vi would find out whatever she could about him, fully aware that at twice her size with impressive instincts, the big black soldier could become much more than an unexpected, unwelcome, variable.

He might instead turn up on an assassin's hit list.

An assassin named Violet Winters.

"Hello," Vi greeted the office receptionist. "I'm doing background for a magazine article about the Heart Partners Clinic. Do you think I could grab a couple minutes with your HR director? I only have a few questions I need answered."

The woman at the desk held up a finger to ask Vi to wait a moment while she picked up a ringing phone and put the caller on hold. While she waited, Vi studied the aerial photos of the medical complex that were mounted on the wall behind the receptionist.

"It's quite a large facility," the woman behind the desk said to her after replacing the phone in its cradle. She pointed a finger at one arm of the center. "We're in this section, right here."

She moved her polished nail across the width of the map. "The Heart Partners Clinic is way over here on the far side of the campus. It's in our newest medical offices wing. I think that's where the neurophysiology lab is located, but other than that, it's all nine-to-five offices. A real tomb after hours, I guess. Oh—you asked about Ms. Bremers, our director."

Vi nodded, filing away into her memory all the woman's chatter about the layout of the medical center.

"Unfortunately, she's out of the office today, but our assistant manager, Ms. Anderson, could see you."

"Is she the one who just spoke with the fellow I met out in the hall?" Vi lied.

"Yes," the woman answered, "she is."

Vi smiled shyly. "That would be wonderful."

CHAPTER FIFTEEN

Ami sat at her desk in her office and scrolled through the list of eighty-plus waiting emails that demanded her attention. Not even five minutes into the task, there was a soft knock on her door, and Ami looked up to see the night janitor, standing just outside her office.

"Mr. Nguyen," she said, rising from her seat.

"No, no," he waved his hands at her. "You sit."

"Come in, please," Ami invited him. "What can I do for you?"

The old Vietnamese man stepped into her office. "May I shut the door for a moment, Dr. Kim?"

A hint of alarm crossed Ami's face, but again Nguyen waved his hands at her.

"I am fine, Dr. Kim. My heart is good today, thanks to you. The door?"

"Yes, of course," Ami responded, a little wave of relief passing over her.

The old man had been one of her first patients to participate in her research trials, and though his advanced age had been a concern originally, his heart condition continued to improve with the treatment. He didn't know it yet, but once her results were completed and published, he would become an overnight medical sensation, if he so chose.

Knowing Chinh Nguyen as well as she did, however, Ami was certain that the humble man would adamantly refuse that option.

"What can I do for you?" she repeated.

Nguyen gently closed the door, the quiet snick of the lock sliding against its seat in the doorframe. He walked across the room to stand in front of Ami's desk.

"Last night, I find Dr. Villome in your office when I clean. I tell him I check for trash. He say I stay out. This your office, Dr. Kim, not his."

His eyes met Ami's.

"He lock himself inside while I finish cleaning the examination rooms."

Ami's smile froze on her face.

Niles had been in her office.

Uninvited.

Definitely unwelcome.

The bastard.

With deliberate effort, Ami forced herself to remain calm for Mr. Nguyen's sake. She didn't want to upset him with her response to his clear evidence of Niles' duplicity because she feared that the elderly fellow might interpret some of her anger as being directed towards him, rather than toward her treacherous partner. Ruthlessly suppressing the explosion she could feel gathering inside her, Ami extended her hand to the janitor and thanked him for letting her know.

"I will take it up with my partner immediately," she promised Nguyen. "You did the right thing to tell me."

"I have bad feeling about it," he confided. "It is dishonorable."

"Yes," she agreed. "It is."

The old man nodded and walked quickly out of her office, leaving her door slightly ajar as it had been before he had entered.

Ami counted three beats and then charged across the room to shut her door once more. She leaned back against the hard oak of the door and tipped her head to stare at the ceiling.

He'd been raiding her files.

She was going to kill him.

All these months, she'd been giving him bare outlines about the research she was doing just to keep him off her back and wrangle some free time out of her busy schedule to focus on the work, and now he'd actually sold that same research out from under her. When he'd fumbled that out late last night at her apartment, she'd convinced herself that he was, as usual, jerking her around, trying to make her feel guilty for going to Orlando, for having an absorbing interest in something other than the great Dr. Niles Villome. She'd reasoned he couldn't possibly have enough information from the snippets of research she'd shared with him in her monthly reports to even consider approaching a pharmaceutical company with a drug development proposal. She'd even gone so far as to deliberately omit key points of the protocol in her summaries as her own extra measure of self-protection. Niles wasn't a researcher, and he'd never had the aptitude or the patience for it, so Ami had felt secure that he would only give her work a token glance. Mostly, she assumed, he used her research project as an avenue for lodging complaints about her decreasing contributions to the clinic's billable hours.

But now, thanks to Mr. Nguyen's disclosure, Ami saw, in her mind's eye, a freight train barreling toward her.

If Niles had accessed her personal files, he could have filtered out enough information for a proposal and padded it with some of the test trial data she stored on her computer. Without a doubt, the data was impressive enough to catch any drug manufacturer's eye, and Ami now realized what a mistake she had made to let Niles think she was testing an already-FDA-approved drug. Not having to run Phase I, II, or III trials would mean that a company could make a quick turn-around and market a new application for a drug with considerably less expense compared to developing an entirely new product.

And while the research costs would be much lower for the producer, the profits would be much, much higher.

Ami groaned.

Obviously much, much, much higher if Niles's comment last night held any truth.

'We're going to be richer than sin," he'd said.

"No, we're not, Niles," she told the ceiling. "Because there's something really important here you don't know."

A rapping sound at her back made her turn around and glare at the door, and Ami knew before he spoke that it was Niles on the other side.

"Are you in there?" His voice sounded hoarsely through the door.

Ami briefly debated giving herself another moment of space before confronting her partner, but decided against it. Niles deserved all her fury, and she was going to let him have it.

She jerked her door open and roughly grabbed the front of his suit coat. Before he could register what she was doing, she gave a hard tug and pulled him into her office, almost pulling him off his feet in the process.

"You bastard," she snarled. She reached around him to slam the door shut with enough force to rattle the diplomas hanging on her office walls.

"You hacked into my computer and copied my private files, didn't you?" she accused him, her voice rising. "You pieced together just enough to sell some drug company on my work, and now they're expecting a goldmine from it. Aren't they?"

Niles stood his ground in the middle of her office, straightening his jacket sleeves from her rough handling.

"That's exactly what I did, Ami. Because you were holding out on me, weren't you?" he accused her. "You've been giving me monthly reports that told me just enough to convince me that your research was valuable, but you've never included the raw data of the trials, or the names of your patients, so I could follow up with them. Partners don't keep secrets from partners, Ami, but you seem to think nothing of it, so yes, I helped myself to your computer."

"That's private property, Niles! You stole my research!"

Niles held his hands out in a conciliatory gesture. "Ami, you need to think this through here. Your work belongs to our clinic. Of course you'll get all the credit for the research—I wouldn't dream of taking that from you. But we both know you have a history of being overly cautious when it comes to treatment therapies. Even though you were holding back on me, I could see where this project of yours was going, and I didn't want you to have to wait to get the funding or recognition you deserve."

Ami folded her arms across her chest.

"Oh, really? So you figured that the best way to help me was to steal from me, lie to me, and make promises you can't possibly keep to some pharmaceutical giant because you really don't have a clue what I'm working on? Brilliant, Niles! Thank you very much! Because you are the most self-centered man on the face of the planet, you have just destroyed any future I may have had in medical research, not to mention my cardiology practice."

"What are you talking about? Your research is going to make us millions, Ami."

Niles reached out to put his hands on her shoulders, but she backed away from him. His features began to cloud with confusion.

"A cure for heart disease! We're going to be in the history books, Ami. How is that going to ruin your life?"

He was totally clueless, Ami realized. Of course he would be, since she'd never detailed exactly what she was running trials on. In all of her notes, she'd named the therapy NRT, and she'd known that Niles would assume it was a drug, which worked well for her since it kept him happy and out of her way.

But if Niles had promised a drug formulation to someone— a formulation she couldn't possibly deliver—her professional career would be dead with her name forever attached to a drug research scam.

Or maybe she'd just end up dead in a hotel lobby.

She looked up at Niles, her knees suddenly feeling like they couldn't support her weight.

"Because there is no drug, Niles," she answered. "In fact, NRT eliminates drugs."

Niles could feel the rush of his blood from his head. He stared at Ami, refusing to believe he'd heard her correctly. She turned away from him and walked stiffly to her chair behind her desk, his eyes following her every step of the way.

"You don't mean that," he choked out, frantically searching for a reason behind her bizarre comments.

He knew there was a drug. He'd seen her reports. NRT was an FDA-approved drug for the treatment of personality disorders. Ami had stated that in her reports, and Ami was nothing if not obsessively meticulous when it came to medical records.

And then it hit him.

Ami's comments were payback for last night.

Breathing a ragged sigh of relief, Niles rubbed his brow with his hand and then dragged his fingers back through his hair.

"Okay, okay. I get it," he told her. If an apology was what it was going to take for him to get the name of the drug from her, he'd do it. No one else was in the room to hear it, so his unchallenged authority with the office staff wouldn't suffer. He held up his hands in a gesture of surrender.

"I'm sorry I showed up at your apartment last night. I should have called first."

Ami sat in her chair, silent, her eyes pinned relentlessly on his.

Niles cleared his throat and clasped his hands at his heart.

"Yes, I probably had too much to drink, but I just wanted to assure myself that you were all right."

"Because you were afraid that someone had tried to kill me because of my research which you stole from me and sold to a manufacturer." Ami's voice was cold, measured.

Niles cleared his throat again.

"Yes."

Ami's voice floated to him in a whisper.

"Get out."

"I will."

He held up his hands again, this time in defense against her anger.

"I know you need some time for this, but trust me, you're going to see that what I did was really for the best—for both of us. But first, please tell me that no one in Orlando tried to get close to you."

He could tell from Ami's face that she was seconds away from yelling at him, so he spit out the rest of his words as fast as he could.

"Because yes, I'm afraid that the hotel shooting wasn't random, and that some rival pharma company has found out about your work, and they're trying to stop you from finishing it. Why do you think I brought you a gun last night? You need to protect yourself, Ami. You hold the key to a miracle cure—a billion-dollar miracle cure! Who wouldn't kill for that? So I ask you: did you talk to anyone—anyone at all—on this trip about it?"

Ami's furious words lodged in her throat.

Rafe.

She'd talked to Rafe Greene.

She'd joked with a total stranger in the hotel gift shop, and the next thing she'd known, there was a bullet plowing past her as that stranger tackled her to the floor. Rafe had saved her hand, maybe her life. Then they'd caught the shuttle to the airport together and he ended up on her crowded flight, seated right beside her in the first-class cabin. He'd talked her through the post-shooting adrenaline drop. He'd made her laugh. They'd gone to dinner. They spent the evening talking.

About anything and everything.

Including her research.

Now that she thought about it, Rafe Greene's incredible timing had been perfect from the moment she'd met him.

Too perfect?

After all, she never did see that laser dot on her hand that sent Rafe knocking her down in the gift shop.

"Ami?" Niles prodded her.

She refocused on her partner's treacherous face.

"Get out," she whispered again.

CHAPTER SIXTEEN

Philip Arden took another sip of his double espresso and sat back in the rich leather armchair in his suite at the Grand Hotel. The room was dimly lit by a small table lamp across the room, the heavy drapes still closed over the big windows that looked out over a gray February morning in downtown Minneapolis.

Philip hated the Midwest. He hated the cold in the winter and the blinding glare of sunlit snow. He hated the ridiculous upbeat attitude of the people who lived here, who claimed to enjoy the frigid temperatures and the challenge of battling the elements. Most of all, he despised the cherished family values they were known for, along with their unremitting trust in the goodness of their fellow human beings.

Trust.

Philip could feel the bile rising in his throat. Compared to his contempt for trust, his hatred of the Midwest was a mere annoyance.

Trust brought people closer to God, and that was a problem for the Devil himself, a problem he couldn't—wouldn't—allow to continue.

And thanks to Ami Kim, he now had the perfect solution.

Philip closed his eyes and laid his head against the soft cushion of the chair's headrest. A smile crossed his lips as he played out the months ahead in his imagination. Within a few weeks, the petite cardiologist would successfully complete her drug trials and her partner would hand over the miracle cure to Calyx. On Pieter Hallenstroem's command, Diedrich would immediately push CardiaZone into production and distribution, securing Calyx's financial future and giving new hope to a hurting world.

At which point, he, Philip, would secretly have the drug's formulation slightly altered, so that all those who had come to trust their very lives to the Calyx cure would not only find themselves betrayed, but also dead.

He could almost hear the human howl of pain that would circle the globe when the new wonder drug suddenly went bad.

He shivered in delight at the prospect.

Success was so close.

Philip opened his eyes. He set his half-empty cup on the antique table beside the chair and walked over to the covered windows. With his left hand, he parted the room-darkening drapes a few inches only, just enough to grant him a slice of a look down to the crowded sidewalk outside the hotel.

How many of those people on the street had heart problems, he wondered. How many would rush to the medical salvation of a CardiaZone?

He focused his attention on a woman in a purple down-filled coat, her hand raised to call a taxi.

She fell to the sidewalk, her hand clutched to her chest.

In seconds, a crowd began to gather on the icy street, and Philip let the drapes fall closed. A minute later, he heard the wail of approaching sirens beyond the cold windows. Car horns began to honk and tires screeched as curious drivers tried to avoid rear-ending the cars in front of them. Muted voices rose from below in anger, fear, and confusion.

Chaos was so reliable.

Philip picked up his coffee and drained the cup.

He thought again about the months ahead.

The tampered drug's death toll would reach staggering proportions before it was pulled from the marketplace. Even then, it would continue to be sold in back alleys as unscrupulous dealers insisted that their supplies were untainted. Meanwhile, physicians who had prescribed it for their patients would be shell-shocked, pronounced incompetents, and sued in enough malpractice suits to cripple the entire field of cardiac medicine for years to come.

Pieter Hallenstroem, boy genius, would probably kill himself out of guilt alone, if not in response to his total financial ruin.

Who says that vengence belongs to God? Philip chuckled to himself. *Vengence is mine, saith the Devil.*

He would have to share that little observation with Diedrich, he decided. The two of them could have a good laugh about it.

Or at least, they would have several months ago. Now, Philip wasn't so sure.

Something odd was going on with Diedrich.

For the first time in their long association, Philip was uncertain if he could depend on his second-in-command to do his bidding. Diedrich had, after all, failed to inform his employer about his hospital visit and the subsequent diagnosis. Not only that, but in recent weeks, Philip had also noted a lack of Diedrich's usual enthusiasm for his assignments. Advancing age had a way of doing that, The Gentleman knew. Not even the hardest men were able to completely avoid the encroaching fears of mortality and death, especially after a surprise stay in a hospital. It seemed that no matter how blasé a man had been in life about the future of his immortal soul, when death and damnation came knocking, the stakes of the game suddenly changed.

Maybe Diedrich was ready to fold.

If so, Philip decided, perhaps it was time to deal him out.

A soundless vibration in the pocket of his trousers interrupted his musings about Diedrich's fading loyalty. He extracted the cell phone, noted Vi's number, and answered the call.

"Everyone loves Ami," Vi's melodious voice informed him. "From the human resources director at the hospital to the lab techs in the adjoining medical suites, everybody thinks she's a saint. And if they didn't before, the local news last night practically canonized her for them for her courageous response to a 'drive-by shooting' in Orlando. I can hardly get through the hallways outside her clinic because of all the reporters grabbing every patient or hospital employee who walks by, just so they can get a sound bite about the talented and modest Dr. Kim."

"Why, Vi," Philip said into the phone, "I do think I detect a tiny note of sarcasm in your charming voice. Has the good doctor done something to offend you?"

"You mean other than dropping out of my laser sight?"

"Yes, I suppose there is that," The Gentleman granted her. "I can imagine she's not on your list of Best Friends Forever right now."

Vi's soft chuckle carried over the connection.

"You imagine correctly, Philip. I've never missed a target before, and I don't like the feeling it gives me: ineptitude. So I'm sure it colors how I feel about Dr. Kim. Although I do happen to know she's not quite as virtuous as her admirers claim."

She paused a moment and Philip could hear the clamor of voices in the background.

"I saw her partner Dr. Villome take an elevator up to her apartment last night," Vi continued as the background noise diminished. "It was late, Philip. Very late. Too late for discussing clinic business, if you get my drift."

"So you think she's romantically involved with her business partner. Not exactly a crime, Vi."

"Not exactly saint-like behavior, either, especially considering she was cozied up on the plane here to Minneapolis yesterday with the man who happened to push her out of my gun sight in Orlando. The same man, who, coincidentally enough, just applied for a job here at the same medical complex where

Dr. Kim works. Really, Philip, I don't see how the woman can possibly get her research done if she's so busy juggling men."

"Meow."

Vi's musical laughter came over the connection again. "Yes, I'm being catty. And you can't fool me, Philip—I know you love it. Just like you love the fact that I'm keeping such close tabs on the little doctor for you."

Her voice dropped to a mere breath in his ear.

"I know what you're going to want, Philip, because I want it, too."

Philip closed his eyes, relishing the quick spear of desire that Vi's assurance sent through his body. Without a doubt, Vi was a gem—smart, discrete, disciplined, and as amoral as anyone he'd ever met. And while those traits in an employee were very appealing to him as an employer, he had to admit that Vi's quiet confidence, along with her uncanny ability to anticipate his next move and his next need, held an unquestionable attraction for him. For the first time in his memory, he actually felt intrigued by a woman.

"Philip? Are you still there?"

He opened his eyes and focused on the task at hand.

"Yes, of course. I was just thinking about how much I enjoy working with you, and if you might be free for lunch with me?"

More noise came over the phone connection.

"Where are you, Vi? What's going on there?"

He heard her apologize to someone at her end.

"I'm outside Heart Partners—that's Kim and Villome's clinic. There must be five different news crews here in the hallway, setting up lights and microphones. I have to keep moving around to stay out of their way so I don't get knocked over by some camera guy. I was hoping to get inside the reception area to get a feel for the office layout, but it looks like nobody's getting in now. Oh, wait a minute—Villome just opened the door."

Philip waited for her to continue.

"I'll be damned," she whispered into the phone.

"What?"

"Just now, when Villome came out to talk to the reporters, I caught a glance inside the clinic."

"And?" he prompted her.

"The man's here. The big black man that Kim brought home with her from Orlando. The one who knocked her down in the hotel so I missed my shot. The same one who just applied for a job here."

Philip could practically feel her smug smile over the phone.

"He's sitting in her reception area," she said. "Isn't that sweet?"

CHAPTER SEVENTEEN

R afe watched the clinic's front door slowly swing shut behind the man who had gone out to meet the press of media people in the hallway. He'd only gotten a quick look at the man's features as he bustled out the door, but it didn't take a face-recognition program for Rafe to match the man with the imposing framed portrait of Dr. Niles Villome that hung on the reception area's wall next to Ami's own professional photograph.

Of course, the man in the portrait looked serenely capable and relaxed, whereas the man who'd just left the clinic was anything but.

Whether the doctor's discomfort was a reaction to the noise of the unexpected company in the hall, or from the yelling match that had leaked down the clinic corridor to the few people waiting in the reception area, Rafe couldn't be sure. All he knew for certain was that he was awfully glad that he'd beaten the bunch of newshounds to Ami's office, because if he'd only been arriving now, there was no way he would have made it inside. Less than a minute after he'd walked into the clinic and taken a seat, the first reporter had approached the receptionist, and she'd politely asked him to wait outside in deference to the clinic's clients.

When a second and third reporter came in and were likewise asked to wait outside, a nurse was dispatched to the hallway to monitor the traffic, refusing entrance to anyone but patients. The receptionist behind the desk had finally asked Rafe why he was there, and when he said he'd made a lunch date with Dr. Kim, she'd smiled and told him he was in for a wait, since it was barely eleven in the morning.

"I was a Boy Scout, ma'am," he informed her, deliberately letting his native southern drawl creep into his voice. "I believe in being prepared. And early."

He flashed her his big white smile. "I know Dr. Kim is a busy woman, and I wouldn't want her to have to be waiting on me."

At which point the yelling from down the corridor had interrupted their conversation, causing the receptionist to throw Rafe an embarrassed smile. Before she could say anything, however, the nurse in the hall stuck her head around the clinic door and called out to her.

"Would you please get Dr. Villome out here? I don't think I can hold these people off much longer. They want to speak with Dr. Kim, and I know she'll refuse."

Fortunately for the harried nurse, Dr. Villome appeared in the corridor at almost the same moment, and, hearing his name, walked into the reception area.

"I need you over here, Doctor," the nurse told him, clearly relieved to turn her post over to her employer. "There's a mob of media people out here all wanting to talk to Dr. Kim about the shooting yesterday. You need to make a statement or something."

The doctor had straightened his jacket and gone out the door. Rafe and the receptionist exchanged a glance.

"He's very good with the media," the woman assured Rafe. "Dr. Kim is camera-shy, so he's always the spokesperson for their practice. Do you want me to let Dr. Kim know you're here?"

"If it's not too much trouble, ma'am," Rafe nodded. "I'd appreciate that."

The receptionist rang Ami's office line.

"I just wanted to let you know that your lunch appointment is here," she said, sending a smile in Rafe's direction. She hung up the phone and turned to him. "She'll be right out."

"Thank you," he replied, "but I didn't mean to interrupt her morning."

"Between you and me, I think she's already been interrupted." She tipped her head meaningfully towards the door which Dr. Villome had just closed behind himself. "I have a feeling that Dr. Kim isn't going to get much accomplished here in the office today, anyway."

The sound of a door opening in the corridor caught Rafe's attention, and he immediately stood up when he saw Ami coming towards him. He was struck again by her petite size and thick black bangs, her intense dark eyes and her confident poise. The smile he liked so well was missing, though, and in its place her lips formed a grim line.

"Not such a good morning, I'm guessing?" he said when she reached out her small hand to greet him with a handshake.

"Not exactly," she agreed. "Would you come to my office, please?"

She turned her back on him and walked back down the corridor. Rafe gave the receptionist a small goodbye wave and followed Ami to her office, where she stood holding the door open for him. As soon as he was inside, she closed it and leaned her forehead against the honey-hued wood.

Rafe waited.

After a few seconds, Ami turned to face him.

"Please tell me you are not an industrial spy from a pharmaceutical company who set me up for, and then saved me from, a near-miss shooting so that I would trust you enough to not only tell you about my research, but also admit to a personal ability that will absolutely scuttle any future I may have in serious medicine."

Rafe blinked.

"What?"

Ami licked her lips and stared at Rafe's handsome face. "My partner thinks the reason someone shot at me yesterday was to stop my research."

"I thought you said no one knew about your research."

"I was wrong."

She continued to pin Rafe's eyes with her own.

"Unknown to me, my partner sold my research to a pharmaceutical company, and now he believes that other drug companies know about it, and either want to completely stop the drug's development or want to obtain the formulation for themselves. So, please tell me you didn't become my constant companion yesterday because you're working for some pharma company as a spy. You know, save the little lady, become her new best friend, let her spill her guts and every secret she has?"

"I'm not a spy, Ami."

"Like you would even admit it if you were."

Rafe gently laid his hands on her shoulders, wondering if she would twist away from him, but she didn't.

"I'm not a spy, Ami," he repeated. "I think I'm your guardian angel. What do you think?"

Ami dropped her gaze to the broad chest that stood exactly at her eye level.

"I'm not sure."

She could feel the warmth of his hands stealing down her arms, across her back, unknotting the tension she'd built up during her fight with Niles. She'd been so blindsided by his betrayal of her professional trust that she hadn't been able to think a lucid thought since she'd thrown him out of her office. She knew in the depths of her heart that Rafe wasn't her enemy, but Niles' deceitful admissions and awful suspicions had shaken her badly, and in the aftermath of their yelling match, she'd found herself second-guessing every decision, every conclusion she'd drawn the day before. When she'd walked into the office this morning, the only thing she'd wanted to do was get caught up on her email and case load and enjoy the anticipation of seeing Rafe again for lunch.

She hadn't anticipated uncovering research theft and becoming a target for industrial espionage before noon.

"Ami?"

She looked back up into Rafe's concerned eyes.

"I trust you," she whispered. "And I think I need your help."

Rafe lifted a hand to lightly cup her cheek. "Hallelujah."

"But you don't even know what I'm going to ask you to do," she protested. "I'm not even sure what I'm going to ask you to do."

"Doesn't matter. I'm on your team, Ami."

"And which team is that?"

She searched his eyes, wondering where this man had come from, why he'd suddenly become her ally, and what kind of fool she must be to think that one person could help her make right again everything that had just tumbled down around her ears.

"The healing team, Ami. The medical miracle team. You've got a cure for heart disease, maybe cancer. How could I not want to be a part of that?"

His fingers left her face, his smile warm.

"You and I—we have healing gifts already," he said. "But this—your research—is something else. It's a path into the future, Ami. You cure heart disease and cancer, you give millions of people a future they didn't have. You make people whole again."

"And 'wipe away every tear,' is that it?" she pressed. "You think this is part of some grand scheme of God's?"

She could have sworn that Rafe's brown eyes burned with a sudden intensity.

"You never know," he quietly told her, his thumb tracing a line over her lower lip.

The door behind her flew open.

"What the hell is this?" Niles's voice erupted into the office.

"Who are you?" he shouted at Rafe.

Ami spun around to face her partner.

"He's a friend," she said tightly. "Now get out of my office."

Niles's glance bounced from Ami's face to Rafe's, then back again to Ami's.

"We need to talk," he commanded her, his voice unnecessarily loud in the small room.

"She asked you to leave," Rafe reminded him.

Niles looked the big man over. The guy was tall, broad-shouldered and equally broad-chested. As a backdrop to Ami's small figure, he couldn't have looked more like a brick wall if he had tried.

"This is my clinic. This is my partner." Niles glared at the man, fighting his body's automatic reflex to lift his chin to better address the taller man. No way was he going to make even that tiny concession towards the interloper. "If you'll excuse us, we have business to discuss."

"We have nothing to discuss," Ami sharply corrected him. "Please leave, Niles."

"Who is this guy?" Niles jerked his head in Rafe's direction.

The man stepped around from behind Ami and extended his hand to Niles.

"Rafe Greene."

Niles gave the outstretched hand a quick glance and deliberately stuck his own hands in his pants pockets.

"Dr. Kim is busy, Mr. Greene. In case you're not aware of it, she's been out of town for a few days, and I know she has a lot of work to catch up on. I suggest you come back later in the day."

"For crying out loud, Niles!" Ami exclaimed. "Could you be any ruder or more comical? 'I suggest you come back later in the day,'" she mimicked him. "I'm a grown woman, Niles, not to mention your partner in this practice, which also makes this clinic mine as well as yours."

Before he could snap off a retort, the huge man moved closer, crossing into Niles's personal space.

Niles couldn't stop his involuntary reflex.

He stepped back.

"I know Dr. Kim has been out of town," the stranger informed Niles. "We met yesterday in Orlando. I knocked her out of a laser sight."

Again, Niles's eyes darted back and forth between the two of them. He settled on Ami's face. "You met him in Orlando? Do you recall the conversation we just had in this office a short while ago?"

"Believe me, Niles, I'm not about to forget it. And no, Rafe is not an industrial spy."

"You can't know that for sure!" he hissed at her. "You met him yesterday. In Orlando. And now he's here in your office? Are you out of your mind?"

"You realize I'm standing right here, don't you, Doctor?"

Niles threw another glare at Ami's new friend. "I'm quite aware of it. And I think you should leave before I call security."

Ami snagged her purse from where it sat behind her desk. "Don't bother, Niles, because we were just leaving. Come on, Rafe."

"What are you doing?" Niles choked out. He caught Ami's elbow as she walked past him. "How much does he know?"

Ami jerked her arm from his grasp. "Enough to recognize a crazy man when he sees one."

She headed for the door with the giant on her heels.

"Ami!" Niles tried one last time. "You're in danger! He's dangerous! He only wants the name of the drug!"

She turned in the doorway and looked back at him. "I already told you, Niles. There is no drug."

She walked out of her office with Rafe Greene behind her.

"You're lying, Ami," he whispered a moment later in the empty room. "I've seen the data, and I know you too well. There's no way on earth you've poured your time and energy into documenting fraudulent research. Integrity is your middle name, except for when it comes to dealing with me, obviously. How very petty of you, Dr. Kim."

Reassured by his assessment of the situation, he turned to face her desk.

Somewhere, she had to have the name of the drug. He stepped behind her office chair and imagined himself in her place.

When it came to research, Ami was scrupulous. She took total control of any project, from interviewing the potential subjects to proofreading final reports. Every detail came under her nose, and only when she had signed off on it, would it be allowed to move ahead. Suppliers were carefully screened and . . .

In a flash of blinding clarity, Niles knew where he could find the name of the drug.

Silently berating himself for his stupidity, he logged onto Ami's computer and pulled up vendor billings. When he'd taken over the business end of their practice a few years ago, he'd purchased the financial records software because it was virtually self-operating. Since then, he'd rarely given it a thought since it performed so well. He typed in the name of the practice's pharmaceutical rep, opened the files and scrolled through the orders, looking for ones authorized by Ami. Finally, he hit the one he was looking for. It had been made out almost two years ago, and Ami had noted on the form that it was the protocol drug for her personal NRT research.

Niles read the item description and felt the blood drain from his head.

Sucrose tablets.

Niles blinked.

He wasn't reading it right. Sucrose tablets were sugar pills. Placebos. Ami must have misspelled the drug's trade name. That would make sense. It was a drug for personality disorders, not cardiac treatment, so of course Ami wouldn't be as familiar with the name as she would be with the usual drugs of her medical field.

He needed to keep looking.

He spun the cursor down the page of order entries that appeared on the computer monitor until he found another one that had Ami's notation for her NRT research.

Sucrose tablets.

Frantically, Niles minimized the screen and pulled up a list of drug trade names that he'd had installed on every computer in the clinic.

There was no drug for personality disorders that even came close to the word "sucrose."

Stunned, Niles looked again at Ami's drug orders.

Sucrose.

Sugar pills.

Placebos.

Ami had been using placebos in her trials, which meant she had told him the truth.

There was no drug.

I am so screwed, Niles thought. *Thanks to you, Ami.*

CHAPTER EIGHTEEN

Chinh Nguyen squinted as he searched the medical center's expansive cafeteria for his grandson Hung's smiling face.

On any other day, the old man would have been at home with his wife Thanh at this late morning hour, watching her make the stock for tonight's soup. Since he'd come in to the clinic during his off-shift to share his concern with Dr. Kim, however, he'd found himself already in the center when his grandson had called him on his cell phone to join him for a cup of coffee. Chinh had never taken a liking to the American addiction, but he did enjoy a cup of tea on a cold day, and so he had readily accepted Hung's invitation.

Besides, it always made him proud to spend time with his grandson who had worked so hard to enter the pharmacy school at the university.

His family had indeed come a long way from toiling in the rice paddies of Vietnam.

Spotting Hung sitting along a side wall, Chinh navigated through the maze of tables and people that filled the space. As he approached his grandson, he noted that a white ceramic cup was already waiting on the table for him, the tag of a tea bag hanging over its side.

"Grandfather," Hung greeted him, pointing to the cup. "Your tea is already brewing."

Chinh glanced at the paper tag. "Green tea. You remember for me."

Hung flashed a handsome smile. "How could I forget? You remind all of us every day that since you had your heart attack,

134

you only drink green tea. You'd think that the green tea saved your life, not Dr. Kim's therapy."

His eyes darted beyond Chinh's face.

"I want you to meet someone, Grandfather."

Chinh turned to see a well-dressed older man just a few feet away. He watched while Hung stood up and shook the man's hand.

"It's good to see you again," Hung greeted him. "This is my grandfather, Chinh Nguyen. Grandfather, this is the man I told you about a few months ago. He's very interested in your treatment with Dr. Kim."

Chinh measured the stranger. His body was erect, his shoulders back. The slight smile on his face was not genuine. In the dark days of the war that had ravaged his homeland, Chinh had met many men like this one—worn, haggard, exhausted. Hung's friend was someone else's soldier, a man doing what his duty called him to, even though he had lost the heart to do it any longer.

Hung's friend had lost his soul.

"I'm hoping I'll be able to help Dr. Kim bring her research and heart treatment to people all over the world," the silver-haired man said, extending his hand to Chinh. "I'm Diedrich Mahler."

CHAPTER NINETEEN

F orgive me if I'm out of line here, but why are you partners with Niles Villome?"

Ami and Rafe were sitting quietly in Ami's car after their quick exit from Ami's office. Bracing her palms on the steering wheel, Ami pushed herself tightly back into the driver's seat cushion and closed her eyes. Where could she even begin to answer Rafe's question?

"I'm sorry. It's none of my business," he began to apologize.

"No," she interrupted him. "It's all right. I've been asking myself the same thing an awful lot lately. When we opened the practice years ago, it made sense for us to work together. We'd met in medical school and then did our residencies here. Just when we were finishing up, one of our instructors was retiring and offered us the clinic, which meant we wouldn't have to start our practice from scratch."

She turned to face Rafe. "Believe it or not, Niles is an excellent cardiologist. He just has some . . . issues."

"As in he thinks it's okay to appropriate your research and sell it to a drug company without your knowledge?" Rafe shook his head. "I'd say that's more than an issue, Ami."

Ami let out a long sigh, feeling some of the tension that had gripped her shoulders ebbing away. "You're right. It is. But unfortunately, I can't undo what he's done. I can only try to clean up the mess."

Rafe's eyes narrowed as he considered her. "You sound like that doesn't surprise you. I take it you've cleaned up after your partner before."

It wasn't a question, but a statement, and Ami acknowledged its truth with a nod.

"Yes. I have cleaned up after Niles before. He's an alcoholic, Rafe. He may be a skilled physician, but he's killing himself with booze, and everything that comes with it."

"He thinks the world revolves around Niles Villome," Rafe suggested. "He has special permission to do what he wants. He's never at fault. He believes he can control everything around him, and if he can't, then he lies to himself about it . . . and to everyone else, too. Am I getting close?"

Ami smiled sadly. "Spot on, I'd say. Do you know an alcoholic?"

Rafe nodded. "I did. My dad. As long as he didn't drink, he was the greatest guy in the world. He was in rehab twice. He didn't make it in a third time, though—he died in a car crash, driving drunk."

"I'm so sorry."

"Me, too. He missed me playing in the state championship my senior year in high school. For a long time, I felt it was my fault. If he hadn't been on the way to the game . . ."

His voice trailed off for a second, and Ami reached over to lightly touch the big shoulder that was only inches away from her own in the front seat.

"You know what I learned?" he continued.

Ami shook her head.

"That life and death happens, and all we can do is live a good life. That's all God asks of us, really. The only thing we can control is who we are and what we do with it. The rest is out of our hands."

He covered Ami's small hand on his shoulder with his own big one.

"You can't fix Niles, Ami. He's got to do it himself."

Ami looked at Rafe's dark hand holding hers. "I know that. I do. I just want him to do it sooner, rather than later."

She caught a little smile tugging at Rafe's lips.

"What?"

Rafe laughed. "Nothing. For a second there, I thought maybe you might have a little control issue, too. 'I want him to do it sooner, rather than later,'" he chided her.

Ami pulled her hand away and put it back on the steering wheel.

"You bet I do. Because look where he's landed me. He's contracted us—me—to hand over a drug that doesn't exist."

She put the car in gear and drove out of the parking garage.

"But you told me you'd developed a cure for heart disease," Rafe pointed out as she took an entrance ramp for the interstate that cut through the heart of Minneapolis. "Doesn't that involve a drug?"

"I'll show you what it involves," she replied. "If you're seriously going to help me with this mess, you need to meet my trial technicians."

Four vehicles behind her, a white rental car followed Ami's every turn. Her hands locked on the wheel, Violet Winters alternately cursed the sloppy road conditions and blessed the little tracking device she'd affixed to Ami Kim's car last night in the condo building's underground parking garage. Before she'd ended her phone call with Philip, she'd agreed to meet him for lunch. Then, when she'd finally gotten inside the clinic, the receptionist had informed her that Dr. Kim had left early for her own lunch date, and Vi had hustled out to her rental car.

She punched in Philip's number on her cell phone.

"What would you say to a 'chance' encounter with Ami Kim over lunch?" she asked him. "A little up-close and personal time?"

"I'd say, 'what a wonderful idea,'" he replied.

"I'll call you when I've got the location." Vi signaled to exit the interstate, following Ami's car.

"Vi?"

"Yes?"

Philip's voice was warm and intimate in her ear. "Just out of curiosity, how quickly could you remove Niles Villome from our little game?"

Up ahead of her, Vi could see Ami's car slowing down for a stoplight at the top of the exit ramp.

"That depends," she replied, her voice as silky as his, "on how quickly you want it done."

"This afternoon?"

Vi smiled and cranked up the heater in her car. Philip Arden was so predictable. She'd figured it was only a matter of time before he decided to get rid of the pompous doctor.

"I'll see what I can do," she promised and ended the call.

Five minutes later, she parked across the street from where Villome's partner had pulled into a small gravel lot.

"This is a lunch spot?" she wondered aloud. She looked again at the snow-covered building beside the lot and read the letter-board sign posted out front that listed events in the building.

From what she could see, Dr. Kim and her new friend were going to have a long wait for something to eat, since the only meal the First Assembly Church of North St. Paul advertised was a Friday Night Fish-Fry.

And it was only Monday morning.

CHAPTER TWENTY

As Diedrich expected, Hung's grandfather hesitated to shake the strange hand that was offered to him. For a split second, the Calyx executive wondered if the small Vietnamese man was going to turn and flee, or spit in his face.

In the long course of his career, Diedrich had developed a sharply honed instinct that could almost instantly predict how an encounter would go, but right now, that same instinct was faltering.

There was more to the old man than met the eye.

Though Hung's grandfather was obviously frail, Diedrich was convinced he detected a hidden core of steel looking out at him through those weathered eyes. Not only that, but he could sense the man's reluctance to accept his hand went beyond cultural differences—the old man's critical gaze was clearly assessing him, but for what, Diedrich wasn't quite sure. He apparently passed the silent examination, however, because the elder Nguyen finally took his offered hand in a firm grasp.

Warmth traveled up his arm.

How odd. Diedrich hadn't even realized he was cold.

"You own drug company?" Chinh asked him.

"No, but I work for one," Diedrich told him, momentarily distracted by his visceral response to the elderly man. He motioned for the two Nguyens to take a seat. "Please, enjoy your tea."

"Can I go get you something?" Hung offered. "Coffee? Tea?"

"Coffee would be fine. Just black. Thanks."

He watched Hung head back towards the cafeteria line and coffee station, then turned his attention to Chinh.

"He's a fine young man, Mr. Nguyen. You must be very proud of him."

Hung's grandfather nodded in agreement, his gaze on his ceramic cup. "He is hard worker. He has done well."

"I don't know if he told you how we met. I came to represent my employer at a hiring fair for the pharmacy students here, and I was most intrigued by your grandson's old-fashioned work ethic. I don't see that kind of dedication very often anymore, to be honest with you."

Diedrich studied the quiet man sitting across the table from him. Nguyen sipped his tea and kept his eyes on his cup.

"I remember he told me that he had learned it from you," the Calyx executive continued, "that you had never missed a day of work since you were hired here at the medical center. No matter what else was going on in the lives of your extended family, you always showed up for a full shift. That's quite a role model, Mr. Nguyen."

The man shrugged in humble acknowledgment. "Hung is good boy."

"I'm sure he will be a fine pharmacist, too," Diedrich added.

He waited a beat or two for the old man to comment, but after a few moments with no forthcoming conversation and no visible response to his remark, he decided to plunge ahead.

"He also shared with me how he'd chosen his career path because of your own experience with heart disease treatment."

Again, Diedrich waited for the man to say something, but when only silence hung in the air between them, his patience began to wear thin. Whether the elder Nguyen was quiet by nature, or just cautious about what he said in regards to the treatment, Diedrich didn't know, but he was going to get the information he'd come for, and it wasn't going to take him all day.

He discarded the oblique approach and went directly to his point.

"I'm intrigued by the incredible results you had in Dr. Kim's drug trials," he said, speaking bluntly, hoping to spark some kind of reply from the man on the other side of the small table. Chinh's eyes finally lifted up from contemplating his steeping tea.

"Yes, Hung has told me," Chinh said, speaking slowly, carefully. Clearly, the older man was very aware of his limits with his adopted tongue and was working hard to use the language correctly. And from what Hung had told him about his grandfather's insistence on family honor, it didn't surprise Diedrich that the elder Nguyen was making the effort to present himself so formally. Diedrich could respect that, too, even admire it, but if the old man didn't get to the point very soon, he would have to restrain himself from reaching across the table and pulling the words out of the man's throat.

"He did not ask my permission to speak of this with you," Chinh said, a hint of anger frosting his tone, "and I was not happy when he told me he had done so. Dr. Kim ask me to not tell anyone beyond my family of my treatment, and Hung broke that trust speaking to you. You will understand I do not blame you, but my headstrong grandson."

Simultaneously relieved that the man had spoken and afraid that he might say nothing more, Diedrich jumped to the younger man's defense. "Please don't blame him too much, Mr. Nguyen," he countered. "Especially since his information has convinced me that Dr. Kim has made a brilliant breakthrough in cardiac disease treatment, and I hope to provide her with the funding she needs to finish her research to bring it into production. Her treatment will save millions of lives, Mr. Nguyen."

Hung returned and set Diedrich's cup of hot coffee on the laminated tabletop, then sat down next to his grandfather.

"I know you are mad at me, Grandfather, but please listen to what Mr. Mahler has to say," he pleaded. "He can help Dr. Kim move ahead with her work. This is how progress happens in medicine. The right word in the right ear can lead to great discoveries. I know you want Dr. Kim to succeed, and this is the way she can do that. Mr. Mahler and his company will make her dreams come true."

Diedrich watched Hung's earnest face as he tried to appease his grandfather's sense of betrayal. There was no way that Hung could know that he was actually heaping lies upon lies by repeating what Diedrich had told him over the last few months. When he'd met the younger Nguyen at the recruiting fair on campus, he'd been hoping to find someone with connections to the Heart Partners Clinic whom he could use for collecting information on Niles Villome and his CardiaZone trials, but he never imagined to find a relative of one of the actual trial participants virtually dumped into his lap. Since then, he'd routinely checked in with Hung to see how the grandfather was doing and what new progress Dr. Kim was making, since it was clear that her partner was only sharing partial information with Pieter Hallenstroem.

From his conversations with Hung, it had also become clear to Diedrich that Dr. Kim was unaware of Dr. Villome's deal with Calyx and the fact that her research was already being financed by the pharmaceutical company.

As a result, Diedrich had let Hung continue to believe that Dr. Kim's work was still a private project, rather than a pending multi-million-dollar drug introduction.

That way, Diedrich could be sure that Hung's reports about the trials were factually correct, and not another fairy tale designed by Dr. Villome to keep Pieter Hallenstroem's wallet open and the funding flowing.

After his unexpected encounter with Philip Arden yesterday, however, Diedrich had made a last-minute change to his travel plans and decided to do a little more digging into the actual drug trials being conducted by Dr. Kim. Though he didn't like to admit it, Philip's presence had rattled him on several levels. Yes, he hated to think that his employer was spying on him for health reasons, but even worse was the sobering recognition that Diedrich no longer got the buzz from doing Philip's dirty work. On top of that, Diedrich knew that for Philip to show up in the Midwest—an area for which he'd developed a deep loathing in the last year—there had to be a compelling reason that trumped his employer's aversion.

After mulling it over during the dark hours of the night, Diedrich could think of only one reason that fit that bill.

Philip was smelling success.

How had he phrased it? Oh yes—if he gave the world a cure for heart disease, everyone would trust Philip Arden.

I own them.

Sitting in the cafeteria with Hung and his grandfather, for the first time in his long career with Philip, Diedrich wasn't sure he wanted to make his employer happy.

He, of all people, knew what it felt like to be owned by Philip Arden, and it wasn't always a pretty picture. In fact, more often than not, it had been ugly, and lately, more and more of those memories had been surfacing in his dreams. He saw the slaughtered villagers and the child soldiers he had helped create when he'd brokered weapons deals for Philip with the guerrillas in Sierra Leone. He recalled the tortured men and women that littered the Latin American landscape thanks to the drug traffic that Philip insisted on supporting through his various enterprises. On his worst nights, Diedrich swore he could hear the crying of mothers as they held their starving children in their arms while humanitarian aid disappeared into the coffers of corrupt governments, thanks to his own discrete tutelage.

No matter the outcome in terms of human suffering, Diedrich had complied with his employer's directives. He was, he ruefully reflected, the ultimate company man.

Philip's company man.

Without thinking, Diedrich rubbed the dull ache that was beginning to rise again in his chest, reminding him that he still needed to make that appointment for a heart exam and stress test. He adjusted his position in the hard plastic chair and felt some relief. He needed a hot soaking bath and a week in the sun, he decided.

But first, he wanted something from Chinh Nguyen.

After combing again through all of the reports that Niles had provided him, Diedrich simply couldn't believe that no other researchers had caught the heart-healing effect of a drug used for personality disorders. There was only one way to guarantee that no one else had a patent pending on the formulation of the drug that would make Calyx the provider of a medical miracle, and that was to get the name of the drug that Dr. Kim was testing.

"Mr. Nguyen," he addressed the old man. "Hung is right. We will make Dr. Kim's dreams come true. But I need one thing before we can proceed. Can you tell me the name of the drug she prescribed for you?"

The old man and his grandson exchanged a concerned look, the alarm in the elder Nguyen's eyes so forceful that it hit Diedrich with physical impact.

Something was wrong.

Hung leaned in towards him.

"This is where it gets really weird," he said, his voice dropping to a whisper. "We did a drug analysis exercise in class one day, and I brought in one of Grandfather's heart pills to analyze."

Hung gave his grandfather another look of hesitation, but the old man nodded, stern-faced and commanding, urging him to finish his comments.

"It was a placebo, Mr. Mahler. A sugar pill."

Diedrich blinked.

"A sugar pill?"

"Yes," Chinh said. "It has no properties of healing."

The Calyx vice president blinked again, his mind gone blank. He faintly registered a shooting pain in his shoulder.

"But your heart disease, it's gone, right?" He struggled to make some sense of what he was hearing, his hand instinctively massaging his chest. "You had some kind of treatment from Dr. Kim that healed your heart."

"Yes," Chinh said again. "I thought it was the pill, but when Hung told me it was not, then I realize why Dr. Kim required me to visit the neurology lab in the hospital three evenings a week."

"Neurology lab?"

Chinh nodded. "For six months, I take my pills on Mondays, Wednesdays, and Fridays, then I go to the neurology lab and Dr. Kim hooks me up to the monitors, here," he pointed to the sides of his head just above his ears, then to his heart, "and here. She tells me to relax and think happy things. And then her technicians—they are on the other side of a glass window—they watch the monitors and me, and they talk together."

Diedrich drew in a ragged breath, suddenly aware that he had broken out in a cold sweat.

"She has a bunch of technicians watch you?"

"Yes!" the old man said, his eyes gleaming. "And after six months, I realize they are not talking about the monitors. They are moving their mouths, but they are not talking. They are chanting."

"Chanting?" Diedrich croaked.

"They pray, Mr. Mahler," Chinh explained. "Dr. Kim's technicians pray for me. The sugar pill does not heal my heart. The prayer does."

Diedrich toppled to the floor, unconscious.

CHAPTER TWENTY-ONE

A mi led Rafe down a narrow staircase into the church basement, his broad frame barely fitting into the width between the walls. One bare ceiling lightbulb followed by another six feet further down threw dim shadows on the steps. A thick glass window coated in dust and backed by a metal window well marked where the building's cement block foundation began.

"I'm assuming you don't have, like, zombies for technicians, right?" Rafe asked. "Because I have to tell you, this is a pretty creepy spot for medical research."

"No zombies," she assured him, flashing a smile over her shoulder. "It gets much nicer down here, really. There's just not much you can do about an old stairway in a building like this. You really can't rebuild it or move the wall."

"Maybe you could find somewhere else for your technicians to work?"

"Actually, this has turned out to be a perfect place for this particular group. It's close to where they all live, so it's really convenient for getting together."

At the bottom of the stairs, more lights automatically came on as soon as Ami's foot touched the carpet. A hall stretched along the length of the basement, with four doorways leading into large classrooms. Rafe noticed that light and voices floated out of the door at the far end of the corridor. Ami headed in its direction.

"Do you remember when I told you on the plane that with the right stimulus, the brain can heal the body?"

Rafe remembered. Her short course on how the brain could rewire its neural pathways with magnetic stimulation had piqued his interest. He'd heard a little about the plasticity of the brain in some of the classes he regularly took to update his paramedic training, but he'd never considered the possibilities that the idea of plasticity might yield in other medical specialties. Even reports of paralyzed patients regaining use of limbs hadn't seemed especially noteworthy to him, since he knew lots of physical therapists who could achieve what seemed like miracles through the intensive rehabilitation of patients' damaged limbs.

When Ami recast the idea of rehabilitation into one of reshaping neural connections, though, Rafe had immediately realized that cochlear implants were only the tip of the medical miracle iceberg that might be neurophysiologically-based. Given the brain's plasticity and its own electrical energy, what physical function of the body couldn't be improved with intentional manipulation?

"'Then the eyes of the blind shall be opened, and the ears of the deaf shall be unstopped. Then shall the lame man leap as an hart, and the tongue of the dumb sing: for in the wilderness shall waters break out, and streams in the desert.' Isaiah 35:5-6," Rafe quoted. "It's biblical. Rewiring neurons is God's healing."

Ami came to an abrupt stop ahead of him, catching Rafe so off-guard that he almost tripped over her. He caught her shoulders in his hands to steady them both and she turned to face him.

"Is that what it is, Rafe? I know you think that God is behind the healing power in your hands, but what if it's just a new medical frontier that's opening up before us? Like I told you last night, I can explain it with energy—call it *chi*, like the Chinese, or call it neurophysiological reprogramming—but either way, I can put it all in scientific language to explain the cause, effect, and process. God doesn't have to be a part of it."

"But where does the energy originate, Ami? You said yourself that the confirmation of the eleventh dimension's existence helped you put all the pieces into place for your own work. Ever since he made his announcement, Carilion has insisted that the eleventh dimension is heaven—the spiritual dimension, the throne of God—so why can't you accept God's place in your work, just as Carilion did?" Rafe argued.

"Because I can't," she argued back. "I don't live in an eleventh dimension, Rafe. I live right here and right now."

Rafe tightened his hands on her shoulders.

"So does God, Ami. Right here. Right now."

Ami raked her fingers through her long bangs and blew out a short sigh of frustration.

"You don't understand, Rafe. The medical world doesn't want mystery. It wants data, statistics. Cause and effect. Saying that God is the key to my treatment plan would destroy everything I've accomplished. I would be tossed out of the medical establishment in a heartbeat!"

"Because you've found the key they refuse to use?" he challenged her. "Who are you really listening to here, Ami? The medical establishment or your own heart?"

His voice softened.

"And which one, in the end, do you really need to be loyal to? You know, the reason God whispers in your heart sometimes is because everyone else is making too much noise. Especially those people who don't want you hearing anyone other than them."

For a moment, she wanted to believe him.

She wanted to believe that she could share the truth of her cardiological success with her colleagues, survive their skepticism, and revolutionize modern medicine.

She wanted to be able to trust her own conviction that she was doing the right thing, that doing what seemed to be so right healed everything that was going wrong.

But the last time she'd followed that little voice in her heart, she'd made the biggest mistake of her life and married Niles Villome.

A mistake she was still grappling with.

She pulled away from Rafe.

"And sometimes that whisper isn't God at all," she told him bitterly. "Sometimes it's self-deception wearing the mask of selflessness. Leave it alone, Rafe. God doesn't work through sinners like me. I fell off any heavenly radar a long time ago, I'm sure. The world of medicine is where I live and work, and if science is the only way I'm allowed to contribute to healing, then that's how I'm going to do it."

"I think your science could benefit from some faith, Ami," he told her.

"Faith is overrated," she retorted.

"How can you say that? You're a cardiologist. Tell me that you don't encourage your patients to have faith—in your skill, in your treatment of their disease, in the power of life itself," he demanded.

"I ask them to have faith in their own bodies' ability to heal," she replied. "And then my technicians teach them how to do exactly that. How to let their bodies heal themselves. And they learn to do it by using cutting edge medical science, not by appealing to faith healers at tent revivals."

She glared at Rafe.

"I don't make promises I can't keep, Rafe. No matter the consequences."

Her eyes dropped from his face, hoping he hadn't caught the bitterness that had surfaced in her voice.

"You should probably know that about me," she added.

The hall seemed unnaturally quiet as she waited for him to respond.

"I'm glad to hear it, Ami," he finally answered. "I feel the same way . . . about promises. Thanks to my mama, I knew the meaning of *Semper Fi* long before I joined the Marines. And, FYI, I have yet to make an appearance at a tent revival. That's something you should probably know about me."

Ami could feel a hot blush spreading across her cheeks. Her crack about rural faith healers had been unkind and unwarranted. Rafe had been nothing but accepting of her own unorthodox ability to intuit medically, and now she had returned the favor with a thoughtless, prejudiced remark that was both insulting and demeaning.

True, she had yet to witness Rafe's gift in action, but comparing him to healing charlatans had been a low blow. She wouldn't blame him a bit if he turned on his heel right now and walked away from her, back up the stairs and out into the Minnesota cold. But before she could utter a word of apology, he walked past her toward the room at the end of the hall.

"Kind of warm in here with all these lights on," he noted, unzipping his jacket as he walked. "Don't you think?"

It didn't take a degree in neurophysiology to see that he'd hit a nerve with Ami, Rafe reflected as he neared the open door at the end of the hall. Somewhere along the line, his brilliant companion had been badly hurt either professionally or personally and she was still suffering its effects.

He knew what that was like—on most days, he continued to feel the loss of his brother Samuel like a recurring punch in his gut. In his more introspective moments, Rafe even suspected that his unresolved guilt about his brother probably helped fuel his need to keep changing jobs and avoid putting down new roots. As long as he kept telling himself he needed to move on, he couldn't get attached; if he didn't get attached, he couldn't get hurt.

Ami, on the other hand, had apparently sucked up her hurt and was living with it.

Judging from the anger Rafe had just heard in her voice, though, her solution to dealing with it hadn't succeeded any more than his had. They were a pair, all right. Maybe they should be out looking for a support group this morning instead of spending time with her medical technicians. *Lord knows we could both use it,* he thought.

He stopped at the entrance to the room and waited for Ami to lead the way in. As she passed him in the doorway, he noted that the heat had faded from her cheeks and she'd put that lovely smile he liked so well back on her face.

The lady was back in control.

"Hey, Dr. Kim! It's not a patient review day, is it?"

Rafe looked at the tall, older man greeting Ami with a handshake. With his gray hair tied back into a long ponytail, Rafe would have expected him to be dressed in a flannel shirt and jeans instead of the well-cut business suit the man wore. Standing with him were two other men, whom Rafe guessed to be in their thirties and forties. Not as stylishly dressed as their older companion, they wore dress slacks with shirts and sweaters. A quick glance around the room revealed that none of the eight people there had on anything like the clinician garb that Rafe had expected medical technicians to be wearing.

Instead, he saw denim jackets, suitcoats, sweatshirts and jeans.

"Could everybody sit down for a minute?" Ami asked the small crowd. "I brought someone I'd like you to meet. I know this is your work time, but I promise to keep it short."

Chairs were dragged into a circle and the men and women seated themselves, looking expectantly at Ami.

"This is my friend, Rafe Greene. I want him to hear from you what it is you do when we treat a patient for heart disease."

Rafe looked at the faces in the circle. Old and young, men and women, they seemed as disparate a group as any he'd ever encountered in a small classroom. Several of them dropped their eyes to the floor at Ami's request, while others broke out into wide grins. One woman looked especially uncomfortable in her chair, shifting repeatedly as Rafe glanced around the group. A boy who looked to be in his late teens seemed fixed on the hands he had folded on his lap.

The pony-tailed man broke the silence. "We rewire patients' brains to improve their heart health," he gently explained. "We do the 'T' in Dr. Kim's NRT treatment plan: Neurological Rewiring Therapy."

"You're brain surgeons?"

Even as he blurted the question, Rafe knew that wasn't correct. There was no way a teenaged boy had finished medical school, let alone a neurological residency.

Chuckles rippled around the group, and Rafe could feel some of the shyness slip away from the men and women.

"No, we don't use any kind of invasive procedures," a white-haired woman assured him. "We pray."

"We meditate, Alice," a younger woman next to her amended. "We focus our mental energy on redesigning patients' neurological maps, and then we teach them to maintain the practice."

"You can call it what you want," her neighbor easily granted. "But to me, it's prayer."

Rafe looked at the two women.

"So . . . you're psychics?" He threw a quick glance at Ami before he continued. "Faith healers?"

A wave of smiles went around the circle.

"My name is Jim, Mr. Greene," the pony-tailed man introduced himself. "And I'm an alcoholic. Welcome to our Monday morning AA meeting."

CHAPTER TWENTY-TWO

For a second or two, Rafe was sure the man was joking. But then he caught Ami's eye, and her silent nod convinced him otherwise.

These people were all alcoholics.

"Do you know about the Twelve Steps?" the woman next to Alice asked him.

Rafe nodded. "It's the core of the Alcoholics Anonymous recovery program," he said. "It's about acknowledging that there is a Higher Power greater than yourself who can help you, and then you turn your life over to the care of that Power. For a lot of people, that Higher Power is God."

"It's definitely God for me," Alice said. "But the key of the program is that we accept that God is who each person understands Him—or Her—to be, and we support each other in that understanding."

"And our Eleventh Step directs us to meditate, or pray," Alice's neighbor said, "to improve our conscious connection to our Higher Power, so we can know more clearly what we are asked to do and have the strength to do it."

Illumination burst over Rafe like the first lightning bolt of a summer storm. For just a moment, he wondered if anyone else had heard the thunder roll in his head as Ami's miracle therapy began to take form in his imagination.

Recovering alcoholics depended on their link to a Power—to God!—for their very lives, which meant they dedicated themselves to becoming spiritually fine-tuned. They became, basically, prayer experts: people who trained themselves to be highly receptive to God's presence and communication.

But there was another benefit to that spiritual discipline, Rafe realized. In order to develop the habits of a deep spirituality, a person's mind had to cooperate by practicing its own mental discipline. Skilled meditators, or people who prayed powerfully, could, with practice, learn to use that same mental discipline to develop a heightened awareness of, and connection to, their own physical bodies.

In fact, anyone who had heard about the yogis of India who could go without food for long periods of time, or walk on hot coals without being burned, was already familiar with the phenomenon: intense concentration could control physical response.

Rafe had even read about exhaustive studies that attempted to unmask the yogis' abilities as elaborate frauds, but instead uncovered a whole new field of research. When scientists brought these wonderworkers into their labs, they discovered a solid physiological basis behind the phenomena: yogis and other mystics could actually control, through mental effort, what the world had believed to be the involuntary processes of the human body.

Yogis could will their bodies into lower metabolic rates to eliminate the need for food.

Mystics could change the flow of blood into their arms and legs to alter their sensory perceptions.

Brain scans of Buddhist monks, Catholic nuns, and members of Protestant Pentecostal congregations revealed that the lobes of their brains reacted in markedly different ways in periods of deep prayer, as compared to the average person's neural activity during a similar period of quiet.

By capturing images of little electrical storms in those lobes with their high-tech monitors, scientists concluded that something previously unobserved was happening—that these spiritual masters and mistresses were deliberately forging new modes of accessing energy in their brains. In other words, the research with the mystics provided hard evidence of a mind-body relationship that could be materially manifested.

Kind of like biofeedback, only with huge repercussions.

And Ami had taken the next leap—deliberately using that connection of mind and body to affect heart function.

"You've got them teaching your patients to pray," Rafe concluded. "You found the most spiritually dependent people you could find and enlisted them to teach their skills to heart patients."

He caught the eyes of several members of the group.

"The Twelfth Step of the AA program asks alcoholics in recovery to help others," he continued, his excitement building. "That's what you're all doing. You're teaching the sick to pray."

He turned again to Ami, and his voice dropped to a tone of awe-filled realization. "You're using the mind to heal the body, and the stimulus you said could do it is . . . prayer."

"Meditation," Alice's neighbor corrected him.

"Your name for it," Alice reminded her. "I call it God—God right here and right now."

The echo of his own words to Ami just a short while ago reverberated in Rafe's mind, and he threw a quick glance in her direction. Judging from the faint look of surprise he saw on her face, he guessed she was recalling his words, too.

"You've just about got it right, Mr. Greene," Jim said. "Except for one part. We don't start with teaching patients to pray. That comes later."

Rafe looked at the man, his eyebrows raised in anticipation. "Later?"

Jim folded his lanky hands in his lap.

"Like Sandy already said, first we focus on redesigning patients' neurological maps to address their health problems. We do that in the clinic by watching their brain scans and manipulating synapse connections for them."

Rafe's eyes flew back to Alice. "But I thought you said there was nothing invasive."

"It's not invasive in physical terms, Rafe," Ami explained. "And all the patients have consented to the therapy, so it's not invasive in that way, either. The only way it's invasive is that we get inside the patients' neural circuits. My techs basically tap into the energy of that eleventh dimension that Dr. Carilion located, and then they focus that energy to retrain the brain to heal."

Once again, Rafe's eyes traveled around the roomful of faces, letting Ami's words sink into his understanding of her heart-healing protocol.

"You're talking about intercessory prayer," he said, his voice still awed.

A few heads bobbed in agreement.

"Okay, I know that some of you don't call it that," he quickly added for the benefit of those who looked uncomfortable, "but all the new research shows that the eleventh dimension is where the line blurs between physical and spiritual definitions, because its energy is tangible, but many-sided. Sort of like the way white light has a whole spectrum of color in it, yet it's still white light."

He caught Ami's eyes and held them.

"I know there's blue in there, and you know there's red, but the fact is, it takes all of the colors to make the white that lights up the world."

He waited for her to argue with him, but she remained silent. Somewhere in the depths of her dark eyes, he imagined that he saw a flicker of acknowledgment, a tiny relenting of her insistence to keep her work firmly rooted in the science of physical reality.

"Intercessory prayer," he repeated softly. "But you've refined it to . . . a science. You can actually locate specific neural circuits in the brain and then manipulate them to heal. How is that possible?"

Across the circle from him, Jim cleared his throat. "Tell me, Mr. Greene, do you know anything about physics? In particular, quantum mechanics?"

CHAPTER TWENTY-THREE

Someone was talking to him.

Diedrich slowly opened his eyes and watched the grooves in the ceiling assemble themselves into a pattern of tiles. There was a sheet over the lower half of his body, an intravenous line tucked into the inside of his left elbow, and a small field of monitor patches stuck to his bare chest. Curtains hung from rods formed two walls of a cubicle around him, and standing beside him was a man dressed in light blue scrubs.

"Mr. Mahler, I'm Dr. Sutter," the man told him. "You're in the emergency room at the University Medical Center. You've had a heart attack, and I think we're going to want to put a stent into one of your arteries. Do you understand me?"

Diedrich focused on the doctor's face and thought the physician looked too young to be an experienced cardiologist. He blinked and nodded.

"I hear you," he rasped.

The doctor smiled.

"You picked the right place to have a heart attack," the man told him. "The cafeteria's just down the hall from here. Your friends must have had at least four cardiologists practically on top of you before someone got you on a gurney for the short ride in. Did you know you have heart disease, Mr. Mahler?"

Diedrich shook his head. "I've been meaning to get an exam," he said.

"But you've been too busy," Dr. Sutter finished for him. "We hear that a lot in here. I don't want you to leave without a cardiac cath procedure to check out your heart, Mr. Mahler. You're stabilized for now, but I don't want to release you without having a look. I'm pretty sure you have a blocked artery. I know your friends said you're not from the Cities, but without treatment, you're in immediate danger of sudden death. Is there anyone we can call for you before we go to the cath lab?"

Diedrich fixed his eyes back on the ceiling tile.

He had no family, no friends to notify, and as long as he used his medical insurance through Calyx, he was reasonably certain that Philip wouldn't hear about it for at least a little while. From what he'd heard of the standard angioplasty procedure, he'd be discharged in a day or two, and if need be, he could hire a nurse to care for him at the hotel until he was able to fly back home. He'd take the drugs the doctor prescribed for him and . . .

Drugs.

There was no drug in Ami Kim's miracle cure.

The moments before he'd passed out in the cafeteria came back to Diedrich in a rush.

The drug was a placebo.

Chinh Nguyen's heart had been healed, but he insisted it was through prayer, not pharmaceutical magic, which meant that the drug trials were a fake. The only thing Ami Kim had proved was that sugar pills were as effective—no, immensely better—than every other medical protocol currently being used to treat heart disease.

CardiaZone was a fraud.

He had to tell Philip.

Even as he reached that conclusion, though, his brain sent him another signal.

But Ami Kim's results—even with a placebo—were phenomenal.

An uncontrollable shiver began to move through Diedrich's body.

Chinh Nguyen said it was prayer.

"I want to talk to Dr. Kim," Diedrich choked out.

"Our Dr. Kim?" Dr. Sutter asked. "Dr. Ami Kim? If you want a second opinion, I can guarantee that she'll advise angioplasty."

"Fine. Angioplasty," Diedrich replied, feeling dizzy. "But I want to get into her treatment program. Afterwards."

"I'm not aware of any treatment program, but then I work in the emergency department, not cardiology."

Another scrubs-garbed doctor entered the draped enclosure, and Dr. Sutter turned away from Diedrich to greet the newcomer.

"Dr. Villome," Dr. Sutter said, "just the physician I wanted to see. We've got somebody here who's in need of a stent. This is Mr. Mahler."

Diedrich looked into the panicked eyes of Niles Villome.

"Hello, Doctor."

CHAPTER TWENTY-FOUR

Rafe shifted his attention to Jim. "Quantum mechanics? I know it has to do with the actions of sub-atomic particles," he answered.

"*Actions* is the key word there—quantum mechanics deals with the behavior of matter in the world of the ultra-small," Jim explained. "Which, when you get down to that level, is really about energy—photons and electromagnetic radiation, for example. The problem with those kinds of energy, however, is that when scientists first began trying to analyze them, they found that the principles of classical physics didn't apply, so they had to come up with new ways of understanding and predicting the behavior of those atomic particles. In fact, Max Planck came up with the first theory of quantum physics in 1900 when he published his explanation of the full spectrum of thermal radiation."

"Get to the entanglement part, Jim," Alice interrupted. "That's where it gets interesting."

Rafe threw the older woman a questioning glance.

"Entanglement?"

"Absolutely," Jim agreed. "Very interesting, indeed."

He leaned back in his chair and straightened his suit coat.

"To make a long story short, scientists found that when they began exploring at this quantum level, particles retained connections to each other even when they were physically separated. In other words, if one particle of a pair behaved in a specific way, the other particle of the pair likewise reacted, even when it was physically distant. Just two years ago, scientists at

162

a research center in Japan observed two paired photons behaving in that exact manner. They proved that entanglement is very real."

He raised his hands in the air and held his palms facing each other, but separated by about a foot of distance. When his left hand tilted backwards, his right hand leaned forwards, as if he were clutching an invisible ball. He repeated the motion a few times and smiled at Rafe.

"Even particles that are separated have an effect on each other, as if they are somehow enmeshed in one medium. Entanglement is a quantum fact of life. And that's the foundation of Dr. Kim's therapy: since people are ultimately made of subatomic particles, which are connected, so, too, are we all connected in invisible, powerful ways, like a massive web of life."

The holy web of life.

The words rang in Rafe's head, accented with his mama's rich tones.

'God gives us our gifts in this holy web of life for good reasons, and you got to respect that, Rafe."

The holy web. Wasn't that really just another way of saying entanglement?

When he was a kid, he'd thought his mama had made a lousy choice of words to describe life—when she said "web," all he could think about were the massive spiderwebs he'd find spun out in the woods beyond his childhood home. If he stumbled into one unaware, he'd be picking sticky goo off his arms and face for an hour later. The idea of a web being something he wanted to get into was ridiculous.

But the idea—the reality—of entanglement could shed a whole new light on that holy web. Scriptural admonitions to care for one another, to be responsible for each other, weren't just pleasant platitudes recorded in sacred texts, but, from the perspective of entanglement, hands-on operating instructions for human life. If what Jim was saying about the connections between particles and people were true, then it made perfect sense to see the universe as one vast web, where even a touch of a hand, a healing thought, could have repercussions that traveled across that web.

And the medium that Jim had just mentioned? The one medium in which all those connected people and particles were connected?

It was God.

Love.

The Holy Spirit.

The Holy Web, with a capital H and a capital W.

"And prayer is the path of that connection," Alice was saying, drawing Rafe's attention back to the group's conversation. "What did Einstein call it, Jim? 'Spooky action at a distance' or something like that?"

Jim laughed. "You should be one of my students at the university, Alice. I can lecture for weeks and some of those kids still don't get it. 'That's impossible!' they say, even when we have the research to prove it. Poor Einstein never got to see that proof because we didn't have the technological abilities back then to test entanglement in the lab, but because the phenomenon was predicted by his mathematics, he insisted it existed."

"Blessed are those who have not seen, yet believe," Alice reminded him. "It sounds like Christians aren't the only ones in that boat."

"Judging from the history of science, I think it could be researchers' universal mantra," he agreed. "More often than not, theories pave the way for research, which then leads to proof. Unfortunately, though, science has hamstringed itself with its own prejudice: only the physical, observable world is eligible for investigation. Anything else doesn't exist. Which is a real problem, since cosmologists now tell us that 70 percent of the universe is dark energy. Another 25 percent is dark matter. Dark energy and dark matter are the words we use because we don't even know what it is! And if you're doing the math here, by now you're realizing that there's only 5 percent of the universe left. That's right—only 5 percent of the universe is ordinary matter, and that's what we've based our science on. Five percent!"

Jim shook his head and leaned back in his chair. "I'm appalled every time a scientist pronounces something doesn't exist or it's impossible because he can't prove it. What about the other 95 percent of creation?"

"More room for God," Alice said.

"That's a whole lot of room," the teenage boy commented, and the room fell silent.

Rafe surveyed the faces of the group again. "How do you do it, exactly? I understand the theory, but how does it work in real life? With patients?"

"The first month we meet in the lab," the woman named Sandy said. "Dr. Kim has her study participants come in, usually in the evenings, so we can work undisturbed."

"It's an hour-long session three to five times a week," Ami clarified. "I hook up the patient to brain scanning equipment, and we track the activity on monitors through the use of functional magnetic resonance imaging. It's a real-time recording of what's happening in the brain and what lobes or structures are being stimulated. We all sit in a room adjacent to the patient, where we can observe through a glass partition, and we focus on stimulating those parts of the brain that are responsible for producing the enzymes and hormones that will heal the heart."

"It's like we have a map overlay on the brain that displays on the monitor," Sandy added. "Our goal is to get certain parts of the brain to light up. By focusing on the path through the brain's anatomy that we know we need to get to light up, we forge new neural circuits."

Beside him, Rafe noticed Ami lifting her left wrist to check her watch.

"Once we get those new pathways established for the patient, we back off of the intensive work, and each patient is taught how to maintain the new circuits with personal prayer," Jim said. "Eventually they get weaned from the placebos and Dr. Kim gets to add another success story to her research."

"But you are the secret to my success," Ami reminded the group. "Without you, the NRT technicians, I would have nothing. You are the healers here, not me."

"Healers?" Alice shook her head in denial. "I think of it as facilitating. What we do is help patients create alternative options for improving their heart's health. You came up with the method, Dr. Kim, but I know it's God who's doing the real healing."

She held up her thumb and index finger and spread them about an inch apart. "We just made a little shortcut for Him," she laughed.

As soon as the chuckles in the room subsided, Jim addressed Ami. "I saw you checking the time. You're not interrupting our meeting, Dr. Kim. It's good for us to talk about the work we do. It keeps us sober and strong. Motivated. Your heart patients aren't the only ones benefiting from this program, you know."

Ami threw him a grateful glance. Rafe thought something else passed between the doctor and the man, but he couldn't be sure what it was. Mutual respect, certainly. But there was an undertone of another emotion that Rafe struggled to identify.

A shared sorrow?

Comfort?

He was about to ask Jim to elaborate on his remark, but Ami cut him off.

"We really do need to go," she told the group. "I just wanted Rafe to hear from you about your role in my research. We all know how crazy it can sound to someone who isn't working with us, and I thought this would be the best way for him to get a feel for the—shall we say—unorthodox treatment protocol. Thank you."

She stood up and hitched her purse strap over her shoulder.

"We'll leave you to what's left of your Monday meeting. See you later, everyone."

Out in the hallway, Rafe caught Ami's upper arm in his hand and turned her to face him. "Whatever made you think to recruit recovering alcoholics as technicians to help you with brain rewiring? I mean, I get how they've retrained their own neural synapses to change their lives, but where did you get the idea to go to them in the first place? Other researchers have called on people everyone expects to be adept at prayer, but why did you think of AA members?"

Ami's eyes held an echo of the unknown emotion that Rafe had seen flash between her and Jim.

"I met these folks years ago, Rafe. Back then, I was hoping they could help me save my husband from himself, but it didn't happen."

She looked him square in the eye. "He couldn't give up the addiction. I think he never really wanted to."

Rafe thought of his own father's struggle with alcohol, and his grip on Ami's arm relaxed. "I'm sorry."

"Me, too," she smiled sadly. "But I never forgot how earnest these people were, and how hard they worked to open themselves to healing. They knew how to let . . . energy . . . flow into them. Once I made the connection between the eleventh dimension and energy medicine, it only made sense to me to draw on their expertise for my research. And they've been more than great. As far as I'm concerned, they're brilliant. They're going to revolutionize the way the medical establishment understands disease."

Rafe's hand lingered on Ami's arm, his thumb lightly stroking her jacket sleeve.

"And the way we understand healing," he added. He lifted his hand to touch her cheek.

"Ami, I have to ask. What happened to your husband?"

Ami's smile disappeared as lines of tension pulled at her lips.

"I work with him. I'm married to Niles, Rafe."

CHAPTER TWENTY-FIVE

Hospital security was a joke. It had only taken Vi a few minutes to locate an empty employee lounge in the sprawling facility and help herself to somebody's forgotten scrub jacket. Then it was a simple matter of following the directional signs that were so helpfully placed around the medical center. Less than ten minutes after she'd walked back into the Heart Partners Clinic, Vi found herself standing outside the cardiac procedure unit that was attached to the center's emergency department. While she waited for the doctor to make an appearance, she imagined the surprise that would spread across Philip Arden's handsome face when she told him that the Villome job was already done.

Anticipating the need of her client was one of Violet Winters' special talents.

Although, she had to admit, this particular need hadn't been hard to foresee. In her experience with Philip, she'd repeatedly witnessed his propensity to clean the slate after one of his projects was completed. In fact, if the assassination job last month had gone as planned, she'd still be occupied with the collateral kills that Philip had planned to follow the demise of the president. As it was, she'd only had the one additional target to take out: the unlucky source who had given Philip the incorrect information. A stealthy midnight visit to the man resulted in headlines the next morning recounting a fatal self-inflicted gunshot wound; by noon, Vi was on her way home for a massage and a pedicure, glad to be leaving New Hampshire's snow behind her.

Philip's less-than-subtle inquiry an hour ago about the doctor had kicked her hunting instincts into high gear, and so she'd only waited five minutes outside the church into which Dr. Kim and her companion had disappeared before deciding to move on. Since Villome had suddenly moved to the top of her boss's list, she saw no reason not to make a swift change in her own day's agenda. Besides, she could always catch up with Dr. Kim later, thanks to the bug she'd planted on her car.

In her business, thinking ahead was just as necessary as being prepared.

Vi smirked. She would have made a hell of a boy scout.

When she'd returned to Villome's clinic and asked to see the doctor, his receptionist had informed her that the doctor was temporarily unavailable.

"He had a call to perform an emergency stent procedure in the medical center," the woman had told her, then, apparently noting the disappointment Vi had been unable to hide, she added, "but it doesn't take that long if you want to wait. The procedure, I mean. Dr. Villome should be back within the next forty-five minutes."

Vi's mood had immediately brightened.

"Thanks," she'd said to the receptionist. "Actually, I'll just come back then."

She'd left the clinic and gone in search of the smock.

The door to the cath lab suite swung open and two nurses walked out, one of them pushing a small cart loaded with medical supplies. Vi glanced at the ID badge of the one not occupied with the cart, and waved her hand to catch her attention.

"Is Dr. Villome still in there?" Vi asked.

The nurse nodded. "He'll be out in another minute or two." Then she resumed her conversation with the other nurse as they made their way down the corridor and away from Vi.

Quickly, Vi pulled on a pair of latex gloves that she had snagged from an unattended nurses' station on her way into the emergency room. From her jeans pocket underneath the stolen smock, she withdrew a small pouch, opened it and took out the jar that was inside. Flicking her glance one more time around the corridor to be sure she was alone, she carefully unscrewed the jar's lid and dipped one gloved finger into the odorless cream that filled the tiny container. She popped the lid back on, tightened it and dropped it back into the bag, which she then returned to its hiding place. With a swipe of her coated finger, she smeared the drop of cream across her opposite gloved palm.

Almost immediately, the door to the cardiac unit opened again and Niles Villome stepped out into the hall wearing his short-sleeved surgical scrubs.

Vi waited till the doctor was a good six feet past her, then called out to him.

"Dr. Villome?"

He stopped to look back at her.

"Yes?"

Vi hurried up to the man and placed her smeared palm on his bare forearm. She gave him a quick squeeze with her gloved hand and a bright smile.

"I'd heard how skilled you were, Doctor," she gushed, "but it was amazing to be able to watch you in action in the lab."

Vi could feel him searching her face for some sign of familiarity. She had banked on the idea that the arrogant doctor probably didn't keep up with the changing shifts of nurses in the unit, and that she could capture his attention for just the moment or two she needed for the cream to begin its deadly journey through the layers of his skin into his bloodstream.

"Thank you, Miss . . . " His eyes traveled over Vi's chest, searching for a name tag.

"Danforth," she supplied, her hand still on his arm.

He returned her smile. "I'm sorry, but I need to go."

Vi removed her hand, and nodded, then turned and walked briskly in the opposite direction that Villome was headed. As she walked, she carefully stripped the gloves from her hands and then ducked into the nearest utility room, where she found a container marked for biohazard waste disposal. Dropping the gloves into the container, she turned to find the nurse she'd spoken with earlier outside the cath lab suite.

"Did you see Dr. Villome?" she asked.

"No," Vi lied easily. "I'll catch him another time."

"He might have stayed in the suite a little longer than normal, I think," the other woman told her. "I heard that he knew the patient."

"Really?"

Vi's eyes darted to the door of the lounge. She needed to get out of the suite before Villome went down and someone sounded an alarm.

"Apparently, they were working together on some research. Can you imagine—working on someone you work with? But I guess Mr. Mahler—that's the patient's name—insisted that Dr. Villome do the procedure. Said he wanted the best, which you can imagine how Dr. Villome ate up."

Vi nodded, filing away the name. Now she had two surprises for Philip the next time she saw him: a done deal and new information.

"Got to run," Vi told the nurse and left the lounge.

Niles's brain was racing. He'd never, in a million years, have expected to find Diedrich Mahler in the emergency room at the medical center, let alone in dire need of immediate heart treatment. If he'd known who was waiting for him, he would have told the emergency department doc to find another cardiologist. Yet once he'd arrived, Mahler had expressed complete confidence in Niles's capabilities; if the Calyx man harbored any suspicion about Niles's integrity or the CardiaZone project, it certainly didn't show itself.

On the contrary, Mahler insisted that Niles do the procedure . . . and that afterward, he be admitted into Ami's therapy as soon as possible.

Ami's therapy that Niles now knew to be a placebo-driven fraud.

Niles stumbled in the hospital corridor and felt a painful headache building behind his temples. The next time he saw the man, he'd have to tell him there was no CardiaZone. Mahler would call Hallenstroem and Niles's career would be over.

Losing the new Beemer would be barely a speck of frost on the tip of the iceberg once Calyx's lawyers set their legal sights on Niles.

He stumbled again and rubbed his forearm with his opposite hand.

That nurse must have had something on her gloves. At first his skin just felt a bit damp where she'd clutched him, but now it seemed to sting.

Some kind of residual disinfectant?

Niles decided he needed to say something to the unit manager about doing a better job of training the nursing staff. Sloppiness had no place in the cardiac unit.

He wiped his hand on his scrubs and turned into the changing room where he'd left his street clothes. As he approached the wall of lockers, his stomach clenched violently and he stumbled against a bench. A moment later, he slid to the floor, the blood in his head pounding uncontrollably.

In five minutes, he was dead.

CHAPTER TWENTY-SIX

D iedrich Mahler stood up and looked down at the body in the bed.

I look terrible.

Then he realized he'd made a mistake. It had to be someone else anchored to the bed with tubing and monitors, because he was standing up.

Wasn't he?

The Calyx vice president glanced around the brilliantly lit room, wondering where the lights were coming from, since he couldn't see any fixtures on the ceiling of the cardiac procedure recovery room.

He could, however, see right through the walls of the spacious cubicle to the adjacent recovery units, as well as out the hallway and around the corner to the nurses' station and the alcoves where the physicians sat recording their notes after completing procedures. Not only that, but he could clearly make out the words of several simultaneous conversations that were going on around the hospital floor.

A nurse was talking with a lab tech about her dinner plans.

Two cardiologists, hunched over a CAT scan report, were comparing their observations.

A husband and wife, up before dawn this morning, were wondering why her procedure had been delayed yet another hour.

For some reason, Diedrich had become hyper-conscious, his senses incredibly sharpened. Taking a final look at the body he'd assumed was his, Diedrich began to move irresistibly toward the source of the light that now seemed to be on the other side of the room's exterior wall.

Without warning, he felt tears tracking down his cheeks.

"You can't come yet," the light told him in the same moment that Diedrich began to reach his hand out towards it. "You have to ask for something first."

Diedrich looked around, but found no one in the room besides himself and the inert patient. The scent of a thousand flowers suddenly filled the space.

"I want to come home," he whispered, the words surprising him as they seemed to rise out of his throat of their own will. He could feel his cheeks growing wetter with moisture.

"Ask and you shall receive," the light gently urged him.

Diedrich strained to break through the invisible barrier that kept him from the warmth and the sweepingly beautiful music he could sense swelling just beyond his arm's length.

"Ask what?"

His voice sounded stripped, raw in his confusion.

An answer floated into the air around him just as a new sensation broke over him.

Pain.

A leaden weight lay on his chest.

Diedrich slowly opened his eyes to see the anxious faces of two nurses and a doctor hovering above him.

"Mr. Mahler? We've got you," the young man in the surgical scrubs assured him. "Your heart wanted to quit on us there for a moment, but we convinced it to keep pumping. You're going to be fine."

Diedrich closed his eyes in despair as the light's last word lingered in his mind.

Forgiveness.

A single tear wound its way down his face. Like a scratchy old piece of film, faces of the people he'd destroyed for Philip Arden flew through his thoughts, and he knew, with utter certainty, that he was never going to be "fine" again, no matter what the doctors told him. He'd finally learned what it was that he really needed to survive, what it was that his life was so sorely lacking.

He didn't know how to love.

And without love, how could he ask for forgiveness?

His heart might be pumping life-saving blood again, but it was still a heart made of stone.

Diedrich closed his eyes again, but this time, he closed them in defeat.

There was no way on earth he'd ever find that much for-giveness.

CHAPTER TWENTY-SEVEN

Y ou're married to Niles."

Ami could tell by the slow way Rafe repeated her words back to her that he didn't quite believe her statement. To his credit, he didn't immediately question her or burst into laughter, but Ami was certain that one of those two responses was only a breath away. Rafe had witnessed her relationship with Niles up close in her office, and she'd even vented some of her frustration with her partner directly at Rafe.

If anyone had a reason to doubt Ami's bond with Niles, it was Rafe.

But even more than his disbelief, it was the stark look of disappointment on his face that caught at Ami's heart.

The man wore his heart on his sleeve, she realized with a start, and her announcement of her marital status had just cut a slice into it—a slice that clearly revealed that her growing attraction to Rafe was reciprocated. And though it still wounded her to admit the disastrous mistake of her marriage, she already cared too much for Rafe to protect her pride any longer with the same half-truths she'd been feeding everyone else for the last decade.

"We separated," she added. "Ten years ago. The practice was just getting off the ground, and we were paying off school debts, so we decided not to incur the costs or the hassles of a divorce. The marriage was over almost as soon as it started, Rafe, but the clinic took off, and I wasn't about to let that fail, too."

Ami felt a rush of heat fill her cheeks as Rafe continued to study her silently.

"It's not just about your successful practice, though, is it, Ami?" His voice was quiet in the empty church basement corridor.

She met his appraising gaze with a defiant one of her own. The man was too intuitive, she realized. She may have been the one with the gift of medical intuition, but Rafe Greene's ability to see into her soul was uncanny.

"No," she finally conceded. "It's not just the money. My family would be shamed by a divorce, and I refuse to do that to them. I know it's old-fashioned, but it's the way I was raised. I hold a responsibility to my family, Rafe, to my community, and if I have to make a personal sacrifice to meet that responsibility, then that's what I'll do. The people I love will not lose honor because of me."

She hitched her purse strap over her shoulder. "Do you still want to go to lunch?"

Rafe nodded, his eyes locked on hers.

"Absolutely," he said. "I need the carbs. And, for the record, Ami, I'm right there with you when it comes to honor and commitment. I didn't join the Marines for the great chow and travel opportunities, you know."

"*Semper Fi?*" she asked.

"Yes, ma'am," he said. "Always Faithful. But it didn't take the Marine Corps to drill that into my head. I learned it from my mama first."

He stopped talking long enough to line up the edges of his jacket, then dragged the zipper up to his collar.

"When I started growing into my body," he continued, "she couldn't drum enough into my head about responsibility and honor. 'You got to respect your gifts,' she said. 'You got to watch out for the little guy.' Seriously, that woman should have been paid a salary as a Marines recruiter, if not a drill sergeant."

A smile made a brief appearance on Ami's face.

"You know what else she pounded into me?"

Ami shook her head. "I have no idea."

"She said that God gives each of us gifts for a reason."

He tipped his head back towards the AA meeting room.

"That's quite a reason, Dr. Kim."

As Ami drove them back in the direction of the medical center, Rafe tried to puzzle out the woman behind the wheel. Ami Kim was a medical genius, yet she feared the criticism of her colleagues and the censure of her own family so much that she felt compelled to hide the truth of her revolutionary therapy. Instead of shouting from the rooftops that she had harnessed spiritual healing, she allowed the medical establishment to dictate what she might claim as cure. Even worse, Rafe reflected, was that by disguising the truth, Ami denied people everywhere an understanding of the human condition that would ultimately redefine disease as more than a physical event.

In fact, if all of her work were brought to light, the human condition itself would be redefined.

But Ami refused to go the distance. She was paralyzed by her fear of her peers' condemnation.

Or, at least, she had been, until Niles had appropriated her work and sold it to Calyx.

Now, thanks to her partner's premature—not to mention unethical—actions, Ami was not only paralyzed, but caught in the crosshairs of a sniper.

Almost unconsciously, Rafe checked the car's mirrors to see if any vehicle shadowed their route.

Guard duty first, he reminded himself. Analyzing Ami could wait until he was sure she was safe.

A few blocks later, satisfied that no car tailed them, Rafe risked a final comment on Ami's revelation.

"Maybe it's time to let go a little, Ami. Let go of Niles, of your family's expectations—of everyone's expectations—and just do what you're doing best right now: using your gift to save lives."

She let out a small, bitter laugh. "Haven't you noticed that is what I do best: disappoint other people's expectations? I failed a husband and my parents. If I announce that my cardio miracle cure is prayer—yes, Rafe, I know that's what it is, no matter how many ways I want to say it differently—I'll be a pariah to my colleagues, and then I'll disappoint my patients."

She threw him an angry look.

"I've even disappointed you, haven't I? You barely know me, but you still decided you could trust me. In fact, you trusted me so much, you told me the one thing you've never shared with anyone else—that you can heal with your hands!—and what did I do? I lied by omission. I didn't tell you I was married even when I could see you were attracted to me. Smooth move, Dr. Kim, right? Lead the guy on and only mention that little fact when he's already getting too close for comfort."

She made a quick turn into a parking lot, slipped the car into a slot and killed the ignition.

"We're here," she said, her voice clipped and brisk. "They've got great soup and sandwiches."

Rafe laid his left hand on her right one before she could drop her keys into her purse. Slowly he curled his fingers around her own. His voice was husky in the car.

"Too close for comfort for whom?"

Rafe watched Ami's pupils dilate as he leaned closer to her in the car. With his right hand, he unsnapped his seat belt and angled his body to lightly brush his shoulder against hers.

"We haven't come nearly close enough for my comfort, Dr. Kim."

Ami's eyes were locked on his as he lifted his hand to cup her jaw.

"And you haven't disappointed me." He let his thumb stroke her lower lip. "Don't be so quick to judge yourself, Ami. You're not the only one with a painful secret."

"Really? What's your deep, dark secret, Rafe?" Ami's voice was cynical, but Rafe noted that she didn't pull away from his touch. "Don't tell me that being able to heal miraculously is painful."

"It's not," he assured her. "It's pure joy. What's painful is when you can't heal. Especially when it's someone you love."

Rafe paused as the familiar face rose in his mind's eye.

"Samuel—my brother—died in my arms, Ami. And it was my fault, because for once, I couldn't work a miracle. That's my dark secret."

Sadness rolled into Ami like a slow tide from Rafe's hand on her cheek. Startled by the emotion's intensity, she felt the wet track of tears across her own cheeks and quickly reached up to wipe them away, but Rafe caught her hand in mid-air, his eyes widening in sudden knowledge.

"You can discern spirits," he whispered. "Medical intuition isn't your only gift, is it, Ami?"

Ami froze, all her interior alarms ringing wildly as she felt her last shred of defense being breached by the man beside her.

When had she let herself become so vulnerable, so transparent, that she'd forgotten to shield herself from experiencing someone else's spiritual state to the point of visible emotion? Even as a child, she'd learned not to let others know she could read their spirits along with their bodies; it had taken only one shaming reproach from her father to teach her to keep her intuitions to herself. Then, when she'd entered medical school, she'd found that her gift—scientific or not—gave her an edge over her colleagues, and she determined to find some kind of "real" explanation for her uncanny medical insight. The spiritual discernment piece she ignored, uncertain of its place in her life, and yet she never quite banished it from her private contemplation of her life's work of healing the sick. Being a medical intuitive was tough enough to explain, let alone a discerner of spirits. Better to walk away from it than let it destroy the good work she could do.

But now, with Rafe's eyes on her, she felt the world shift, an enormous sense of relief beginning to pour throughout her body, unleashing a recognition that she had ruthlessly repressed for most of her adult life.

She was gifted by God.

Her ability to read the human body's ills and to discern the spiritual wounds of others wasn't a figment of her imagination or a random arrangement of her neurophysiological transmitters. She had a purpose on earth, and if she was going to accomplish all that she could, she needed to step outside her comfort zone of medical science and embrace the mystery of her own gifts.

Right here and right now.

And who better to admit that to than the man who saw those gifts in her? A man with his own unique gifts, a man who could heal with his hands, a man whom she'd already trusted with her greatest fears and achievement?

From the moment she'd seen him in the hotel gift shop, she'd felt inexplicably drawn to Rafe Greene, almost as if life itself was pulling them together, and for the first time she could remember, she'd allowed herself to imagine what it would be like to share with someone the awesome mystery of spiritual skills.

To share a mission to heal up every wound.

Ami looked at Rafe's hand covering her own and felt a sense of power and peace waiting for her just beyond the precipice of accepting her own giftedness.

"No," she calmly replied, taking the leap and feeling her own spirit soar. "It isn't. I can read hearts as well as bodies."

Rafe smiled. "Then I think we should have us some lunch, and you can tell me more about your prayer protocol, Dr. Kim, because you are going to change the world of medicine, and I want a front-row seat."

Violet Winters cruised slowly past the small café where Rafe and Ami sat framed by the large front window, drinking soup and eating sandwiches.

"I'm guessing she hasn't heard the news yet," Philip Arden said from the passenger seat of Vi's rental car. "Either that, or she's a cold, heartless woman to go out to lunch when her partner is found dead in the hospital."

Vi turned into the café's lot, looking for an empty parking space. "I doubt she knows. By the time the police get around to notifying the victim's business partner, it'll be hours from now. It's not like she's next of kin."

She exited the small lot and parked on the street a block down from the café. "Shall we meet the very recently deceased Dr. Villome's partner?"

"What a wonderful idea."

Arden got out of the car and stepped over a small snowbank to wait on the sidewalk for Vi to join him.

"I think we need a diversion, though—a plausible reason we might know she's a doctor. Otherwise, she might think it odd that two strangers just happen to walk into this no-name diner and recognize her from last night's newscast. For all we know, she might be very suspicious of anything unusual today. She was, you know, in a very frightening incident just yesterday morning."

Vi smiled. "So I've heard. And what do you suggest, Philip?"

Arden offered his arm to Vi. "I think we should witness the good doctor in action." He closed his eyes briefly, then opened them wide. "Shall we?"

He led Vi to the café's door and pulled it open. Just as they crossed the threshold, the sound of crashing dishes and panicked screams disturbed the quiet diner. In a booth near the back wall, a woman cried out in anguish.

"Help! Somebody, help us! Is there a doctor in here?"

CHAPTER TWENTY-EIGHT

Without a word, Ami and Rafe both dropped their spoons in their soup bowls and dodged the tables and chairs between them and the panicking server.

"I'm a doctor." Ami's eyes darted to the middle-aged man sprawled across the bench seat behind the table. His eyes were closed, his breathing erratic. She bent over the man and found Rafe right at her elbow.

"Touch him and tell me what it is," he told her, his voice too low for any ears but hers.

She laid her fingers on the man's carotid artery and closed her eyes. She could feel Rafe moving behind her, shoving the table completely out of his way so he could also reach the man. Beyond them, the alarmed voices of a waitress and other diners dimmed as Ami let her intuition search the man's body for the cause of his collapse.

"An aneurysm," she breathed. "Near the base of the brain in the back. It's leaking. He's having a stroke."

She felt Rafe's big body slide into the space beside her and when she opened her eyes, she saw his hands spread wide on the man's chest.

For a split second, she thought he was going to start pumping the man's heart, and she knew she had to stop him before he started CPR and sent more blood pouring through the man's already splitting blood vessel. But before she could utter a sound, she felt a searing heat rising right through the man's artery beneath her fingers. Startled, she pulled her hand back and glanced at Rafe's face, which was rigid in concentration. The vein in his right temple stood out against his dark skin and his eyes were locked on the unconscious man's face. His hands lay gently on the man's chest, and Ami could see a slight tremor in Rafe's extended fingers.

She took another quick look at Rafe, and caught her breath, momentarily stunned.

His body glowed.

"Block anyone's view," he instructed her, his voice barely audible, his eyes still on the afflicted man's face.

Ami shook off her shock and stood upright. She turned to face the small crowd that was standing a few feet away. Taking a step forward, she spread out her arms and waved the people back.

"We need some room here," she directed them, her voice filled with authority. "Has someone called 911?"

"Yes! They're on the way!" the waitress called out. "Is he going to be all right?"

"We're doing everything we can," Ami assured him, her eyes briefly scanning the crowd. "We need an open path for the EMS when they get here. Please, everybody, make some room to the door."

She moved her hands in the air, clearing an imaginary corridor across the café.

"Dr. Kim," Rafe's voice came from behind her, "would you check the man's pulse again?"

Ami turned.

And froze.

The man's eyelids were fluttering, his Adam's apple sliding up and down as he swallowed big gulps of air. Beads of sweat lined his hairline and upper lip, but the man was clearly recovering from . . . a ruptured aneurysm?

Impossible.

Ami slowly turned her head in Rafe's direction. He was down on one knee beside the booth's bench seat, his right hand still grasping the man's forearm. He gave Ami a small smile.

The glowing was gone.

"Good call, Doctor," he told her. "He's going to be okay." Ami searched Rafe's face, her own suffused with awe and confusion, and just a touch of fear.

"Who *are* you?" she whispered.

Standing just inside the café's doorway, Philip Arden grabbed Vi's arm and spun her back outside with him into the cold February air.

"What are you doing?" she complained. "I thought you wanted to meet Dr. Kim. This is our chance."

"I changed my mind," he abruptly explained, practically dragging her back to the car.

Along with his mind, Philip's whole demeanor had undergone a transformation, Vi noted. Before they'd stepped into the café, he'd been his usual collected, commanding self, cruel and calculating. When he was like that, Vi thought he was invincible, and nothing appealed to her more than a masterful man.

But then something had happened while they watched the little drama unfolding in the café.

In a heartbeat, Vi had watched Philip's cool self-confidence turn to tension, and then fury. Watching his reaction to Dr. Kim and her companion's quick response to the incapacitated man, Vi could feel her employer's fingers clamping onto her arm, digging deeply into her coat sleeve. His silver eyes had gone almost black and his jaw had clenched tightly.

And then she'd seen a fleeting glimpse of something she'd never imagined that she'd ever see crossing his face.

Fear.

The next thing she knew, they were back on the sidewalk outside the café heading towards her rental car.

"What about Dr. Kim?" she pressed him as she tried to keep up with his long strides.

"Kill her," he snapped, throwing his answer over his shoulder to her.

Vi quickly scanned around her for any listening ears, shocked that Philip would be so careless to even speak of her profession in public. Granted, no one else was on the sidewalk with them, but Vi had not succeeded so long in her work by making stupid assumptions or tolerating loose lips.

Nor had Philip.

Which only confirmed for Vi how distraught and off-balance Philip had suddenly become.

Opting to keep her own mouth shut until they were in the privacy of her car, Vi whipped around the back of the white rental and popped open the locks before Philip reached for the handle of the passenger door. Sliding into the cold driver's seat, she immediately turned on the ignition and car heater while Philip got in and closed his door.

He still wouldn't look at her.

"Did I do something wrong?" she finally asked as the moments went by, silent.

"Not yet," he tersely answered.

"Not yet?" she repeated, making it a question. "Philip," she said in her softest, most intimate tone, "have I ever disappointed you? Tell me what you need, and you know that I'll take care of it."

To her complete surprise, Philip Arden tipped his head back and roared with laughter.

"Do you, by any chance, know the name of the man with Dr. Kim?"

Thrown off-balance by Philip's lightning mood swing, Vi took a second to study Philip. Lines of tension still creased his handsome forehead, his blonde-streaked hair looking a little washed-out in the reflected white haze of the snowbanked streets. Almost as if he sensed her appraisal, he turned his head and met her eyes.

Where Vi had grown used to seeing bright silver in his glance, there were only dark shadows.

"His name is Rafe Greene," she told him. "He's an unemployed paramedic looking for a job. The woman in Human Resources I talked with this morning at the medical center was just bubbling over about him when I mentioned I thought he looked familiar and asked who he was. Why? Do you know him?"

Philip leaned his head back on the headrest behind him.

"In a way," he said. "And not a good one."

He turned his head toward Vi.

"You're going to have to kill him, too, you know."

CHAPTER TWENTY-NINE

Rafe and Ami stood aside while the emergency medical technicians who'd arrived with the ambulance secured the man to a stretcher and wheeled him out of the café.

"Lucky guy," a man behind Rafe said. "Lucky for him that you two were here."

Rafe turned around, and the man extended his hand to him to shake.

"Tom Carlton," he introduced himself. "I'm the owner. Thanks for helping out. It's not really good for business when patrons drop dead at their table."

Rafe shook the man's hand and smiled at his effort to lighten the mood. "Rafe Greene. I thought the soup was good—or at least mine was." He nodded toward Ami. "This is Dr. Kim."

Ami and Carlton shook hands.

"Thanks, Dr. Kim," he told her. "Lunch is on the house."

He tilted his head in the direction of the ambulance outside. "Is that fellow going to be okay?"

"I think so," she replied, though to Rafe's ears, her voice sounded uncertain. He watched her gaze shift from the departing ambulance to his own face before she turned again to Carlton.

"I told the paramedics that the hospital would want a full workup on him once they get him to the emergency room. More critical conditions can sometimes be masked by a . . ." she slid her eyes again to Rafe, then back to Carlton, "a fainting episode like this one."

"Fainted, huh?" Carlton asked, then shook his head. "Sure scared the wits out of my waitress."

"She did the right thing, calling for help," Rafe said. "A quick response is one of the most helpful things anyone can do in an emergency like that."

He laid his hand on Ami's shoulder. "I think we need to get you back to your office, don't we? Something about seeing patients or doing paperwork?"

For a second or two, Ami's eyes looked blank to Rafe, like she hadn't quite recovered from the adrenaline rush of tending to the collapsed man.

Come on, Ami, he silently urged her, *work with me here.*

Her eyes regained focus and locked onto Rafe's brown ones.

"Yes," she said, her answer brisk and clear. "We need to get back. Goodbye, Mr. Carlton."

She turned on her heel and headed for the door.

"I'm out of here," Rafe told the man, waving a quick goodbye. He followed Ami out the door, wondering what was going through her mind and feeling pretty sure it wasn't good. He hadn't missed that note of distrust in her voice when she'd asked him who he was after he'd healed the man in the café. Even though he'd known Ami for only a little more than a day, Rafe didn't doubt that the woman's defensive reflexes were already kicking back in big-time despite the progress he'd made in knocking them down.

Something he'd said or done had upset her, and he needed to know what it was, because without her complete confidence in him, he didn't see how he could keep her safe from whatever or whoever was ultimately behind the attack at the hotel in Orlando. When he'd decided it was his job to watch her back while she finished her research, he hadn't anticipated it would take the literal form of her walking rapidly away from him after he'd performed a miraculous healing. The woman had trust issues, he reminded himself, and with good reason.

He just couldn't think of any reason she should have trust issues with him.

Pulling his passenger door open, Rafe slipped into the car at the same moment Ami slid into the driver's seat.

"You want to talk about it?" he carefully suggested.

Ami's eyes were wild when she turned to face him.

"You glow when you heal. Who are you?" she asked again.

"I glow?"

"Yes, you glow!" she shouted. "Your whole body gets wrapped in this . . . this . . . light . . . and I could feel the healing happening. It was like fire beneath my fingers. It's not . . ."

"Normal?"

Ami recoiled in the seat, a small gasp escaping from her lips.

"I think we're way past 'normal' here, don't you, Ami?" Rafe quietly reminded her. "You can intuitively read the human body for illness and discern spirits. I can heal with my hands. You already knew that about me. Didn't you believe it?"

"I did! I did believe it, but seeing it happen . . . it was . . . I can't even . . . and you glowed! You didn't tell me you glowed."

"I didn't know that I did."

Rafe thought it over, but couldn't recall ever noticing any kind of light change around himself when he healed others, nor had anyone mentioned it. And somebody would have said something, he was sure. Only Ami had seen it.

He grinned, suddenly certain why Ami alone had picked up a glow. "You're a medical intuitive," he said, "and you can read spiritual energy. That's what you saw—the pure energy of healing."

Ami shook her head.

"No, Rafe. It was more than that. Your whole body glowed, not just your hands. When I looked at you saving that man's life, you looked like . . . an angel."

Rafe reached over and folded her cold fingers into his own warm hand. His voice was soft in the car.

"What would you say if I told you that you were right?"

CHAPTER THIRTY

Y ou want to say that again?"

"I'm an angel, Ami. I know it sounds crazy, but it's true."

Ami locked her eyes on Rafe's.

"You're an angel," she repeated slowly.

She inhaled deeply and then blew out a long sigh, her breath momentarily frosting in the chilled air in the car. She scrubbed her free hand over her eyes and face, holding her forehead in her hand. Somewhere deep inside her mind, she heard a hushed voice telling her that Rafe's words were indeed crazy. Maybe even certifiable. Miraculous healing was one thing, but a different form of being?

"I just don't know how much more of this I can do," she whispered. "I don't think I can stretch this far."

Rafe's hand tightened on her fingers.

"You can, Ami. I know you can. Hear me out."

She took another deep breath and let it slide out of her opened lips. Her eyes returned to Rafe's face.

"Okay, I'm listening." Her voice was calm and even. "Explain to me how you can be an angel."

Rafe looked deeply into her eyes. "I'm not sure I can, actually. I don't know exactly how or why it happened, but I can tell you what I do know. I can spontaneously heal other people in the name of Jesus Christ. I've never had a vision or visit from God or any other heavenly being, so it's not like I got struck down on the road to Damascus ... or New Orleans ... and when I got up, I was a whole new person who just happened to be able to heal miraculously. I was born in Leesville, Louisiana, the seventh child of CeCe and Randall Greene, and my mama fed me faith along with baby cereal. I was a twenty-two-year-old medic in the United States Marine Corps when I found out I could keep soldiers from dying just by putting my hands on them. Airplanes wait for me, buses stay on schedule, and I can always find a taxi when I need one."

Ami lifted her eyebrows in question. "And that makes you an angel? Healing with your hands and getting taxis?"

Rafe smiled ruefully. "St. Raphael is the patron of travelers," he explained. "If you want to make sure your luggage makes a connection, stick with me, Doctor."

Ami couldn't stop the small smile tugging at the corners of her mouth. The man was an incorrigible charmer, if nothing else.

"And I've got a great sense of humor, too, just like St. Raphael, according to what I've read on some Internet sites," he added. "And—get this—supposedly you see sparks of light around St. Raphael. Green sparks. I'm Raphael *Greene*, Ami."

Ami's smile froze.

She could have sworn she'd seen green dots of light dancing around Rafe in the diner when he touched the man.

She swallowed past the sudden lump in her throat and licked her dry lips.

"And this is why you think you're an angel?" She could hear the disbelief melting away in her voice. "Sorry. An archangel?"

Rafe squeezed her hand, which had now warmed in his grasp.

Archangel or not, she suddenly realized that she'd never felt more secure or safer in the company of any other person. If Rafe wasn't a member of the heavenly host, he'd certainly become her own angel in the last two days.

"This is the way I see it, Ami," Rafe said, his voice growing solemn. "The archangels all had—have—tasks to accomplish in God's scheme of things. Michael defends heaven. Raphael heals. Gabriel is the messenger. When you think about what they do, you can also see them as role models. Archetypes. So every time God heals a hurt using my hands, I am, in effect and in truth, doing the work of St. Raphael, but it's work that God has given to me. And so that's my gift, my call—to be Raphael for today."

He laid a finger under Ami's chin and gently raised her head so that her eyes met his.

"And if I can help you heal, if I can help you convince others that prayer is the miracle cure, that it's the path to wholeness, then I'm on a mission for God, too. I'm your archangel, Ami."

"I was just thinking that," she breathed.

Rafe smiled, his head dipping towards her, his eyes on her lips.

Ami's cellphone rang in her purse.

"I have to get that," she told him, her voice unsteady. "I'm a doctor."

Rafe released her chin and laughed. "I noticed."

Ami pulled the phone from her handbag and answered the call. As she listened to the voice at the other end of the line, she could feel the color draining from her face, her head beginning to swim.

"I'm on my way," she told the caller and dropped the phone back into her purse.

Her eyes welled with tears as she searched for her key in her bag. Once she found it, she tried to fit the key into the ignition, but she didn't seem able to coordinate her hand with the key-hole. Rafe's hand suddenly closed over hers, and she looked through the veil of tears in her eyes at his concerned face.

"Niles is dead," she told him. "I have to go."

Rafe pried the key from her hand. "I'm driving."

CHAPTER THIRTY-ONE

There was someone in the room with him.

Diedrich Mahler swam slowly up into consciousness and cracked open his tired eyes. Listlessly, he scanned the room until he found the face of the man in the corner.

"What are you doing here, Philip?"

He watched his boss approach the bed, his hands tucked into the deep pockets of his tailored overcoat.

"I heard you had collapsed, Diedrich. I was worried about you." He shook his head slightly in reprimand. "Why didn't you tell me you had a heart problem?"

The Calyx vice president swallowed, his throat dry and sore.

"I didn't want to trouble you, Philip," he lied. "You're a busy man."

His eyes wandered across the ceiling, his focus blurred. Then, without willing them, more words came out of his mouth. "To tell you the truth, I didn't know myself how bad it was."

If the admission surprised him, Arden didn't show it to Diedrich. Instead, he pulled a chair up to the side of the bed and sat down.

"So I hear from the nursing staff," he noted. "They say you're a lucky man to have a heart attack in the hospital cafeteria. Help was—literally—within reach."

Diedrich shut his eyes in fatigue. "I know." He vaguely recalled the moments before he collapsed, aware that there was something important he needed to tell Arden—something about CardiaZone. A moment or two passed before he found the right trail in his memory, and when he did, he turned his head to look at Arden.

"The drug," he said, his lips feeling heavy and numb. "It's a placebo. There is no CardiaZone, Philip."

He felt Arden's eyes fasten on his own with an almost physical intensity that rocked him to his core. Diedrich knew that look, and for all the years of his association with Arden, he'd never failed to feel the visceral thrill, the heady promise of danger that lay behind it. It was that promise, that challenge of walking on the razor's edge, that had fueled his employment with Arden for almost forty years. It was his drug, his addiction.

Until this moment.

In this moment, Diedrich felt nothing but a bone-deep weariness.

"What do you mean, Diedrich?" Arden's cool tone snatched Diedrich abruptly back into the present, back into the hospital room filled with monitors and wires.

"You gave me the reports yourself," Arden reminded him. "The trials are all documented. Dr. Kim has a revolutionary heart treatment on her hands."

He nodded at Diedrich's prone figure in the bed. "I think your condition is impairing your memory here, my friend."

"No." Diedrich's voice came out as a rasp. "No, Philip. I know it now. The reports are faked. I thought they were too good to be real, and they are. There is no CardiaZone," he repeated.

Arden continued to hold Diedrich's stare. "Dr. Kim is a fraud?"

"No," he said again, trying to hold on to his thoughts as they seemed bent on scattering. Why couldn't he concentrate? What kind of drugs had Villome pumped into him during the procedure? All he needed to do was tell Philip about the janitor—the old man who was Dr. Kim's patient—and how his heart had been healed by the prayer of the lab techs.

Not CardiaZone, but prayer.

"She uses prayer," he said, the effort exhausting him. "She's found a neurological explanation for faith healing, and she's using it to heal heart disease."

Silence filled the room.

"Did you hear what I said?" Diedrich asked the man in the chair.

Then, for a terrifying moment, Diedrich thought he was hallucinating. Philip Arden, the man whom Diedrich had known for his entire professional career, didn't look like Philip Arden. As Diedrich looked at his employer, the handsome tanned face shaded deathly gray and the eyes became the hollows of an empty skull. Fire licked at Arden's temples and his entire face lost its three-dimensionality, distorting itself into a flat mask of horror.

"Prayer?" the mask hissed.

Diedrich felt his brain begin to explode inside his head. He squeezed his eyes shut to block out the impossible vision he'd imagined.

"What else haven't you told me?"

The pain inside his head abruptly vanished, and Diedrich opened his eyes to see Arden's once-again familiar face. His voice, too, had regained its normal smooth tone, and the air no longer burned around his head. Diedrich stared at the man, afraid of what he might see next, but nothing happened. He could feel the beads of sweat on his brow, feel his own labored breath.

Definitely drugs. Powerful drugs.

Maybe too powerful.

"What else?" He repeated Arden's words, trying to read his boss's mind, trying to find what he had missed.

What else could there be? He needed to be sharp for Philip, just as he had always been, but he knew he was failing miserably, and that knowledge alone almost broke him.

He'd never failed Philip Arden.

Never.

Again, he searched his memory, but nothing surfaced that he thought Philip would find valuable.

"I just found out about the placebo before I collapsed," he carefully explained, appalled at how hard he had to focus to make each word clear and distinct, hoping he would stumble on whatever answer Philip was waiting for. "One of her trial subjects—her janitor—told me the whole story. His grandson, a pharmacy student, realized the drug was a sugar pill."

He watched his employer's brows knit together in concern. His reply was curt. "We'll have to get rid of them."

"The sugar pills?"

"The janitor," Arden corrected him. "The grandson."

Even through his confusion, Diedrich could hear the impatience in his boss's voice. He just couldn't follow the conversation; his clouded brain was lagging too far behind.

"What are you saying?"

"They know the truth," Arden admonished him. He leaned towards Diedrich, his hands clasped, his elbows braced on his thighs.

"Now here's the new plan: we're not going to let anyone in on this little caveat, Diedrich. We'll let Calyx sell CardiaZone sugar pills to a million miserable heart patients and then watch them die. Without the 'neurology' that goes with it, it's just a placebo, right? Calyx won't survive the lawsuits. Pieter Hallenstroem will be the newest mass-murdering villain on the planet, and I get exactly what I want."

His voice filled with satisfaction. "Revenge, death, and destruction. Again."

Diedrich fought against a new wave of exhaustion that rolled over him, even as Arden's dulcet tone seemed to pull him more deeply under the wave.

What was Philip talking about?

The janitor and his grandson weren't the only ones who knew the truth of Dr. Kim's research. There were the lab techs, and Dr. Kim herself.

The patients who had been healed.

"You can't kill them all," he whispered to Arden. "Too many know. It's too late."

He glanced at the monitors keeping guard over his own ravaged heart, then turned back to the man at his bedside. The word *forgiveness* echoed in his head. He pulled in a ragged breath, and decided, for the first time in his life, to question his employer's directive.

"Let it go, Philip," Diedrich said, his voice finally gaining some semblance of strength. "We've buried more than enough bodies over the years. We can still come out on top of this. Let Dr. Kim's miracle cure make millions for all of us—we'll patent the sugar pill and the prayer protocol that goes with it. Why not cash in on it? It's just words—it can't hurt. A prayer will cost us nothing, Philip. Nothing at all."

Without warning, unmistakable rage flooded into Arden's face. "That's where you're wrong, Diedrich."

His voice went low, deadly.

"A prayer will cost me everything."

He leaned close to Diedrich's ear, his words barely audible. "Why didn't you tell me about Rafe Greene?"

Diedrich turned his head and found Arden's face only inches from his own.

"Who's Rafe Greene?"

"My enemy," he breathed. "I just saw him in action, making a miraculous save. You failed me, old friend. You let him slip right in under my nose."

Diedrich blinked, his thoughts pulling apart again before he could really grasp them. Damn medication. Damn Philip. Diedrich had just barely escaped death, and the man was talking in riddles.

"What are you talking about?" he managed to ask.

"Dr. Kim's companion. This isn't just about healing hearts, Diedrich. With Rafe Greene in the game, it's about saving souls."

Arden straightened back up in his chair beside the bed. "Although, come to think of it, you wouldn't know anything about that, would you, Diedrich? After all, you sold your soul to me a long time ago."

He stood up and stalked across the room to the door, then turned back to look at Diedrich. "*Let it go, Philip?*" he mimicked Diedrich's earlier remark. "I don't think so. You have no idea what's at stake, old man. For some unfathomable reason, you've gone soft on me, and there's no room for someone like that in my empire. I don't, however, give out pink slips, as you well know."

He held up his right hand and twisted it into a tight fist. "I'm doing collections, today, Diedrich. Welcome to hell."

He turned and left the room.

Behind him, every monitor attached to his former employee's body screamed in alarm as Diedrich's heart stopped beating.

CHAPTER THIRTY-TWO

Almost blind with fury, Arden strode down the hospital corridor while nurses and doctors ran past him to answer the frantic summons of the alarms in Diedrich's room.

He'd been deceived.

Again.

He'd been so focused on exacting his revenge on Pieter Hallenstroem's defiance that he'd neglected to look more closely at the Belgian boy-wizard's pharmaceutical find. He'd handed the project over to Diedrich, confident that his second-in-command could spin the drug's development into a coup at Calyx that would—one way or another—result in Hallenstroem's destruction. He'd never imagined he'd find an archangel waiting in the wings.

Fool! he silently raged at himself. *A cure for heart disease? Impossible. Only God can heal hearts.*

Arden swept his hand across his temple, shoving his blond hair back off his face. He should have listened to Diedrich, who had been suspicious all along, saying it was too good to be true, that no one could cure heart disease. Yet medical researchers were solving impossible puzzles every day. Prostheses could make the lame walk again, cochlear implants allowed the deaf to hear, and ground-breaking sensor technology was allowing the blind to see.

Ha! So much for prophecy, Philip silently sneered. It didn't take a Savior to work miracles anymore. Just cutting-edge medicine. Even the regeneration of the spinal cord was just around the corner. When he'd first heard Diedrich's doubts, he'd simply assumed that his employee hadn't realized how fast medical science was advancing.

Arden came to a sudden halt in the hallway.

Diedrich had said something about a neurological explanation for CardiaZone—for the doctor's supposed prayer therapy. If that were true, then there was still a chance that Arden could orchestrate damage control. If Dr. Kim laid her success at the feet of neurology and medical science, then the world would have no reason to turn to God for healing.

Maybe, just maybe, he could still salvage this mess.

And then he remembered the archangel he'd seen in the diner, pouring God's own healing grace into the man that Arden had chosen as the handy excuse to meet Dr. Kim.

The angel he'd immediately recognized as St. Raphael.

That damn green glow.

And that could mean only one thing, as far as the Devil was concerned: Dr. Kim was in league with the angel, which meant she not only knew the truth about prayer, but that she had, indeed, put it to work for her.

Prayer was her miracle cure for heart disease.

Unable to contain his frustration, he slammed his hand against the elevator call button. Within two seconds, the doors slid open.

He looked down into the face of Ami Kim.

CHAPTER THIRTY-THREE

O ver there!" Rafe urged Ami.

He'd heard the hospital code for cardiac arrest over the loudspeaker in the elevator just as the doors slid open. He'd taken off at a run down the corridor, unaware that Ami had frozen in the car behind him. If someone's heart was fibrillating, there was a chance he could still save the patient's life. But every second counted, and Rafe didn't think twice about what he had to do. He raced down the hallway, pushed his way into the room already crowded with fast-moving medical personnel, and lunged for the dying man's hand.

Ami couldn't breathe. A mind-bending cold gripped her body and closed her throat, while darkness swirled around her. Instinctively, she took a step back from the man who had locked his eyes on hers. She didn't recognize him; she was sure she'd never seen him before, yet her body was reacting with such revulsion at the sight of him that she had to struggle against the nausea rising inside her.

Nausea . . . and a terror which she'd never before experienced in her life.

The man extended his hand towards her, and she shrank even further back into the elevator.

"Dr. Kim," he said, his voice rich and deep. "I've been looking forward to meeting you. I'm Philip Arden. I'm . . . associated . . . with Calyx, the company that's funding your research. Do you have a moment?"

No! NO! Get away from me!

Even over the sound of the roar that was growing in her ears, she could hear her heart hammering and her mind screaming at the man. Who was he that he could affect her like this? What was going on?

Rafe, I need you!

She began to stammer out an answer. "I . . . I . . ."

"Dr. Kim?"

Ami turned her head to see the nurse who had materialized next to the man in the hallway.

"I'll show you where Dr. Villome is," the nurse told her. "I'm so sorry."

Ami could feel the man moving aside without even looking at him. The air around her seemed suddenly warmer again, and her lungs spasmed into a deep breath.

"Another time, Dr. Kim," the stranger told her. He turned on his heel and was gone.

"I'm sorry," the nurse apologized again. "I didn't mean to interrupt your conversation, but I saw you when the elevator doors opened. I can't imagine how awful this must be for you, and I just wanted to help out if I could. Can I get you anything?"

Ami shook her head, rendered speechless by her violent physical response to the man who'd introduced himself as Philip Arden. He was a stranger, yet every nerve in her body had screamed into overload as soon as she'd looked into his eyes. Her legs were still shaking.

Evil. Pure evil.

She had read the man spiritually, and it had brought her, almost literally, to her knees.

Philip Arden was evil incarnate.

She had to tell Rafe.

This time, Diedrich was ready.

He waited for the light to approach from beyond the hospital room's walls. The sweet bouquet of flowers filled the air again. He looked at the medical personnel crowded around his body in the bed and silently thanked them for their efforts. When the light broke into the room, he bowed his head in a clean sorrow that rose from the depths of his heart.

"Forgive me, Lord," he begged. "Do with me as You will."

He felt a searing pain and the light went out.

"Got it!" the cardiologist yelled as a heartbeat began to trace its shaky pattern on the EKG monitor in the hospital room. "This guy is one lucky son of a gun," he told the team of nurses and doctors clustered around the patient's bed. "This is the second time he's arrested since he got out of the cath lab. That makes three cardiac events in less than one day. He just doesn't want to die, I guess."

A few steps behind him, Rafe leaned against a bank of monitors, fatigue closing his eyes for a moment's respite. He always felt the jolt when healing power traveled from him into a dying person, but it had never felt quite this intense before. Something else had been going on, he was sure, though he had no idea what that something may have been.

"Only God knows," he quietly muttered to himself.

He froze in dumb realization.

It was true. Only God knew everything that had just transpired as Rafe held the dying man's hand.

Just like only God knew why Rafe could save so many, yet lose his own brother. Rafe could replay his brother's death a thousand times in his mind, question his every move, second-guess his every instinct, but the truth was, he'd never have an answer to why his brother had died in his arms.

Only God knew.

Because He was God.

Not Rafe.

A thousand memories flooded through his head as he re-called all the times he'd healed since the first time he'd discov-ered his gift. Miraculous healings. Minor healings. Healings so impossible that he'd had to quit his job and move on before an-yone could question him too closely. Healings that he'd at-tempted and failed. Losses for which he'd blamed himself. They'd all been part of the same road down which his gift had led him, Rafe realized.

A gift over which he, ultimately, had no control, because he was just the instrument, not the Healer himself.

God was the Healer, and He used Rafe's hands to do it.

And wasn't that exactly what his mama had always told him? That God worked through the hands and hearts of His people, and that Rafe had to respect that?

And now all those healings and losses, including Samuel's death and even Rafe's discharge from the Marines, had brought him to this place, to this moment in time.

To Ami's side in her moment of need.

Like the recovering alcoholics on Ami's prayer teams, Rafe needed to respect God's wishes and surrender his own illusion of control.

And he needed to surrender that control to God.

His eyes still closed, Rafe bent his head in his own silent prayer.

Your will—whatever it is—be done.

And with that simple acceptance, Rafe felt his guilt melt away and his own heart begin to heal.

"Heartrate stabilized," the nurse watching the monitor across the room from Rafe announced. "Blood pressure is 120 over 76 and holding."

The crisis over, a murmur of relief circled the room as the doctors and nurses slowly drifted out the door to return to other patients. Next to Rafe, one of the nurses checked the IV bag hanging from its hook and threw him a curious look.

"Are you new here?" she asked. "I don't think we've met."

"I'm a paramedic," he told her, still feeling a little disoriented. Whether it was from his unusually draining physical response to the healing or his newfound spiritual peace, he couldn't say. "I heard the code, and I came running."

"You and everyone else," the nurse said, adding a syringe of medication to the suspended line. "It's been crazier than usual on the floor today. Not only has this patient kept us on our toes, but his cardiologist collapsed and died right after the procedure. It's kind of spooky, if you know what I mean. One minute the doctor is performing a delicate procedure, and the next thing you know, he's dead."

She removed the empty syringe from the tubing and placed it in the sharps box. Rafe watched her practiced motions, feeling almost soothed by the predictable medical routine he himself knew so well and performed so often when he was riding in an ambulance with a patient.

"I heard that they knew each other, too," she added. "The patient and his doctor. I guess they were working together to develop some new heart drug."

Heart drug.

The words caught in his mind and sent a hot burst of adrenaline through his body. Instantly alert, Rafe focused his attention on the nurse.

"The cardiologist," he said. "What was the name of the cardiologist?"

The woman threw him another curious look. "Dr. Niles Villome. Did you know him?"

"I just met him this morning," he answered, suddenly sharply aware that he'd lost track of Ami since he'd run out of the elevator. "That's why I'm here. I was with Dr. Kim when she got the call about Dr. Villome, and I brought her over. Actually, I need to go find her now."

He excused himself and left the room with a growing sense of uneasiness.

Niles had unexpectedly, and literally, dropped dead in the hospital.

The man in the bed—Dr. Villome's patient—had just come a breath away from dying . . . for a third time.

Spooky coincidence? That's what the nurse had called it.

But Rafe's gut told him something different. Both Niles and his patient knew about Ami's research; one was dead and the other barely hanging on.

Death was stalking Ami's project . . . in the hospital.

Rafe looked to his left and to his right, but the corridors were empty.

Where was Ami?

Rafe's uneasiness vanished.

In its place was cold fear.

He took off like a shot down a hallway.

CHAPTER THIRTY-FOUR

Vi tried the phone number again.

"Thank you for calling Janklow Cleaning Services," the recorded voice of a woman repeated. "We are currently assisting another caller, but your call is important to us. Please leave a brief message, and we'll get back to you as soon as we can."

Vi tapped the cell phone's cancel button. She didn't want to leave a message. She wanted to speak with a breathing body, preferably one who would gladly give her the name of Ami Kim's office janitor. Philip was desperate for the man's name, and she aimed to please her employer. She dialed the number a third time.

While she waited for the call to be picked up, she began reviewing her options for killing the janitor. Philip had been insistent that she do the job immediately, which meant she would have to use what she had on hand. She automatically rejected the deadly toxin she'd used on Villome—she had no desire to risk the kind of attention that two identical kills would create among the local law enforcement agencies. Even though she was working far outside the local cops' radar, she still held a great deal of respect for their investigative abilities, and she hadn't acquired her reputation and her record of success by making stupid, ultimately very costly, mistakes.

That left either the small handgun she had picked up this morning at a decrepit pawn shop or the stiletto she wore sheathed along the inside of her left arm.

Either way, she'd have to get up close and personal with her mark. Once she knew where the janitor was working, she could watch for a break to make the hit—when the man stepped outside for a smoke, or when he moved between offices. Worst case, she could catch him when he left work for the day, tired, unobservant, and easy prey. For Vi, this kill would be a no-brainer.

Or at least it should have been, except for the other request Philip had made.

"I need the name of his grandson," her employer had instructed her. "He's a pharmacy student. He has to go, too."

Vi listened to the phone continue to ring. At the rate he was assigning her jobs today, Philip was going to make her rich by the end of the day, Vi decided. Maybe she should call it quits, then, and head for that sunny spot on the Pacific side of Costa Rica that she'd had her eye on for a while now. Just as she wasn't stupid about the tenacity of good detectives, she harbored no illusions about the probability of longevity in her career. She'd always thought the advice to quit while you were ahead made a lot of sense, and maybe, after this Minnesota murder spree, it would be the right time to take that advice and hang up her gun. And her toxins. Her stiletto . . .

"Thanks for holding. How can I help you?" the perky voice at Janklow Cleaning Services asked her.

"Hi. I'm new at Heart Partners Clinic, and I needed to know the name of our Janklow janitor. I think he left his coat here after he finished cleaning, and it's so cold out today, I'd hate for him to be without it," Vi improvised. "Can you tell me where he'd be now, so I can track him down and get it to him? Or maybe where his grandson is, and he could come pick it up? He's a pharmacy student, right?"

"Just a sec," the woman replied. "Let me check our work schedules. You said Heart Partners Clinic, right? Okay, it's coming up on my computer. And I think you're right about Mr. Nguyen's grandson, too," she continued. "I know he was here in the office once to pick up a paycheck for his grandfather while he was recuperating from his heart attack, and he said something about his classes at the pharmacy school."

Piece of cake, Vi congratulated herself. *Amazing what a little human kindness will get you. Although in this particular case, it's going to get the Nguyens dead.*

"He must have left his coat last night," the woman informed Vi. "Chinh Nguyen works a late shift, after the offices close for the day. I bet he's missing that coat plenty," she added. "That air is frigid out there today."

Vi immediately revised her plans. She was going to have to make the kill a little later than she had originally thought if the man wasn't already on the medical campus.

"Maybe I can catch him when he comes on tonight? Do you know when he'll be here? Or his grandson—do you know his name?"

"Hang on," the Janklow receptionist said. "Let me just pull up Mr. Nguyen's contact information and see if it's there."

Vi held her breath, hoping the woman wouldn't suddenly think twice about giving out so much information about a company employee to a total stranger. She decided to pile on a little more goodwill just to be safe.

"This is so nice of you," Vi said, injecting as much gratitude into her voice as she could. "I really appreciate your taking the time to help me out. I just hate to think of such a sweet old man going without his coat in this cold."

"He cleans your offices at 8 p.m.," the woman told her. "And his grandson's name is Hung Nguyen. Would you like his cell phone number?"

Vi grinned.

"I'd love it."

CHAPTER THIRTY-FIVE

Rafe skidded around a corner into another hallway just in time to see Ami approaching a doorway at the far end of the floor's corridor.

"Ami!"

She turned at his shout.

"Wait for me," he called to her, relief pouring through his body.

If he hadn't already been convinced that Ami was in danger, he couldn't possibly deny it now. Someone wanted to shut down the research project, and along with it, the key players.

And even though no one had said as much to Ami, Rafe was sure they were about to find out that Niles's death wasn't the result of natural causes. The man was too young to die so abruptly, unless he'd had an undiagnosed health issue, or he'd suffered an aneurysm, like the man in the diner.

Rafe almost stopped in mid-stride as he covered the distance down the hallway to where Ami stood by the doorway.

What were the chances that both Niles and the man in the diner had had aneurysms?

For that matter, what were the chances that he and Ami just happened to be in the right place at the right time in the diner to save the man's life?

An icy finger of certainty trailed down Rafe's spine.

Rafe didn't believe in chance.

Somehow, Niles's death and the two near-deaths were connected.

How they were connected, he had no idea, but when it came to why, he was convinced that the reason was standing at the end of the corridor: Ami. And there was only one thing Rafe could think of that might have made her a lightning rod for death: her miracle cure.

A cure that promised to revolutionize medicine.

A cure that would change the world.

An even deeper, blacker, certainty chilled Rafe to the bone.

Whoever wanted Ami's cure would also want her dead, and unless he discovered who it was, and stopped him, Ami would be the next victim of "chance."

Ignoring the reprimands he got from several nurses to keep his voice down, Rafe kept his eyes on Ami, consciously breathing away the fear for her that threatened to paralyze him. Some guardian angel he was turning out to be, he berated himself. He'd left her alone in the elevator and completely lost track of where she was, here where her own partner had mysteriously collapsed and died just hours ago. If he was going to save this woman's life, along with her research, he needed to get a lot better at protecting her, a whole lot faster.

As soon as Rafe reached Ami, the nurse on her other side directed them into the room where Niles's body lay inside a clear plastic bag on a gurney. Rafe took a quick look at Ami's face. Her already porcelain complexion was now a shade paler. Rafe wrapped his arm around her shoulders and pulled her closer to his side. Together, they approached the body, while the nurse quietly filled them in.

"No one saw it happen," she told them. "He collapsed in the changing room and another doc found him there. He was already dead. I'm so sorry, Dr. Kim."

Ami nodded, her eyes welling with tears. Rafe made her sit down in the plastic chair that the nurse pushed his way, then took the nurse's arm and led her out of the room.

"No marks on the body?" he asked her. "There's no possibility he hit his head when he fell and trauma is the cause of death?"

She shook her head. "Not that I've heard."

Rafe caught a trace of hesitation in the woman's voice. "What, exactly, have you heard?"

The nurse's eyes darted to the left and then to the right before she settled them back on Rafe. She seemed visibly nervous.

"I heard there were some indications that Dr. Villome may have been poisoned," she whispered. "With some kind of a contact neurotoxin. We're expecting a medical examiner here any minute. Everyone wants to keep it quiet until they know for sure."

A neurotoxin?

Rafe let out a low whistle. A hospital was the last place that wanted a biotoxin scare on its plate, and especially in connection with a practicing doctor. The ensuing chaos would be devastating for everyone concerned. Patients would be terrified and every clinic associated with the medical center would be shut down or swamped with government inspectors and regulators. Ami's practice—the Minneapolis Heart Partners clinic she'd shared with Niles—would never recover.

Overkill, Rafe thought. *Scorched earth policy.*

Clearly, not only did someone want Ami dead, but he wanted no trace of her research to survive, either.

Ami, however, had living proof of her cure. She had patients who had been healed of heart disease, and she had her technicians, the recovering alcoholics, who knew her protocol. Someone aiming to wipe out Ami's work would have a host of witnesses to eliminate, even if Ami herself were killed.

Scorched earth policy.

A yawning abyss began to open before Rafe.

Ami wasn't the only target.

Not by a long shot.

CHAPTER THIRTY-SIX

Vi waited outside the classroom in the university building. She'd called Hung's cell phone number and was immediately forwarded to his voice mail, which she guessed meant that he was in class with his phone turned off. Being the resourceful assassin that she was, she'd immediately headed for the pharmacology college's main office and explained to the receptionist there that she urgently needed to contact Hung Nguyen about a family health crisis. Although the young man behind the desk gave her a suspicious glance, he'd dutifully checked his database for Hung's course schedule and then directed Vi to where the class was being held.

"There really is a medical emergency," Vi had reassured him, unhappy that the young man was taking his time looking her over. In her line of work, Vi never wanted people to remember her, and she especially didn't want them remembering her making inquiries about people who later turned up dead.

"I work over at Minneapolis Heart Partners," she'd added, trying to gain the receptionist's confidence and throwing in a little misinformation for good measure. She read his name on the medical center ID card that was clipped to his collar. "It's Brad, right?"

The young man nodded.

"We have Hung listed as his grandfather's emergency contact, Brad. I tried his cell number, but he's not answering, so Dr. Kim said I should try to find him in the pharmacy building."

The receptionist held up his hands in mock surrender. "Okay, okay. I believe you. I didn't think you looked like Hung's type anyway."

She gave him a curious look. "Excuse me?"

He shrugged lightly and gave her a lopsided grin. "Hung's always got girls chasing him down. What can I say? I thought maybe you were one of the crowd. Sorry."

Vi forced a smile.

Maybe I should just lean over and kill this kid now. She could pick up the heavy, old-fashioned stapler on his desk and slam it into his windpipe. She could reach over and shut off the blood to his brain with a hard strike from the side of her hand right on his carotid artery.

Instead, she thanked him for the help and walked out of the office and down the nearest stairwell to another floor of the building. Now, as she waited for Hung's class to let out, she considered how close people came to death every day without even realizing it.

Like Brad, the idiot receptionist in the college office.

Others, she imagined, clearly saw the black maw of death approaching, like Philip's employee Diedrich Mahler, who'd suffered a heart attack and lived to tell the tale. Vi wondered what else Mahler had confided in Philip when his boss had shown up in his recovery room in the hospital, since Philip had sounded especially peeved when he'd called her to order the two additional killings.

Whatever Mahler had had to say, it hadn't made Philip Arden happy.

It was, however, going to make her richer. Costa Rica was getting closer by the minute.

She checked her watch and leaned back against the solid wall outside Hung Nguyen's classroom. As soon as he came through the door, she'd grab him and hustle him off to the family "emergency." Once they were outside the building, she'd move in close to him and slide her stiletto right up under his ribs and into his heart.

Vi guessed that there wouldn't be any girls chasing after Hung then.

CHAPTER THIRTY-SEVEN

Philip stormed into his hotel room at the Grand, slamming the door shut so hard behind him that the expensive paintings on the wall shuddered on their hooks. He tore his expensive overcoat off and threw it across the room,where it knocked over a crystal lamp, sending it into the wall with a crash.

Furious, he raised a clenched fist toward the room's ceiling. "This is not over!" he roared. "I will find them all, and I will kill every one of them! Not a single one will survive to tell the truth! Do you hear me?"

There was only silence.

Arden lowered his fist and raked his fingers through his hair. "Of course you hear me," he hissed. "You hear everything, don't you. Tell me, oh Mighty One, did I surprise you by killing Diedrich? My own faithful, loyal minion, and without a second's hesitation? Unlike someone I know, I don't tolerate weakness in my organization."

He looked at the broken lamp on the carpet and picked up the room phone that sat on the antique credenza in the suite.

"I need housekeeping," he snapped into the phone. "There's broken glass in my carpet."

The Gentleman dropped the phone back into its cradle and pulled open the door of the small refrigerator that was built into the credenza. Finding only a variety of bottled water, he picked up the room phone again.

"I need a bottle of the most expensive bourbon, as well."

Remembering then that he'd not eaten since breakfast, he likewise ordered a focaccia sandwich from the room service menu propped on the top of the credenza.

"But send the bourbon up here now," he instructed the concierge on the other end of the line. "Get it here in the next five minutes, and I'll tip you as much as it's worth."

Comforted by the thought of food and drink on the way, Philip walked over to the suite's big windows that looked out over the city.

"How can people live here?" he muttered. "It's freezing. It's ugly."

He recalled the mountains of dirty snow he'd seen piled in parking lots during his taxi ride back to the hotel from the hospital. The city looked gray and anemic, like an aged newsreel. He'd called Vi on his way out of the medical center and tersely told her to kill the janitor and his grandson, and that he'd take a cab to return to his suite. The whole ride back he'd fumed silently, cursing Ami Kim, Rafe Greene, and that idiot Niles Villome who'd apparently been clueless as to the real significance of his partner's research. If it hadn't been for the man's opportunistic appropriation of Kim's work and the wealth he imagined it would produce for him, there was probably an excellent chance that years would have passed before the woman found anyone willing to give her even a hearing about her miraculous protocol, let alone someone who would risk funding its FDA approval.

Instead, Villome had virtually leapfrogged the research into the near release of a clinically proven product, even though it was nothing more than a sugar pill.

Of course, it wouldn't have been the first time a placebo shook up the medical establishment with its "curative" powers. Diedrich, suspicious from the beginning of the project, had shared with Philip countless reports of drug trials that proved no more effective in medical treatment than the sugar pills provided to the control groups in those same trials. One report in particular came to his mind—the article that had appeared in the *Washington Post* back in 2002 that revealed that placebos were as effective, if not more so, in treating depression than the

FDA-approved products marketed by the pharmaceutical giants. Another report cited the impressive effectiveness of placebos in treating gastric or duodenal ulcers.

Yet despite the growing evidence of the placebo effect, the idea of the mind-body connection was still rejected by traditional physicians as a viable option for developing medical treatment. Chemical concoctions were the therapeutic drugs of choice, and doctors who attempted to circumvent that conventional wisdom found themselves ostracized from their profession.

The Gentleman, on the other hand, was delighted by the medical establishment's stubborn insistence on scientific proof as the measure of healing. Every time Diedrich brought him another report denouncing the brain's role in physical health, he celebrated.

Because as long as no one was looking for an alternative path to healing, no one was going to find it.

No one was going to realize that healing was, at its heart, the work of the spirit, and in a deeper reality than anyone guessed, the work of the energy of God.

And that energy was prayer.

Or at least, no one would have guessed it if it hadn't been for Ami Kim's visionary work and Niles Villome's greed.

A knock on his suite's door interrupted Philip's gloomy musings. Pleased with the concierge's prompt response to his request, The Gentleman peeled a hundred-dollar bill off his money clip and handed it to the delighted hotel employee.

"Tell me," he asked before the man could turn away, "how can anyone live here? It's colder than a witch's—"

"You have to see the spring, sir, and the summer, and the fall, to understand," the man cut in. "They're breathtaking. Glorious. Of course, a lot of Minnesotans live for the winters, too, you know. They think it's just as wonderful as the rest of the year here."

Philip shook his head. "I certainly don't see it."

"Not everyone does," the man agreed. "Have a good day, sir."
He turned and walked towards the elevator at the far end of
the floor.

"Not very likely, I'm afraid," The Gentleman whispered at
the back of the concierge. He inspected the label on the bottle
of aged bourbon and closed the suite's door.

From the other side of the room, a single ray of blinding
light suddenly penetrated the windows, making a feeble attempt to light up the hotel suite. Philip looked at the ray in disgust and dismissed the wintry city skyline with a wave of the
bottle in his hand.

"He's right," he told the empty room, "not everyone sees it. I
know I certainly don't."

With a deft twist of his wrist, he opened the bottle and
poured the golden liquid into a crystal tumbler sitting on the
credenza.

"Just like I didn't see Rafe Greene coming. How pathetic is
that? Blindsided again by an archangel."

He lifted the glass to his lips and drank the bourbon down.

"But you're too late, St. Raphael," The Gentleman cheered
himself as he refilled the glass. "The damage is done. Our Belgian boy-wizard is going to produce CardiaZone, thanks to the
dearly departed Niles Villome's treachery and the enthusiastic
stamp of approval from the likewise dearly, and oh-so-recently,
departed Diedrich Mahler. With any luck, millions are going to
die from our little sugar pill before it's pulled from the market.
So, regardless of your role in this miracle cure, Rafe," he jeered,
"I'm afraid you're going to have to change your job description."

He raised his glass in a mock salute.

"Farewell, oh healing one. Hello, Angel of Death."

He took another deep draught of the bourbon, then smiled
as one last comforting thought occurred to him.

"And you don't even see it coming, do you?"

His smile went hard and cold.

"Don't you just hate it when that happens?"

CHAPTER THIRTY-EIGHT

The classroom door beside Vi swung open and a handful of students entered the hallway, each intent on juggling books and laptops. She looked quickly into each one's face, searching for the Asian features that would identify Hung Nguyen, but to her chagrin, all she found were northern European types—big-boned blond women and men.

Where was Hung Nguyen?

Vi could feel her blood pressure rising. Killing the old man and his grandson should have been a simple task. They should have both been right here in the university medical center, where all she had to do was find them and kill them.

But so far, she was striking out.

The old man didn't come in to work until eight o'clock at night.

The grandson wasn't where he was supposed to be.

How could Vi do her job when people were unpredictable?

In a last-ditch effort to try to locate the younger Nguyen, Vi stepped into the classroom to speak with the instructor who was still gathering her materials into her briefcase sitting open on a table. Before she reached the woman, though, Vi came to an abrupt halt when she realized there was another person in the back of the room who was just standing up to leave.

An Asian student.

"Excuse me," she asked the young man. "Are you Hung Nguyen?"

"Yes," he replied.

Vi smiled, relief and the beginning of a cold anticipation flooding through her veins.

"Can I speak with you for a moment?"

CHAPTER THIRTY-NINE

Rafe handed Ami a plain white ceramic mug filled with steaming coffee and sat down beside her on the couch in the doctors' break room.

"It's NRT, isn't it?" Ami's voice was very quiet in the empty lounge. "Niles didn't have any heart issues, Rafe. I know that for a fact."

She stared at the dark liquid in her cup.

"He was murdered, and it has to do with my research."

"There's speculation that a biotoxin was involved," Rafe told her. "A very fast-acting, very deadly, biotoxin."

Ami sighed, still staring at her coffee. "Yeah, I figured that one out. There's only one reason you encase a body in that kind of material. I'm surprised they'd let anyone in that room until they knew for sure what's involved."

"Hospitals have pretty good protocols now for that kind of stuff, Ami," Rafe reminded her. "Ever since that anthrax scare a decade ago, procedures have been in place to identify and handle cases of biotoxin exposure."

He lightly circled his arm around her shoulders and gave her a small hug.

"It's not your fault, no matter what you think."

Slowly, she lifted her eyes from the mug in her hands to meet his somber gaze.

"I know that, Rafe. I do. But I still can't ignore the fact that it's my research that has . . ." She broke off her words to swallow past the emotion that was crowding her throat.

Niles was dead.

Even though it had been a long time since she had loved him, she never, never, had wished him any ill.

She'd just wanted him to get better, to recognize and defeat the demon that drove him.

She'd wanted him to recover from his alcoholism.

But he'd never quite managed it.

And now it was too late.

". . . that has brought a killer into the hospital," she finished. She shook her head in disbelief. "Biotoxin? Not quite your run-of-the-mill murder, is it? Who carries around deadly poisons?"

"An assassin?"

Ami felt the blood drain from her face in a rush as she recognized the utter seriousness in Rafe's expression. In her hands, the coffee cup shook.

"Maybe you want to wait to drink that," he said, taking the mug from her fingers and placing it on the end table beside the couch. He took her hands in his and Ami immediately felt a rush of warmth that surprised her—she hadn't realized her skin had gone so cold, despite the fact that she'd been holding a steaming cup. A sudden image of the man in the elevator filled her head.

"I had the weirdest experience," she said, her eyes on their joined hands and her voice soft. "Just when we got here, and you ran for the coding, there was a man in front of the elevator."

She shivered as she remembered the man's face, the soul-searing pain she'd felt in his presence.

Her terror.

The evil.

Evil incarnate.

She looked into Rafe's brown eyes, and she knew he'd understand. Not only did he believe that she possessed the ability to discern spirits, but he also believed that he, himself, was an archangel. Who else could possibly accept the supernatural truth of what she was going to tell him?

"I met the Devil today," she told him, stunned by her own realization. "He was right here. His name is Philip Arden."

CHAPTER FORTY

S ay again?"
   Rafe could have sworn that Ami had just said that she'd met the Devil in the hospital. Given the shock of seeing her ex-spouse in a body bag, Rafe had been expecting some kind of meltdown to occur, but Ami hallucinating hadn't been at the top of his list. After all, he'd seen Ami cope brilliantly after a bullet missed her by a hair, pulling herself together in record time and turning her concern to other innocent bystanders. The woman had steel for a backbone.

"The man in front of the elevator," she repeated. "I couldn't breathe. I thought I was going to pass out."

Rafe could see the panic beginning to rise in Ami's eyes even as he felt her body begin to shudder violently beneath his hand on her shoulder.

"Breathe with me, Ami," he said, taking her chin firmly in his free hand and forcing her to look at him. "Breathe."

He inhaled deeply through his nose, then pursed his lips as he slowly exhaled. To his relief, Ami immediately matched her breathing to his, and within a minute, Rafe could feel the tension leaving her shoulders.

"All right?" he asked her.

She nodded slightly, her chin still cupped in his hand.

"All right."

Rafe relaxed his grip on her face, brushing his fingers gently over the line of her jaw.

"You've had a terrible day, Ami. You're under too much stress. You need—"

"You don't believe me."

Though whispered, Ami's words hung heavily in the sudden silence of the lounge. Rafe scrambled to find the right answer to give her, an answer that was both honest and yet reassuring, but he kept coming up empty. The fact was that he'd just seen classic signs of early shock rolling through Ami—the uncontrolled shaking, the panicked breathing—and to his trained paramedic's eye, those were totally understandable in Ami's situation.

But claiming that she'd seen the Devil?

Even for Rafe, that was pushing the boundaries of belief too far.

He reached out and tenderly brushed her long black bangs off her left temple.

"Ami, I just think it's hard for you right now, and—"

She pulled away from his touch, and like a physical wall rising between them, Rafe felt Ami's withdrawal and hurt closing him out. Even worse than that, he felt the bond of trust that they had so quickly forged begin to weaken, his own balance starting to shift within him.

Distrust was going to tear them apart, now, when they needed each other more than ever.

Not going to happen, Rafe vowed.

He clamped his hands on Ami's shoulders and pulled her roughly against him, his mouth covering hers in a kiss that was equal parts frustration, repentance, need . . . and love.

This is the man I've been waiting for.

The words rang so clear and true in Ami's mind that she could have sworn she'd said them aloud, except that her lips were pressed tightly to Rafe's as the tidal wave of his deepest feelings roared through her. Never had she felt so sure of another person, so totally in tune with life itself as she did at that moment. Yet even as she savored the touch of his mouth, she knew it wasn't a kiss alone that had crumbled her last bit of resistance to trusting this man.

Rafe Greene was a man of faith. He knew exactly where his incredibly unique gifts came from, and he wasn't afraid to use them.

And neither am I. Not anymore.

The thought flared in her mind with abrupt clarity.

She'd faced the Devil himself . . . and survived.

God was with her.

Right here and right now.

He had given her incredible gifts for a reason, and it was her responsibility to use them. For the first time in her life, she didn't need the permission of the medical community, or her parents, or anyone else. God had called her and He was faithful.

"Tell me what you're thinking."

Rafe's voice, soft and deep, wrapped itself around her.

She realized she was gripping the front of his jacket and slowly eased her fingers out to lay her palms flat against his chest.

"I was thinking about getting permission," she told him, her eyes on her fingers splayed just below his jacket collar.

"I didn't ask for any."

"I noticed."

"Is that a problem?"

Ami lifted her eyes to his and caught the faintest flicker of uncertainty in his gaze.

"No," she assured him. "It's not. Not with me. But I just realized it's been a problem for me—seeking permission. My whole medical career, I've wanted someone to say it was all right to be a medical intuitive, that my gifts were good, that I had some kind of official validation to do what I know I can do."

She smoothed her hands over the soft leather of his jacket.

"But now, for the first time in my life, I don't need it anymore."

A slow smile fanned across her face.

"You've opened my eyes, Rafe. You believe in me. I don't have to hide who I am anymore. And because I can be who I am, and do what I can do, I'm not afraid anymore of what anyone else might think or say."

She laid a soft finger on his lips.

"You've given me my life back because you have faith in me, Rafe. Niles took that away from me a long time ago, thanks to his constant criticism. I hadn't even realized what I'd lost until you helped me find it again."

His eyes fixed on hers, Rafe took her hand and dropped a kiss on her knuckles.

"Ami, I want to tell you something."

She could feel the heat of his body reaching for her as if it were a physical force. Her senses reeled. Her breath left her lungs.

But her heart . . . her heart leapt.

"I know we just met—yesterday?—but I—"

"Rafe."

Her voice was a whisper.

Rafe's hand tightened on hers, his eyes instantly alarmed.

"Give me a little time, okay?" She added a smile to reassure him, and she felt his fingers relax their grip on her hand.

Her smile broadened. "Yesterday or not, that wave of emotion that you just sent crashing over me almost knocked my lights out. Or maybe I should say my neurological circuit board."

She watched the concern on his face turn to momentary confusion, then to realization.

"Yes, Rafe, I know how you feel about me," she confirmed, "but that's part of the deal when you're spending time with someone who can discern spirits. I may not always know what you're thinking, but I can certainly tell how you're feeling. Is that a problem?"

She threw his own question back at him, her eyes laughing, because she already knew his answer.

"No, ma'am," he replied, dipping his head to kiss her again. "It's definitely not a problem."

A few moments later, he cupped her cheek in his big hand. "Can we start over now?"

Ami opened her eyes and leaned back on the couch so she could watch Rafe's face. "From which point?" she asked, feeling the floor beneath her feet growing solid again.

Rafe rubbed his thumb over her still-sensitive lips, then took her hands in his own. "From where you told me about the Devil in the elevator."

He fastened his eyes on hers.

"I'm listening, Ami. This time, I'm listening to you."

CHAPTER FORTY-ONE

I *keep waking up,* Diedrich marveled. *Every time I think I'm dead, I end up opening my eyes again.*

He watched the nurse move around the room, checking monitors and making notes on the clipboard she carried with her. She reached towards the IV bag hanging near his head and pulled back with a sudden gasp, her eyes wide as she realized that Diedrich's were open.

"Oh my," she sputtered. "I didn't realize you were conscious. You nearly scared the life out of me."

He wanted to tell her that he was finding out from personal experience that life wasn't an easy thing to scare off. His, at least, just kept hanging on.

"Dr. Kim," he managed to rasp out.

The nurse cocked her head and considered him, then checked the clipboard in her hand.

"Dr. Kim isn't your doctor," she told him. "But if you want to see her, I might be able to find her for you. I think she's on the floor right now. Give me a few minutes and I'll see what I can do."

Diedrich nodded and closed his eyes. The moment he'd floated up from unconsciousness, a single thought had commanded his attention: he needed to meet Ami Kim.

He needed to warn her.

Because if anyone in the world might listen to what he'd come to realize about Philip Arden the last time he saw him, Diedrich had to believe it would be the petite researcher who healed her patients' hearts with prayer.

"Dr. Kim?"

Rafe looked up at the nurse who'd just walked into the doctors' lounge. He was still processing what Ami had told him about her reaction to the man at the elevator, trying to accept the fact that the Devil himself might physically exist, let alone that he had been within Rafe's own arm's reach as he'd raced out of the elevator to help the coding patient. As impossible as it seemed, Ami had met the Devil—and thanks to her gift of discerning spirits, she had been able to see through his human veneer and recognize him for who he truly was.

That alone was bad enough.

But it got worse.

Arden, the Devil, had told Ami that he was associated with Calyx, the company that Niles had been working with to produce what he thought was Ami's pharmaceutical miracle cure.

What did the Devil want with a heart drug, a medical miracle that would save millions of lives and in so doing, change the world itself?

The nurse stepped into the lounge. "I'm sorry to intrude, Dr. Kim," the nurse apologized, "but I have a patient who's asking for you. Do you have a minute?"

Ami slipped her hand out of Rafe's and stood up.

"Of course. Who's the patient? I don't think I have anyone admitted right now."

The nurse tilted her head in the direction of the hospital corridor outside the lounge.

"The fellow who was coding a while ago."

She gave Rafe a curious look.

"Are you the paramedic who was in the room when they revived the patient? I heard about you, how you slipped in and nobody even asked you who you were. So much for our security on this floor, I guess."

Rafe put his hands up in reassurance. "I won't tell if you won't."

The nurse laughed. "Spoken like a true hospital veteran."

She turned to leave the room, and Rafe stood up to follow Ami out into the hallway.

"I go where you go," he told her when she gave him a questioning look. He lowered his voice to a whisper and leaned down to place his mouth near her ear. "Don't forget that there's an assassin on the loose, Ami. Not to mention . . . Philip Arden. You may not have thought you needed a guardian angel yesterday, but from what I see today, you're not going two steps without me for the foreseeable future."

"Are you going to be the angel on my shoulder, Rafe?" she whispered back, her eyes searching his.

He straightened up and smiled. "Yes, ma'am, I am." Gently, he threaded a strand of her dark hair behind her ear.

"Actually, I'm going to do even better than that," he added, his voice filled with serious intent beneath his joking tone. "I've got your back, Ami. As long as you need me, and want me, I'm going to be right here."

He watched a pink blush rise on Ami's cheeks and figured that she was remembering his kisses as clearly as he was. She did, as she had recently reminded him, have the gift of discerning spirits.

Now if they could just discern where it was going to lead them, he'd relax. No way was it a good thing to find the Devil in your path.

"Mr. Mahler?"

Ami walked into the room, quickly assessing the condition of the man lying in the bed. She guessed he was in his sixties, and though his pallor looked as ashen as she had expected a multiple-heart-attack victim's to look, there was a clear spark in his eyes that told her that this particular patient intended to keep his heart beating for quite a while yet.

"I'm Dr. Kim," she introduced herself. "This is my colleague, Raphael Greene. I understand you wanted to speak with me?"

The patient's dark eyes alternated between Ami and Rafe, almost as if he were trying to remember where he had met them. But Ami was sure that the man was a stranger to her, and aside from the meager amount of information that Rafe had provided before they'd entered the room, she knew nothing of the man's medical history. As Niles's partner, she would, of course, assume care of the patient since Niles was . . . wasn't . . .

She pushed thoughts of Niles away and focused on Mahler, waiting for him to tell her why he had sent the nurse to find her. Instead of addressing her first, though, Mahler's attention seemed to zero in on Rafe's face, his eyes narrowed.

"Raphael Greene," Mahler repeated. "Rafe Greene."

His eyes traveled up and down Rafe's body, like he was searching for something.

"Who are you, exactly, and why does Philip Arden hate you so much?"

Ami's heartbeat stumbled. She sharpened her own gaze on Mahler.

"You know Philip Arden?"

Mahler turned his head slightly on his pillow to look at her. Even from where she stood, she could clearly feel the remorse and pain that clung to the man.

"He's my boss," he said. "Or at least, he was. He tried to kill me, so I think it's safe to say that our association is over."

His eyes returned to Rafe.

"He said you were his enemy, that he'd just seen you do something miraculous, and that you have something to do with saving souls."

Ami looked at Rafe, her eyes filled with questions.

Rafe knew Philip Arden?

And he saved . . . souls?

Mahler was still speaking. "And then he said he was collecting mine, and I went into cardiac arrest—again. Just like that. It was like he was holding my life in his hands and he simply crushed it."

He glanced at Ami. "You think I'm crazy, don't you? Delirious. Doped up. I'm saying crazy things that can't possibly be true."

Ami shook her head as she felt Rafe come around the side of the bed to stand next to her. "No, I don't think you're crazy, Mr. Mahler. Right now, I can't say how much of what you're telling me is true, but I met Philip Arden myself just a little while ago, and I know . . . who he is."

She drew in a deep breath, willing away the icy chill that seemed to seep into her very spirit every time she recalled her encounter with Arden.

"What I don't know," she continued, "and what . . . concerns . . . me, is why he's here, and why he's interested in me."

Mahler's earlier comment to Rafe barreled back at her.

He said you were his enemy.

"Wait a minute. Is he interested in me?" She looked to Rafe for an answer. "Or is it you? You know Philip Arden?"

Rafe shook his head. "I've never met the man."

Ami looked back to Mahler. "You said that Arden saw Rafe do something miraculous? Where?"

Mahler returned her stare. "He didn't say. He just said I'd let Rafe slip past me. I had no idea what he was talking about—then."

She watched him give Rafe another narrowed glance as she tried to make sense of the man's remarks. Arden had recognized her in the elevator, so he must have seen Rafe with her. Yet Arden hadn't been in the room when Rafe had revived Mahler, so he couldn't have witnessed that. The only other time that Rafe had used his gift today was . . . at the café.

Ami and Rafe had been together at the café, and Rafe had stopped the man's bleeding aneurysm and saved his life.

Philip Arden had been there?

Cold slid down her spine.

Almost as if he were reading her mind, Rafe's arm circled her shoulder and pulled her snugly against his side. He leaned down to whisper in her ear.

"I don't think that man's collapse was an accident, Ami. I don't know how or why, but I think Arden set us up. Set you up," he corrected. "He couldn't know me from a hole in the wall. But he obviously knew who you were, and where you were."

Ami shuddered, her throat dry and tight. The implications of Rafe's words slammed into her.

She was being followed . . . by the Devil.

Why?

Rafe turned to Mahler. "I've never met your boss—former boss, that is—and I'm a paramedic, not some spiritual guru, so I have no idea what he's got against me. But I can tell you one thing: if he ever comes anywhere near Ami again, I absolutely will be his enemy."

He rubbed Ami's shoulder reassuringly, and she let herself lean a little more heavily into his solid body.

"So what can you tell us about Philip Arden, Mr. Mahler? What do we need to know to keep all hell from breaking loose?"

"Funny you should put it that way," Mahler replied, although Ami could clearly hear from the tone of his voice that he didn't find anything at all comical about Rafe's remark. "Because that's exactly what Philip is up to. He plans to use CardiaZone as the highway to hell for every human being with heart disease."

"CardiaZone?"

"That's what Niles wanted to call the drug he assumed I was testing in my trials," Ami explained to Rafe.

"Except that there is no drug," he finished for her. "You let him think that just so he wouldn't shut down your research."

Ami nodded.

"So how could Arden use a drug that doesn't exist?" Rafe asked Mahler.

"By marketing the same placebo Dr. Kim has tested," Mahler answered. "Dr. Kim's drug trials are the proof that CardiaZone works, so Calyx—the pharmaceutical firm that Dr. Villome had contracted with—will put the drug into production. You think they care if it's a sugar pill? As long as the documentation shows the pill is a success, they'll produce it. It won't be the first time that a useless drug has been prescribed for patients. Look at the list of antidepressants on pharmacies' shelves—research has shown several of them to be no more effective at treating depression than placebos."

Mahler sighed. "It'll be like any other prescription medication—you have to read the fine print to find out how to properly use it."

His shoulders lifted in a small shrug. "How many people do you know who take the time to read all the fine print? Quick fixes are what people expect today. If a drug is approved and available, it must work. Even if the prayer protocol instructions were included—and my guess is that Philip plans to make sure that part of the medical directive is missing—too few patients would read it and use it correctly and consistently."

"But without prayer, there's no healing," Rafe objected. "The reason Ami used a pill at all is to give it to people who need something material to trust in while they do the hard work of transforming themselves neurologically and spiritually. It's a crutch—a temporary crutch."

"Which is exactly what Arden wants," Ami guessed. "He wants people to trust in the drug alone, the crutch itself, so that they don't apply themselves to the hard work of changing."

She saw Mahler nod his head in agreement with her.

"Arden doesn't want anyone to be healed, Rafe," she concluded, her voice taut with a growing anger. "He wants people to trust in the wrong thing, because then they'll die, and he wants people to die."

She looked at Mahler.

"Including you."

"I know," he replied. "I finally jumped ship, and he didn't like it at all."

Ami studied the man in the bed, noting that his color was already improving. Surviving multiple cardiac events in one day was nothing short of amazing, but to argue with the Devil himself and live to tell the tale?

That was miraculous.

"Why did you jump ship, Mr. Mahler?"

As Ami waited for his response, she realized that Rafe had gone perfectly still beside her, as though Mahler's answer was the one piece of information he'd been waiting for since entering the man's room.

"An odd thing happened to me when I thought I was dying . . . the second time, I think it was," Mahler said. "I saw a light that I can't even begin to describe to you, and I heard a word: forgiveness."

He closed his eyes for a moment, then reopened them.

"Considering my long and dedicated career as Philip's right-hand man, the last thing I could expect to find in this world would be forgiveness for all the sins I've committed. But I still didn't really understand just how much was really at stake for me until Philip told me I'd sold him my soul a long time ago."

Mahler shook his head.

"I thought he was being melodramatic, but suddenly it all made sense. Terrifying sense. The growing doubts I've had about working for him in the past few months . . . Philip's rage when he told me that the prayer protocol would cost him everything . . . his fury about some enemy coming on the scene who could save souls . . . the hatred that disfigured him, literally. I realized three things: evil is personal, his name is Philip Arden, and the only way I wanted to die was to be embracing light, not darkness."

He took a deep breath and blew it out through parted lips.

"I found out I was right, you know. Forgiveness was the last thing I found in this world. But now that I have found it, I'm hanging on to it."

His eyes sought Ami's. "Will you teach me your prayer protocol, Dr. Kim? My brain needs rewiring, now that my heart . . . and soul . . . is beating again."

He focused his attention back on Rafe, again narrowing his eyes.

"Do you always throw off those green sparks like that, or just after saving someone's life?" Mahler frowned. "I can't say I was happy about it at the moment, but that was quite a jolt you gave me, St. Raphael, and I thank you nonetheless."

Ami felt her eyes widen and her mouth fall open.

Mahler smiled at Ami's surprised expression. "Almost dying will do that to you, Doctor. You suddenly see things from a whole new perspective. Trust me."

He again addressed Rafe. "And the wings, Rafe—they're a dead giveaway—no pun intended. No wonder my old boss was upset—an angel showing up couldn't possibly be a good thing when you're the Devil."

Ami turned to Rafe, but his eyes were glued on Mahler. When he spoke, his words were so soft, only she could hear them. "I felt it," he whispered. "I felt the moment he was forgiven."

His voice dropped even lower. "I think I'm learning to discern spirits, Ami."

Before she could say a word, though, Mahler interrupted.

"Don't underestimate the Devil, Dr. Kim. He wants you dead, whether or not there's an archangel at your side. And the Devil almost always gets what he wants."

"He wants more than just Ami dead, though, doesn't he?" Rafe pressed. "He wants every trace of her research wiped out, because he can't allow the truth about prayer to become public knowledge. Prayer would cost him everything. If people knew the power of prayer, they'd turn to God in droves. The Devil would be obsolete, and he can't let that happen."

Ami's gut began to knot in fear as she sensed where Rafe was heading. "The assassin," she whispered. "You think the assassin is Philip Arden . . . the Devil?"

"What assassin?" Mahler asked.

Ami noted the fatigue in his voice and knew they couldn't quiz him much longer. The man desperately needed rest.

"Niles was murdered, here in the hospital, just after he finished your angioplasty." She swallowed past the lump in her throat. "He was killed with a fast-acting biotoxin."

"And then Philip tried to kill me," Mahler added. He looked up at the ceiling. "He's cleaning the slate."

"But there are so many people involved in my work," Ami protested. "He can't possibly go after all of them."

Mahler let out a bitter laugh.

"Oh, no, Dr. Kim, he won't go after all of them himself. He has help. He always has help. He used to have me. I have no doubt he's got someone else on his payroll now—probably the assassin who killed Dr. Villome. Philip wouldn't risk getting anywhere near a biotoxin himself."

He winced, whether from pain or memory, Ami couldn't be sure.

"He's a survivor, Dr. Kim," Mahler reminded her, his voice beginning to slur. "If nothing else, he's a survivor."

Ami put her hand on Rafe's arm, intending to steer him out of the room so Mahler could sleep. But before she could take a step, the man in the bed seemed to rally, his eyes suddenly sharp on hers.

"The Nguyens," he said. "He knows about them. That's where he'll start."

Ami's hand tightened on Rafe's arm, fear clutching at her heart.

"That's impossible," she told him. "He couldn't possibly know about them. Niles didn't even know about them."

"He knows," Mahler assured her, "because I told him. I've had an eye on you and your research as long as Philip has. Longer, actually. The Nguyens are dead men, Dr. Kim."

She turned on her heel and marched straight into the room's bathroom.

She didn't care who heard her retching into the toilet.

CHAPTER FORTY-TWO

Brad Elefsson pulled up the collar of his jacket and headed out to the parking lot that was closest to the pharmacy college buildings.

"One more year," he muttered to himself. "One more year of class and I can take my boards, find a sweet job in some nice warm drugstore, and hang up my diploma on the back wall. Goodbye minimum wage and hello nice salary with benefits."

He looked out over the lamplit lot and its sea of cars, trying to remember exactly where he'd parked that morning. Piles of dirty snow edged the lot on all sides, and Brad involuntarily shuddered at the idea that spring was still a long way away. Despite its low pay, Brad liked his part-time receptionist job with the pharmacy college; not only did it make the time go faster between classes, but it helped pay the bills while he finished school, and he'd made a lot of contacts with the pharmaceutical bigwigs who visited the university on a regular basis. With a little luck and probably a multitude of phone calls, Brad was pretty confident he'd land that first job quickly enough once he graduated.

He rubbed his hands together, folded them into one fist, and brought it against his lips for a shot of warm air from his mouth. When he'd left the apartment for his first class of the day, he'd been running late as usual and forgotten to grab gloves from the hallway closet. Fortunately, his parking place wasn't much further, and he could already imagine how good that heater was going to feel on his hands and feet. He shifted the backpack he'd slung over his left shoulder and saw the flashing lights of a vehicle parked a few rows over from his own car. At first glance, he assumed it was the parking patrol checking for cars without authorized tags hanging from their rear-view mirrors, but then he realized that the throbbing lights on the vehicle's roof were the red and blue of an emergency vehicle and not the yellow of the parking attendants. There was some kind of trouble in the parking lot.

He kept walking towards his car, his neck craned to one side trying to get a glimpse of the scene.

He never saw the brown-haired woman approaching him from between the cars as he passed. By the time he registered that someone was right behind him, it was too late. The silenced bullets knocked the wind out of him and he dropped to the parking lot's surface.

Dead.

CHAPTER FORTY-THREE

Rafe heard the quiet click of the bathroom door shutting itself behind Ami.

"You can't let him win this, Rafe," Mahler rasped, his eyes drooping closed. "You have to stop him."

"I know," he replied. He touched the man's shoulder gently. "Pray for us, Mr. Mahler. We're going to need it."

In mid-nod, he fell asleep, and Rafe sat down in the chair by the bed. He threw a glance towards the bathroom, where he could hear water running into a sink. He'd give Ami a few minutes to pull herself together before he'd go and knock on the door to check on her. The good Lord knew she needed a few moments to herself right now.

Just like Rafe did.

He leaned forward in the chair and cradled his shaved head in his hands. Where should he start sorting through everything that had happened in the last few hours?

He'd met a roomful of recovering alcoholics and discovered that Ami had harnessed the power of prayer to heal damaged hearts by applying cutting-edge research in neurophysiology.

He'd saved the lives of two men; in so doing, he'd painted a target on himself with the first miracle and almost been knocked to the ground the second time by the saving grace of God in action.

Ami's partner—her husband—was dead, and now she and her patients were also on a killer's to-do list.

Last, but certainly not least, the Devil himself was on their trail, with plans to make Ami's medical breakthrough the newest scourge of the earth.

And Diedrich Mahler had told Rafe he had wings.

Yes, sir, that just about covered it.

Except for the part where he realized he was in love with Ami Kim and that she already knew it.

Minneapolis sure had a lot going on, Rafe ruefully told himself. That winter festival thing that Ami had mentioned on the plane yesterday was sounding pretty good right about now. He'd much rather be cuddled up with Ami in a blanket watching some dogsled races on the Capitol's lawn in St. Paul than be sitting here in a hospital next to a man who'd won only a brief reprieve from his former employer's deadly attention.

Because there was no doubt in Rafe's mind that when—no "if" about it—Philip Arden learned that Diedrich Mahler was still alive, he'd be back to finish the job, along with anyone else who got in his way.

Which added one more person to the growing list of people that Rafe needed to protect from the Devil.

He walked over to the bathroom door and tapped on it lightly, then pushed it open to find Ami standing in front of the room's small sink, wiping her face with a moistened paper towel.

"We need to get out of here," he told her, meeting her eyes in the mirror over the water basin. "We need to put together a plan, and we needed it yesterday."

He noted the red rimming her eyes as she wiped her nose and then turned towards him. "I'm responsible—"

"For curing heart disease," he said over her, cutting off the words he knew she was going to say. "That's what you're responsible for, Ami. For healing. For teaching patients how to use their minds, their spirits, to touch God. You're not responsible for this . . . evil . . . that's pursuing you."

He took her hand and drew her out of the tiny bathroom with him.

"He's in danger, too," he said, his head tilting in Mahler's direction. "So you're going to tell the nurses to put a lid on any information about him. Nobody says anything to anyone about Diedrich Mahler until you say so. You can do that, right?"

Ami nodded.

"Then we're going back to your office," he told her. "We're going to put together a list of every patient you've had in the drug trials, every technician you've recruited, and the name of every person who works with you in the hospital or lab."

Ami's white face went even paler. "He can't possibly—"

"Yes, he can," Rafe cut her off again. "Mahler warned us about underestimating Arden, and we're not going to make that mistake. I'm sick and tired of feeling at least two steps behind this guy, Ami. From here on in, we're on the offense, not the defense."

He gave her hand a hard squeeze. "I'm going to do this, Ami. I told you I'd keep you safe, and I meant it. Even if I have to beat the Devil to do it."

He turned away and headed into the hospital corridor, almost colliding with two nurses hurrying towards the floor's central nursing station. One of them was the same woman he'd spoken with earlier in Mahler's room after the rest of the cardiac team had moved on.

"Sorry," he said, quickly sidestepping to avoid knocking her down.

"Don't worry," she called back. "Like I said, it's been a crazy day in here, and now it sounds like it's contagious. Two critically wounded men were just brought into the ER downstairs. One shot, one stabbed."

Rafe felt Ami's fingers clutch at his left bicep. He looked down into her face, fear stark in her eyes.

"We'll find out," he promised her in answer to the question he knew she needed to ask, but couldn't bring herself to voice. "We'll find out who they are, Ami. Talk to the nurses about Mahler, and we're out of here."

Without a word, she walked briskly to the station to talk to the charge nurse about assuming care for her deceased partner's patient. Ami was bucking up, Rafe noted with relief. The doctor was tough.

But then, he already knew that. From what he could see of the supervisor's reactions to Ami's directions, it was also plain that Dr. Kim had the respect of her coworkers. Neither the charge nurse nor the other personnel at the desk seemed surprised at Ami's instructions that information about her patient should be released to absolutely no one; the only comment the supervisor made was to offer her sympathies to Ami about Niles.

Rafe didn't catch Ami's reply, but he could see her briefly nod to the woman before she signed the paperwork for Mahler. A moment later, they were hustling down the stairwell on their way to the emergency room.

"It's faster than the elevator," Ami said, her hands barely skimming the railings as she led Rafe to the ground floor facility, taking the stairs at a quick clip. "I know it's probably hard on that knee of yours, but it's the shortest route, too."

"No apologies necessary."

He pounded down the stairs behind her, looking up into the corners of each landing as he swung by, reassured to find security cameras recording their passing. He didn't think they were in any danger in the empty stairwell, but just knowing that someone else had an eye on them was comforting.

As long as it wasn't the eye of Philip Arden.

Then Rafe thought of something else that would be even more comforting to him at this particular moment.

A gun.

If he was going to be tracking down an assassin, that cold metal would feel awfully good in his hand. Rafe was a sure shot, a skill that had been tested more than once during his tours in combat zones. As a medic, he'd only fired when fired upon, but he had no doubt that if he came face-to-face with the assassin that was tracking Ami, he wouldn't hesitate to pull the trigger first. Protecting Ami was his mission, and even if he wasn't a bona fide guardian angel, he was going to keep her safe.

Even if he had to die to do it, which would really be a shame since he was in love with Ami and was already wondering what the housing market in Minneapolis looked like.

He could call his mama, invite her up here. She'd no doubt find the perfect spot for Rafe and Ami and her future grand-children.

Rafe took a corner too fast and banged his hip against the iron railing.

"Ow!"

"Just two more flights," Ami called back to him.

Focus, man.

He wasn't going to be any good to anyone if he didn't stay focused on what lay ahead. What had Mahler said?

Don't underestimate the Devil.

Right. He was going to have to keep each one of his brain cells on red alert if he was going to pull Ami and himself through this nightmare. How did you fight the Devil, anyway? Was he even physically real, with substance, flesh and bone? Or was he just a clever mirage, a trick of a hologram?

Rafe watched Ami fly down the stairs just in front of him. She'd met Philip Arden only momentarily and recognized him immediately for who he was, thanks to her gift of spiritual discernment. Mahler had worked with Arden for decades, but had never guessed his true identity until he'd cheated death a third time and experienced forgiveness.

Until he'd embraced the light and saved his soul.

And Rafe had felt it the moment it happened.

Another remark of Mahler's popped into Rafe's head. He'd said that Arden had claimed that Rafe could save souls.

But that was a lie.

Rafe was a healer, a modern-day St. Raphael. There was only one Savior.

He clutched the stairway railing as he rounded a landing, and his mama's voice popped into his head.

'That's true, baby boy, but He works through the hearts and hands of his people, right here and right now, and that includes you. Don't you ever forget it, you hear me?'

"Yes, ma'am," he responded under his breath. "I hear you."

All right. So Rafe Greene was not only an archangel, he was a channel of peace.

Although if that was true, why did he still wish he had a gun?

God helps those who help themselves?

In front of him, Ami skidded to a stop and yanked open the door to the ground floor emergency department.

"Where can I get a gun?"

Her hand still on the door handle, she turned to look at Rafe. "A gun?"

"Yes. A gun," he repeated. "If someone's going to try to kill us, I want a fighting chance, Ami."

She paused for a second on the threshold.

"There's one at my apartment."

She didn't wait for his response before she turned and strode into the emergency unit.

Rafe stared after her in surprise for only a moment before he followed her inside.

Everyone in the department was in motion.

Nurses and doctors darted in and out of curtained cubicles while technicians rolled in carts loaded with diagnostic equipment. Two police officers were questioning the paramedic who had apparently brought one of the victims in, his shirtfront covered in drying blood. While he talked, a nurse passed by and handed him a clean scrub top. He laid it on a nearby desk so it would stay clean until he could get himself washed up. Another man, this one wearing the medical center's security uniform, was walking in tight circles near the triage desk, raking his hands through his hair, murmuring something to himself.

Ami walked up to the security man and laid a hand on his arm. "I'm Dr. Kim," she said. "Do we have the names of the two men who were attacked? I need to know if they're patients of mine."

"They're not patients," he told her. "They were in the designated parking lot for the pharmacy college. That's where we found them."

Ami felt dizzy with relief. Not her patients. Not Chinh Nguyen.

But Hung was a pharmacy student.

And Mahler said the Nguyens were dead men.

Ami's stomach clenched and she spun to face the row of curtained cubicles that lined this side of the ER suite. Which ones held the men from the parking lot? Out of the corner of her eye, she saw a doctor she knew pulling one of the curtains tightly closed behind her before she headed in Ami's direction, her head bowed over a clipboard.

"Karen."

Ami stepped directly in front of the ER doctor.

"I'm looking for a pharmacy student. His name is Hung Nguyen. Is he in here? Is he one of the men being treated from the parking lot?"

Karen shook her head. "Nobody's being treated, Ami."

"But I heard that one was a gunshot victim and the other was stabbed."

"They're not being treated because they're dead. Both of them."

Ami took a step back, momentarily stunned. "The names? Do you have their names?"

"I only know the name of the . . . patient . . . that I just left: Brad Elefsson. He's . . . was . . . a student at the pharmacy college. Apparently he had a work study job in the college's offices and had just gotten off his shift."

"What about the other man?"

Again, Karen shook her head.

"I don't know. I think we're all in shock that something like this happened right on our doorstep. Makes you not want to leave the building, almost. Either that, or never come back in." She nodded toward the nurse at the triage desk behind Ami. "If the other man's been identified, Ronda will know."

Before Ami could turn to the nurse to ask, however, Rafe appeared at her elbow and steered her towards the exit door.

"We need to leave," he told her.

"But I need to find out—"

"Hung Nguyen is dead, Ami. Someone slipped a stiletto right through his ribcage and into his heart."

Ami would have tripped over her own feet if Rafe hadn't been almost dragging her out the same door they'd used to enter the unit. She looked up at his face, his eyes dark and his expression grim.

"I heard the police and the paramedic talking about it," he said. "Whoever was parked next to Hung's car spotted him lying on the ground. He thought maybe Hung had fallen on the ice and knocked himself unconscious, until he noticed blood seeping around the body. He called 911 and the whole crew hightailed it out to the lot."

Cold air smacked Ami's cheeks as Rafe pulled her through the outside exit door opposite the emergency department entry from the stairwell and out into an already dimming dusk.

"Next thing everyone knew, there was another body a couple rows away," Rafe continued, still hustling her along. "That one had a bullet hole blasted through the back of the coat. Nobody heard any shots, but that's probably not a surprise given the commotion surrounding Hung's body."

He glanced down at her and slackened his pace. Ami gulped in a chilly breath of air and tried to figure out exactly where they were in the medical complex. As best as she could tell, they were going in the opposite direction of her office.

"Or more likely," Rafe added, "the killer used a suppressor and took advantage of the confusion to shoot his victim. That's what a professional would do."

Ami stopped trotting alongside Rafe, planting her shoes firmly on the sidewalk.

"You think it's the assassin, don't you? Arden's man?"

"Yes, I do," he said. "Hung Nguyen was killed, Ami, only yards away from a building full of people, and no one even knew it was happening. That's not some knee-jerk, random act of violence—that's coldly calculated murder. Mahler told us both Nguyens were targets. Why wouldn't I assume it was Arden's hired gun that killed Hung practically in plain view?"

"Because I don't know the other victim!" she said in frustration. "If these murders are because of my NRT research, why would someone I don't know get killed?"

"Because he was in the wrong place at the wrong time?"

Rafe grabbed Ami's hand and started pulling her along again.

"Maybe this Brad kid saw the killer with Hung, and maybe the killer saw that Brad saw him and wasn't about to leave any witnesses. This isn't a game with rules, Ami. This is scorched earth, and anyone who treads on it is going to be burned."

"We have to find Chinh, Rafe," Ami protested. "Now. Mahler said the Nguyens were dead, and he was right. Hung's dead. We have to find Chinh and warn him, make sure he's safe."

"Do you have his number on your cell phone?"

"No, but it's in my office."

Rafe paused for a moment. "You've got a receptionist on duty till five o'clock, right?"

"Yes."

"So no one is going to go through your files while she's there, and with a common name like Nguyen, Arden or his assassin won't be able to single Chinh out from any listings in a phone book," he reasoned. "My guess is that since they know he's a janitor, they're just going to wait for him to come into work. They knew where Hung would be, so we have to assume they've got Chinh's schedule, too."

"We have to call Chinh and tell him to stay home."

Rafe shook his head."No, we want Chinh to come in, Ami. Because I'll be waiting with him."

She looked up at his profile in the dusk.

"You think you're going to set up a trap for an assassin? Are you crazy?"

"Not crazy," he said. "Desperate. I can make this work, Ami. I have the skills, believe me, and if we can grab the assassin, we can get to Arden."

Again, Ami came to a halt.

"I'm not letting you risk Chinh's life or yours, either, Rafe. We're calling in the police."

"No, we're not," he argued. "Think about it. The police have their hands full with three murders in the last few hours. You think they're going to drop everything to listen to us explain that the Devil has a hit list right here at the medical center? And even if someone would listen, by the time we could explain what's going on, it'll be too late. Chinh will be dead and Arden's assassin will already be targeting the next person on the list." He paused. "Which could very easily be you."

He took Ami's shoulders in his hands and met her worried gaze.

"This is the best chance we've got to stop this massacre before it goes any further. We can do this, Ami."

She searched his eyes for assurance and thought about the three dead men.

"I don't want anyone else to die," she whispered. "Not Chinh, not you. Not anyone."

"Neither do I, and that's why I'm going to make this work. So we need to hustle."

He steered her away from the direction back to her clinic.

"Where are we going?" she asked. "My office is back there. I thought you were going to set up an ambush."

"I am, but first we're catching a cab to your condo. I need your gun, Ami."

He glanced up at the sliver of moon that was already rising high in the sky and led her towards a parking ramp. "There's a cab stand on the other side of the ramp. It's where I was dropped off this morning. And if you're wondering why we're not taking your car, it's because I'm pretty sure Arden must have placed a tracking device on it somehow, since there's no other way he could have known we were in that café for lunch."

Five minutes later, Rafe held the door open for Ami as she climbed into the back seat of the taxi he hailed. He slid in next to her, his body heat instantly warming the small space, filling Ami with a sense of profound security that she really didn't want to analyze at the moment. It was difficult enough for her to acknowledge how attracted she was to Rafe after such a short time—knowing for a fact that he had strong feelings for her, too, only served to set off a louder alarm in her head. The only other time in her life that she had thrown caution to the wind in a matter of the heart was the day she'd married Niles, and the outcome of that had been a disaster from which she still carried emotional scars.

But now Niles was dead, and Ami would have to wrap her understanding around what that would mean for her, both professionally and personally.

At least, she hoped she would have a chance to figure it all out.

But first, she had to make sure that she, Rafe, and her patients survived Philip Arden's scorched earth policy.

Ami felt Rafe's strong hand cover hers, reminding her she was not alone in this battle. She looked out the taxi's side window already beginning to frost with her breath and watched darkness fall on the city.

CHAPTER FORTY-FOUR

I have some good news and some bad news," Vi said when her employer answered his phone.

"What is it?"

Vi held the phone away from her head to look at it. Judging from his snapping tone, Philip's foul mood had not improved since the last time she'd spoken with him. She knew that his visit with his man Mahler had upset him, adding fuel to whatever fire Philip had been stoking after leaving the café where Dr. Kim and her companion had done their medical duty. Why that particular scene so infuriated Philip, Vi had no idea. He obviously knew the woman was a doctor, so to find her exercising those skills shouldn't have come as a surprise, yet Philip's reaction was clearly that: surprise.

Surprise, but with a strong dose of anger thrown in.

And fear.

Vi wondered again at that brief ghost she'd seen in Philip's eyes as they'd hurriedly left the diner. He'd plainly seen something that troubled him.

And then Vi remembered something else.

Philip had known that Dr. Kim was going to be involved in an emergency situation in the diner . . . before it happened.

They were walking to the restaurant, trying to decide how to introduce themselves to the cardiologist, and Philip had said something about a diversion. Then he'd said they should "witness the good doctor in action."

And then a man collapsed the moment they walked into the place.

How weird was that?

"The good news is that I just gave you a two-for-one deal," she said into the phone, deliberately ignoring his rude greeting and hoping her news would lighten him up even a little bit. "The bad news is that one of the two wasn't the janitor."

Silence filled the phone line.

Vi waited.

"When can I expect the janitor?" he finally asked, his voice back to its normal velvety tone.

Vi smiled. "In plenty of time for me to meet you for a late"— she paused for emphasis—"intimate dinner."

She heard Philip's rich, low laughter at the other end of the connection.

"You think you can make me happy, don't you, Vi?"

Vi checked her watch. It was almost five o'clock. She needed to get into position for her next kill, which meant inserting herself into the Heart Partners' offices just after their receptionist locked up. She'd take some time to familiarize herself with the clinic's layout before she decided on her method for killing the janitor and the subsequent cleanup.

Then, over that late dinner, Vi would spell out for Philip how Dr. Ami Kim was going to be involved in a fatal car accident sometime during the night. She didn't have all the details worked out yet, but it wasn't going to take much, especially when she knew exactly where Kim's car was, thanks to the little device she'd attached to it last night. It was the dead of winter, after all, and everyone knew that icy roads could be treacherous.

Murderous, even.

As for the big man who'd been at Kim's side all day, perhaps Vi would luck out and he'd be in the car with the doctor at the time of the accident. If not, Vi would just have to see what else she had in her bag of tricks for him. One way or the other, Rafe Greene wasn't going to live past the next twenty-four hours.

"I don't think it, Philip," she corrected him, returning to their conversation. "I know it. And after tonight, so will you."

She cut the connection and drove out of the pharmacy college's parking lot. The yellow crime-scene tape that blocked the lanes a few rows over gleamed dully under the soft lights of the parking lot lamps. As she exited the lot, she removed the parking tag that she'd attached to her rear-view mirror and slipped it under the driver's seat. Students really should remember to lock their cars, she reflected. It didn't take much for a thief . . . or an assassin . . . to steal a tag when the car was left unlocked.

CHAPTER FORTY-FIVE

Ami led Rafe out of the elevator to her condo door, where she began to fish in her shoulder bag for her key. When she pulled her keychain out, Rafe plucked it from her fingers.

"I'm going in first," he told her. "I want you to stay out here until I tell you to come in."

"Are you joking?"

In reply, he pushed her gently away from the door, so that she would be standing with her back to the wall next to the doorframe.

"I wish I were," he said. "It's not exactly my preferred style of entrance into a woman's apartment, but given our experiences today, I'll make an exception. Where are the light switches when I get inside?"

"To your immediate left."

He put the key in the lock and soundlessly opened the door just wide enough for him to slip into the condo. Ami pressed her ear to the wall and strained to hear him moving around inside, but heard nothing other than the accelerated beat of her own heart.

Could an assassin be waiting for them?

In her own home?

Rafe was convinced that Arden had planted a tracker on her car, which was unsettling enough, but when she tried to figure out when Arden could have done that, all she could come up with was an even more disturbing idea: the easiest place to bug someone's car would be in their own garage. Anywhere else, how would someone know which car was Ami's? Even if someone followed her into work at the medical center, that someone would still have to find an opportunity to plant a bug when no one was around, and that was virtually never.

Her underground condo lot, on the other hand, was usually deserted, and each slot was labeled with its corresponding unit number. A quick look at the front lobby's wall of mailboxes with occupants' last names clearly marked on them would be all it took to identify Ami's assigned spot.

Which meant that the Devil not only knew where she lived, but had gotten access into her garage.

And if that were possible, then so was entry into her condo itself.

Maybe it was time to start looking for a new place to live.

Even as the thought occurred to her, the lights inside her home went on, and Rafe pulled the door wide open.

"All clear, ma'am." He stepped back to let Ami into the small foyer. "Except for the kitchen counter. I think you might want to toss that milk that's been sitting out since your breakfast."

She stepped into her condo, and despite Rafe's assurance that nothing was amiss inside, she couldn't quite banish the feeling of uncomfortable vulnerability that had suddenly taken hold of her imagination. Supposedly, her condo building was secure. Entry was only possible with a key to the front door or with the code to the underground parking garage. Yet Niles had shown up at her door last night—an obvious clue that a key and a code weren't nearly enough to keep out those who didn't belong there.

And if an inebriated Niles had been able to gain entry, what was there to stop someone else from doing the same?

Especially if that someone was an assassin.

Or the Devil himself.

Ami dropped her purse near the front door and deliberately pushed away her disturbing thoughts. In an effort to dispel the haunting idea that her home might no longer be a safe space for her, she tried to match Rafe's levity.

"Oh, so now you're the kitchen police along with my security patrol? Please tell me you didn't see the bathroom yet."

Rafe grinned. "Sorry to embarrass you, but yes, I did. Hey, don't worry about it," he said as she felt a hot blush rise on her cheeks. "I have a bunch of sisters, remember? They always had their underwear drying over the shower rod."

He threw the deadbolt on the front door.

"Though I don't recall any of them having the colors you've got."

It took Ami a minute to find her voice.

"I'm getting the gun."

Rafe laughed. "Uh-oh. Did I say the wrong thing?"

She threw him an icy look. "It means I'm changing the subject. If I'm not mistaken, we did come here for a reason other than to comment on my housekeeping skills, or lack thereof."

Rafe's eyes bored into hers, his tone suddenly serious. "Yes, we did, and that brings me to my next question: why do you have a gun?"

She turned and headed for the kitchen.

"It's not mine," she said over her shoulder.

"Gee, that makes me feel better," he called after her. "Does that mean you're just keeping it for a friend?"

When she didn't reply, Rafe followed her into the kitchen he'd already checked out before letting her into the condo. In the darkness, it had been a smooth wall of appliances and cabinets circling a center island; in the brightness of its strategically-placed track lighting, the kitchen looked like a spread from a home decorator's magazine.

"Wow. This is beautiful," he told her. "You must love cooking in here. If my mama saw this, she'd think she'd died and gone to kitchen heaven."

"That's what I thought when I bought the condo," Ami said, pulling out a drawer on the other side of the island. "I actually like to cook, but I've been so busy with my research, I barely have time to make a peanut butter sandwich in here."

"So you just use the kitchen to store your friends' guns, now?"

She made a face at him and pointed at the open drawer. "I don't want to pick it up, if you don't mind."

Rafe came around the side of the island to stand next to Ami and then reached into the drawer.

The gun was a Heckler and Koch P2000. It fit neatly in Rafe's hand as he turned it from side to side to examine its features. Smaller than most of the pistols he'd learned to shoot as a Marine, the P2000 was designed primarily for police officers and commercial users. Pointing it down and in the opposite direction from Ami, he unchambered the round and popped out the magazine, emptied the bullets into his hand, then reassembled it empty.

"Nice gun."

He dropped the bullets into his jacket pocket.

"But you don't want to store it with the bullets loaded, Ami. It's just not a good idea."

"Niles brought it over here last night," she said.

Rafe could feel his eyebrows rise in surprise. "Last night?"

Ami nodded, her eyes on the gun in Rafe's hand. "He showed up really late, drunk. He said he was worried about me, that he'd seen the newscast on television and wanted to be sure I was all right."

Her voice trembled, and Rafe waited for her to continue as he watched her bite her lower lip and try to stem the tears that were forming in her eyes. When she seemed to be losing the battle, he carefully laid the gun on the island's countertop and wrapped his arms around her shoulders.

"You should go ahead and cry, Ami. Now is a good time for it. Nobody else is around, and I'll hold you as long as it takes."

He felt her arms slip around his waist and her face pressed into his chest. Quiet sobs filled the designer kitchen as Ami's grief washed over Rafe. Without willing it at all, he could feel tears in his own eyes and his chest tightened with sorrow. He hadn't known Niles at all, yet he could feel Ami's emotions almost as sharply as if they were his.

Well, this part of discerning spirits isn't a big plus, he thought, wondering if there were any way he could control which spirits he discerned. *I'll take the happy thoughts, thank you very much.* Especially since he already had plenty of bad ones rolling around in his head.

He looked at the gun lying on the counter and wished it had come with a battalion of Marines. Maybe then he'd at least have a chance at protecting all the people associated with Ami's research. As the odds stood, though, he figured only one person had a good shot at walking away from the Devil alive, and that was going to be Ami.

No matter what it took, he was going to make sure of it.

Too bad his mama wasn't going to get to see this kitchen, though. It really was nice.

In his arms, Ami sniffled and lifted her head to look into his eyes. "A gun isn't nearly enough, Rafe."

"I know," he said, "I was just wishing I could call in some reinforcements, but I don't know anybody in the Twin Cities. It looks like we're the only game in town."

Ami stared into his shirt front, her eyes narrowing in concentration.

"No," she said slowly, "we're not."

She looked up at him again, her eyes firing with excitement. "We do have reinforcements, Rafe. And, even better, we have something that Arden can't fight."

She broke out of his arms and ran back to the front door. A moment later, she was back in the kitchen, her cell phone in her hand.

"We're not thinking this through, Rafe," she said, her voice rising with excitement. "You said it yourself when we spoke with Mahler: prayer would cost Arden everything." She began punching in numbers. "And I just happen to know a whole boatload of people who are proven prayer experts."

He watched her put the phone to her ear, waiting for it to be answered at the other end of the connection.

She truly believed that prayer was going to save them.

But she was wrong. Prayer was neither fool- nor bullet-proof. Rafe knew that for a fact after watching his brother die in his arms. Some things, he'd finally learned, were held only in the hand of God.

"Ami," he gently told her, "I know you want to believe that anything is possible with prayer, and, in a way, your research is proving that, but believe me, prayers won't stop a bullet. Even if you have a roomful of your prayer technicians working at it."

She gave him a confused look, held up a finger for silence and listened to her phone. A second later, she snapped the cell phone shut and grabbed Rafe's arm.

"That was Jim, the professor you met this morning. Or rather, it was his message machine. He's not there, because he's at the lab for a therapy session tonight. With everything else today, I totally forgot about it."

"He's at the medical center?"

"Yes. He and his group. If everyone shows up, there will be seven technicians. This is perfect!"

Ami began tugging Rafe out of the kitchen towards the front door of the condo. He grabbed the gun off the counter and stuck it into his inside jacket pocket.

"I must be missing something here, because I would think the last place we want anyone associated with your research to be is anywhere near the medical center," he said as they went out into the building's corridor. "Ami, what is going on?"

She stopped in front of the door to the stairwell at the end of the hall. "I'm sorry about your knee, Rafe, but we've got to take the stairs again. They're faster."

She reached out to open the door, but Rafe caught her arm and turned her to face him. "Did you hear what I said?"

His voice was low, his eyes hard. "Prayer isn't going to stop the Devil, Ami. You're asking your prayer team to walk into the line of fire."

She grinned back at him. "We're not going to pray our way out of this, Rafe. We're going to call our way out. We're going to have every member of the NRT team calling as many media outlets as they can to tell their story about participating in my research trials. We're going to throw such a floodlight of attention on what prayer is doing in my lab that not even the Devil can withstand the glare of that much truth."

Rafe looked at her in growing astonishment as her strategy crystalized in his own head.

"It's the one thing he can't defeat," he said. "Truth. And the truth is that prayer heals."

"Yes! When you said we were the only game in town, I realized you were right, as long as we were talking about brute force. But then it occurred to me that deep down, that's not the game that Arden is playing. What matters to Arden is much, much bigger: the truth. Don't you see? He needs to keep prayer buried, and if the only way he can do that is to bury bodies along with it, so be it."

She laid a slim hand on Rafe's cheek. "There's only one way to fight his scorched earth policy, and that's to proclaim the truth."

"Shout the news from the housetops?"

She smiled. "Absolutely."

Rafe laid his own hand over hers. "No fear of reprimand or expulsion from the medical establishment?"

Her eyes glittered with joy. "Not at all. This research, this neurological knowledge, is my gift to give, and I'm going to give it whether or not the Devil himself approves."

Rafe turned his head to place a kiss in her palm.

"Now just keep me alive long enough to do it, St. Rafael," she said and slipped into the stairwell.

Rafe lifted a hand to check the pistol in his pocket and hustled down the steps behind her.

CHAPTER FORTY-SIX

Vi watched the receptionist lock the front door of the Heart Partners Clinic at five minutes past five o'clock in the evening.

She loved it when people kept the hours they advertised. It made her job so much easier.

As soon as the woman disappeared from view down the building corridor, Vi counted slowly to fifty before she gave herself the "all clear" to move towards the clinic door. A few seconds more and she had the lock picked and the door opened. Once inside, she quietly closed the door behind her and slipped soundlessly through the darkened lobby. She headed directly for the hallway she'd noted less than an hour ago when she'd "mistakenly" entered the clinic and claimed she was looking for the Health Partners offices.

"That clinic is on the opposite side of the medical center complex," the afternoon receptionist had informed her. "I'm sorry you came so far out of your way, especially so late in the day. Would you like me to give them a call and tell them you're on your way?"

"Oh, no," Vi had replied. "But thanks, anyway. I didn't have an appointment. I'm a new sales rep, and I'm still learning my way around here. I'll drop in on them tomorrow."

"Sorry again for the confusion," the receptionist said. "You know, the names of the clinics are so similar, I'm surprised we don't have more people showing up here by mistake."

Vi wasn't sorry at all, though. In the two minutes she was inside the clinic, she had memorized the lobby's floor plan and the location of the hallway that led back to the examination rooms and offices. She'd also scanned the In/Out board on the wall to the right of the woman at the front desk and mentally filed the fact that there were seven people on staff in this office, only two of whom were physicians: Doctors Villome and Kim. That told her that the other five people were nurses or clerical staff, making it highly unlikely that they'd linger in the offices past the clinic's regular hours. And that meant that when Vi came to work, she'd have the place to herself, which was exactly the way she liked it.

Once she was inside the hallway, she flicked on a penlight to guide her exploration of the clinic's interior rooms. A quick glance inside each of the examining rooms revealed a wall-mounted desk equipped with a sleek computer, two chairs, a sink and cupboards, and an exam table. Curious, she opened the drawer at the end of the table to find an assortment of medical tools and a box of disposable gloves. Deftly grabbing two of the gloves, she immediately pulled them on, then lifted an edge of her jacket to wipe the handle of the drawer. So far, she hadn't left any fingerprints anywhere that might link her to the day's three murders, but extra caution was never excessive in her line of work. Only the foolish or the arrogant thought they'd never get caught, and Vi was neither.

Niles Villome, on the other hand, had been both.

According to what she'd learned from Philip, the doctor had not only stolen the groundbreaking work of his partner, but he'd foolishly sold it to Calyx before all the test trials were complete. Exactly why Philip had wanted the doctor dead, she wasn't sure, nor did it matter. As long as Philip wired the money into her Swiss bank accounts, she was happy to take his assignments, no questions asked.

Although she did wonder what Ami Kim had done to earn Philip's ire, especially since it was her research that had produced the wonder drug that Philip aimed to own. Had the woman threatened to scuttle her research when she discovered her partner's betrayal? Or did Philip want her killed to insure he had sole control of CardiaZone?

Yet he had wanted to meet her earlier in the day. To Vi, it had even seemed that he was eager to forge some kind of working association with Kim. Not until the chaotic scene at the diner when she and her companion, Rafe Greene, assisted the collapsed man, did Philip lose his interest in making the doctor's acquaintance.

Again, Vi recalled Philip's furious response. It seemed . . . personal . . . somehow.

Impossible, she told herself.

In the few years she'd worked for Philip, she'd never seen the man get personal about anything. That, in fact, was part of his allure for her, Vi had to admit. She'd never met anyone colder, more calculating, or as invulnerable as Philip Arden. He was power personified, and Vi loved power. Every time she killed, she felt the rush of total control flooding through her body, filling her with a sensory thrill the likes of which she'd never found in anything else. The more she'd worked with Philip, the more she began to fantasize what it would feel like to bring his power to heel before her, to control the man himself. She was certain he was likewise attracted to her, yet before she'd witnessed his momentary lapse when they left the diner, she'd feared she'd never find the crack in his armor that would enable her to breach his own defenses.

But now she knew the crack, and it was named Rafe Greene.

And she was sure, if she played this just right, that crack was going to be her ticket into an incredibly close and personally gratifying relationship with Philip Arden.

By the time this whole Minneapolis job was over, in fact, Vi planned to own her boss, body and soul.

Because not only was she going to get rid of Ami Kim for her employer, but she was also going to serve him Rafe Greene's head on a silver platter.

All she had to do was figure out how.

Fortunately for her, Vi was exceptionally good at figuring out "how."

She returned her attention to exploring the corridor linking the examining rooms and the doctors' private offices. Two doors led to closets stacked with medical and clerical supplies, while a third door was marked "Office Manager." Beyond that room were the doctors' offices—one for Villome and one for Kim. Vi didn't bother with the dead doctor's space, guessing that when the janitor came, he would probably avoid it after learning of the man's death. Instead, she picked the lock on the remaining door, and once inside, she closed it softly behind her. Her hand brushed the wall until it located the light switch and flipped it on.

A cursory look around the room was all it took to convince her that she'd found the perfect spot to wait for Chinh Nguyen's appearance. She turned the lights out and walked across the thick, sound-absorbing carpet to the massive desk that dominated the room. When it grew close to eight o'clock, she would walk over and stand where she'd be hidden behind the door when the unsuspecting janitor swung it open to begin his nightly cleaning duties. As soon as he crossed the threshold, Vi would step out from around the door and loop a deadly garrote around his neck. A tight tug, and the man's windpipe would be shut off. If he struggled too long, she'd use the same stiletto she'd put into his grandson in the parking lot to finish it off.

Trailing her gloved fingers along the edge of the desk, Vi worked her way around the piece of furniture until her legs encountered the leather chair behind it. She sat down in the chair, relishing its firm support and surprisingly comfortable fit for her slight frame. Usually desk chairs were too big or stiff for her, but Ami Kim's chair fit her like a pair of favorite old shoes. She briefly recalled the subtle pastels she'd noted in the carpet during her brief look in the light, and silently complimented the doctor on her choice of décor. Hopefully, she wouldn't have to resort to the stiletto.

Bleaching blood stains out of that carpet would be almost impossible.

A moment later, Vi stood up and walked back into the clinic lobby. Remembering the layout she'd memorized earlier, she made her way across the dark space to a counter along the far wall. Shielding her penlight's tiny illumination with her hand, she located the small refrigerator situated beneath the counter and quickly reached inside to grab a bottle of water. Thanks to her busy day, she'd missed lunch, and the only food she'd eaten had been two peanut butter granola bars from a vending machine in the pharmacy building. She unscrewed the cap and just as she lifted the bottle to her lips for a drink, she caught a distant sound beyond the office walls.

Someone was coming in this direction.

She darted for the inner corridor back to her hiding place in the doctor's private office.

CHAPTER FORTY-SEVEN

I thought you said that everyone would be up in the neurology lab by now," Rafe reminded Ami as she hurried down the deserted hallway to the Heart Partners Clinic. "So why are we making a detour to your office first?"

Ami halted in front of the clinic's door and rummaged in her shoulder bag for a second or two before pulling out a key ring.

"I need the list of media contacts we keep. Believe me, we'll be more successful in reaching the right people by using the list than by trying to locate reporters through staff directories, especially after regular working hours like it is now."

She inserted the key and pushed the door open.

"Niles spent years developing those contacts, trying to find the most direct route to becoming the media's medical darling. Whenever I said he was wasting his time, he said it was an investment in the clinic's future—that any time the press needed a sound bite about a cardiology breakthrough, he wanted to be the expert they called. It was good PR, he said."

She flipped the bank of switches on the wall to the up position and the clinic lobby lit up.

"He always said you never knew when you were going to need a PR cheat sheet. Turns out he was right," she added. "Except that I'm the one who needs it, not Niles."

She walked over to the doorway that led to the corridor between the examining rooms and offices.

"Let me just pull a hard copy from the filing cabinet, and we'll be on our way upstairs," she told him. "Do you need to rest your knee? This might take a minute or two."

"I'll survive," Rafe said, looking around the vacant lobby.

When he'd been in here earlier in the day waiting for Ami, it had been bustling with clients, and the press had been clamoring outside the door. Now, in the silence of the empty room, the space seemed eerily hushed, almost as if it were a presence itself, holding its own breath, as if he had interrupted something. For a split second, he even thought he felt the fine hairs rising along the back of his neck.

"That's weird," he said to himself. He pulled the gun from his pocket, dug the bullets from another, and loaded it again.

"Did you say something?"

Ami was poised in the doorway, half-turned to head down the corridor to her office.

"Nothing," he replied. "I just don't like the way it feels in here at night."

He tipped his chin in her direction. "Get the file and we'll go."

She turned and left the lobby.

Rafe scanned the room again, but this time around, his eyes latched onto the plastic bottle he'd seen lying on the carpet in front of the small refrigerator.

Water was dripping from its open mouth.

He sprinted across the room and into the corridor to Ami's office.

Vi breathed calmly through her nose, slowing her heart rate, readying herself for the moment Dr. Kim's office door opened. She was behind the door, in the dark, literally and figuratively—she'd heard both Kim's and Greene's voices when they'd entered the clinic, but she had no idea if they would both enter the doctor's private office or not. If they did, Vi would be hard-pressed to kill them both at once, because one of them would have the precious seconds he or she would need to react defensively while Vi was finishing the other. If Kim entered first, Vi's stiletto would make a clean kill, but then she'd have Greene on her, and she had no doubt that her chances of walking away would shrink exponentially. Rafe Greene might be an unknown as far as she was concerned, but she'd seen the man in action yesterday morning in Orlando, and his quick reflexes were enough to convince her she didn't want to mess with him in close quarters.

If, on the other hand, Greene walked in first, Vi could probably inflict some serious damage on the big man, but she wasn't confident it would be enough to stop him or give her the time to deal with Kim.

Which left Vi with only one solution to her situation.

She pulled her gun out of her pocket and released the safety. It wasn't going to be neat and tidy, but two fast headshots would guarantee that she'd once again be the only one waiting when Chinh Nguyen showed up to clean the clinic.

Just as Ami pushed the office door open, Rafe grabbed her by the shoulders and spun her away. When she landed against the wall five feet away from the door, Rafe's body pressing tightly against hers, she looked up at his face, her eyes wide with fear.

"I think there's someone here," he said, his voice barely a breath. "Don't move."

Ami felt him carefully lifting his body away from hers and watched, transfixed, as he inched his way back towards the open door, Niles's gun in his right hand. A second later, he was gone, dropping to a low crouch and spinning across the office's threshold.

Ami squeezed her eyes shut, waiting to hear the report of the gun.

Nothing happened.

She opened her eyes and leaned a tiny bit away from the wall, trying to see into the open doorway.

And then Rafe was standing there, whole and unharmed, the gun still in his right hand down at his side.

"There's no one in here," he said. "I thought someone was here in the clinic because I saw a bottle . . . never mind."

He stepped back to let Ami into the office, and though she felt unsteady on her feet, she managed to walk past him and over to the oak filing cabinet behind the desk.

Niles's desk.

"I didn't realize the list was in here," Rafe told her. "I'm sorry, Ami—I know it's got to be hard for you to be in Niles's office right now. If I'd known, I would have offered to get it for you."

"You wouldn't be able to find it," she replied. "Niles is . . . was . . . awful at organization—it's going to take me a minute or two to track it down as it is."

She rifled through one drawer, slid it shut, and then pulled out a second. Notes in Niles's handwriting sat loose in the front of the drawer, and Ami had to swallow past the lump that rose in her throat.

He'd been brilliant.

He'd been a tragedy.

So much to give, and so much wasted.

Again, Ami pushed thoughts of Niles out of her head. There would be time later for grieving. Right now, she needed to stay focused on the task at hand—finding the media list and putting her prayer therapy technicians on the phones as fast as she could to spread the truth about the indisputable healing bond between body and soul. Only a storm of media attention could possibly stop the killing that had already claimed three lives, and though she clearly knew that a full disclosure of her NRT protocol might jeopardize—or even destroy—her own career, she was willing to take the risk.

Besides, as much as Rafe's false alarm in Niles's office rattled her, it also reminded her of the stakes in this insane confrontation with evil incarnate—stakes that not only included the lives of all her research associates, but hers and Rafe's as well. Until they were surrounded by the glare of publicity, nowhere was safe. For all she knew, the next door she opened could place them directly in the sights of a killer.

"Got it!"

She lifted the stapled sheets from a file and waved it at Rafe.

"Our key to victory," she said. "In the face of the media spotlight, and the testimonies of my patients and technicians, Philip Arden won't have a prayer."

"Amen," Rafe agreed.

Ami glanced at the pistol in his hand. "Put the gun away, Rafe. We're not going to need it in the neurology lab. The most threatening thing we'll have to face in the next three hours is busy phone lines."

She headed into the hallway and paused while Rafe closed the door to Niles's office behind them. A hard shiver traveled down her spine and her stomach clenched.

Adrenaline, she thought.

Rafe caught her free hand and held it against his chest, concern creasing his features. "You okay? Your hand is like ice."

Ami curled her fingers around his own warm ones. "I'm fine. Let's get up to the third floor, and get the crew working the phone lines. Just a few more hours, Rafe, and we've got the Devil beat."

"From your lips," he said, touching Ami's mouth with his own in a brief kiss.

"To God's ears," she finished for him.

They hurried out of the clinic.

Less than five feet away from where they'd stood in the hall, Vi remained glued to the wall inside Kim's office, her ear pressed to the tiny crack between the office's door and its frame. Once she heard the muffled thud of the clinic's front door closing, she detached herself from her listening post and silently reviewed what she'd overheard.

For the next several hours, Kim and Greene would be in a neurology lab right here in the medical center, along with whoever Kim called her "crew." They planned to spend that time making phone calls in some kind of media campaign to expose something that involved Philip.

What had Kim said?

'Philip Arden won't have a prayer."

Vi mulled over what terrible crime her employer might have committed, but she didn't know where to start with the possibilities, since she knew from her own business transactions with him that he was capable of almost anything anyone else would consider horrific. Kim had also mentioned testimonies—proof, Vi guessed—from her patients. Given Kim's occupation, that could imply that Philip had perpetrated some kind of terrible medical fraud or been behind an alternative treatment that Kim opposed.

Yet he'd initially wanted to meet Kim and bypass her partner Villome in forming some kind of relationship with the Korean doctor. Had he then learned that Kim's drug trials posed a threat to his master plan, and he'd bargained on persuading her to work with him, instead of against him? Perhaps that's where Greene—whose mere presence had sent Philip into a rage—played into what was going on. Perhaps he and Philip had faced down before in a similar scenario, one in which Philip did not emerge the victor.

That, Vi reasoned, would certainly explain her employer's sudden change of heart regarding Kim and his subsequent urgent need for multiple murders; if Vi killed the people who could expose his fraud or destroy his scheme, he'd walk away with impunity, his plans unopposed, with no one the wiser. Vi had always perceived Philip's nearly rabid insistence on remaining an elusive figure both personally and professionally as a character quirk, but now she wondered if it was more a strategy for self-preservation. Just as he'd used Mahler to manipulate Calyx and Pieter Hallenstroem, Philip was an expert at masking his behind-the-scenes involvement in any of his projects, which certainly contributed to his longevity, if not his success, in the shadowy world in which he operated.

But if Kim and Greene held him up to a spotlight?

'We've got the devil beat," Kim had said.

Caught in the glare of publicity, Philip Arden, master of manipulation, would be exposed. He'd become visible, vulnerable, and, ultimately, powerless.

But Ami Kim didn't know about Violet Winters.

Nor did she know that Vi now held the key to the one thing that Philip Arden needed most in the world: to remain invisible.

And she also couldn't know how very much Vi wanted to give her employer what he needed.

"Say your own prayers, Dr. Kim and Mr. Greene," she whispered into the darkness. "Chinh Nguyen will have to wait, because you've just hit the top of my list."

Soundlessly, she opened the office door, but then turned back to grope along the wall where she'd been hiding. Her hand found the coatrack she'd noted earlier in her brief inspection of the room, and she lifted a lab jacket from its peg. She shrugged it on and slipped out of the office, through the clinic's lobby, then out into the empty building corridor.

A quick glance around the area assured her she was alone. She stashed her gun in the deep pocket of the lab jacket where she could easily access it.

Because that was one more thing she'd learned from Kim's and Greene's conversation.

The doctor's companion had a gun, too.

CHAPTER FORTY-EIGHT

S *omeone else was in that office.*

Over and over again, Rafe's instincts butted into his concentration as he hustled up the stairs to the neurology lab on Ami's heels. Ever since he'd felt the hairs on his neck bristle when Ami walked into her office's corridor, Rafe had been convinced that someone else was in the Heart Partners Clinic. The dripping bottle had been a warning, a siren, really, that something wasn't right.

Yet Niles's office was empty, and no one had come bolting out of any of the other rooms.

Neither would I if I'd been hiding there. I'd be holding my breath, hoping no one would discover me.

But why would anyone be hiding in Ami's clinic?

The answer hit him like a fist in the gut.

Because Chinh Nguyen would be there at 8:00.

Why hunt down the prey when it's going to come to you?

"I've got to go back to the clinic," he said, snagging Ami's arm before she could take another stair. "There's something I've got to check out."

She turned her face to look over her shoulder at him. "Rafe, I've got to get upstairs. They're waiting for me. We both agreed we can't waste any more time."

"I know, but I've got to check this out."

He prayed she wouldn't ask what or why. No way on earth was he going to take her back into that clinic with him when he thought an assassin was waiting inside.

He glanced at the door on the landing just ahead of them.

"This is the floor for the lab, right? Go. Go to the lab. Get everyone on the phones. Lock yourselves in. You hear me? I'll be back as soon as I can."

He spun on his heel and flew back down the stairs.

His knee was killing him, but he ignored it as he took the steps down two at a time, skidding around the landings. He pulled the door open onto the first floor and barely missed knocking over a woman in a lab coat as he made a sharp turn towards Ami's clinic. Instinctively, he reached out to steady her.

His spine went to ice at the same instant he saw the gun in her hand.

Rafe didn't think. His right foot shot out, kicking the gun from the woman's hand as it discharged with a muffled pop. She and her gun tumbled across the hall, and he felt the heat of a bullet graze his left temple. At the same time, he thought he heard the snap of cracking bones in the woman's wrist, but he couldn't be sure, because he was down on the ground himself, his left knee throbbing in excruciating pain.

Helpless, he watched the woman pull a long thin blade from inside her lab jacket's sleeve with her other hand.

It was a stiletto.

Arden's assassin was a woman.

Without another moment of hesitation, Rafe pulled the gun out of his own jacket pocket and aimed it at her heart.

"I'll shoot to kill," he told her, "and I won't miss."

The assassin gave him one look and jumped up, sprinting for the open door into the stairwell.

He should have taken a shot at her, but he didn't.

He couldn't.

Assassin or not, she was a woman, and Rafe couldn't pull the trigger. He'd always figured that those good manners his mama had drummed into him were going to be the death of him some day.

But not today.

Not when Ami was two flights above him with an assassin close on her trail.

He heaved himself up to stand on his bad knee and tested it for a step.

Pain seared through the joint, but it didn't buckle.

Rafe headed back into the stairwell, his body hugging the wall, his pistol raised.

Four floors above Rafe, Vi quickly walked down the hallway, hoping desperately she'd find a women's bathroom. Her injured hand was stuffed deeply into the pocket of her stolen lab coat, her teeth locked against the crushing pain.

He'd broken her wrist.

Not only that, but his quick reflexes had cost her the gun.

And even worse, her cover was blown. He'd be watching for her from now on.

Part of her said she needed to pull back and regroup, come back and kill another day.

But the other part of her refused to give even that much quarter to her prey. She hadn't, after all, spent years honing her skills to be deflected by a broken bone and an unexpected attack when she was so close—only two floors away, to be precise—to achieving her objective. She was, after all, a very resourceful woman, and she wasn't nearly ready to call it quits now. The big man's kick had accomplished exactly the opposite, in fact—now Vi had an even bigger personal score to settle with the man, and it trumped even her desire to please Arden.

Greene was going to die, all right, and she was going to make sure it hurt.

But right now, she needed privacy and a couple of minutes to pull herself together and come up with a new plan, and the only place that sprang to mind was a private stall in a bathroom.

So far, the human resources receptionist had been right about the medical offices wing: the building was deserted at night. What were her words for it? Oh yes—a tomb after hours. Other than Greene and Kim on the first floor, Vi hadn't seen or heard another person in the building, and on this floor, large empty conference rooms lined both sides of the hallway. Hoping her luck held, she passed a few more empty rooms before she found a restroom. Blowing out a breath of relief, she reached for the door with her good hand, her eyes scanning further down the brightly lit hall for any indications that she might not be alone.

No one was there. The hallway was empty.

But as she pushed open the door, she found out the bathroom was occupied.

"I cleaning here!" a man called out from the other side of the door.

And then the bathroom door was jerked completely open by a small Asian man, and Vi found herself staring straight into the night janitor's eyes.

She read his name tag pinned onto his overalls.

Mr. Nguyen.

CHAPTER FORTY-NINE

He was a fool. The moment he'd seen that dripping water bottle in the lobby, he should have grabbed Ami and shoved her out into the corridor beyond the clinic doors. Then he should have pulled his gun and gone room to room to find her, the assassin. Instead, he'd disregarded the bottle and ignored his own uneasiness, the chill he'd felt across the back of his neck. Even Ami must have registered something amiss, he realized, remembering how icy her hands felt. Hadn't she said she'd felt a terrible coldness when she'd come face-to-face with Arden?

Great, he castigated himself, *we both have the ability to discern spirits but we were too busy to pay any attention when it really mattered. God, have mercy on us idiots.*

He slid around another landing, his gun still in his hand.

Where had the woman gone?

By the time he'd gotten into the stairwell, she was so far ahead of him, he had no way of knowing if she'd gone up the stairs to a higher floor or down to the basement. No steps rang in the stairwell and the doors were all tightly closed. Rafe had had to choose: up or down? Since he figured that the woman had been hiding somewhere in the clinic while he and Ami picked up Niles's' media list, he gambled that she must have overheard their conversation. That meant that the woman—Arden's assassin—now knew she could find a whole slew of her targets upstairs in the neurology lab. And whether or not he'd injured her enough to send her running away from the clinic, Rafe didn't know, nor was he willing to bet on it.

Not with Ami's life riding on it.

He'd gone up the stairs.

With each step, he'd cursed his knee for collapsing beneath him when the assassin had taken her shot. If it had held, he could have pinned her to the floor before she'd had the chance to draw her knife, and Rafe could have restrained her until help had arrived. As it was, he'd lost her, along with any opportunity that she might have led them to Arden. Dressed in a lab jacket, the assassin could blend in anywhere in the medical center, making her worse than a wolf in sheep's clothing.

At least with a wolf, you knew how it killed; with this assassin, it was anyone's guess. As she'd already proved once today, all she had to do was shake your hand or touch your arm and leave a little biotoxin behind.

Rafe shivered. Maybe it was just as well he hadn't gotten close enough to pin her. If he had, maybe he'd be dead right now.

I change my mind, God. Bless this knee forever and ever. May it always fail me in my moment of need.

Or at least whenever an assassin is pointing a gun at me.

Less than two minutes after he'd entered the stairwell, he stepped out of it onto the third floor, his pistol swinging in an arc to cover the hallway.

It was empty.

"Ami!"

Ten yards away, a door opened and one of the men he'd met that morning at the AA meeting leaned out.

"Get back inside!" he yelled at him.

The door slammed shut.

Again with his back to the wall, Rafe quickly worked his way down the hall to the door that had opened, scanning the area and swinging his gun all the while. When he reached the lab, he turned the handle.

It was locked.

He rapped twice on the door before Ami's face appeared in the door's small window.

She unlocked the door and Rafe was inside.

Without a word, he pulled her into his arms and held her tightly against his chest.

"You're all right," he breathed, relief and thanksgiving pouring through his body.

Ami's small hands framed his face as she looked at him with concern. "And you're not," she replied. "I can feel it, Rafe. What happened?"

"I finish up here," the janitor told Vi, pushing his cleaning cart past her out into the hall.

"Wait!"

The old man turned to face her.

Glancing at his narrow chest, she read the name tag again.

Mr. Nguyen.

A night janitor in the medical center.

Her target.

"Something you need?" he asked.

Yes, she wanted to say, *I need a stiff drink, because I'm obviously delirious with pain and I'm imagining that I literally stumbled into my next mark on an abandoned floor with no witnesses anywhere in sight.*

She felt his stare, questioning, but she was too stunned to speak. Irrationally, she wondered if he could see through the material of the lab jacket to the stiletto stashed in the pocket. Clean kills didn't just present themselves out of the blue, Vi argued with herself. That was why people hired her—to script the conditions that would lead to a murder no one could explain. To be handed an opportunity like this just didn't happen in her line of work, especially when she'd just made a total mess of her encounter with Greene downstairs. No way could her luck turn that fast.

Could it?

She wet her dry lips, the blinding pain in her wrist momentarily forgotten.

"I'm sorry, but are you Hung Nguyen's grandfather?" she asked. "The Hung Nguyen who attends the pharmacy school here?

The old man's eyes bored into hers, then dropped slowly to the ground. "No," he told her. "I not that man. Chinh Nguyen mourns tonight with family. His grandson is dead. I substitute for him. They give me Chinh Nguyen's overalls and tag for tonight so I can do his work. Many Vietnamese people working for Janklow Cleaning Services now."

Vi let out the breath she hadn't been aware of holding.

Of course, this man couldn't be her mark. The odds against it were astronomical. That she'd even considered the possibility just proved how frustrated she was by the debacle with Greene. With that thought, the pain in her wrist came roaring back, and she clenched her jaw to control it.

"I go now," the janitor said, his eyes sliding one more time over Vi's lab jacket.

She watched him walk away, fitting what little nuggets of information she'd learned from the man into her newly revised plan for the evening.

If Chinh Nguyen wasn't coming into the center tonight, she would have to make alternate arrangements to complete that part of Philip's assignment tomorrow. She had a feeling her employer wouldn't be happy with the delay, but he was going to have to live with it for once. Surely, if the old man was missing work to grieve with his family, he would be no threat to Philip for the next twenty-four hours at least, and that would be all the time Vi needed to add his murder to her current job's count.

Besides, she had a much bigger plum just waiting to fall into her lap right where she was: Kim and Greene.

Knowing that the doctor and her friend were practically within arm's reach was the only thing that was keeping Vi's adrenaline surging enough to keep her lucid through the pain in her wrist; with her targets so close, she wasn't about to give up the kill. All she needed was a few minutes to think it through, and she knew she'd have a strategy for success. After all, the only moment she had really sweated was when she'd leaped into the stairwell to escape Greene's gun barrel pointing at her. If the man had taken the shot, she'd probably be bleeding out in the stairwell right now. But since he hadn't, she'd been able to tear up the stairs to safety, and when she hadn't heard his footfalls behind her in fast pursuit, she'd known that she'd won the key advantage in tonight's deadly match.

She knew exactly where to find Greene and Kim.

In the third-floor neurology lab.

And labs were usually filled with all kinds of lovely things she could use to kill, even if she had to do it one-handedly.

The squeak of the janitor's cart called her attention back to the man making his way to the end of the hall.

"Excuse me!" she called after him.

He turned back to look at her.

"Would you by any chance have some aspirin with you? I have a splitting headache," she lied, "and I don't have anything with me to take for it."

The janitor shook his head as he touched the button on the service elevator.

"No aspirin. Sorry."

He and his cart moved into the elevator, and Vi watched the doors slide shut.

"Thanks for nothing, buddy," she muttered, but the old man was already gone.

She carefully pulled her damaged hand from her pocket and winced to see it beginning to swell. She needed to put some ice on it or find a bandage to wrap it. Even the simplest splint would help support the broken wrist and relieve some of the intense pain she was feeling.

Testing her limited range of motion, she tried to turn her wrist and almost doubled over from the burning jolt that lanced up her arm. Biting her tongue so she wouldn't cry out, she waited for the blackness to leave her vision, then stumbled into the women's bathroom. She turned on the tap, let the water run cold, then stuck her damaged wrist under the faucet. Only when her hand was numbed past feeling did Vi finally admit to herself that she needed help. For the first time in her career, she couldn't finish the job alone.

But hell would freeze over before she let even that stop her.

Fumbling beneath the lab coat with her good hand, she dragged out her phone and dialed her employer's private number.

"I need you," she told him when he answered her call.

"Why, Vi," he replied, his voice smooth and warm. "I never pegged you as the sentimental type."

"I need your help, Philip."

The line went silent.

"My help," he echoed.

Vi winced at the sound of disappointment in his voice. Steeling herself against her own self-loathing over her failure, she focused on the task at hand. She already had a clear idea of how to salvage the job, along with her reputation, but she needed to convince Philip to do one thing for her.

"Kim and Greene are here in the center, virtually steps away from me in the third-floor neurology lab, along with some of her assistants. I can make a clean sweep, Philip—kill them all right now—but I need you to bring me something to make that happen."

Another moment of silence passed.

Vi felt sweat beading her hairline. Whether it was from the pain in her wrist or in fearful anticipation of Philip's response, she couldn't be sure.

The quiet stretched out. Vi could hear her pulse pounding in her head.

Come on, Philip!

"What is it?" he finally asked.

Vi felt the relief pour through her.

He was going to do it.

He was going to help her finish this job.

She was going to owe him for this small favor, but in the long run, she was certain it would bind them together even more securely. Because after she pulled this massacre off for him, after she guaranteed him his anonymity, she wouldn't just owe Philip Arden.

She would own him.

"Bring me a match," she told him.

In the service elevator, the elderly janitor watched the floor numbers on the control panel count down as he descended to the third floor. Pushing his cart into the darkened hallway, he turned left and hurried halfway down the corridor. When he tried to open the door to the suite of rooms he was searching for, he was startled to find it locked even though light spilled through its small window. It was a therapy night, and even though the floor was deserted, he'd never before found the door locked when he arrived.

He pressed the small button on the wall next to the door and heard the buzzing noise inside. While he waited for someone to come open the door, he wondered about the woman upstairs, and why she'd been wearing a lab coat with Dr. Kim's name stitched on the pocket. Maybe she thought she could fool other people, but there was no way she had fooled him.

He, on the other hand, had clearly fooled her, though it had required a lie from him.

From the moment he'd learned about Hung's murder at the medical center, Chinh Nguyen had felt the presence of evil hovering near. Refusing to stay home and cower in fear of the unknown, he had reported to work early and begun his cleaning rounds ahead of schedule in hopes of finding Dr. Kim and her technicians in the lab. He wanted to share his foreboding with her and tell her about his tea with Hung and the pharmaceutical man. More than anything, though, he wanted to ask her forgiveness for speaking about her research without her permission. Hung had claimed it would help her, and he had believed his grandson, but now Hung was dead.

And on what should have been an empty floor of conference rooms, a brown-haired stranger wearing Dr. Kim's jacket had appeared and asked him if he was Hung's grandfather.

Chinh shivered in the hall outside the lab.

Evil was coming closer.

CHAPTER FIFTY

W e're splitting up the list," Ami told the five technicians
in the lab as she ripped the papers she'd found in Niles's
office into seven pieces. "Let's put together the talking points
before we start calling, so we're all on the same page. Remember, we don't have to go into much detail at this point. The idea
is to get the media contacts on the line and give them the high-
lights, and refer them to me."

"Then you shouldn't be calling, Dr. Kim," Jim pointed out as
he rolled a whiteboard across the room for Ami to use. "You
need to be able to move around the room and talk with whoever we can get on the lines."

Rafe found a marker on the whiteboard's ledge and removed
its cap. "Jim's right, Ami," he said. "You've got to be the free
agent in the room. Whoever finishes their list first can pick up
that last piece in your hand."

He poised the marker against the board. "First talking
point?"

"Prayer heals."

Rafe looked at the speaker and recognized one of the
women from the morning's AA meeting.

"I'm Alice," she reminded him. "We met this morning."

Rafe smiled and nodded. "I remember."

"That's way too vague," Jim commented. "And if you say
'prayer' right off the bat, you're not going to have anyone staying on the line to hear the rest of what you have to say."

"That's a shame," Alice said.

"But true," added another man from the morning meeting. "If you start with the spirituality part, they're going to toss you in the New Age bin."

"That would be at best, Eldon," Jim said. "Worst case, they're going to call you nuts."

Rafe's eyes met Ami's. His unspoken question hung in the air between them.

Are you sure you're ready to do this?

Ami nodded in silent reply.

"We need to make this about science," Ami told the group, then raised her hands to cut off the protests beginning to erupt around the room. "And once we've done that, established our scientific credentials, then we can move into the more challenging territory of physically effective spirituality."

She pointed to the whiteboard.

"Number one: Neurophysiological research study here in Twin Cities confirms mind-body connection in reversing heart disease."

"Too long."

"Boring."

"We've got to have a real attention-getter here," Jim said. "Something that will grab them by the throat and not let go."

"You're absolutely right." Ami took the marker from Rafe and quickly wrote on the board as she read it aloud. "Heart disease reversed with breakthrough therapy."

"Make it simpler," Alice said. "Cure discovered for heart disease."

"The real deal: the end of heart disease," Eldon tossed out. "That's really what this is all about: saving lives."

A loud buzzing noise broke into the discussion.

Rafe looked at Ami in confusion.

"It's the door," Jim explained. "When it's locked, you have to buzz for someone to come open it. It's probably Diane or Stuart. I'll get it."

"Wait!" Rafe commanded. "I'll go."

Throwing a warning glance at Ami, he walked to the door that led out of the lab suite. As soon as his back was to the group gathered around the whiteboard, he slid his hand into his jacket pocket and wrapped his fingers around the gun that was hidden there. He lifted it along his right shoulder and cautiously approached the door. Through the small window, he could see an elderly Vietnamese man standing beside a cleaning cart in the hallway. Rafe read the name tag on the man's shirt.

Mr. Nguyen.

The dead Hung Nguyen's grandfather?

Rafe tucked his gun back in his jacket.

"Who can identify Mr. Nguyen for me?" he called back to the technicians.

Alice joined him at the door and peered through the glass.

"Yes," she said. "It's Mr. Nguyen. Chinh Nguyen," she added for Rafe's benefit.

Rafe unlocked the door and admitted the old man. Once Nguyen was inside the suite, Rafe relocked the door and turned to find the shorter man staring up at him.

"Lock is good idea," Nguyen told Rafe in his broken English. "This evil place tonight. I think Dr. Kim in danger."

Rafe's heartbeat accelerated and he returned the man's stare. "Why do you say that, Mr. Nguyen?"

The old man pointed towards the locked door. "Upstairs, a woman ask me if Hung is my grandson. She wearing Dr. Kim's coat."

Rafe remembered his fleeting encounter with the assassin. She'd been wearing a white lab jacket.

"Where did you see this woman?" he asked.

"On seventh floor. I clean bathroom and she walk in."

The assassin had fled up, not down, the stairs after he'd pulled his gun on her. She was still in the building.

Not good.

Not good at all.

That could only mean one thing, Rafe reckoned. Even with a busted hand—and Rafe was sure he'd damaged her hand when he'd kicked the gun out of it—the woman wasn't giving up. Reflexively, Rafe turned towards the locked door that was all that stood between him and Ami and the assassin.

"I talk to Dr. Kim now," Nguyen said.

"We'll both talk to her," Rafe amended. "She might think we're already in the frying pan, but the fire's getting hotter, and everyone needs to know it."

He caught Nguyen's confused look.

"It's an expression, Mr. Nguyen. It means that the situation is rapidly deteriorating, and it's probably going to get worse before it gets better."

If it gets better at all, Rafe grimly acknowledged to himself.

Arden's assassin was on the loose, right here in the building, and based on her track record so far today, the woman was a clever, efficient killing machine. That alone was enough to send every nerve in Rafe's body into overdrive, but to make matters even worse, if the woman had overheard any of Rafe and Ami's conversation in the Heart Partners Clinic—and Rafe didn't doubt she'd heard plenty—she now knew exactly where her targets were sitting.

In a lab suite with only one access door, three stories up from the ground.

The good guys needed help.

Rafe pulled his cell phone from his pocket to call the police, but his fingers froze over the keypad.

He didn't have any service.

"This floor. It stops cell phones," Nguyen told him, nodding at the phone in Rafe's hand.

"The lab is specially shielded," Alice added.

The sound of the older woman's voice beside him startled Rafe. He'd been so focused on the janitor's report about the assassin that he'd forgotten someone else was listening.

Alice continued her explanation. "Because of the nature of the neurological research they do here, they wanted an interference-free space that couldn't be compromised by any kind of electrical or magnetic transmissions."

She suddenly stopped talking and her face drained of color. Her eyes flew to Rafe's.

"We can't use our phones in the lab," she announced. "Dr. Kim must have forgotten. We have no way to contact the media as long as we're on this floor."

Her eyes swung over to the locked door and then back to Rafe.

"It's not safe for us to leave, either, is it?" she asked. "This woman upstairs, the one with Dr. Kim's coat—she's one of the people you said was trying to stop us, isn't she?"

Rafe nodded and stuck the dead phone back into his pocket, his mind churning furiously for a solution.

"Who you want to call?" Nguyen asked.

"The cavalry," Rafe replied, his voice as flat as his attempt at humor.

"It's that bad?" Alice whispered.

Rafe thought again about the assassin waiting somewhere beyond the door.

"Yes, Alice," he said, "it's that bad."

"We better start praying, then," she told him. "God's a lot closer than any cavalry." She walked back across the room to deliver the bad news to Ami.

Rafe glanced towards the windows of the suite and did as he was told.

He prayed.

Anytime, Lord. Light up the sky with that big neon sign telling me what to do because I . . .

He looked at the windows again and the darkness on the other side of the thick glass. If only he had a flare. Just one flare like the ones he'd often lit as a medic calling for an airlift evacuation during his days in the Marines. He'd break that window

open to the freezing air outside and shoot that flare straight up.
It would light up the night and . . .
He turned back to the elderly janitor.
"What kind of cleaning fluids do you have on your cart, sir?"

CHAPTER FIFTY-ONE

Philip Arden leaned casually against the wall near the elevator on the darkened first floor of the medical center office wing. He lightly tapped the edge of his gold-banded watch to activate the luminous dial and checked the time. In another forty seconds, the elevator doors would slide open and Vi would be inside, waiting for him and the box of matches he'd picked up for her from the bar in his hotel. What was going to happen after that, Philip didn't know, as Vi had refused to fill him in on her complete plan until they were alone in the elevator. She'd promised him it would make him very happy, though, especially since one Rafe Greene was going to end up dead at the end.

Vi was right. A dead Greene would make Philip very happy. One less archangel would mean one less big headache.

Except that Vi wasn't going to be the one doing the killing, because The Gentleman had a plan of his own. A plan that would wipe out this whole miracle-drug-cure fiasco in a clean sweep.

Philip looked again at his watch. The razor-sharp edges of the face gleamed dully in the dim hallway.

Violet Winters wasn't the only assassin with secrets.

She was, however, the most intriguing killer he'd ever met. Until her call for his help, he'd even considered taking her with him when he left this miserably cold excuse for a city. In many ways, Vi was almost his equal—she had his cunning, his patience, his perseverance, his total self-interest. Yet at the same time, Philip could sense a fire in her belly that she barely managed to conceal with her icy control, and it was called ambition.

Poor Vi, Philip thought. She'd never realized that when it came to The Gentleman, ambition on the part of anyone—other than him—was risky business.

Wasn't history littered with the tales of ambitious men and women brought to ruin?

Didn't Vi see the delight in his eyes every time he ordered another hit on someone who'd sold his soul in exchange for Philip's assistance in securing coveted success?

The reality of life was that selfish ambition was as much a cancer as any physiological one; pride, called by any other name—including ambition—was still pride.

And only Philip Arden was allowed to claim its crown.

The elevator door slid open and Philip looked down into Vi's face.

"Your match," he said, presenting her with the pack he'd brought from the bar.

Vi brushed her fingertips lightly over the pack offered in his hand and gave him a luminous smile. She stepped back so he could enter the elevator. As soon as he was inside, she awkwardly jabbed the seventh-floor button with the side of her right hand.

"What happened to your hand?" he asked, already knowing he wasn't going to like her answer.

"Greene damaged it," she replied. "I pulled a gun on him and he kicked it out of my hand."

"You pulled a gun and didn't shoot him?" He didn't bother to hide his disgust with her failure.

"He's fast, Philip. Incredibly fast," Vi defended herself. "I practically walked right into him before I saw him. When I lost the gun, I pulled my stiletto, and he caved. He had a gun, too, but he couldn't shoot me. His delicate conscience, I guess. I had no choice. I ran to regroup."

Philip looked over Vi's head to calm himself. Two opportunities to kill St. Rafe and she'd blown them both.

Two opportunities!

He was right. This was his job to finish.

Feigning concern, he cupped Vi's chin in his hand and looked down into her eyes. "What's the plan now?"

He saw the lines of tension in her face relax slightly. At least she'd known enough to fear his reaction, he told himself sourly.

"Right now, we're riding up to the seventh floor while we talk. When we get there, you can get off and go back to the hotel. I'm riding back down to the third floor, where Greene, Kim, and a handful of her technicians are holed up in the lab. Greene has to be expecting me, so there's no way I can get into that lab. But with this," she said, lifting the matchbook, "I can get them to come out to me."

"You're going to set off the fire alarm on the floor," he guessed. "And then what? They're going to stand in line while you stab each one of them?"

Philip could feel Vi's physical recoil at his tone of voice, and grasped her chin more tightly.

"No," she whispered. "As soon as I have them in the hall, I'm going to mow them down."

She dropped the matches into her lab coat pocket.

"But you lost your gun, Vi."

"You're right, I did," she agreed. "But I didn't lose this one."

Philip felt the barrel of a gun jam up against his lower ribcage. He released Vi's chin and looked down to see a small gun in her left hand, its nose buried in his expensive overcoat.

"You're ambidextrous," he noted. "I can see where that's a real plus for an assassin."

"That, and always having a second gun on my body."

Philip covered her good hand with his right one and raised it, along with the gun, to his lips. He kissed the soft skin between her thumb and forefinger and held her dark eyes with his own silvery ones.

"What are they doing in the lab, Vi? Besides waiting for you?"

"Apparently, they plan to make phone calls."

The elevator came to a stop, but he turned and laid his finger on the control button to keep the door closed. Vi returned the gun to her pocket.

"For what?" he asked.

"From what I could gather, to expose something about you. I overheard Kim and Greene say you wouldn't have a prayer after their group made the phone calls."

The world lurched under his feet, and bile rose in his throat. Kim and Greene were calling in the press.

They were releasing her research, announcing the miraculous and medically proven healing power of prayer.

They were tearing apart his lies.

They were destroying him.

"I know how important your anonymity is to you, Philip," Vi was saying, though her voice sounded dim and distant to him. "And while I don't know what it has to do with Greene or Kim's so-called miracle cure, I'm going to make sure you keep it."

Infuriated beyond measure, Philip ripped the watch off his left wrist and slashed its honed edge across Vi's throat.

Stunned and voiceless, Vi dropped to the floor of the elevator, her fingers clawing desperately at the blood gushing from her throat. At that moment, the doors slid open and without a second's hesitation, Philip grabbed her small form and heaved her out into the corridor. He stooped over her just long enough to retrieve her gun from her jacket.

"Bye, Vi," he told her curtly. He pushed the button for the third floor.

CHAPTER FIFTY-TWO

Rafe looked up from the wad of rags he was winding around the handle of Mr. Nguyen's mop to find Ami staring at his handiwork.

"Low-tech, I know," he said, "but it's going to get us out of here in one piece, Ami. Think positive."

"I can't believe I totally forgot about the phone blackout up here," she replied, frustration still clouding her face. Rafe had lost count of the number of times she'd said those exact words in the last five minutes. As soon as Alice had mentioned the blackout to Ami, she'd sprinted over to Rafe and castigated herself profusely for her lapse in memory.

"I should have remembered!" she'd insisted, anger and fear riding her hard. "I can't believe I forgot about it, tonight, of all times! It's my fault, and now everyone in this room is—"

"Ami."

He'd placed his fingers over her lips to seal them shut.

"Listen very carefully to me. This is not your fault. You are not responsible for the design of this floor. You didn't plan to have a professional hitwoman on board tonight during a therapy session in this lab. None of these things is because of you. This is life, and sometimes, things get crazy."

She'd rolled her eyes and he'd smiled somewhat sheepishly.

"Okay, maybe crazier than usual."

He'd gently lifted his fingers from her mouth. "Do you hear what I am saying to you, Dr. Kim?'

"Yes," she'd answered, though Rafe could still hear a note of defiance in her voice. "This is life, and I don't control it. But I still can't believe I forgot about the phone blackout up here."

Rafe had sent her back to her technicians then, shooed Alice and Nguyen away from him, and, pistol in one hand, unlocked the lab door. Dropping to a crouch, his gun again raised by his shoulder, he'd slowly eased the door open just wide enough to accommodate his body, and then angled himself through to squat behind the cart Mr. Nguyen had left in the hall. Moving carefully and deliberately, he'd inched around the side closest to the wall in order to check for any assailant hidden by the mound of janitorial supplies, but to his great relief, found no one in the hall. Slipping quickly back to the front of the cart, he'd snagged it with his free hand and pulled it backwards into the lab with him. As soon as the rear of the cart cleared the lab's threshold, Nguyen darted forward, closed the door and locked it.

In less than a minute, the two men had emptied the cart of all its rags and polishing cloths and selected the cleaning supplies that would flame the most reliably on the makeshift signal flare Rafe intended to make. Lacking any means of propulsion, his flare wouldn't be able to rise above the building, but when held out the window of an otherwise darkened building, he was confident its flame would stand out in the icy night. Mr. Nguyen had assured him, too, that the rags coated in cleaning solvents would burn brightly for at least several minutes, and since he knew the rounds of many of the night security staffers during his own work hours, he was certain the torch would attract someone's attention.

With no one else to confirm Nguyen's information, Rafe had no choice but to trust the old man. Besides, the elderly janitor was clearly devoted to Ami, as well as beholden to her for his recovery from heart disease. Even so, Rafe wondered what the odds were of someone seeing the burning torch in time to call in a rescue for all of them in the lab. Knowing that the assassin was probably closing in at that very moment only deepened his concern that time was running dangerously short.

He wound the rags on the mop handle faster.

"Think positive," Ami repeated, breaking into his chain of grim thoughts. "I, of all people, should know what thinking positively can accomplish, shouldn't I? Physical healing. The reversal of disease. The rewiring of neurophysiological circuitry. Given time and intensity, positive thinking can literally change a person's body. But you know what, Rafe?"

He threw her a glance as he finished with a rag. Her face was drawn, but not defeated. He'd been right about her from the start: she was a trooper.

"Here's the real secret to all that thinking," she continued. "It's not thinking at all. It's talking. Talking with God. Prayer. The more people do that, the more they come to know God, and the more their souls change. And that's what will change the world."

She handed him a final piece of cloth for his homemade torch.

"In the end, that's what this is all about, Rafe. Changing the world, body and soul."

He looked at the material in his hand, recognizing it as the flannel shirt he'd seen on one of the technicians while they'd brainstormed their talking points for the media.

"Eldon figured it would do us all more good burning like a beacon on your mop handle than staying on his back," Ami explained, accurately reading the question on his face. "I guess he wants to let his shirt shine for all to see."

Rafe felt the corner of his mouth twitch into a tiny smile at Ami's remark.

The woman was making a joke.

Man, would his mother love her.

He gave the arms of the shirt a final tug into a tight knot around the heavy padding that now crowned the top of the mop. Carrying it towards the windows, he plunged the homemade torch into the first of the two buckets of fluid that Mr. Nguyen had poured out from his cleaning drums, allowing the solution to soak into the rags. Beside him, Jim dragged open the heavy lab window, then popped the screen out from the frame. Frigid air blasted into the lab, but Rafe didn't feel it as he hoisted the dripping mess from the first bucket and then dunked it into the second container of solvents from the janitor's cart. The combustible bundle would burn rapidly as soon as he put a match to it, and he didn't want to waste a precious moment of flare time because he wasn't closer to the window.

Someone was going to see his signal.

Someone had to, or else they were all going to be dead, and Ami's work, her revolutionary prayer therapy, would be lost.

Not going to happen, he promised himself. God had led Ami to her work for a reason, and that reason was to heal people—right here and right now—by teaching them the true power of prayer.

And it wasn't just Ami's mission any longer, either, Rafe knew.

It was also his.

With a silent prayer on his lips, he lifted the heavy mop and watched Jim hold a lit match to the saturated rags.

Flames erupted, and Rafe raised the fiery beacon out the empty window frame.

Behind him, the blare of the fire alarm sliced through the lab.

CHAPTER FIFTY-THREE

Ami looked around the suite in confusion, the sound of the fire alarm ringing in her ears. No flames licked the walls. No wisps of smoke filtered in through the ducts and vents. Rafe's torch was burning, but it was outside the window, too far from any sensor to set off the piercing signal.

Something wasn't right.

"The building's on fire!" Eldon shouted from near the lab door. "There's smoke in the hall!"

The other technicians in the room began to scurry, grabbing up coats and winter scarves.

"We have to get out," Alice said, tugging on Ami's arm, trying to move her toward the lab's door. "We're three stories up. We can't wait for the fire department. We'll have to risk the hallway no matter who might be out there."

"Ami, don't!" Rafe yelled to her from the window. He kept the torch extended into the cold night air, and Ami could see the strain of its weight pulling on the muscles of his back even through his leather jacket.

The alarm blared.

"Keep everyone inside!" he shouted. "Don't go out in the hall!"

She looked up at the sprinkler heads that were positioned across the ceiling in strategic locations. In the event of a fire, they were programmed to spray water streams across the room to protect the expensive equipment used in the state-of-the-art neurophysiology lab.

But the sprinklers weren't activating.

And Ami knew why: there was no fire in the suite.

The alarm must have been triggered somewhere else in the building. Wherever the fire was, the sprinklers nearest it would release water to douse the area and contain the flame. For now, they were safe in the suite.

She turned her head to yell to Eldon to move away from the door . . . but she was too late.

The NRT technician threw the door open and stepped out into the hall.

In the next second, part of his head was blown away by a bullet and a silver-eyed man stepped into the lab.

Waves of paralyzing evil rolled over Ami as she recognized the man she'd met outside the elevator on the cardiology floor of the hospital.

Philip Arden.

The Devil had arrived.

Unable to move, Ami watched him aim the gun in his hand directly at her head.

CHAPTER FIFTY-FOUR

It was like watching a movie in slow motion. Rafe saw Eldon open the door, cross the threshold, and get his brains blasted out of his skull. The well-dressed stranger appeared in the doorframe and moved smoothly into the room, a gun held down at the side of his overcoat. He closed the door behind him, and his oddly gleaming eyes traveled around the room until they landed on Ami. He lifted his gun, a feral smile on his lips.

Alice screamed.

Rafe dropped the burning torch, its flames shooting into the darkness like a falling comet. He dove for Ami, his arms stretched out to infinity.

The gun roared in the lab.

The elegant stranger had not seen him hiding behind his cart when he'd entered the suite and closed the door, but Chinh Nguyen had known at once that this was the evil he'd sensed approaching, the mortal danger that had haunted him all day and finally revealed itself in his grandson Hung's death in the parking lot. The woman upstairs—the one in Dr. Kim's jacket— she had directed this man to the lab, Chinh was sure, and now another victim lay dead in the hall.

Trapped between his cart and the wall, he watched the stranger point his gun at Dr. Kim.

He was going to kill her.

With a wild cry that poured strength into his old bones, Chinh launched his body towards the man.

She was falling. Screams and alarms filled her ears, a heavy pressure slammed into her chest. More shouts, more gunshots. Ami couldn't breathe.

Darkness washed over her. She'd pushed past the very frontiers of medicine to blaze a path into a new world of healing, and this was what she got in return.

Death, not life.

And not just her own death. Thanks to her, every person in this room was going to be killed, and NRT—healing prayer—would be buried with them. Faced with her final, colossal, failure, she felt the icy fingers of despair clutching at her heart.

It's not your fault. This is life.

Like a beacon in the night, Rafe's words floated in her mind. He'd been right. She couldn't take responsibility for everything. She didn't have to.

She wasn't God.

Too bad she hadn't figured that out sooner.

She felt a trickle of hot liquid slide down her cheek and the weight lifted.

It felt like heaven.

Rafe shot up from the floor from Ami's body with a roar of pain, swinging hard with his right, landing a bone-shattering smash on Arden's left cheek. Vaguely aware that Mr. Nguyen had latched himself onto the man's back and was valiantly beating his enemy around the head with his own fists, Rafe aimed an uppercut at Arden's belly, but only glanced the blow as the man twisted nimbly out of his range.

"Watch out!" a woman's voice shouted.

The gun roared again and one of the big windows on the lab's outer wall exploded, wicked splinters of glass flying everywhere.

"He's still got the gun!"

The noise was deafening. The alarm continued to blare and people were shouting. Out of the corner of his eye, Rafe saw Jim hurtling in his direction, making a run straight for Arden, a metal lab stool raised as a shield in front of him. Mr. Nguyen continued to flail at Arden's head. Rafe looked for the gun in his enemy's hand, but it was out of his reach as Arden raised it and fired off a shot straight at Jim.

Jim fell to the ground. In the same moment, Arden reached behind him with his left hand and tore Mr. Nguyen from his back, tossing the old man across the room as easily as flicking a fly off his shoulder. He turned to Rafe and spit. His handsome features contorted into a grinning grimace and his voice was a growl only Rafe could hear in the chaos around them.

"How does it feel, St. Raphael, to be an agent of death, instead of life?"

Arden circled him slowly, just out of the range of Rafe's clenched fists.

"This is your fault, you know. If you hadn't shared your healing secret with Dr. Kim, none of these people would be dying right now. I'd be lying on a beach somewhere, enjoying my dominion, idly plotting more intrigue and deception to hold fast my kingdom. But no, you had to interfere. You had to tear away my illusion that the body and soul are separate."

Arden whipped his hand out to his side to viciously backhand Jim, who had staggered to his feet.

The man dropped to the floor.

"What do you say, Rafe?" the Devil taunted him. "Do you want to join my team?"

Rafe kicked out a foot and sent the gun flying from Arden's hand. His hands closed around the clammy throat and he watched in horror as the face before him dissolved into a hideous death's head.

"Tell your Lord that you have failed," Arden hissed.

He raised his own hands to Rafe's neck and locked them in a steel grip.

"There is no healing prayer. It's just another of my lies."

Rafe pounded a knee into the man's groin.

Arden's face instantly reverted to its human form, and he screamed in agony, crumpling to the floor.

Rafe staggered, breathing hard, pain streaming through his knee.

Darn MCL was going to kill him yet.

He looked up to see Mr. Nguyen holding the gun on Arden, who was still writhing on the floor.

"If he so much as opens his eyes, shoot him," Rafe said.

"Her heart is stopping!"

Ami. Dear God, not Ami. She'd been fine. The bullet missed her—I knocked her out of the way. She . . .

But it wasn't Ami.

Rushing over to the windows, Rafe found Ami kneeling beside Alice, frantically performing CPR. Blood pooled beneath Alice's hip.

"The window, when it shattered," someone was saying. "A piece of glass. It was like it was drilled into her stomach."

"She's in shock," Ami said between breaths. "She's losing too much blood."

Rafe took Alice's slack hand in his own and closed his eyes.

The familiar roar of power gathered in his body.

Behind him, he heard the words of a prayer.

It was Mr. Nguyen's voice.

And Jim's.

Rafe let the healing pour through him.

Ami sat up, startled.

"She's breathing again," she whispered, awed. "Her heart's beating."

She turned to see Rafe at her side, his eyes closed. A green glow surrounded him.

It was going to take some getting used to, that glow.

Without warning, Philip Arden shot up from the floor, flew across the room and dove out the broken window.

Stunned at his prisoner's lightning-fast escape, Nguyen made the sign of the cross on his chest. For the first time since he'd discovered Dr. Villome in Dr. Kim's office, the old man felt light again, the danger and evil he had sensed approaching vanished.

Just like his prisoner.

He joined Jim and another technician at the window, where they craned their necks to see if they could spot the intruder's body on the snowy ground below, but the darkness was too deep to penetrate.

"He had his hands over his ears," Jim said, his eyes still searching for a trace of the man who had leapt to a certain death. "Just before he went out the window, I could see he had covered his ears."

He turned to Nguyen.

"I just realized the fire alarm stopped. What didn't he want to hear?"

The old janitor looked past Jim and out into the night. "Our prayer," he said. "He not like it."

"Geez, it wasn't that bad," Jim protested. "We've done a lot worse in some of our therapy sessions."

Nguyen nodded. "This time, it enough."

Two blocks from the medical center, Philip Arden collapsed onto a park bench.

He could have taken all of them out.

He had been so close.

Even the archangel's kick to his groin had only been a momentary setback. He'd been just about to rise from the floor and set the whole lab afire with his own fury when he'd been slammed back to the ground by the healing Presence that had invaded the suite. The Gentleman knew that Presence just like he knew that St. Raphael had called it down, and he'd folded. It had taken every last bit of strength he had to get out of that lab before he was totally crushed.

He had lost the battle.

Healing prayer would circle the earth. The crippling chasms he had cleverly engineered between bodies and souls would be breached as men and women began to understand their two-fold, but integrated, natures. Humankind would grow closer to God, and his own kingdom would diminish.

It was time to move on, he decided, and leave this disaster behind. After all, he did have other rows to hoe, he reminded himself. Losing his leash on medical science wasn't the end of the world.

Not by a long shot.

Rising to his feet, he looked back at the lights of the medical center that illuminated the Minnesota night and cursed Rafe Greene.

Then he pulled his collar up against the cold and vanished into the darkness.

CHAPTER FIFTY-FIVE

Rafe stood to the side as the paramedics wheeled Alice out of the lab on a gurney, Jim trailing along behind it.

Out in the hallway, a police officer directed traffic around the spot where Eldon's body lay; when he'd initially burst into the suite, gun at the ready, he'd taken only a second to survey the wreckage and survivors before radioing his dispatcher for assistance. Within minutes, the paramedics had arrived and prepared Alice for her short trip to the emergency room on the other side of the medical center campus while other trauma personnel evaluated the physical conditions of the rest of the people in the suite. Police officers began showing up moments after that, and Rafe had heard the first policeman tell the others how he'd seen a fiery torch planted in the snow outside the building as he drove by on patrol and decided to investigate. He'd had to drive a block to find an open entrance to the wing, but once inside, he'd heard the fire alarms blaring and followed them to the third floor.

"He saw your signal."

Rafe looked down as Ami lifted his arm and slid underneath it. The white bandage on the side of her head where she'd been grazed by Arden's bullet contrasted starkly with her jet-black hair. He gently touched the covered wound.

"I thought I'd been fast enough," he murmured. "I thought his shot had completely missed you. When I saw that blood running down your temple after we brought Alice back from the edge, I almost passed out."

"No worries, big guy," she told him, pressing her side into his. "You and me, we've got this healing thing going for us."

310

Rafe smiled. "Yeah, we do, don't we?"

"Speaking of which, you ought to get off that knee. That MCL is killing you."

He started to protest, but she laid her fingers on his lips. "Don't argue with a medical intuitive, mister," she said. "I know these things, remember?"

Rafe lightly kissed the tips of her fingers. "Yes, ma'am, Dr. Kim, you're right. I could really use a sit-down right about now."

He hugged her shoulder closer to him and tried not to limp too much as she led him to a chair by one of the monitors in the suite.

"I hope no one's watching this," he said. "The big Marine leaning on the little lady doctor. It's bad for my image, you know."

Ami carefully eased him into the chair. "I think your image will survive, Rafe, along with the rest of you. It appears that archangels don't die easily. Thank God."

"Dr. Kim?"

Rafe looked past Ami's shoulder. Mr. Nguyen's left arm was in a sling, and a bruise was beginning to rise on the side of his face.

"The police look outside, they say no one there. They say no footprints in snow, no body." His eyes met Rafe's for just a moment before returning to Ami's face. He lowered his voice. "Where he go?"

"We don't know, Mr. Nguyen," Rafe answered for both of them. He reached out for Ami's hand and folded it in his own. "But I don't think he'll be bothering us again."

The old man nodded. "I think this also. This man powerful, full of evil, but I not afraid of him. My heart strong, thanks to Dr. Kim and my prayers."

Rafe held up the palm of his hand for a high-five from Mr. Nguyen. The janitor looked confused for a moment, then a smile broke over his face as he slapped his right palm against Rafe's.

"My brother," he said.

"Amen," Rafe replied. "You're the first man I'm calling the next time I'm in a tight spot, Mr. Nguyen. You can have my back anytime."

The old man's smile widened. "But I not jump on it." He rubbed his lower back vigorously. "I too old to do again."

He gave them a little wave and walked out the door of the lab, where Rafe could hear the noise of a crime scene investigation unit arriving.

"The media won't be far behind," he warned Ami. "Do you think Mr. Nguyen will mind becoming America's newest and oldest hero?"

"I think Mr. Nguyen will just want everyone to leave him alone." She lifted his hand, wrapped around hers, to her lips. "He has a grandson to mourn."

"I'm so sorry about Hung," he said.

Ami nodded. "He—Arden—was two steps ahead of us from the beginning. Niles, Hung, the pharmacy student."

Her eyes widened in alarm.

"The assassin—the woman you almost caught—I forgot about her."

Rafe squeezed her hand in reassurance. "It's over, Ami. She's out of the picture. She's not a threat to any of us anymore."

Ami studied his solemn face. "She's dead, isn't she?"

He nodded. "While you were getting your head wrapped, I talked with one of the police officers. As soon as the first policeman radioed in, they sent out a team to secure the whole building."

He paused for a moment.

"They found a woman's body up on the seventh floor just outside the elevator. She was wearing your lab jacket. I'm guessing that Arden and his assassin had a conflict of interest, and his interest prevailed."

"Scorched earth?"

Rafe nodded. "I'd guess so."

Ami pulled up a chair beside Rafe and sat down. For a few minutes, neither spoke.

"This is all a pretty heavy price to pay for finding a miracle cure," Ami finally said. "If I had known—"

"You didn't," Rafe reminded her. "There's no way anyone could have told you this is where your research would lead." He squeezed her hand again.

"You know, it's kind of funny almost," he reflected. "For some reason, Arden thought I was responsible for your NRT."

He could feel Ami's eyes on him as he replayed his encounter with Arden in his mind.

"This is your fault, you know. If you hadn't shared your healing secret with Dr. Kim, none of these people would be dying right now. But no, you had to interfere. You had to tear away my illusion that the body and soul are separate... It's just another of my lies."

"He said I'd shared my healing secret with you—that the body and soul aren't separate."

Rafe looked into Ami's dark eyes.

"But I never fully realized that until I met you. God gave you that knowledge, Ami. Not me."

Ami smiled her beautiful smile. "So maybe the Devil isn't as smart as he's cracked up to be," she said. "Maybe he's delusional, ignorant of the fact that God works through the gifts we're each given to build up the kingdom, just like your mama always told you, Rafe. Or maybe the Devil is just sexist, and he can't accept that women have brains. If someone came up with a miracle cure, it had to have been a man."

Rafe returned her smile. "If he believes that, he really is in denial."

He could feel Ami's laughter bubbling up like it was inside his own body. It felt like lights winking on beneath his skin, making him glow in a thousand places. It felt warm, life-giving.

"He is the master of deception, isn't he?" Ami was asking him, though he was rapidly losing interest in anything having to do with Philip Arden. "Self-deception included?"

Rafe leaned in her direction, his eyes locked on her lips.

"Yes, ma'am," he said, though he honestly wasn't sure what she had just asked him.

"Are you listening to me?"

Rafe shifted his gaze to her eyes. "Absolutely. I'm hanging on every word here." Her laughter was so close to the surface, he couldn't help but grin. He knew exactly what it was that he was discerning in her.

Faith.

Hope.

Love.

"What did I just say?"

Rafe blinked. "You said, 'Are you listening to me?'"

Ami put her hand on his chest and stopped him from leaning closer.

"Before that."

"Is this a test? Because if it is, I've got a better question to ask."

He covered her hand on his chest and cleared his throat. "Will you go to the Home & Garden Show with me? I'm going to find a house here in the Twin Cities. I'll probably want to do some remodeling, or something. And I really should have a doctor with me in case I go into a coma—a diabetic coma—when I'm comparing—oh, I don't know—paint swatches?"

Ami hesitated.

Paint *swatches?*

It was a good thing her NRT trials were so close to being finished. If Rafe thought that paint samples came in swatches instead of chips, she really had her work cut out for her. She shook her head in exasperation.

"Rafe, you don't—"

"No, don't say no," he interrupted. "I know you need time, but I can wait, Ami."

His face was earnest, confident.

"I want to wait," he said.

"You'll have to wait till next January, then, because that's when they hold the home show."

She watched the parade of emotions flying across his face, but she didn't need to read them to know how he felt about her.

Especially since she knew he could read hers just as well.

Faith. Hope. Love.

Ami fisted her hand in his shirt and pulled him back towards her. "I was going to say, before I was interrupted, that you don't call it a swatch, Rafe. It's a paint chip. And if you think I'm going to wait till next January, you're wrong."

She brought her lips close to his.

"Forget about finding a house, Rafe. Just come home to me."

"Home," he murmured. "Do you have any idea how good that sounds to me?"

She smiled as his happiness washed over her, surrounded her with his warmth and joy.

"As a matter of fact, I know exactly how good that sounds to you."

"Kiss me," he said.

She did.

Rafe gathered the woman into his arms, marveling at how right she felt nestled against him. He wasn't going to be moving on anymore, now that he'd found right where God wanted him to be. He and Ami had a world of healing to do, a new mission before them. He wasn't so naïve to think that there wouldn't be obstacles ahead, or antagonists to confront, but he had no doubt that together, he and Ami could succeed.

They had gifts to give. Gifts of faith, hope, and love.

And the greatest of these was Love.

Rafe lifted his lips from Ami's and opened his eyes. A fine shower of light embraced them.

"What color is it?" Ami whispered, her eyes still closed.

Rafe's voice filled with awe. "It's green."

"I love green," she told him. She opened her eyes and smiled into his. "In fact, I think I'm going to redo my condo in it."

"Sounds like a plan," he replied. "When do we start?"

Ami smiled that smile he liked so well.

"I'm thinking that right here and right now would be good," she said.

"I couldn't agree more," he said, and kissed her again.

AUTHOR'S NOTE

Writing has always been a journey of discovery and blessing for me, and *Archangels Book II: Heart and Soul* has been no exception.

In the course of writing this book, I have had the amazing opportunity to research and speculate about the connections between science and faith. My reading list included books about spiritual healing, alternative medicine, Taoism, alcoholism, neurophysiology, and psychology, and I was intrigued and fascinated by all the ways science and faith share common territory in these fields. One of the best outcomes of writing this book is how my research is deepening my own Christian faith and offering me new portals for recognizing the presence of God in our world. I hope readers have a similar experience—as the celebrated geneticist Francis S. Collins notes in his book *The Language of God,* "For those who believe in God, there are reasons now to be more in awe, not less."

As far as acknowledging the wonderful help I received during this particular creative journey, I have several people to thank for giving me so much of their time and expertise. I relied on my dear friend Karen Karn, MD, to explain the intricacies of clinical drug trials to me, and I depended on my high school buddy Katy Hadduck, BSN, RN, to make this book as accurate as possible in all things concerning emergency medicine. My daughter Nicole was my primary sounding board and cheerleader, who provided me with key texts from her own bookshelf in psychology when I was struggling to find the critical connections I knew were out there somewhere. Thanks, ladies, for the contributions you have made to this novel, and, more importantly, for the friendship and love you bring into my life. Likewise, my daughters Rachel and Colleen continue to inspire me to become the best writer I can be by believing in me at all times, as do their brothers Tom and Bob, and my wonderful husband Tom—I regularly thank God for the gracious gifts that each of you are to me.

Finally, I am blessed with my agent Greg Johnson, who has kept the faith in my *Archangels* series from the very beginning of our association, and the excellent editorial assistance of his colleagues Sarah Joy Freese and Keely Boeving. I am a better writer thanks to all of you. Thank you.

ABOUT THE PUBLISHER

FH Publishers is a division of FaithHappenings.com

FaithHappenings.com is the premier, first-of-its kind, online Christian resource that contains an array of valuable local and national faith-based information all in one place. Our mission is "to inform, enrich, inspire and mobilize Christians and churches while enhancing the unity of the local Christian community so they can better serve the needs of the people around them." FaithHappenings.com will be the primary i-Phone, Droid App/Site and website that people with a traditional Trinitarian theology will turn to for national and local information to impact virtually every area of life.

The vision of FaithHappenings.com is to build the vibrancy of the local church with a true "one-stop-resource" of information and events that will enrich the soul, marriage, family, and church life for people of faith. We want people to be touched by God's Kingdom, so they can touch others FOR the Kingdom.

Find out more at www.faithhappenings.com.

Made in the USA
San Bernardino, CA
16 February 2018